**Praise for the breathtaking novels of
Jane Goodger**

Dancing with Sin

"Deep, insightful. Ms. Goodger's talents lie in presenting a different picture of the era and following through with themes that are as relevant today as they were a century ago."—*Romantic Times*

"Jane Goodger deserves gold stars. Reminiscent of some Hitchcock movies, *Dancing with Sin* presents a portrait of an ordinary woman caught up in extraordinary circumstances."—Ellen Edwards for Amazon.com

Anything for Love

"Simply wonderful. A beautiful, touching story of a second chance at life and love. Goodger has created a winner."
—*Romance Communications*

"*Anything for Love* shows that time-travel romance is in good hands with the talents of Jane Goodger."
—*The Romance Reader*

Memories of You

"An exciting and sensuous tale."—*Romantic Times*

"Hours of joyful reading . . . exceptional characters, blazing passion, and a humdinger of a plot."—*Rendezvous*

Into the Wild Wind

Jane Goodger

A SIGNET BOOK

SIGNET
Published by New American Library, a division of
Penguin Putnam Inc., 375 Hudson Street,
New York, New York 10014, U.S.A.
Penguin Books Ltd, 27 Wrights Lane,
London W8 5TZ, England
Penguin Books Australia Ltd, Ringwood,
Victoria, Australia
Penguin Books Canada Ltd, 10 Alcorn Avenue,
Toronto, Ontario, Canada M4V 3B2
Penguin Books (N.Z.) Ltd, 182–190 Wairau Road,
Auckland 10, New Zealand

Penguin Books Ltd, Registered Offices:
Harmondsworth, Middlesex, England

First published by Signet, an imprint of New American Library,
a division of Penguin Putnam Inc.

First Printing, August 1999
10 9 8 7 6 5 4 3 2 1

Prologue

March 4, 1852

James MacRae was getting married. The man she loved, the man she had almost died coming home to see, was getting married. To someone else.

Hannah Wright let out a small sound, not quite a laugh, not quite a sound of anguish, as she carefully placed the New York *Tribune* back on her delicate rosewood desk. Hannah sat for a long moment allowing herself to absorb the truth. He was lost to her, and it was all because of her stubbornness, her selfishness. Now she knew how James had felt when he'd begged her to marry him and she had said no. Hannah closed her eyes against the image of him waiting for her in vain. Despite that memory, she felt his betrayal was a bit worse than hers, for he'd known soon after they'd met that Hannah was already engaged. He knew. She'd never made promises. She'd never even told him that she loved him. Though God above knew that she did.

"Oh, James," she whispered brokenly. Her nose prickled, and her eyes burned from tears that threatened as her eyes were once again drawn to the article announcing that Captain James MacRae, master of the clipper ship *Windfire,* would marry.

Despite herself, Hannah couldn't help but be immensely proud of him. The article portrayed him as a hero, the catch of New York, describing him in lavish terms, both his physical and mental attributes. It was all heartbreakingly accurate. He would marry Sandra Sheffield, the "lovely and demure daughter of wealthy shipowner Maxwell Sheffield. Her mother is the former Alice Stanhope of the Boston Stanhopes."

Lovely and demure. Hannah had never been described as demure, that was for certain. She could not picture a demure woman with James, a girl who would shrink from him if he raised his voice or blush if he swore, which he often did. According to the article, Sandra Sheffield was the product of two society parents, raised mostly in private boarding schools whose objective was to graduate marriageable girls. She would likely look up at James with complete adoration, eyes wide, pretty lips slightly pouted just the way she'd no doubt practiced for hours in the mirror. Hannah shook her head, realizing she was engulfed with jealousy over a girl she'd never met.

A girl James, *her* James, was going to marry in just four months' time.

Sandra Sheffield certainly must be something special, Hannah thought with a severe frown. After all, she'd captured him in less than a month. Then Hannah's face crumpled, and the tears she'd been holding back since seeing the article came in full force. James certainly hadn't loved her as much as he'd claimed if he was so ready to marry another. All during her journey from California, through the maddening delays, through her long and frustratingly slow recovery from yellow fever, she'd never thought in her wildest imaginings that James MacRae would fall in love with another. He'd gone thirty years without forming a lasting attachment to a female, and then, in a matter of months, fell in love twice.

Hannah hastily wiped her eyes upon hearing a knock at her door.

"Yes?"

"It's me." Her father, Austin Wright, stepped through the door, his eyes immediately going to the newspaper still on her desk. Hannah prayed she had wiped away any trace of tears from her face, for her father did not know she had succumbed to the immense and fickle charms of Captain James MacRae. She didn't want him to ever know.

"Captain MacRae is getting married," she announced with a broad smile. "To a Sandra Sheffield. Do you know of the girl?"

"I know her father." He looked at Hannah with an intensity that was mildly disturbing, then he seemed to relax, and Hannah let out a silent breath of relief. "I probably met the daughter, as well, somewhere along the way, but I cannot recall for certain. So you are happy about the announcement?"

Hannah forced herself to give a casual shrug. "As happy as I would be to read that any of my friends or acquaintances was about to marry." Hannah couldn't stop herself from saying aloud the next. "I certainly never took Captain MacRae as a man who made such life-changing decisions so hastily."

Again, Austin Wright gave his daughter a long look. She spoke without thinking, only knowing that she had to deflect the curiosity and doubt she read in her father's eyes. "We should invite them to supper," she said, her voice bright, almost harsh. Calming herself with forced effort, Hannah continued. "We should have a congratulatory party. Invite several couples. I haven't seen the captain since my return, so it could be a reunion of sorts, as well. Perhaps Allen would come."

"Yes. Allen." She could hear the irritation in her father's voice.

"He has been a good friend to me. I could do worse than to marry Allen." She hadn't yet told her father that she realized weeks ago she would never marry a man other than James.

"Have your party, then. Invite Allen. I've done all I could do." Hannah lifted her head at her father's bitter tone.

"What do you mean?"

"Hell, girl. You must know I have never thought Allen Pritchard a good match for you. And now that we are more fully aware of his dire financial straits . . . Ah, but I've never held a man's empty pocketbook against him. Come here, Hannah." Hannah stood and walked to her father. He placed his big hands on her upper arms. "You are so much like your mother. Full of spirit and intelligence. Call me vain, but I'd hoped you'd find someone more like me, someone with a passion for life, with a fire in his soul."

"A sea captain," she said woodenly.

"Perhaps," he said, dropping his hands and stepping away. "You can't even cross-stitch," he shouted, and Hannah laughed and shook her head. Austin looked a bit sheepish, and Hannah's heart swelled with love for her cantankerous father.

"I suppose now that you're both to marry other people, there's no harm in telling you that I had hoped you and Captain MacRae would fall in love."

"You *what?*"

Two spots of red formed on her father's cheeks. "He seemed to be the right man for you. Trustworthy. A damned good captain. Women find him attractive, I believe. I thought two attractive young people with a shared love for the sea couldn't help but fall in love."

His words sliced into her. "I hope that is not the reason you allowed me to sail to San Francisco with the captain." Hannah watched with dismay as those two spots grew brighter.

"Not the only reason. But I cannot lie. Partly I agreed to allow you to go because I had hoped for a match."

Hannah sat down, completely deflated. Her father hadn't allowed her to go because he had faith in her abilities or because he understood her need to find Allen, but because he was playing matchmaker. "Oh, Papa," she said, disappointment clear in her voice.

"I just wanted you to be happy, Hannah. Like your mother and I were happy."

"I know." Their marriage had been a happy one—when Austin Wright was in port. He never saw his wife's lonely vigils, the sadness during those long, long months when he was at sea. He never knew she carried one of his old pipes in her skirt pockets so that his scent would always be with her. Hannah watched as her father left her bedroom, his face filled with sadness over thoughts of his lost love.

Yet she couldn't become angry with him. The reasons he had allowed her to sail to San Francisco didn't matter. The only thing that did matter was that James was marrying another woman. And Hannah would marry no one. She refused to acknowledge that those thoughts only made her miserable. Poor Allen. He was one of only a few people who knew how much she loved James, and he was still willing to marry her, convinced that in time she would come to love him. But he was so, so wrong. She would never stop loving James. How had she ever thought she could let him go?

Now, foolish, foolish woman, she had invited the man she loved and his fiancée to dinner. Blast and damn.

She folded her arms on the newspaper and lay down her head so that the words to the engagement announcement became illegible blurs. "James, how could you?" How could he not? She had made herself quite clear the day he sailed from San Francisco. If he had loved her, she had certainly broken his heart. The day he'd left San Francisco harbor seemed like years ago, their journey to California, a lifetime ago. So much had happened. So much. Despite her misery, she smiled, as she often did when she thought of her sea captain. Even that first day, when he'd been so disagreeable. Even then, part of her knew she was falling in love.

Chapter One

July 12, 1851

Captain James MacRae was blustering again, waving his arms and pounding his fists in a way that would make many a man quake upon seeing it for the first time. But his first mate, George Wright, already knew with one look into his captain's piercing blue eyes that he was not angry. Far from it. Captain MacRae loved a challenge, and the fact that they were scheduled to set sail in three days and were still without a navigator was simply another challenge to be met. Captain MacRae was one of those rare men whose expression often appeared fierce, but whose eyes twinkled with good humor. Indeed, since George had been hired on two months ago as first mate to the clipper ship *Windfire,* he had never seen Captain MacRae truly angry.

"I've got a ten-thousand-dollar bonus on the line, Mr. Wright, and I've got little chance of collecting it without a navigator." The captain, a strapping man with broad shoulders who stood a head over most men, strode to his dusty office window and looked out at the forest of masts along New York's East River. Then he turned and glared at George. "Why the hell did I hire you as mate?"

George suppressed a smile. "Because, sir, there is no one who knows how to set canvas better than me. Present company accepted, sir."

James muttered a curse. "Hell, the *Flying Cloud's* probably laying dock in San Francisco as we speak," James said, tapping his fist against a muscled thigh in thought.

"Or the *Challenge,*" George said, fully knowing his captain's opinion of that over-canvassed monstrosity. Sometimes it was amusing to watch Captain MacRae bluster.

"With that crew of cutthroats?" James shouted, happily rising to the bait to discuss his favorite subject. The much-publicized race between the two clipper ships was all the seafaring crowd could talk about since the ships departed in June. It was unlikely either ship would make it to San Francisco until September or November, and it was maddening to James to have to set sail without knowing how fast the ships were making the fifteen-thousand-mile trip. The *Windfire* was fast, his crew was well trained and well paid, and his stomach curled with the excitement of trying to set a speed record around Cape Horn.

"You know my opinion of Captain Waterman, the man's a sadist, but he can skipper a ship. I'll give him that. And only that," James shouted and pointed a finger, as if George were about to argue. Then he burst out laughing, a hearty and contagious sound. "Did you see that crew? Did you, lad?" he said, wiping his eyes, his Scottish burr deepening in his mirth. "I stood on the dock and listened to the first mate explain where the bow and stern were. He had 'em shifting from one side of the ship to another, repeating 'starboard, port.' " More gales of laughter. "They'll be lucky if they make it around the Horn, never mind beat Captain Creesy and the *Flying Cloud.*"

James suddenly sobered. "We need a navigator, Mr. Wright. My skills and your skills will get us to port safely— hell, they could probably get me that bonus—but I want to set that damned speed record. We can do it. The *Windfire* can do it. She's a fine ship, she is." He glanced out the window where the *Windfire*, a sleek clipper ship, lay at berth on Pier 6, her prow jutting high above South Street. She was a beauty. Her mainmast soared one hundred ninety feet into the sky, her spars carried ten thousand yards of sail. Her bow arched up like a woman well pleased, bending a few feet higher than her stern. She was painted a deep blue and trimmed in gold, and never had James beheld a more beautiful sight than the *Windfire*. He only wished he owned more than just a few shares of her.

James had sailed the *Windfire* from Boston, where she was built by the most successful clipper ship builder in the world, Donald McKay, and launched two months ago with much fanfare. On that short trip, he worked his crew, driving them to obtain speeds of fourteen and fifteen knots on that small strip of the Atlantic. By the time he berthed the ship in New York, he was confident his crew, many of whom had followed him from his former ship, would make *Windfire* fly.

"Any answers to that ad we placed?" James asked.

"No, sir. Not any that I would send your way."

"Three days. We'll not find anyone in three days if no one has come forward yet." James pounded his thigh lightly. "Ask around, Mr. Wright. Six ships have made port in the past week. One of them has to have a disgruntled mate willing to sign on."

After George departed, James spent a long moment gazing at his beloved *Windfire* before turning to a stack of charts unfurled on his desk. Captain MacRae glanced up from the charts to see a stylishly dressed woman navigating around the puddles left by last night's rain. She looked remarkably out of place as she gingerly sidestepped a large pile of horse manure, hefting her many petticoats in an attempt to keep them clean. The woman was a splash of color in her sky-blue dress and bonnet in a place that was mostly brown—brown mud, docks, and water. Behind her, the East River piers were filled with the frenzied movement of dockworkers, stevedores, ships' crew members, and passengers heading toward their ships laden with bags and trunks. But the small strip of mud-filled ground between South Street and the offices of shipowners Haywood & Bennings was

devoid of anything but that pretty splash of femininity that
appeared to be making its way directly toward him.

On a ship, James MacRae was not a man who was easily
distracted. But on land, his active mind had a tendency to
wander to the sea or into the bedroom of some lovely lady
he'd been with sometime in the past. To James MacRae, life
was meant to be lived. A man didn't breathe, he inhaled until
his lungs were filled to the brim with fresh salt air. He did
everything with the vigor of a man who expects this day
might be his last. Though he did not dwell on it, his profession as clipper ship sea captain made that philosophy of life
a practicality, for his was a dangerous profession. He
grinned widely when he heard the knock of a small fist on
his office door.

Hannah Wright, her stomach a nervous flutter, knocked
determinedly on the captain's office door. Captain James
MacRae was her last hope. Standing on the outside second-
floor landing of the three-story brick building, she clutched
a newspaper clipping in one gloved hand, willing herself not
to peruse it again to make certain she was at the correct office. She knew she was, but her heart was in her throat for
what she was about to do.

Hannah Wright was a desperate woman. Leave it to me,
she'd thought on more than one occasion, to lose a fiancé.
Allen Pritchard had left for San Francisco eighteen months
earlier to go work for her uncle and had not been heard from
since. Hannah was bound and determined to find him, and
Captain MacRae and his *Windfire* were her last chance of
getting to California before the end of the year. When the office door swept open, she lifted her head sharply, for she
needed to appear confident and brave, and her eyes settled
on the bluest, most beautiful pair of eyes she'd ever seen on
a man. His tanned face and thick black hair only made those
eyes seem even bluer, and for a moment Hannah could only
stare as she was inclined to do whenever she saw something
beautiful.

"Can I help you, miss?"

Hannah immediately noticed the faint Scottish burr, as well as the obvious admiration in his gaze that swept up and down her form in what should have been an insulting manner, but which somehow was not. "Are you Captain MacRae?"

He bowed, his eyes crinkling. "At your service, miss." Hannah could only think: He has smiling eyes, the kind that twinkle, the kind that are easy to read. Right now those eyes were telling her they liked what they saw, and Hannah stiffened. She was a woman on a mission and had no time to be flattered by admiring glances, especially not those from a sea captain. The captain, wearing well-fitted brown trousers tucked into gleaming black boots and plain white shirt that was open at the neck, stepped back and waved an arm welcoming her into the rustic office. The whitewash walls were nearly obliterated by ropes, charts, and tackle nailed to the wall to make the most of the cramped space. He turned to his desk, appearing to search for something, then fingered his discarded cravat, as if deciding whether he should put it back on. Dropping the piece of cloth, James settled one hip on his desk and indicated that Hannah should take the only chair in the office. Ignoring his gesture, Hannah remained standing already intimidated by the man's height and muscled bulk.

Taking a deep breath, she announced, "I've come to apply for the navigator's position, sir." She watched as the captain's easy grin faded and his mouth dropped open. And then he laughed, a loud, hearty, back-slapping sort of laugh that had Hannah inexplicably fighting the urge to join in. She struggled not to smile as she said, "I'm quite serious, sir."

Still laughing, the captain managed, "I'm sure you are."

Hannah narrowed her eyes, no longer finding amusement in her predicament. "I must get to San Francisco, sir. As I cannot afford the exorbitant fee as a passenger, I find the only other alternative is to sign on as a crew member. You may test me. You'll find I'm quite knowledgeable."

James finally controlled his laughter, but his eyes smiled still. "I'm sorry, but you must know that is impossible."

Hannah jutted her chin up even higher, feeling anger and the tiniest tinge of desperation boiling just beneath the surface. "Captain MacRae," she said as authoritatively as she knew how, "I am aware that you have been offered a substantial bonus to reach San Francisco within one hundred days and more if you make the trip in record time. I am also aware that you will be unable to do that without the help of a knowledgeable navigator. Perhaps you haven't noticed, but thanks to the Gold Rush, there is a dearth of qualified seamen in New York. Beggars, sir, cannot be choosers."

"Sea*men*," James shouted, taking his hip off his desk and coming to his full height to loom over her. "A man is what I need. Not some little miss who is looking for an adventure."

Hannah flinched at the man's loud volume and felt a tingling of fear along her spine at the derision she heard in his voice. And then she looked at his eyes. He wasn't angry. Far from it. He was still maddeningly amused, and Hannah instantly wished he were truly angry. She could handle an angry man better, she thought, than someone who thought every word out of her mouth was vastly funny.

"You seem to think this is a joke, Captain," she said, well pleased that he narrowed his eyes at her perception. "Well, it is not. I must get to San Francisco. I must." Hannah balled her fist and set her mouth stubbornly.

"Take a steamship to Panama."

"Perhaps you were not listening. I haven't the funds for a clipper ship, never mind the money to pay for two steamships, hotels, and transportation across the isthmus."

James looked her up and down, and Hannah knew he was taking in the richness of her clothes, the pearl buttons, the expensive lace. "You seem to be a woman who can afford passage. And if not, the cross-land route is quite inexpensive."

Hannah had thought of that, but instantly discarded it. It was already July, far too late to cross the continent. And besides, it would take too long. "I must get to San Francisco quickly." Hannah smiled, thinking that perhaps flattery would help her cause. "You have a reputation as a good captain, and your ship is being touted in the papers as the fastest to be launched since the *Flying Cloud.*"

"Faster," James shouted, sweeping one fist through the air. "We did fifteen knots on Block Island Sound."

Hannah had to force herself not to flinch at his outburst. "Fine sailing, Captain. And a fine ship. I saw her as I was walking to the office. How much sail does she hold?"

James narrowed his eyes again, a look that told Hannah he knew what she was doing and found it, too, amusing. She wanted to slap his smug face. "Ten thousand yards of canvas snapping overhead. Ten thousand yards of sail pushing the sleekest, most beautiful ship ever built. A ship," he said, pointing a finger at Hannah, "that won't be navigated by a woman."

Oh, this stubborn, stubborn, smiling man! What had she expected, after all? That the captain would welcome her with open arms? That he would kiss her boots and hand over his sextant? She must convince him, she thought, battling the panic that was threatening to undo her. She must.

"Captain, a man's life is at stake. If I do not reach him in time, I do not know what will happen. He may already be dead, for all I know." Hannah turned away and pretended to dab at her eyes. She'd tried reason, flattery; now she thought she'd see if this brute had a heart susceptible to a woman's tears.

"You cannot help a dead man."

Hannah could not quite believe he had said that. No, she was certain even this man would not have been so callous. "What did you say?"

"If the man's already dead," he explained patiently, "it'd be a monumental waste of time and energy to go after him, now, wouldn't it?"

Hannah spun around, so angry she forgot she was supposed to be crying. Laughing. He was laughing at her. Oh, not out loud, not even with his mouth. But those eyes were crinkled at the corners, so filled with mirth he might as well have been doubled over and letting out gales of laughter.

"Don't you dare laugh at my pain," Hannah said dramatically. He studied her for a long moment, apparently looking for signs of pain.

"I wasn't," he concluded, and Hannah was certain he meant he saw no pain in her to laugh at.

"Why are you being so stubborn?" she said with venom. After all, she had not tried anger yet, and she was truly feeling that darker emotion. "You need a navigator. I need to get to San Francisco. I must get there, Captain. You're just being stubborn. You, sir, are obstinate and bullheaded."

A smile quirked at his lips, making another wave of anger surge through her. "Tsk, tsk," he said mildly. "Perhaps you should try flirtation instead of insults."

Oh, he could see right through her, the cad. "You are . . . you are . . ." She thought and thought, scanning her mind for some of the colorful language she'd heard over the years. "A bastard. Yes. You are one of those . . . what I just said." She nodded her head.

Instead of making him angry, the smile that had been quirking on one side of his mouth, bloomed into a full-fledged grin. He sighed. "Miss . . ."

"Miss Wright."

"Wright?" And James's brows snapped together. At that moment his first mate strode into the office, eyes lighting up at the sight of the woman standing in his office.

"Hannah," George said, crossing over to her and drawing her into his arms in an enthusiastic greeting. "What the devil are you doing here?"

"Applying for the navigator's position," James stated, eyeing the two with interest. "I take it you two know each other?"

"Cousins," George said heartily. "And I haven't seen Hannah in, what is it, two years?"

"Nearly three," Hannah said warmly, stepping back so

that she might get a better look at her cousin. "Are you on the *Windfire,* too?"

"Too?" James asked, one eyebrow shooting up.

Hannah and George ignored him. "First mate," George said with pride.

"My mate and navigator got himself killed in a ballroom brawl. Now I have a mate but . . ."

George interrupted, ". . . but as you know, Hannah, I'm no navigator. I'm willing to learn, but this is not the trip for novices."

Hannah gave her cousin a friendly smack on the arm. "Why, you were always a fair one with the sextant."

"Fair isn't good enough," James said, beginning to get slightly piqued that he was being ignored. He found it vastly irritating that as soon as George entered the office, the beauty before him seemed to forget he was in the room. James knew women were attracted to him, not only for his good looks but for the near-hero status he had as a clipper ship captain. Women were in awe of him, and if he were honest, he rather enjoyed that awe. That look Miss Wright gave him when she first saw him, now, that was more like what he was used to. He'd seen more emotions cross that woman's face in the space of a few minutes than most women he'd known had displayed in a year.

He watched silently as the two cousins talked animatedly. Beneath her overlarge bonnet, he could see brown-gold hair peeking out. He hadn't been close enough to her yet to determine the color of her eyes. He'd first thought they were brown, but now he realized they were not; they were some other indefinable color, and he found himself willing her to look at him so that he at least might take a look at them. Finally, she did. Ah, he thought. Green. Her eyes are the green of a stormy sea, changeable and mesmerizing.

"Tell the captain, George. Tell him what a fine navigator I am. He won't believe me."

James crossed his arms. "Yes, Mr. Wright. Please do."

George smoothed down his beard with one hand, obviously reluctant to answer. "Actually, captain, she's the best damned navigator I've ever seen. Granted, she's never been around the Horn, but she's been to Europe plenty of times."

James gave his first mate a stunned look. "As navigator?"

"My father is Austin Wright, Captain," Hannah said as way of explanation.

James smiled, flashing his white teeth. "Of course he is." James knew Austin Wright slightly, having met him on a few social occasions. He was a fine captain, though to James's knowledge he'd never captained a clipper ship. His career ended because of some illness, he recalled. But when he sailed, he was known as a solid seaman, tough but fair. Though he did not know Austin Wright well, James believed he was not the sort of man who would allow his single daughter to hire on as a navigator.

"You come from quite a seafaring family, Miss Wright. When was the last time you were aboard ship?"

"Six years ago. When I was sixteen, my father determined I was missing a formal education and I attended boarding school for two years," she said. "But I've been studying Maury's *Charts and Sailing Directions,* and I truly do have a good sense about where to find the wind."

James shot a look to George, who gave a reluctant nod. James could not deny that he needed a good navigator, and here stood his salvation in a pretty little package, literally tied up with a bow, he thought, glancing at the bow at her trim waist. That trim waist which made him look again at Miss Hannah Wright. Hell, he thought, a good gale would knock her off the ship. She barely reached his chin, even with that ridiculous bonnet. It took a hearty soul to take on Cape Horn and survive. A father would have to be insane to allow his daughter to sign on with a clipper ship. James smiled. Austin Wright certainly was not insane.

"I'll tell you what," he said, a pleasant gleam in his blue eyes. "If your father gives you permission to sign on, I'll allow it." He could not suppress a smile at her crestfallen face.

"I'm twenty-two years old," Hannah said drawing herself up so that her bonnet reached perhaps up to his smiling lips. "I do not need the permission of my father to sign on."

"True enough. But that is a condition of hire."

Hannah set her jaw mulishly, but did not argue. She felt defeat cover her like a thick fog. Her father would never agree.

Chapter Two

"Oh, Allen, look what you've done now." Hannah lay upon her bed on her stomach, chin on her fists, legs bent so that her petticoats and skirt formed a frothy pile of material on her backside.

Hannah had been so worried about Allen for so long, the thought that she might never see him again filled her with an awful sense of failure. Allen did not belong in San Francisco, where there were no museums, no opera house, and very little society. Poor Allen. What was she thinking sending him off into the wilderness alone? Hannah could only comfort herself with the knowledge that no one could have predicted that Allen Pritchard, one of the wealthiest men in New York, would have been lured by the gold that had drawn so many foolish men to California.

They were to have been married by now and living together in that western city. But fate and events had shattered Hannah's dreams of forging a home in the newest state in the Union.

"Allen, what were you thinking?" Hannah said aloud, still unable to believe the letter she'd received from her uncle one week earlier. Her father's brother, a former sea captain, had settled in San Francisco in 1849, soon after gold was discovered and the rush to find it began. Richard Wright had been lured by another sort of riches, the kind that came from selling goods to the hoards of people who traveled to California with visions of quick riches in their greedy heads. In two years, her uncle had made a fortune selling building materials and constructing buildings for the people who were arriving in the thousands. By mid-1849, it was clear Richard needed help with his ventures, the kind of help that would not be tempted to head off and try their luck at finding gold. Allen had seemed the perfect choice.

Poor, poor Allen. He'd wanted to please her and her father, and so he had agreed to take the journey to California and begin working for her uncle, despite the histrionics of his mother upon hearing his decision. Hannah refused to go until her father, who suffered a weak heart, was better. Just weeks before they were both to board a ship to California, her father suffered another, more severe attack, and Hannah decided to remain. Allen was to send word to her when he was settled, and she'd planned to join him as soon as her father was faring better. But Allen never wrote.

Hannah expected to hear from him within a year, but as the months passed, she became more and more alarmed. She knew his ship had made it safely to port, so she could not fathom why no word from him came. Each day she checked the post becoming more and more alarmed. Finally, nearly two years after Allen departed, Richard sent word of his fate. Allen had been stricken with gold fever.

"It can't be," Hannah had said, the letter from her uncle held limply in her hand. Her father, hearty and hale once more, appeared to be equally stunned. "Allen is rich. He has no need for gold." Hannah could not picture her refined fiancé toiling in the mud for little nuggets of gold. Her uncle had to be wrong. He had to be. The person she knew would never be tempted to such a life.

Allen was the person who introduced her to the finer things in life. Having spent much of her youth aboard ship, Hannah knew she was a bit rough around the edges and wanted nothing more than to become a real lady. Allen taught her all he knew. He brought her to art exhibits, he showed her fashion plates from Paris and helped her choose the right dressmaker. Allen gave her an appreciation of opera, of symphonic music. He opened a world to her that she'd never experienced, one that she'd thought was out of reach.

She loved his world of fine clothes, of balls and soirees. Allen was everything that everything she'd ever known was not. Allen hated the sea, and his rather delicate constitution made his agreeing to head to San Francisco even more heartwarming. Hannah knew she did not love him, but she loved what he brought into her life. She loved the fact that he was stable. He wouldn't be lured by adventure, taken from her by his love of the sea or the love of anything else, for that matter. At least, she hadn't thought he would be. That was why the letter from her uncle had caused such a panic in her breast. The Allen who had helped choose the very dress she now had on, commenting drolly about the number of petticoats required to obtain the desired volume, could not be the same man her uncle described in his letter.

"He seems to be a rather reckless sort," her uncle wrote. "The man came off the ship with a strange light in his eyes which I've seen other men have with gold fever. He was polite enough and apologized for promises broken. Then was off with a small crowd of young Harvard men to look for gold. I must say I am quite disappointed, for with his background in law and in business, he would have been a great help to me."

Allen? Reckless? It was absurd. Hannah half suspected that someone pretending to be Allen had shown up at her uncle's door with his apology. Her uncle had waited several months for Allen to "come to his senses" before writing Hannah that he had disappeared. She, of course, had been left to tell Mrs. Pritchard that her son was not safely ensconced in what little society there was in San Francisco, but was instead looking for gold. Mrs. Pritchard, as Hannah suspected, blamed her, and because Hannah blamed herself, she could only hang her head and beg the fine lady's forgiveness. She'd felt truly dreadful leaving behind that weeping woman who was as stunned as she that her refined and elegant son would desert everything to prospect.

Hannah had read numerous articles about the vast quantities of gold being discovered. Even she had felt a bit of a thrill when reading about how men were practically shoveling the stuff from riverbanks into bags. But her uncle's missives had drawn a much more realistic picture, and she hadn't thought Allen—of all people—would have fallen for the extravagant stories being told. So many people were flooding the California countryside that few actually were getting rich. Prices were so exorbitant that most people were spending much of what they made just buying supplies and food. Her uncle was proof that the real gold to be made was in commerce, not digging.

Allen knew all that, Hannah thought, pounding a fist into her counterpane. He had read the same articles with snorts of disbelief, he had commented on the "poor fools" who spent their last dime paying for fare on a clipper ship to head to California. What had happened to him? Hannah had to find out, but she was certain her father would never agree to allow her to sign on to the *Windfire*. Lying on her bed, she realized how foolish that dream was. George was expected to arrive for dinner shortly to act as witness to Austin Wright's refusal to allow his daughter to become a crew member. Captain MacRae, she acknowledged bitterly, was not a stupid man. He knew her father would not allow it.

Why, then, had he agreed to this farce to begin with? Hannah wondered. She allowed herself the fantasy of seeing his stunned face if George returned with news that her father had agreed to her plan. Hannah, chuckling, could almost hear him bluster and rant. It would have been a beautiful moment, she thought wistfully. Ah, well, no harm in asking. A knock at the door brought her out of her delicious fantasy.

"Miss, Mr. George Wright has arrived and is waiting in the parlor with your father," her maid informed her.

"Thank you, Joan." Hannah heaved herself off her bed and smoothed down her skirts. Since her meeting with Captain MacRae, she had changed into her favorite brown silk,

with wide stripes of darker brown in the skirt that matched
the large shawl-like collar of her plain bodice. Her white
petticoats peeked out as she walked sedately into the parlor,
where George and her father awaited her arrival. Though
they were uncle and nephew, Hannah thought the two men
looked like father and son. Their similar builds, long and
lean, and their beards—George's a reddish-gold, her father's
red-streaked gray—marked them as relations at any rate.
They sat near a bank of windows, the setting summer sun
streaming in through the fog of the men's pipe smoke.

"Isn't it wonderful to have George to visit," Hannah
asked her father brightly.

"Next time he comes to visit, he'll be a captain for certain," Austin said proudly, clapping his brother's son on the
shoulder.

"Uncle, I'm happy to be first mate. I've still much to
learn," George said modestly. It was modesty, for George
would make a fine captain even now. The only thing against
him was his youth. At four and twenty, it would be difficult
to find shipowners willing to hire such a young man to captain ships that were extremely costly to build.

Hannah smiled at the two men she loved most in this
world. Austin Wright was the picture of health, his cheeks
above his beard ruddy, his eyes bright, but Hannah would
never forget how her father looked that horrible day of his
attack. Lying in the bed where his wife had died ten years
earlier, he looked like he would soon join her. Hannah had
tiptoed in and had been shocked to see the man who lay
abed. He was . . . old. When had her father become this frail
old man? Nearly two years later, Austin Wright looked years
younger than the man who had laid so still on that bed. But
Hannah would never forget the helplessness she felt realizing the most powerful, strongest, and vital man she'd ever
known would someday die.

"I believe I would have made a fine captain as well, had I
been a man," Hannah said, taking advantage of the track of
the conversation.

"Hannah," her father said grandly, "even as a woman, you'd make a fine captain." Hannah beamed. What better lead-in to what she wanted to ask him this evening.

"My thoughts precisely," she said, ignoring the look of panic in George's eyes.

"Papa, you know how worried I've been about Allen."

"Yes, yes," he said impatiently. "But he's a grown man after all."

Hannah grimaced. Her father had never been overly warm toward Allen, and she'd wondered many times if he hadn't been secretly glad of his disappearance.

"I know you do not think Allen is the best choice of a husband," she ventured, and was a bit put out when her father didn't immediately argue. "But I'm very worried and also very determined to find out what has happened to him."

"I thought your uncle's letter was quite clear what happened to him," Austin said, sneaking a wink to George, a gesture Hannah guessed she was not supposed to see.

"But, Papa, don't you find it rather out of character for Allen to have decided to pan for gold?"

"Not particularly."

Hannah pursed her lips at George, who was trying not to laugh. "Well, I do. I must find out what has happened. Or at least why. We would have been married by now. He's my fiancé, Papa, my future husband. I must find him. But I need your help."

Austin shifted uneasily in his chair as he gazed at his only child. He had that look about him, Hannah thought. The one that meant whatever was about to come out of her mouth would be rejected.

"I plan to be aboard a clipper ship when she sets sail in three days."

"Hannah, girl, you know we can't afford the passage," he said with real sorrow.

"I know that, Papa. That is why I've decided to hire on as the ship's navigator . . ."

"No."

". . . so that I may get to San Francisco to . . ."

"No."

". . . find Allen. The captain has agreed," she said quickly to ward off another no.

"Hannah, you know that's not true," George said.

Hannah frowned at the traitor. "He has agreed," she insisted. "As long as you agree, Papa. And you must. For I'll go anyway. I'll go across the continent. I'll join a wagon train and brave all those savage Indians and probably get caught in a blizzard and die a slow agonizing death thinking over and over that I'd already be safe in San Francisco if only my papa had let me . . ."

"I said no." Austin's voice thundered over Hannah's speech. "What are you thinking, girl? A woman as a crew member. Ridiculous."

"Papa, please, don't get overexcited. Your heart."

"If my heart gives out, it's because I am being forced to deal with this insanity."

Hannah looked properly chastised, but her mouth was set stubbornly. "You don't know how much this means to me," Hannah said softly.

"I do. And my answer is still no." Austin sighed wearily. "What captain would have agreed to this farce?"

"Captain MacRae of the *Windfire*," George answered.

Austin shot him a look of disbelief. "James MacRae agreed to hire Hannah as navigator?"

"He made a condition of her hire that she receive permission from you, sir. I believe he was quite certain that permission would not be granted. He was indulging her, Uncle." Hannah let out a little huff of anger at having her suspicions confirmed.

Austin leaned back in his chair and stared at the fire thoughtfully. "James MacRae," he repeated softly. He sat forward again. "The *Windfire* you say? That's your ship, is it not, George?"

"Yes, sir."

Austin Wright was silent a long moment. "I'll decide after

dinner," he said, pushing himself up from the chair with a small grunt.

Hannah leapt to her feet. "You mean you'll truly consider it, Papa? Truly?"

"I'm a reasonable man," Austin said easily.

Dinner seemed to last forever. Austin and George debated about the future of sailing ships now that steamships were becoming more common. Although Hannah enjoyed the conversation, she felt like a child who could only open her birthday presents until after the adults had finished eating. She wanted to know—now. She couldn't believe her father was even considering her request, and she wondered if it was George's presence on the ship that made the idea easier to swallow.

As the servants cleared the dirty dinnerware away, Austin leaned back in his chair and lit his pipe. George followed suit, two men with full bellies and nothing better to do than enjoy a smoke. Hannah wanted to take her glass of water and douse their pipes. Her father must know how anxious she was to hear his decision.

As a maid began lighting the candles on the table, Hannah let out a heavy breath that caused her father to glance in her direction.

"Certainly we can afford to light candles when the sun goes down," he said, raising his eyebrows. Hannah was certain he was purposefully misinterpreting her sigh of impatience.

"Of course not. I'm simply a bit on edge awaiting your decision."

"Decision?" And he had the gall to wink again at George. Austin smiled indulgently at his daughter's look of exasperation.

"If James MacRae is foolish enough to hire on a woman as his navigator, I will not stop him," he said, as if the idea had never given him trouble.

"I have your blessing to go find Allen?" Hannah asked incredulously.

"You have my permission to sail aboard the *Windfire*," Austin amended.

Hannah shot out of her chair and hurried around the table to give her father a neck-wrenching hug. "Oh, thank you, Papa. Thank you."

Austin watched as his daughter happily left the dining room, no doubt to begin packing for her trip, and let out a chuckle.

"Beg pardon, sir," George said. "I would never question a father's decision . . ."

"But you are about to anyway, I gather."

"She will be an unmarried woman alone among a crew of men."

"One of which will be her overly protective cousin."

George nodded. "Yes, sir."

Austin took a series of puffs from his rosewood pipe. "Seafaring men are gamblers, son. I'm taking a gamble, here. I know that. But if I'm right, it will all be for the best."

"If you say so, sir." George's stomach gave a turn. He'd have to tell the captain that his ploy had failed. He was afraid he'd see the man truly angry for the first time, and he wasn't looking forward to it.

Chapter Three

"**D**amn and blast it!" James slapped the top of the ship's railing with a loud crack. "What is the man thinking?" he demanded of George. He'd been right. James MacRae was angry. Very angry.

"I have no idea, sir," George said with a small shake of his head.

"He's been ill. Is it up here?" James asked, pointing to his own head.

George shook his head. "His heart, Captain."

"Well, it affected his brain. I'll not have it. I'll not." James strode about the main deck of his ship, boots sounding loud on the wooden surface, and gazed up at the towering masts as if they could offer up an answer to what he should do. "I gave my word," he spat. "Damn if I'm not the biggest fool God created."

He leaned on the railing, the muscles straining in forearms exposed by his rolled-up sleeves, and looked down the long row of ships. Playing a game with Miss Wright had been enjoyable, one he'd hoped he'd be able to continue—on land. How else would he get the lovely lady to his side if not to indulge her a bit. He saw the look of gratitude on her face when he'd agreed to hire her, and it was nearly that look of awe he'd enjoyed from so many beautiful ladies. If he'd thought for a single moment that her father would agree, he never would have played such a dangerous game. He hadn't known it *was* dangerous. Her father's refusal was a certainty, like finding a gale around the Horn or seeing seagulls dancing in the wind near shore. Ah, she was a dangerous one, with her sea-green eyes and that little stubborn chin that jutted up every time he'd said something disagreeable. God above knew he loved danger most of all.

"The address," he spat. "Give me the address."

"Of my uncle's?"

"Yes, of your uncle's. My God, man. Why *did* I hire you?"

And that is when George knew. He wasn't angry, he was challenged. James MacRae would attack this problem with the joy and vigor he attacked everything else. He'd thought he'd come to know the man, but apparently he had not. James MacRae would hire Hannah, that was a certainty. He would bluster and blow, he would pace and gesture, he would curse and gripe, but he would hire Hannah. And enjoy every minute of it.

George shook his head. "You *want* to hire her," he said.

A slow smile spread on James's lips, and he gazed again at the masts. It seemed that, out of the blue, that is exactly what he wanted. "What a trip this will be, mate. A trip we'll not soon forget. Just tie Miss Wright to the mast if it blows too hard. Hell, a ten-knot wind could tear her from this deck."

"You're still going to talk to her father?"

"Of course. Wouldn't miss it for the world. Not for the world."

The hansom cab left a wake of dust behind as it departed from where Hannah had stepped off, her calling card already in hand. She was certain Mrs. Pritchard would be "unavailable," but she was determined to let her future mother-in-law know that they needed to talk. If Hannah's mother were still alive, she would have accompanied her, but as she was not, Hannah was forced to face many tasks quite alone. Her father absolutely loathed Mrs. Pritchard, and Hannah had to admit she was a bit snobbish. She disapproved of her son marrying someone she did not see as "quality," even though Hannah's mother had come from one of the finest families in New York.

Knowing their disdain, Hannah was at times positively awful in front of her. Instead of getting angry, dear, dear Allen had been amused by her antics. Hannah had not seen Mrs. Althea Pritchard with any regularity since Allen's departure. Her father refused to invite her to dinner, and when Hannah insisted, he pleaded illness, then slipped out the back door to spend the evening at his favorite tavern. Hannah knew and didn't mind, for she found Allen's mother quite tiresome, simply because she was always striving to be so proper with her all the time. But she was Allen's mother, after all, and he truly loved her in his careless way, and so Hannah forced herself to act the way she thought a daughter-in-law should, especially since Allen left.

Hannah turned the doorbell and waited on the marbled entryway for one of the Pritchards' numerous servants to answer the door. Far wealthier than the Wrights, Althea Pritchard, a widow for fifteen years, appeared to enjoy flaunting her dead husband's wealth by hiring more servants than could possibly be needed, even in such a fine home as hers. She seemed to enjoy talking about her servants, the trials of having such a vast staff, the sacrifices she had to make for being unable to find qualified help. The Wrights made do with a cook, one upstairs maid, a downstairs maid, and a butler, who was also her father's valet.

A uniformed butler opened the door, then immediately held out one spotless gloved hand for her card, even though the man knew who she was. Regardless, Hannah silently handed over her card, then handed off her bonnet to a maid, who curtsied nicely. She knew that had she sneezed, yet another servant would have rushed forward with a clean handkerchief. Hannah thought she would never get used to such ostentatiousness, but for Allen's sake she would try. Sun streamed through a high round window above the door,

which cast the large, marbled entrance hall in cheerful light.
A grand, marble staircase with a royal blue runner curved up
to the second floor. Everything about the Pritchard mansion
was grand, which had the effect of making Hannah feel very
small.

The butler, who had disappeared with her card laid in the
very center of a small silver tray, returned with a bow and
led her to Althea's drawing room. It was a sunny, lovely parlor, dominated by rose with gold accents. The marble fire-
place, which Althea had told her with pride was imported
from Italy, was the same rosy hue as much of the upholstery.
A large gold-framed mirror had been hung above the fire-
place. Hannah had always thought the placement of that
mirror impractical, for it was situated so high, no one could
put it to its proper use.

"Miss Wright," Althea said, standing gracefully. Althea
Pritchard did everything gracefully, Hannah thought with
grudging admiration. The older woman had even aged
gracefully, her once-blond hair gradually turning to a soft
white, her figure slim, her face without heavy lines. She was
only a few inches taller than Hannah, but had a way of making Hannah feel as if she were an awkward, mannerless
child. Which, of course, Hannah on occasion was, if only to
irritate the woman. "So good of you to visit. Have you word
from my dear Allen?"

Hannah felt her stomach twist at the hopeful note in the
woman's voice. No matter how she felt about her, Althea
Pritchard loved her son, and Hannah could not fault her for
that.

"No, ma'am, I'm afraid I have not," Hannah said, taking
a seat as Althea lowered herself back into her chair. Though
they had known each other for years, Althea had never given
Hannah permission to call her by her given name, and continued to call Hannah Miss Wright. "I have come here to in-
form you of my plans to search for Allen. I leave on the
Windfire in two days and should arrive in San Francisco before the first of the year."

"I shall go with you," the woman said without hesitation, thoroughly surprising Hannah.

"Oh, Mrs. Pritchard, I'm afraid the ship's long been booked. There are no more berths available, else my father would surely join me." Hannah said a little prayer that God would not be too angry at her small lie.

"I see." The older woman's lips pursed, causing the entire lower part of her face to wrinkle unappealingly. "And who will be accompanying you on this journey?"

Hannah looked down at her hands, hoping Mrs. Pritchard would not see the guilty flush on her cheeks. "My cousin, George, is first mate on the ship. As no one else is available, he will act as chaperon."

"But that will never do." She seemed rather shocked that Hannah had planned such a trip without an adequate chaperon. "A single woman alone on a ship for months . . . Oh, no, it will never do."

"I'm afraid it must, ma'am. I realize the conditions are not ideal, but with ships' berths at such a premium, I was lucky to find a . . . spot on the ship."

Althea sniffed. "Indeed. Well, there is nothing to do but share."

Hannah gulped audibly. "Share?"

"As uncomfortable as it will be, we will simply have to share your cabin."

"But . . . but . . . the beds are hardly large enough for two," Hannah said, desperately casting about for some excuse to make so that she would not have to tell Mrs. Pritchard the full truth. Indeed, she did not know where she would lay her own head as the only woman in an all-male crew.

"We will simply bring a cot. We'll make due. As Allen's fiancée, your reputation must remain intact. I'm afraid a trip alone would taint you beyond redemption. You say the ship is leaving in two days? Oh, much to do. Much to do," she muttered. As she stood and strode toward the bellpull that would likely call an army of servants, Hannah stood, panic gripping her.

"Mrs. Pritchard," she shouted. "Please. You cannot come with me."

The older woman turned ever so slowly, a look of stern disbelief on her face. "I beg pardon."

Hannah sagged back into her chair. "You cannot come with me, Mrs. Pritchard, because I am not going as a passenger on the *Windfire*. I am going as a member of the crew."

Althea made a hasty grab for the back of her chair, as if she were about to topple over from shock. "You cannot be serious."

"I'm afraid I am very serious. It is the only way I can get to San Francisco to find Allen."

The older woman settled back into her chair. "My dear girl, if funds were so low, you could have come to me."

It had never entered her head to ask Mrs. Pritchard for money. Even if it had, she decided pride would have prevented her from asking. "I could not do that," Hannah said with quiet firmness.

"You can and you shall. How much is the passage?"

Hannah set her jaw stubbornly. "Mrs. Pritchard, I cannot allow you to pay for passage. It is one thousand dollars, and besides, there are no berths available."

"None on the *Windfire*, but certainly there are other ships. Steamer ships. I will book us passage on one of the steamers and . . ."

"No," Hannah shouted. Although part of her rebellious mind knew that Allen's mother was making perfect sense, she refused to alter her plans. She was going to be navigator on one of the most glorious clipper ships ever made, and she'd be damned if propriety would stop her.

Hannah did not realize until that moment how important a victory it was for her to have gained permission from her father to become a crew member. She remembered with pride the first voyage to France that she had plotted. How her father had praised her after that trip, boasting to other captains, who smiled indulgently not believing a word. After all, Hannah had only been fourteen at the time—and a girl. She could still recall the sense of accomplishment, that heady feeling that she could do anything, face any challenge. She'd been devastated two years later to learn that her secret girlish fantasy of becoming a ship's captain would never be realized. She would not become a captain, she would become a wife and a mother. By the time she'd left Hudson Finishing School for Girls when she was eighteen, she'd realized those dreams of captaining her own ship were silly, and she'd wanted nothing more than to become that wife and mother. Now . . . well, now she'd gotten a taste of that dream she'd thought she'd given up. Suddenly there was nothing more in this world that she wanted to do but sail around the Horn on the *Windfire*, sextant in hand. After the voyage, she would marry Allen and become that respectable woman Mrs. Pritchard wanted her to be.

"No?" Althea was clearly puzzled by Hannah's adamant refusal.

"Mrs. Pritchard," Hannah said with restraint as she tried to tame her temper. "I am leaving on the *Windfire* in two days. Please understand that this is something I must do. You are correct, there are other ships, other ways to reach California. But this is the quickest route to Allen. I cannot wait for another berth to open on another ship."

Althea's elegant nostrils flared in anger. "Is your father aware of your plans?"

"He is. He has given his permission."

"I can tell you that I am not surprised he has. Has he no concern of your welfare?"

Hannah stood, ready to defend her wonderful father. "My father realizes I am a woman grown and can make my own decisions."

Althea also rose to her feet, taking advantage of her taller height to look down her nose at Hannah. "And your father has no care of your reputation? No care of Allen's? Have you no idea how very improper it is for you to be aboard a ship of men, alone, without a chaperon."

"My cousin is the first mate. He is my chaperon," Hannah repeated.

Althea waved a hand dismissing the notion that a cousin—a male cousin—could offer Hannah any protection. "You leave me no choice but to talk to your father myself. And if he continues to be so obtuse, then I will be forced to speak to the captain of the ship personally."

Hannah smiled at the thought of Althea Pritchard in conversation with Captain James MacRae. "I'm afraid the decision is final, but you may speak to whomever you wish, Mrs. Pritchard. My father and the captain gave their words. They are not men to change their minds."

Althea lifted her head a notch. "We shall see."

Hannah returned home, excitement curling in her belly. Now that the unpleasant task of informing her future mother-in-law of her plans to find Allen was completed, her entire focus was on the trip. No, the race. The race around the Horn. She could do it, she knew she could, she thought, already planning to study her book on wind and sea currents. She'd not let Captain MacRae and the rest of the crew down, she'd find the best route to get to San Francisco. And then, of course, she'd look for Allen. And they would marry, and she would . . . she would . . . Be normal. Hannah faltered as she made her way upstairs to her room. "It's what I want," she told herself fiercely.

She began trudging up the stairs again, allowing herself to be lost in the excitement of packing and planning such an adventure, when she heard a shout coming from her father's study. One hand clutching the teak banister, made from a scuttled ship's railing, she cocked one ear toward the study. Another shout, loud and with a discernible Scottish burr. Why would Captain MacRae be here shouting at her father? Narrowing her eyes, she marched back down the steps and headed for the study, thrusting the door open without knocking.

"My ship is not a training ground for . . ." James stopped his blustering when he saw Austin Wright's head turn toward the door.

"You gave your word," Hannah said, refusing to acknowledge she was hurt by Captain MacRae's attempt to renege on their agreement. The man, looking irritatingly dashing standing there before her father, had the gall to smile.

"That I did," he said, turning his large body fully toward her. "But I had to hear it in person to believe it."

"You thought George lied to you?"

"No. I thought perhaps your father misunderstood your role on the ship. But I was wrong. He seems quite sure what he is about."

Hannah turned to her father, who appeared, to her confusion, to be trying not to smile. He picked up from the holder on the desk his still-smoldering pipe and took a couple of thoughtful puffs, his eyes going from her to Captain MacRae. Her father had a wonderful knack of hiding what he was thinking, so Hannah had no idea whether he was angry with Captain MacRae for doubting George or pleased that the man had come to see him in person.

"It is very urgent that my daughter reach San Francisco safely and quickly, Captain. She is searching for her fiancé, who has gone missing in search of gold."

Hannah frowned at her father's disclosure. She hadn't wanted Captain MacRae to know the precise purpose of her trip. It was none of the man's business why she needed to get to California.

"Fiancé," James said, a knowing look dawning on his face as he crossed his arms over his chest. "Jilted, hmmm? Well, isn't it a mite humiliating to go chasing after a lost man who doesn't want to be found?"

Why, the audacity of the man, Hannah thought, anger surging through her. "I have not been jilted, sir," Hannah managed to say with some civility through tight lips. "It is simply that Allen is not the sort of man who disappears. I am deeply afraid that something has happened to him, and as I intended to go to California to join him eventually anyway, it only makes sense for me to make the trip now."

"I should have known," James said, disappointment clear in his voice. Somehow, Hannah knew the man was mocking her.

"Should have known what?" she asked with hostility.

"That it wasn't adventure or the love of the sea that drove you to want to board the *Windfire*, but romantic fancies," he said with some derision. "I thought you made up that melodramatic drivel about rescuing a man."

"Drivel?" she said, outraged. "And there is nothing fanciful about . . ." Hannah stopped abruptly, knowing full well she was about to fall into the trap the captain had set for her. He was a man who loved conflict, who thrived on it. Well, she'd not give it to him, surely the best way to deflate his sails. She raised her head and smiled without warmth. "You are correct, sir. The only reason I am boarding the *Windfire* is to go to my true love."

This time it was the captain's lips that pressed into annoyance.

"It matters not," he said in an impatient way Hannah had not yet heard from him. "I gave my word. You are signed as navigator. We leave at high tide Wednesday. I expect you aboard and ready at half tide."

"Yes, sir."

James then strode to her father to shake the older man's hand. "Thank you for your time, Captain Wright."

Austin Wright looked directly into James's eyes. "Take care of my daughter, Captain."

"In three months' time, sir, she'll be in her true love's arms," he said grandly.

"I'm counting on it." His words surprised Hannah, for she knew her father didn't truly support the match between her and Allen.

James bowed and smiled to Hannah, then walked from the room. After he'd gone, Hannah turned to her father.

"Thank you for standing by your decision, Papa," she said.

"Have you ever known me to change my mind about anything once a decision's made?"

"You apparently have changed your mind about Allen."

Her father gave a grunt, which Hannah interpreted as confirmation, and stood. "Captain MacRae seems to be an extraordinary man. Did you know he is only thirty years old and yet he's been given one of the best, fastest ships McKay's ever built? I've been doing some inquiring since yesterday. Your Captain MacRae is an extremely competent ship's master with a crew who's loyal and well trained. I want you to know, that had I heard otherwise, I would not have allowed you to go."

"I don't know how he runs a ship effectively. The man is never serious," Hannah grumbled.

Her father's eyes widened. "Is that what you think?"

Hannah gave an unladylike shrug. "He thinks it's a grand joke to have me aboard. Surely you know that."

"That is true." And he laughed quietly. "But he's about to find out otherwise, isn't he?" He chucked the underside of Hannah's chin. "I pride myself on reading men, Hannah. Don't think for a moment he doesn't take this trip seriously. If he thought you would jeopardize his ship, you would not be on it. He came here today, not to complain, but to see if you were as good a navigator as you think you are."

Hannah lifted her head. "And am I?"

He smiled indulgently. "Almost, Hannah. Almost."

Hannah let out a delighted laugh. "I'm that good? My goodness. I think I'll ask the captain for a raise."

Chapter Four

Hannah stepped up the gangplank that led to the *Windfire* main deck feeling almost light-headed with excitement. She walked up it as if she belonged, though she truly felt she did not. Many of the crew were making last-minute checks of lines and sails, Hannah noted as she looked about for Captain MacRae. She could hear him somewhere near the bow shouting about something, but she could not see him past the many crew members that had crowded the deck. The excitement on board and off was almost a tangible thing. Although most people had gathered at Battery Park to watch as the ship headed toward the Atlantic, a fair-sized crowd had gathered at Pier 6, many relatives of passengers or crew. Hannah's own father would soon be part of the crowd, and she scanned the faces to see if he had arrived, but determined he had not. The dock was a bustle of activity as passengers directed servants where to bring luggage. All the cargo, including wagons, construction and mining equipment, flour, sugar, as well as everyday items such as pots, pans, and place settings, had long been stored in the ship's narrow hold. The ship's owners had built a bandstand, and a brass band played foot-tapping music to entertain a crowd no doubt attracted by numerous newspaper articles that touted the *Windfire* as the fastest clipper ship ever built.

And Hannah was a part of it all. Not a spectator, but a participant, and she was filled with pride. Hannah smiled at the crowd and made her way toward the bow, where Captain MacRae was taking care of last-minute details.

"Miss, the passengers' rooms is toward th' stern in the after house. That's toward th' back of th' ship," a young seaman said politely. He had white-blond hair beneath a black cap and sported only the scarcest of beards, a few dark blond spikes erupting from his chin. He was no more than seventeen, Hannah guessed, thinking he must be one of the ship's apprentices.

"Yes. It is," Hannah said. She thrust out her gloved hand. "I'm Hannah Wright."

The boy stared at her hand as if she were offering an object he'd never seen before. "Yes, miss." He stared at her blankly, shifting his feet as if unsure what he should do, and it suddenly dawned on Hannah that the captain might not have told his crew he had hired her as navigator.

"I'm the navigator, seaman. Hannah Wright."

The teenager's jaw dropped. "The *what,* miss?"

"Mr. Engle," came a bellow from somewhere behind them, causing both to jump. The seaman recovered first, and with fear showing clearly in his eyes, hurried over to where the captain stood scowling at him. "You have duties to attend to. Do them. You can become acquainted with our navigator another time. Now, go."

The boy fairly ran from the area, as if fearing the devil were on his tail. Hannah turned to the captain, a smile on her face. "You've got them fooled with all that bluster, haven't you?"

James scowled down at Hannah, irritated that she so easily saw through him. It seemed to be a family gift, to immediately know that there was little bite accompanying his rather formidable bark. His first mate, George Wright, would never defy him, but he sure as hell wasn't afraid of him. He looked down at his navigator, still scowling, as he took in her decidedly feminine attire. If he couldn't frighten this spit of a girl, who the hell could he frighten? Unlike George, who was a good and loyal mate, he suspected Hannah would fight him at every turn. It was best to set the girl straight now, he thought with a bit of regret. It would be the first time in his life he'd attempt to make a beautiful woman fear him.

"Miss Wright. Your opinion of me matters not. What does matter is that you are standing here as if this is a Sunday outing. What the devil are you doing dressed in all your finery? You are a member of this crew, miss. I pray you have something more appropriate to wear than a gown that one good wind would tear from your back." For good measure, he leered at her.

He saw her green eyes snap in anger, and was stunned. Hardly frightened, the girl balled her fists. "I have more appropriate clothes. Do not forget, Captain, I am no stranger to ships. I simply thought for the ceremonial launch that I would dress in my finest. I shall change as soon as I know where I am to sleep." She lifted her chin. "And if you plan to frighten me, you'll have to do a much better job than that." It was all James could do not to throw back his head and laugh, so delighted in her was he. Instead, he deepened his scowl.

"As I rarely sleep in my cabin, that is where you will stay." He saw fear in her eyes for the first time and decided he didn't like it, after all. "You need not worry about your delicate sensibilities, Miss Wright. I will sleep in the mate's cabin when I need to. With the chart room off my cabin, it only makes sense to put you in there." He watched as she bit her lower lip, refusing to acknowledge that he was fascinated by the gesture.

"I don't want to take your berth, Captain."

"You certainly cannot sleep in the forecastle with the men. And as I told you, I rarely sleep in the cabin. If I do require prolonged rest, I will take your cousin's berth."

Hannah nodded. "I will change, then." She looked down at her dress uncertainly. "I thought . . ." Then she shrugged and headed to collect her bag, pulling in her voluminous skirts as close against her as possible.

Blast and damn, James thought, forcing his eyes away from the woman who walked away from him. He looked instead at the broad spars, the pristine white sails ready to unfurl, the crew making ready. It wouldn't do to become distracted by that bit of femininity. He needed to focus on his true ladylove: the *Windfire*. As soon as he gazed up at her towering masts, all thoughts of Hannah Wright were driven from his mind.

Minutes later, Hannah watched as Captain MacRae bounded down the ship's gangplank and swept a middle-aged, rather plump woman into his arms, twirling her about with ease. Even from this distance, she could hear the delighted squeals the woman let out.

"His mother," George offered as he came up beside Hannah. "You really ought to change out of that dress. I overheard the captain grumbling about certain crew members who think they are on holiday and wearing their Sunday finest."

Hannah gave her cousin a crooked smile. "I plan to change, George. But I thought for the ceremonies, I'd look my best. I believe many spectators would find my ship-wear rather shocking, particularly my future mother-in-law. Although, after her disagreeable interview with my father, I doubt she will make an appearance."

The two watched as James gave a hearty handshake and quick hug to a man Hannah assumed was his father. For some reason, she'd not thought of him as a family man, and she wondered if either of the two young women gazing up at him with such annoying adoration was his wife. George quickly supplied her answers.

"The older man is the captain's father. He's headmaster of a boys' school and is still trying to figure out how he managed to raise a sea captain. The young ladies are two of his sisters. There are seven children in the family altogether. I met them all while I was in Boston. Captain MacRae is the oldest. There are five daughters, and then Adam, the youngest. He's the one looking at Captain as if the sun rose and set around him."

"They all look like that," Hannah said dryly, and smiled when George laughed.

"Get used to it. Captain James MacRae is a hero to a lot of people, including many on this ship. Some have been with him for years, and to them he can do no wrong. He's led them through some tight spots, proven he's a fair man. There are very few things the crew wouldn't do for him."

Hannah stared at the captain as he talked animatedly with his family. "Does that include you?" she asked.

George nodded sharply. "It does." Hannah sensed he wanted to say something more, so she turned her thoughtful gaze his way. "I don't know why he allowed you to sign on, but now that he has, I want you to behave."

Hannah stiffened.

"Now, don't get your back all up," George said, putting up a hand to ward off any angry retorts. "This trip is important to us all. It's vital that the captain's entire focus be on this ship. I've never seen him distracted, no matter what was happening in his life. I know I haven't been with him long, but I've heard stories from the second mate, Timothy Lodge. You'll meet him today, I'm sure. The captain had another brother, his first mate years ago. He died of a fever during one trip in the midst of one of the worst nor'easters many had ever seen. He stood by, never leaving the helm, never allowing his grief to jeopardize the lives of his crew and his ship."

Hannah turned her gaze once again to Captain MacRae, and her heart clenched at the thought of that young man losing his brother and having the strength to continue. "If he kept his head during such a tragedy, why would you think I could distract him?" she asked.

George shook his head. "You really don't know, do you?"

Hannah gave him a questioning look.

"You're quite beautiful, Hannah. Beautiful women have been known to wreak more havoc than the fiercest storm.

And Captain MacRae is well-known for attracting beautiful women."

Hannah snorted. "Oh, really, George. For one thing, I am engaged and the captain knows it. For another, I am quite convinced the man dislikes me." She put her hands on her hips and tilted her head, narrowing her eyes at her cousin because it was clear from his expression she had somehow misunderstood him. "Wait one minute. Are you afraid that the captain will find me irresistible or that the captain will be irresistible to me?"

"As I said, the captain has quite a reputation. And I've seen his effect on women firsthand. It is positively amazing," George said with all seriousness.

Hannah let out a delighted laugh and lightly slapped her cousin on the arm. "I will try my utmost to resist the captain's charms," she announced, laughter in her voice.

George frowned. "The captain likes his women, but he'll not become distracted. His ship always comes first. I'm not saying that you'll abandon all principle and . . ."

"What? Fall madly in love with him as we're rounding the Horn and scuttle the ship? Don't forget, the reason I am traveling on this ship is so that I might find my fiancé. Two of the passengers are also women. Do you plan to give them a similar lecture?"

"Forget I said anything," George said, sounding sulky.

"I certainly shall."

"It's not only that you're pretty," he muttered.

"I thought you said 'beautiful.' "

George shot her an exasperated look. "It's that you are disagreeable and stubborn at times. On this ship, the captain's word is gold. Crew members do not question orders, they don't chat about the merits of their assignment. They simply do it."

"I have been on a ship before, George. I quite understand how one is run."

"Don't forget, cousin, I've seen you on a ship. I've heard you argue and debate with your father until he wanted to dive off the highest mast and into the sea simply to escape your tongue."

"That's not true. Well, perhaps a bit. But I was younger then, and the captain was my father, after all. I suppose I felt it permissible to question his orders . . ." Hannah's voice faded as she realized her own arguments were weak. She noticed that George was looking pointedly at her dress.

"I know the captain asked you to change."

Hannah lifted her chin. "Yes. He asked. He did not order. If he had ordered me to . . ."

"You would have stayed in that dress until the wind ripped it from your back, and you know it."

It was Hannah's turn to act sulky, for she knew her cousin spoke the truth. "I will try."

"Men and women's lives are at stake. You must do better than try. This is not some grand adventure, Hannah. This is a ship built for speed, built to earn profits. There is no room here for someone who is not committed to her."

"Oh, enough," Hannah said with irritation. "I am not a child, George. I am just two years younger than you and have been on ships nearly as long."

George softened his expression. "Consider this lecture over, Hannah. I apologize if it was not necessary."

Hannah smiled, graciously accepting his apology, but frowned as George finished his thought. "But I believe it was necessary. Very necessary. Now, I have duties. I suggest you change your clothes, cousin. The captain just looked up here, and he wasn't smiling."

But Hannah did not hear the last admonition. She was already rushing down the plank toward her smiling father.

"Papa. Isn't she grand?" Austin Wright gave the *Windfire* an admiring look, before looking down at his daughter, pride clear in his eyes, and just the tiniest bit of fear. It would be a treacherous journey in more ways than one, and his eyes traveled to the strapping young captain giving final good-byes to his family.

"She's a fine ship, daughter," he said, his voice gruff.

"You miss the sea, don't you, Papa?" She watched as her father's gaze lovingly swept the ship.

"I do. But every captain must someday retire. Even your Captain MacRae will."

Hannah wrinkled her nose. "I wish you would stop referring to him as *my* Captain MacRae."

"But he is your captain."

Hannah said nothing, but crossed her arms and watched with a scowl as the captain charged up the plank, his black hair blowing in the stiff breeze coming off the river. Hannah's thoughts turned to her mother, to all those times she had stood on a dock and waved good-bye to her husband as she tried to hold back the tears. Mary Wright hadn't wanted to upset her husband by letting him know how desperately she would miss him, and so the last sight of her Austin Wright always had was her waving and smiling. And it was all a lie. Hannah remembered watching her mother smile as tears, her father could not see, streamed down her face.

"Will you be all right without me, Papa?" Hannah said suddenly realizing she would not see her father for perhaps years. She'd been so caught up in the excitement of the trip, of her worry about Allen, that she hadn't realized she might not see her father again. He was ill, after all, and if she found Allen and they married in San Francisco, she might never return home again. She whirled about and thrust herself into her father's arms as sobs shook her body.

"There, there, now, girl. I'll be fine," Austin said, patting her back, his face a heart-wrenching mixture of concern, panic, and deep sadness. "Ships' navigators do not cry, Hannah."

"This one does," she said against his neck, her voice filled with tears. "And I don't care who sees." Hannah wrapped her arms so tight around her father's neck, he let out a strangled sound. The exaggerated noise had the desired effect. Hannah started laughing as she apologized for nearly asphyxiating her father.

"I'll miss you, Papa," she said, stepping back and smiling through her tears. As her mother had done so many times.

"I'll miss you, too, daughter. You know that."

"Yes. I know." Hannah gave her father one final hug, then turned and walked up the plank. When she turned back, she waved and her father saluted her making her laugh again. With a heartfelt sigh, she turned to head to her cabin to change.

An hour later the tug that had brought them off the pier was disengaging, and James was ordering the sails unfurled in a voice that carried up and down the East River. Men, already in place on the spars, some so high their features were indiscernible, obeyed the order with a collective shout. It seemed all of New York was on hand, all holding their breaths to watch this glorious ship unfurl acres of pristine canvas as it passed Sandy Hook. In a well-planned maneuver, the sails were dropped as if by a single hand, snapping in the wind as the ship was pushed forward. The twenty-member crew began gustily singing, "Blow, boys, blow, for California, oh; There's plenty of gold, so I've been told, on the banks of the Sacramento."

Had there ever been a more beautiful sight, James thought, than his *Windfire* under sail? Though the ship was majority owned by Haywood & Bennings, he owned a fair share of her, which only deepened his pride. His only hope was that someday the *Windfire* or a ship like her would be his. James could hear the cheers of the distant crowd in his ears as he continued to shout orders, instantly obeyed by his well-honed crew. By God, he was proud of them, he thought, his eyes going from sail to sail, from mast to mast, to make sure all was well. Every face held a smile, every body was ready and fit for the journey of a lifetime. They knew and were proud that they could be part of history. It would be months before they knew whether they had beat either the *Flying Cloud* or the *Challenge,* months of brutal, bone-wearying work, of battling gales and cold that numbed the body as well as the spirit. And James embraced it all with vigor. He strode to the stern, listening to the sails, listening to what his ship was telling him. She sounded well pleased at the moment, a stiff breeze filling her sails. What a beauty she was, he thought, his entire body electrified. Then his gaze fell on Hannah Wright, and the admiration for his ship that glowed in his eyes deepened.

She was wearing well-fitting fawn breeches and a white oversized man's shirt, a blue sash about her waist. On her head, covering that brown-gold hair of hers, was a ridiculously large and flopping straw hat tied under her chin with a scarf of the same color as her sash. She stood near the ship's wheel and her cousin, gazing up at the sails with an expression of pure rapture, unaware that several crew members were looking at her with similar expressions.

He'd known this would happen and was ready for it. "The ship, men," he bellowed, "is your mistress. She cannot be ignored, she is jealous and she is vengeful." The men who had been staring at Hannah quickly turned their heads away and worked diligently on the tasks at hand. By their red faces, James knew the men had gotten the message. Crew members too far away to hear the veiled warning would hear of it from other sailors. Word spread quickly that a woman had been hired on as navigator, and though there had been some speculative looks, James knew his crew was too loyal to grumble about it. If Miss Wright failed, *then* he would hear grumbling.

James ignored the look of gratitude Hannah flashed him. He had a ship to sail.

Chapter Five

The *Windfire* was heading out to sea, and New Jersey was a narrow strip on the darkening horizon. Hannah headed to her cabin and to the chart room to plot her course. A few passengers lingered on the deck after dinner, putting off until the latest possible hour when they would head into their cramped cabins.

The *Windfire* carried eleven passengers, mostly men hoping to strike it rich in the gold fields of California. The two women passengers were nowhere to be found, and Hannah wondered about what had brought them on this journey. Were they married to men who sought their fortunes? Were they, like her, traveling to California to meet a loved one?

Though *Windfire* was a beautiful ship, she was not built for the comfort of its passengers. Tiny rooms had been carved in the after house, which surrounded the mizzenmast as it poked through to the hull. She wondered why someone who could afford the one-thousand-dollar passage would need to go to California in the first place. And then she thought of Allen, and realized the lure of gold was something beyond her comprehension. So many people, thousands, had left all they knew behind—family, friends, jobs—on the chance they could strike it rich. Hannah could understand the lure of adventure, of discovering a new land, of forging a home. Wasn't that what she and Allen had planned?

Above her head a sail snapped loudly, and she could hear the shout of Captain MacRae. She smiled. She was beginning to understand that elusive quality he had that made men listen to him, that made them jump when he shouted at them to jump. It was clear the good humor and enthusiasm the captain had for the sea and his ship rubbed off on the men. He strode with purpose from one end of the ship to another, pausing to speak to crew members, his officers and passengers alike, slapping backs or shaking hands, or bowing at the two middle-aged ladies who had ventured above. There he was now, head bent and expression filled with interest as he listened to one of the ladies on the ship. But Hannah could tell by the tilt of his head that what he was truly listening to was his ship. She watched as he excused himself, then went bounding toward the ship's wheel, shouting an order that the helmsman head farther off the wind. Hadn't the helmsman felt that wind shift? Did MacRae have to man the helm twenty-four hours a day?

"I'll do it, if that's what needs to be done," he shouted, his words holding more challenge than criticism. When the helmsman brought the ship so that the sails had the best benefit of the wind, he slapped the man on the back. "Do you feel it, man? Do you see how she responds? That's what you want. We just gained another knot, I'm damned if we didn't."

Her father had been correct. Captain MacRae was a fine ship's master. Hannah felt the urgent need to please him by finding the best winds and currents, and she headed toward the companionway that led to her quarters. Stepping down, her cabin was immediately to her right, the chart room to her left. Ahead, down the narrow hall, its mahogany wainscoting gleaming in the lamplight, were the first and second mate's cabins. Farther still, it opened to a stately dining hall with soft forest-green carpeting. Here, the walls were a brilliant white, while the furnishings were deep reds and greens, trimmed with gold. The skylight, now darkened with the oncoming dusk, cast only the dimmest rectangle of light on the polished table. One side of the dining hall was lined with the tiny but richly appointed passenger's cabins, the other side with a large pantry and bread locker. Hannah peeked her head into the dining hall and waved at the young, fresh-faced steward who was still cleaning up following their dinner. She would have liked to have chatted with the young man, who would spend much of this trip working alone, but she was far behind on her work and had much to do before the next day.

The captain's cabin, her cabin for now, was already dark, the small portholes letting in only dim circles of rosy light as the sun set. After depositing her hat, she headed to the chart room. She smiled as she remembered to cover the portholes with the heavy canvas that would not allow any light to seep onto the deck. Hannah still remembered her father's anger when she had forgotten this necessity. Even the smallest light hitting the deck could ruin a helmsman's night vision and lead to disaster. Hannah lit a lamp, rehung it, and pulled out the chart of the Atlantic Ocean. She unrolled it and laid it on the slanted teak desk, placing small weights on its corners to keep it unfurled. She smiled, well pleased that the charts were the most recent ones published. Her dog-eared copy of *Charts and Sailing Directions* lay open on the floor.

Hannah closed her eyes, reveling in smells and sounds that filled her senses. Linseed oil, wood, the sharp sea-scent, mingled with the groan of rope, the snap of the sails, the steady cadence of the water smashing against the ship's hull. She could feel the *Windfire* slicing through the sea, almost picture how she would look to another ship passing by, her sails glowing pale rose in the last of the sun's light. She could hear the footsteps of the crew, their muffled shouts, the laughter of the passengers. It was . . . wonderful, she thought, feeling more alive than she'd felt in years. How her father must miss the sea, his ships. Hannah Wright knew she looked like her mother, but she acknowledged her father's blood ran through her veins. With a new sense of enthusiasm, Hannah bent toward the task before her.

Three hours later, James stood frowning at the dimmest of glows coming from the chart room porthole that told him his navigator was up and working. It was past midnight, and Hannah would likely be up with the sun. He didn't stop to think that he, too, would be up with the sun, for James had no plans to sleep at all that night. He never could manage more than two or three hours sleep during the first few days of a journey, no matter how he tried. He could not stop his ears from hearing the wind, the sails, and knowing that he alone was responsible for getting the ship to port on time made it nearly impossible to relax. The ship spoke to him constantly, even in his sleep. The tiniest of windshifts had him bolting upright from a deep sleep. In storms, he never left the deck, choosing instead to lash himself to a deck chair if exhaustion overcame him. How many times had he wished that sleep was not a necessary thing, that he could remain awake throughout the three-month journey?

Though James expected it of himself, he required his crew to be well rested. They worked in twelve-hour shifts, and unless they were in the middle of a gale, crew members were required to get at least six hours sleep each day. Perhaps, he thought, Miss Wright was not aware of this mandate.

James worked his jaw as he debated whether to pay his navigator a visit. He was acutely aware that it was late, that she was in the chart room alone, that she was, well, a *she*. He wanted to get to San Francisco in record time, and he knew that to do so he would require Hannah's entire focus to be on finding the best route. If she were wary of him, she could not do her job well. James had no doubt that he could ignore the fact she was inordinately attractive and focus on his ship. But he was not so certain that Miss Wright, if she were afraid of him, would be able to do the same.

Before he realized he made up his mind, he found himself knocking at the chart room door. "Miss Wright, may I have a word with you."

The door swung open almost immediately. "Yes, Captain, what can I do for you?"

She made no move to let him inside, so James stepped forward, forcing her to retreat. Better to get over any awkwardness between them right now, he thought. She still wore her pants and shirt, though she had removed the sash at her waist so that her shirt hung down to her knees. Despite the floppy hat she'd worn all day, her little nose was sunburned. Though he knew her to be twenty-two, at this moment she looked about sixteen and he had the terrible feeling that he should have refused to hire her. She should be at home wearing a cotton nightdress, tucked into bed, her head against a down pillow. She looked so young, so uncommonly beautiful, that for the briefest of moments, James forgot why he wanted to talk to her. But mostly he forgot he wanted to be businesslike, to set her at ease. What he wanted, before he could push the thought away with dogged determination, was to kiss her.

And then it was gone, with an angry surge, James thrust that thought away. "You are likely unaware that we work in twelve-hour shifts. Crew members are to get six hours rest each twenty-four-hour period, unless there are mitigating circumstances." His words were uncharacteristically clipped.

"There are mitigating circumstances, Captain," she said, waving a hand at her charts. "I am far behind on plotting a course. I'm doing work now that should have been done a week ago." And then the defensiveness was gone, replaced by glowing excitement that had James once again admonishing himself to stop acknowledging how damn beautiful she was.

"Shall I show you what I've done?" Hannah asked, clearly wanting to show off her skills.

James gave a curt nod and followed her to the desk, his hands clasped tightly behind his back. Her hair, he noticed for the first time, was in a single braid that bounced from shoulder blade to shoulder blade when she walked.

"I've relied heavily on my manual," she said, nodding to the book at her feet. "But I thought for this first leg, we'd try to go a little more eastward. It will add more miles to the trip, but the extra wind, I believe, will give us at least another day off the trip, perhaps more if we're lucky enough to hit some real air. That way, when we get to the equator, we'll benefit from . . ." She riffled through some charts, letting out a sigh of exasperation. "It was just here."

James's eyes were riveted on the charts, all thoughts of beautiful women and sunburned noses swept from his mind. "I see what you're doing. It's risky. If the wind isn't fair, we'll lose too many days."

Hannah smiled. "But if it is . . ."

"Plot the course. Get it to me tomorrow." James turned sharply and headed toward the door, his head bent as he made to cross the threshold.

"Captain?"

"Yes, Miss Wright."

"Thank you for your confidence in me."

James paused at the door. "I have no confidence in you right now. But if you're correct, if we gain a day, or even more, then you'll get more than my confidence. You'll get my respect. Good night, Miss Wright."

Hannah hugged herself. She'd get his confidence and his respect.

When he'd first knocked on her door, Hannah's heart had pounded with alarm, her stomach twisting in disappointment. So this is how it's going to be, she'd thought, a midnight visit for an amoral purpose. She wasn't truly afraid, for her cousin, after all, was only two doors down. She felt relatively safe from any unwelcome advances, but she prayed none were made. How could she possibly do her job if she were constantly afraid of groping hands? Now Hannah was ashamed she had even for a few seconds thought unkindly of the captain. She was quite certain he had treated her as he would have treated a new male navigator, and that knowledge pleased her.

Hannah hadn't known how nervous she was assuming this uncommon role until that knock on the door. A part of her had thought he would not listen to her, that he would disregard her advice. What a truly extraordinary man he is, she thought.

"Papa, you were right." Without even realizing it, Hannah put Captain MacRae on the pedestal already built by the rest of the crew. She could still hear George's warning ringing in her ears: "I've seen his effect on women firsthand. It is positively amazing."

Well, Hannah thought, Captain MacRae was an amazing man. And uncommonly handsome, with those blue eyes of his and that wavy black hair and that big body that a woman could fall against and know she'd be safe forever. She shook her head in disgust.

"Hannah Wright, you are a ninny." Here she was, on a ship bound for San Francisco and her fiancé, and all she could do was extol the virtues of another man. A man, she reminded herself, who apparently drew women the way old bait drew flies. How very amusing it would be for the good captain to discover that his navigator had a crush on him. Of course, she didn't. But Hannah knew that unless she was very, very careful, her admiration could turn into something more. She refused to become one of an apparent legion of women who fell for the charismatic captain only to have their hearts broken.

"He's a sea captain. And you're engaged," she said aloud. Her job as navigator would not be very time-consuming once she had finished plotting a course for the journey. She'd take readings twice daily to determine their location and make adjustments as she felt necessary, but Hannah would have quite a bit of free time. Hannah vowed she would not spend that time mooning after Captain MacRae. The ship held two female passengers who would no doubt be grateful to have a friend who could allay their fears when the seas became rough. Too many times she'd seen women cower in fear fed more by ignorance than any true threat. It would be heartening to see another woman on the deck, unconcerned about the rolling sea, the darkening clouds. Hannah smiled, glad to have another mission on ship. Glad to have her mind off the great Captain MacRae.

As the eastern sky was just beginning to hint that the sun would make its appearance, Hannah was brushing out her hair, her stomach a knot of excitement. She had gotten little sleep but felt wide awake, the way she had on the mornings she'd awaken on her father's ship that first time he'd let her navigate. She braided her hair hastily, wrapping the braid around her head so that it would not blow about and would fit beneath her straw hat. Donning her "uniform," she stepped out of her cabin just as George was stepping out of his.

"Sleep well, cousin?" he asked with a smile.

"How could I when I was plotting our course to the equator all night," Hannah said happily. In her hand she held the polished teak box that held her sextant, given to her by her father when she was sixteen years old. It had been her grandfather's and was one of her most cherished possessions.

"Let's see where the captain put us overnight," George said, allowing Hannah to proceed him up to the deck. The sky had gone from black to the deepest of blues, slowly lightening as the earth turned to the sun. Stars still filled the sky to the west, but were rapidly disappearing in the east.

"The captain was up all night?"

"The crew tells me he rarely sleeps. Frankly, I don't know how he is able to function as well as he does if what the crew told me is true. It's one of the reasons I know I'm not ready to captain a ship. I like my sleep."

Hannah saw him near the ship's wheel; his hands were fisted at his hips and his neck was craned back so that he might see what adjustments were needed. A stranger stepping aboard at that moment would have known he was the captain with one look. The only effect of a sleepless night that Hannah could discern was the growth of his black beard, which made him look rather fierce.

"Twelve knots overnight, Mr. Wright. I can't wait to see how well she does in a gale. My best guess is we're one hundred forty-four miles from port, but we'll know better once Miss Wright finishes her plotting this afternoon."

The sun was just beginning to peek over the horizon, a muted golden slice of light against the dark sea. Hannah took her position near the rail, spreading her feet for balance, even though it would be several hours before she would take a reading. Each morning at nine o'clock ship's time, it was Hannah's job to determine the height of the sun. The morning sighting was done to compare ship's time to the mean time—the time in Greenwich, England, at the same moment. Greenwich had the honor of being located at zero longitude, making it the standard for ships at sea. At high noon, Hannah would again stand at the rail with her sextant in hand to call out the precise moment the sun reached its zenith. With both calculations in hand, she would determine the ship's precise location.

"If we averaged twelve knots, that would put us about seventy miles east of Delaware," Hannah shouted so James would hear over the snap of the sails. "We flew last night," she said.

"You haven't seen speed yet, Miss Wright," James said. "Just wait until we're in the middle of a gale and we're hitting eighteen, twenty knots. Then you'll know what it feels like to fly. You'll . . ." He stopped in mid-sentence to shout an order, moving toward the bow with the assurance of a man walking in his parlor. Hannah watched as dozens of crew members rushed to the foremast to do his bidding. When the sails were once again filled, James turned to George, who suggested a minor adjustment. The captain simply nodded and shouted his order, which was carried up the ship until the crew had the order.

Hannah was heartened. Captain MacRae seemed to be a ship's master who was not too proud to ask for advice—or act on it. Perhaps now was the time to remind the good captain about her suggested course. Before she could broach the subject, he started toward her, his steps sure and steady. "Miss Wright. You've got a course in mind? Let's hear it. Mr. Wright, you need to hear this, too. I want a witness." His eyes were twinkling despite his tone, and Hannah smiled.

"Don't smile yet, miss," he admonished loudly, and put on a deep scowl when Hannah's smile broadened.

"I believe if we sail just two degrees farther east than you normally would, you'll pick up a fair wind and make up at least a day, possibly more."

"And how do you come by this plan?" Captain MacRae asked.

"My manual and . . ."

His eyebrows rose. "And?"

"My instinct."

"Instinct! You've never sailed in this part of the world, have you? From where do you draw even the most basic knowledge to act on instinct and to put my ship in jeopardy?"

Hannah was startled. Last night he'd seemed to like the idea. And now he was fighting her.

"As I said, most of the time I draw my conclusions from my manual."

Captain MacRae made to walk to her cabin. "Well, let's see where it says we'll find a fairer wind two degrees east."

Hannah hurried after him, knowing that no matter how long he looked, he would find nothing to collaborate what she said. It was mostly instinct that told her the winds to the east would be stronger and more steady. Her instinct was rarely wrong, but he would not know that. Was this gut feeling enough to put into jeopardy their quest to make it to California in record time? What if she were wrong? Hannah knew, she did not know how, but she *knew* the eastward trek would be better.

"You won't find it in the book, Captain," she shouted at his back. George had simply leaned against the rail to watch his cousin make a fool of herself.

James turned slowly. "Then, I ask again, from where do you get this knowledge, Miss Wright?"

She bit her lip, knowing this was a pivotal moment in her career as ship's navigator. "In here," she said, putting both fists up against her stomach. "It's just a . . . a feeling. I cannot explain it, Captain."

"A feeling." He spread his arms wide and looked up to the now-blue sky as if asking for divine help. When he looked down, Hannah tried very hard to see that twinkle in his eyes, but all she saw was impatience. "Miss Wright. I have thousands of dollars worth of cargo on this ship. I have eleven passengers and forty crew members to protect, not to mention a ten-thousand-dollar bonus if we make it to San Francisco in a timely manner. You want me to endanger all that because of a feeling?" He ended the question in a shout that made Hannah flinch.

"Well," he said, and began to pace. "I *feel* like drinking rum every day. And I *feel* like giving the crew the day off. As a matter of fact," he said, placing one long finger against his lean cheek, "I *feel* like going west and visiting Baltimore right now."

Hannah narrowed her eyes and crossed her arms throughout his monologue.

"Hannah, he's just having sport," George said in a warning tone. She shot him a look that told him to keep out of it, then turned back to the captain.

"You hired me to do a job. If you do not allow me to do it, I will simply become another passenger with rather nice accommodations. Captain MacRae, I am a competent navigator. I am more than competent. My instincts have served me well in the past. Do you think for one moment I would make such an unorthodox suggestion if I believed I was not right? Do you not fathom how very important it is for me to do my job well? I, too, have reason to get to San Francisco in a timely manner. The man I plan to marry is there and could be in trouble." She was pleased to see him frown, her points being well made. "So do not tell me I am being reckless with my suggestion." Hannah let her words sink in before continuing.

"Tell me, Captain. Will I be navigator or passenger?"

She watched as he worked his jaw, his eyes scanning his ship, as if silently asking it permission to do as Hannah asked. He turned to her then, his mouth pressed into a straight line, but the twinkle was back and Hannah relaxed.

"Well-done," he shouted, and clapped her on her back, causing Hannah to stumble forward. "Good girl. Of course you're the navigator. No need to get on your high horse, Miss Wright. Now! Go plot your course and bring it up to me when you are done."

Oh, it was all just a game, the cad. "It's plotted. I'll be right back, Captain. I suggest you make the change now, though. If we don't change course by the forty-fifth parallel, we won't get the benefit of the wind."

As Hannah headed back toward her cabin, she could hear Captain MacRae shout the order for the course change, and began praying she was right. God help her if she was wrong.

Chapter Six

Four days later, the *Windfire* bobbed in seas as calm as glass, its sails hanging listlessly. The crew was subdued, feeling failure hanging over them, eyes searching in vain for any sign of good air. It was approaching noon, the sky overhead a brilliant, cloudless blue. He had allowed the helmsman to leave his station, a loosely tied rope doing the job for him. A ship adrift did not require a helmsman, he thought darkly. Every time he heard the soft thunk of the wheel pulling that rope taught, he was reminded that he was an idiot to listen to a girl who had never sailed farther south than the fortieth parallel. He cursed his impulsiveness, his love of adventure, his need to push all limits. He cursed the fact that he had wanted Miss Hannah Wright aboard his ship. It wasn't that she was so pleasant to look at, though that was a nice little bonus, it was that she simply added another challenge to an already monumental task. Imagine not only beating the record, but with a woman as navigator. By God, it would have been rich. Now he'd be called the biggest of fools by his shipmates, and he'd have to smile and shrug and pretend his gut wasn't twisting.

James watched from his point near the wheel as Hannah walked up onto deck to see the glassy surface and hear the odd silence of the ship, and knew she felt sick. She closed her eyes briefly and clutched her sextant case to her midriff, before heading with determination toward the ship's port side to await the moment when she would begin sighting the sun to determine high noon. He could hear water lapping up against the hull, the halyards banging rhythmically against the masts, as if the *Windfire* were at dock. It was a horrible sound.

"Don't need a reading today, Miss Wright," James said, unable to keep the bitterness from his voice. "We haven't moved a boat-length since last night."

She looked at him, then turned away to gaze again at the placid water. "I was so sure."

"Yes, you were, weren't you." He felt sorry for the girl. He truly did. But they had lost two days bobbing listlessly off South Carolina. With fair wind, they could have been off Florida by now. He braced himself against the rail, strong hands curling around the wood, his eyes gazing out at the calm sea. If he could forget they were supposed to be racing the wind, he might think it was beautiful, this molten water, heaving gently, endlessly. He could not forget, nor could he keep a navigator on who led them to this clipper ship captain's hell.

At ten minutes before noon, Hannah lifted the sextant, ready to give shout when the sun had reached its zenith. Then, the helmsman would beat out eight bells, and the ship, a slave to time and the sun, could stay on its rigid routine. James watched as she stood still, silent in the long minutes before she gave her shout, and saw that her hands trembled just slightly, and he let out a sigh.

"This ship hasn't a place for a navigator who leads us to doldrums where there oughtn't be doldrums."

She remained still, her hands tightening slightly on her instrument. "I understand, sir." Those eyes of hers that were gray and blue and green, never wavered.

George bounded up from below, where he was keeping an eye on the ship's instrumentation. "The glass has been falling all morning, sir."

"High noon," Hannah shouted, and eight bells immediately sounded. She dropped her sextant and immediately joined James and George in scanning the horizon for a reason for the sudden drop in barometric pressure. "Sir? Look at those clouds."

James did, seeing a bank of fast-moving clouds that began as a hazy shadow on the horizon, but which were quickly building into something dark and menacing. Only minutes ago, those clouds had not been visible.

"I'll be damned," he whispered. It seemed they saw it at the same moment as one of the crew members high above them on the mainmast.

"We've got some air coming. Big air," came the shout. It was true. The sea, still so calm where they stood, was broiling beneath a fierce wind not ten miles to the east. It was a fascinating sight, to see the wind rush at them when they stood hoping for a breeze to fill their sails. It would be on them soon enough.

"Get those heavy sails up. Blast it. Have we got time before the wind hits?" James shouted, then answered his own question. "Hell we do. Look sharp, men. Those light sails will be ripped apart in that wind." In a matter of minutes, the sails designed to capture the lightest wind were down, and heavy sails were taken from lockers and being readied. James shouted, rushing about the ship to make sure his crew, after the boredom of the last two days, were ready for a gale. "Johnson, be ready at the wheel. If she's a strong wind, Carpenter won't be able to hold her alone. Untie that damned rope."

He felt his blood surge at the thought of a gale. When he heard the first snap of a sail in the wind, he smiled, his heart so full it was nearly bursting. He strode from one end of the ship to the other, shouting orders, listening to his ship creak and groan and celebrate the wind. He cursed as he realized not all sails would be flying when the wind hit them. A few passengers, hearing the commotion, made their way up on deck.

"What's happening, Captain?" one man said.

James threw his arm to the east and pointed to the fast-approaching storm. "We've got us a gale coming. You'd best stay below if you want to stay dry. But if you want to stay on deck, you may, unless I give the order for you to go below." And then he moved on. This was it, the first test of *Windfire*, the first test of his crew aboard her. Seas, once so calm, were already heaving, even though the wind was still fairly light. That would change, he knew. Rough seas meant a storm was nearby somewhere, and these were getting rougher with every minute that passed.

"Captain." He turned to see Hannah, her straw hat flopping in the wind. "I'm going down below. Some of the passengers, particularly Mrs. Coddington and Mrs. Davis, may be frightened by their first storm. I thought I could do some good by calming their fears."

"Fair idea, Miss Wright," James said, though he wondered if it was Hannah who was frightened by the oncoming storm. "Before I forget," he shouted above the sound of the sea crashing about them. "You're still the navigator on this ship." Then he turned to find George.

Hannah fell against the companionway as the ship was buffeted by an unexpectedly strong gust, bruising her arm. She barely felt the pain, for she could hardly stop herself from jumping up and down in complete glee.

"I was right," she shouted, making a fist. "I knew I was right." Then, silently: Oh, thank you, Lord. Thank you, thank you.

Hannah knew she was getting close to the passengers' cabins when she smelled the sour odor of vomit. Grimacing, she made her way down the narrow passage where the two women aboard were staying. She'd visited them once before, amazed that both had been miserably sick, given that they had been on fairly smooth seas thus far. But she knew that swells, with their slow-heaving movement, were sometimes as debilitating as rough seas. Hannah had felt queasy on board ship only once as a child, when she was already feeling ill and her father insisted she ride out the storm in her cabin, rather than on deck. She'd told the two women it was best to spend as much time on deck as possible, but even the thought of seeing that heaving water was enough to send both heads back into their chamber pots.

Hannah knocked on the door and smiled when she heard a weak, "Come in."

The women, both in their fifties, were huddled together on a single bunk. They were too weak to even light their lamp, and so were in the darkness, clutching each other fearfully as they no doubt realized a storm was upon the ship. Hannah quickly lit a lamp, then seeing the condition of their chamber pot, told the women she would return momentarily. She ignored the sick twist of her stomach as she lifted the sloshing pot, and made her way carefully back up on deck.

The seas had become violent, sending ten- and fifteen-foot waves hurtling against the *Windfire* bow. The ship, lean and sleek, was made for such seas, and she sliced through them with amazing agility. For a moment she stood clutching the rail, feeling the ship heave beneath her feet, letting her face become wet with salt spray and rain. It was glorious, and Hannah wished she could stay atop, but she knew she was needed more down below. Until the skies cleared and she could determine their position, Hannah would not be needed again. After emptying and cleaning the pot, Hannah returned to the two women, who barely managed to hold on to the scarce contents of their stomachs before Hannah returned.

That was how she spent her first gale—emptying a chamber pot into a surging sea and comforting two women who were bewildered to find themselves in such dire straits. Their husbands, who had left for San Francisco more than a year ago to start up a newspaper, had not been forthcoming about the true nature of their journey. Every time the ship crashed over a wave or heeled over in the wind, the women shrieked in terror. No amount of comfort could help them, Hannah knew, but she tried anyway.

"My dear girl, how can you be so brave?" Beatrice Coddington asked. Beside her, Winifred Davis, moaned in her sleep.

"Because I know we are in no danger. We will face stronger storms than this, Mrs. Coddington. I'm telling you not to frighten you, but so that you'll know that this is nothing to fear. Clipper ships are made for storms like this. It is when they are at their best. Truly, do not worry."

"There are to be worse storms?" she asked, clinging to the worst of what Hannah said. "My God, I shall die of starvation."

Hannah laid her hand on the older woman's arm. "There will be fair days. When we get close to the equator, the seas are calm, much like they had been before the storm. If you go on deck, the swells will not bother your stomach nearly so much. It's quite pretty. You'll see. By the time you get to San Francisco, you'll be a regular old salt."

Poor Beatrice. Hannah's speech had little effect. She moaned and once again vomited.

The gale pushed the *Windfire* along with it for sixteen hours before moving to the north, but the southeast trade winds remained strong and steady for several days. When finally the skies cleared and Hannah could take a reading, she was pleased to tell the captain that not only had they made up the two days lost, but they had gained a full day. If the wind continued to be strong, they would gain several more days before hitting the equator and calmer seas. Hannah was brimming with pride and felt absurdly happy to have put that satisfied gleam in Captain MacRae's beautiful blue eyes.

"So," Hannah said, gazing up at the brilliant while sails, "it seems my instincts were correct." She couldn't help but smile smugly as she watched James try to frown. They stood side by side on the main deck between the mainmast and the mizzen, feet spread wide to keep themselves steady as the ship cut through the seas. Hannah grasped the rail with one hand as the ship took an unexpectedly deep plunge into a valley between two waves.

"You are one lucky lady," he said, ignoring her wide smile.

"It isn't luck, Captain. I have a gift."

He raised one black eyebrow at her. "We hit twenty knots during the height of that storm. If you receive any more gifts, feel free to pass them on to me, Miss Wright. I'm well pleased."

Hannah glowed under his praise, but looked away so that he would not see just how much his words meant. Kind words from Captain MacRae shouldn't mean so much, but they did. She wanted to please him, wanted to prove that she was the best darned navigator he'd ever had on board his ship. She wanted to break that record to California, not for glory, not for money, not even to get to Allen. She wanted to break that record for James MacRae. She knew every other crew member on this ship wanted the same thing.

"I don't know how you do it, Captain," she said, giving him a sidelong look that would have been flirtation from any other woman.

"And what is that?"

"You manage to turn everyone on this ship into a puppy dog wanting only to please its master."

He shrugged, his eyes gleaming wickedly. "Everyone, Miss Wright?" Hannah just smiled and walked away as casually as she could manage with the ship rolling through heavy seas.

James couldn't be sure, but he thought he heard her say a melodic "Woof, woof" and his smile broadened. If he wasn't careful, he might fall under that lady's charms. Not only was she beautiful and charming, but, hell, she knew how to find a good gale. He knew that had they not taken her course, they would have missed the storm and the wind it brought. James watched her until she disappeared down the companionway, unaware that he did so, unaware that the main upper topsail directly above his head was snapping and ill set.

George's shout that the sheet be trimmed caused him to snap his head up and scowl at the sail—and at himself. He should have noticed, he would have noticed, if not for his lovely navigator in those enticingly fitting trousers of hers.

"She's quite proud of herself," he heard George say from behind him.

"She should be," James said, looking at the companion-way where she had disappeared, as if he hoped she would step on deck. Hell, he thought with another dark scowl, I'm a man. There's no harm in looking, no harm in liking to look, no harm, he argued to himself, in even wanting to touch.

"Sir? May I speak frankly?"

James frowned, guessing what Miss Wright's cousin was about to say. He found himself slightly irritated that his thoughts may have been so transparent and doubly so that George was taking his job as chaperon so seriously. It wasn't as if he had plans to ravish the girl. Could he help it if he liked to look at her, talk to her? And, yes, if he were honest, he had contemplated what it would be like to kiss those pretty lips of hers. He sighed.

"Speak, Mr. Wright," he said as the two men began walking toward the stern and the ship's helm.

"Hannah is engaged to a man who is very much unlike you. To my thinking, he's rather pompous, a dandy of sorts, I suppose. I've never met him, so I may not be completely fair to the man. But her father isn't very taken with the fellow, and that's putting it mildly."

James, nodding at the helmsman, leaned casually against the ship's rail. "What are you trying to so delicately tell me, Mr. Wright?"

George's fair complexion, already red from wind and sun, turned a bit more crimson. "I know you have a way with the ladies, sir. And even though Hannah is engaged . . . Well, sir, I've seen the way she looks at you already. And we're not even to the equator."

James chuckled. "It's my favorite look, Mr. Wright," he said wistfully.

"Captain," George continued, his tone a bit impatient. "I have been charged to keep her safe. I am asking you . . ."

"Don't worry, Mr. Wright," James interrupted. "I don't mean to be vain, but I am used to such adoring looks. For good or for bad, the New York press has made every clipper ship captain into a hero. Because I am single, it is worse. I cannot tell you the number of mothers and fathers who have introduced their daughters to me, and all have looked at me the same way. I'd like to say I find it annoying," he chuckled, "but I find I like it. Who wouldn't? That is as far as it goes. Especially for Miss Wright."

"Yes, sir. I didn't mean to presume that you would put her in a compromising situation. Hannah is headstrong, and to be honest, I feared . . ."

George's sentence was cut off by a terrible scream, followed quickly by a sickening thud. James's heart nearly stopped, for he knew what that sound meant: A man had tumbled from high on the mainmast.

"Man down," came the shout, but James was already running toward where he could see a man lying still on deck. It was the one thing about captaining a ship that he hated—men would be injured, men would die, and he felt to blame for every mishap no matter how insignificant. While he had been having a nice chat with his first mate about a woman, one of his men had been in grave danger. And he hadn't known it.

When he reached the downed man, he knelt beside him, giving a quick prayer of thanks when he moaned. At first James could not determine where he was injured, but then a small pool of blood began seeping from behind his head. "Go get Doc," he shouted.

"Kelley already went to the galley to fetch him, Captain," one crew member said.

"Mr. Wells, can you hear me?" James asked, placing a gentle hand on the side of the injured man's face.

"Sir," came the weak reply.

"We're getting Doc, son. Lie still." James's heart beat

painfully in his chest. A blasted head wound. He knew those proved to be the most deadly. He lifted his eyes and studied the men who surrounded them. "We've got a ship to sail, men. Mr. Wright, take the lead." The men, who'd come running at the commotion, quickly dispersed, casting quick and worried glances toward the man who lay so still on the deck of the ship.

"What have we here?" Doc Owen asked as he lowered his short, squat form to the injured man.

"Head injury."

"And arm," Doc said, pointing to one arm that was, indeed, bent at an odd angle and already swelling.

"He was conscious, but I think he's fainted," James said, wishing with all his being that he could have somehow prevented the accident. To the few crew members who worked nearby, he asked, "Does anyone know how this happened?" He was startled to see the men grow uneasy. Several eyes shifted to a freckled-face boy who lingered nearby, swaying overmuch for the amount of the ship's movement. His face was flushed, his eyes slightly glazed. He was, James knew with one look, quite drunk. Rage, as he had experienced only a few times in his life, filled him with lightning speed.

Hannah, brought on deck when she heard the scream, too, noticed the crew members' eyes shifting to the young boy who had first greeted her when she came aboard the *Windfire*, and her heart went out to him. He looked frightened to death. When she turned to the captain, she realized why. He looked at the young boy with murder in his glittering eyes.

"You," he barked, and the boy visibly jumped. "You are at fault?"

"Y-y-yes, s-sir," he stuttered rather pathetically. Hannah's instinct was to defend the boy, but she forced herself to remain silent.

"You do know that drunkenness while on duty is forbidden?" The boy bobbed his head in a manner that made it clear that he was, indeed, quite drunk, and Hannah's heart plunged. Punishment for drunkenness on her father's ship was three days in the hold with only bread and water. She imagined the same fate awaited this boy.

She watched as James looked about at the crew members, his gaze intense, his mouth set angrily. "You, Mr. Smythe. Tell me what happened." The man came forward immediately and relayed the story. The boy had nearly fallen from the spar, and the injured man had fallen in his attempt to save the boy.

Hannah could almost see the rage building in the captain's body; he seemed to swell with it. The boy, still swaying, began to cry sloppy tears. Despite what he did, Hannah couldn't help but feel sorry for him. He was just a boy, after all. A boy, she told herself, who had nearly caused the death of another man. The man might still die.

When he sputtered a heartfelt apology, when he sank to his knees and begged forgiveness, Hannah couldn't help but be moved. The poor kid didn't mean anything. The captain only sneered.

He heaved the boy up by his shirt. "Ten lashes," James shouted. "When you are sober. I want you to feel every bite of that whip. And if that man dies, it'll be twenty more. Do you understand, boy?"

The boy was sobbing so loudly, he could not respond, so James shook him, shook him until his head snapped back and forth and he was screaming, "Yes, sir, I understand."

James, his face a mask of fury, thrust the boy from him in disgust. "Put him in the hold with the rest of the vermin," he bit out.

"Ten lashes seems excessive, Captain. I must protest." Oh, goodness, Hannah thought in a panic when his blue eyes lashed at her, did that come out of my mouth? But once said, she intended to stick by her defense of the boy.

"Keep out of this, Miss Wright."

"But he's only a boy."

He stalked to her until he loomed over her. "That boy," he spat, "nearly killed a man. A man with a wife and children."

"But it was an accident," Hannah said, not quite believing she continued to argue with him. Apparently, the captain could not believe it, either, for his face became very red, very quickly.

"Do not question me, lady," he said with quiet fierceness.

"Captain, I must insist . . ."

"Mr. Wright!" he shouted.

George was there in a second, sickly aware of what Hannah was doing. "Yes, sir."

"Get her away from me before I kill her." Then he turned away and was once again kneeling by the injured man, assisting Doc Owen.

George took her arm, none too gently, and led her away. She was aware of the dark looks given to her by the other men, and knew she had committed a great sin. They knew, as she knew, that the boy deserved his punishment. Though she truly believed ten lashes was excessive, another captain might have done worse. Then why had she argued? She knew the answer. She had a soft heart and looking at that poor boy, crying and miserable, had gotten to her. It had been an accident, after all. Part of her knew that if someone had simply related the story of the accident to her, she might have agreed with the captain's punishment. But because she had been there, had seen his tears, had seen how very young he was, she allowed her heart to get in the way of justice. She'd thought Captain MacRae had a heart as well. Perhaps that good-natured, happy, twinkling-eyed act was just that—an act.

Hannah pulled away from George, suddenly angry with the captain all over again. Somehow she felt betrayed, and felt extremely foolish for feeling that way. Her captain's halo, which had glowed so brightly, was tarnished. Perhaps, she thought, it didn't exist at all. She turned, ready to do battle again with the captain but was stopped by a strong grip on her arm.

"Oh, no you don't. I think the captain indeed will kill you if you show your face to him right now." George continued to drag her along down the companionway and into her cabin.

She lifted her chin. "Am I to be kept prisoner?"

"Don't be ridiculous, Hannah," George said with a weary note. "I warned you of this. You said you would try."

"I did try. But that boy . . ."

"Nearly killed a man. Why are you being so stubborn? You know about punishment aboard ship. Hell, your father has sentenced men to worse."

Hannah had no answer for him. She hadn't liked it when her father had punished the men, either. But she'd never confronted his decision in front of his men, she'd always saved her complaints to discuss in private.

"I didn't think Captain MacRae would be so cruel."

"It is not cruel. It is a lesson that boy will never forget. He will be thankful to the captain someday. Mark my words."

Hannah turned away from her cousin's censorious gaze and fiddled with a chart still unrolled on her desk. "He's very angry with me, isn't he?"

"Until that moment, I'd never seen him so angry."

Hannah swallowed painfully. Perhaps it was better that he was angry with her, and that she was angry with him. She was starting to like him much too much. She had been aware for days that her eyes were constantly seeking him out, and that when she did find him, her heart would step up a beat. She had been trying to convince herself that what she was feeling was admiration for a great sea captain, but in her heart she knew better. She knew she was in grave danger of falling for the captain, and a little splash of reality thrown full in the face was the best remedy for a silly schoolgirl crush.

"Why don't you stay in your cabin for a while. Let things cool down a bit."

Hannah turned to her cousin and gave him a weak smile. "I suppose you are right. I also suppose you expect me to apologize to the man. And I probably will. But I'm still too angry at this moment. Fair enough?"

"Fair enough."

Three hours later, when Hannah was being escorted to the deck so that she would be forced to witness the punishment, an apology to Captain MacRae was the last thing on her mind.

Chapter Seven

James watched as Todd Engle, his face white, his eyes bloodshot, no doubt more from tears than drink, was brought on deck and tied to the mainmast. Though to all appearances, Captain MacRae felt little emotion about the punishment to be meted out, he had no stomach for such things. Enforcing discipline was as necessary to being a captain as making sure the sails were trim, but ordering the whipping of a seventeen-year-old boy was not something he relished. He'd already decided, in fact, to stop the punishment at five lashes. The sailor who had fallen would recover with little more than a lasting headache and an arm splint, but would be nearly useless for much of the remaining journey to San Francisco. James knew the man could have died, and was lucky that he did not.

Crew members who were not on watch gathered around the mast, their expressions solemn. None cast accusing or angry eyes at either the captain or the boy. They knew Todd Engle was young, and they also knew their captain was a fair man. James was certain that once the punishment was dealt, the boy would not be ostracized—as long as he took his punishment like a man, as it appeared he would. If he had complained about the sentence or begged that he not be whipped, the crew might have scorned him. Though it was clear the boy was frightened to tears, he remained stoic, accepting his sentence. It wasn't until the ship's lady navigator arrived, dragged to the scene by her stone-faced cousin, that James felt any animosity directed toward him. Even the few passengers who chose to witness the punishment seemed to accept the captain's word.

He spared a quick look to Hannah and was nearly sliced in two by the look in her eyes. No awe in that expression, James thought, ignoring the feeling of loss that nipped at his heart. Hell, it was just as well she hated him. It had been getting damned hard to see that girl look at him with such open admiration and not drag her into his arms.

"For the crime of drunkenness, for nearly causing his fellow crew member to fall to his death, I sentence you, Todd Engle, to ten lashes," he bellowed. Even as he shouted the sentence, he knew he would stop the second mate after five lashes. The poor kid looked like he was going to pee in his pants and surely would never touch a drop of rum on this trip again.

"Ten is too many."

James shouldn't have been surprised when he heard her strident voice, but somehow he was. Damn her. She would force him to repeat the sentence, to follow it through, when he did not want to. He ignored her, clenching his jaw as anger reddened his cheeks.

"Remove his shirt. Mr. Lodge, you may begin."

"Ten lashes is excessive. You know it is, Captain. That man will recover. He is just a boy."

James clenched his fists.

"You are worse than Captain Waterman. You are . . ."

James whipped around to face his tormentor. "One more word and he'll get twenty."

Hannah gasped, but snapped her mouth shut, narrowing her eyes and shaking her head in disgust. James turned back to witness the punishment, shocked that he had threatened to double the boy's punishment for her obstinance—and that she had believed he would carry it out.

The young boy cried out as the second lash sliced into him, leaving behind a bleeding welt. Too damned hard,

James thought, wanting to admonish his second mate not to whip the lad too severely. But Mr. Lodge, also angered by Hannah's outburst, seemed to be taking out his anger on the poor boy's back. The third lash was as severe as the second, and he could hear George say something harsh into his cousin's ear. Damn, he hadn't wanted this, but Hannah had forced his hand. He couldn't relinquish control else lose his men's respect, and certainly he could not bow to a woman. By God, when this was over, he'd make her ears bleed with his furious words.

By the time the whip lashed across his back the fifth time, the boy's head hung low and he was sobbing uncontrollably. It was enough. More than enough, James thought, feeling sick inside.

"I'll do the final five," he bit out, taking the whip from his second mate's hand as he ignored the man's look of surprise. He'd said ten lashes and the boy would receive ten, but the final five would not be the stinging blows of the first five, James would make certain of it. Before laying the whip to the boy's back, James looked at his men. Many knew, he thought, what he was about. Others thought nothing of the captain meting out the punishment and simply waited for him to begin. He gave Hannah a long hard look, ignoring the hatred that shot from her green eyes, ignoring the twist his gut gave when he realized that she would not understand what he was doing.

"Five more, lad," he said, kindness touching his voice. The boy braced himself for what he thought would be brutal blows, and even shouted out when the whip touched his back. But after the first blow, he actually turned his tear-filled eyes and looked at James with confusion, his eyes widening further when his captain winked at him. The blows left puffy little welts behind and no doubt stung like hell, but James in that moment earned that boy's loyalty forever. Todd Engle would climb the mast in a raging hurricane with a single nod from him.

After the punishment was ended, James ordered that he be

unlashed from the mast. Todd stood, his knees only a bit wobbly, and actually smiled at him.

"I deserved my punishment, Captain," he said, then looked at Hannah, who was turned away. "Miss? I don't want no one to get into trouble on my account. I was wrong. I got what I deserved."

Hannah, who had turned away when James had wielded the whip, turned and shook her head at the boy, looking so pale and young she wanted to give him a big hug and send him off to bed with some warm milk. How could he defend such an action? She ignored the part of her that shouted that the punishment meted out was not excessive. But when the captain had taken up the whip himself, it had been too much. What kind of a man wanted to whip a young boy? What kind of a man forced a woman to witness such a thing against her will? James MacRae certainly was not the man she thought he was.

She turned her gaze to the captain, who stood near the boy, the whip still in his hand, looking at her impassively. No twinkle in those lying eyes now, she thought. She watched as he handed the whip to the second mate, his eyes pinning her to the spot. She couldn't have moved in that moment if she'd tried. Hannah felt her cheeks flush in anger, and she lifted her chin. There. You don't frighten me.

"Miss Wright."

Her insides rolled, and the back of her scalp prickled with heat. I'm not afraid, I'm not, I'm not.

"I need to speak to you privately in my . . . your cabin. Immediately."

One look at the crew members who lingered told Hannah she was about to get a dressing down—one they thought she deserved. Even Todd Engle, the little ungrateful boy, looked at her with disdain. Hannah scowled. It wasn't her fault that she felt the need to speak her mind. Well, perhaps it was technically her fault, but she refused to be a sheep, to allow the captain to get away with whatever he wanted simply because he had managed to evoke such loyalty in his crew.

Why, the man could tell them all to jump ship, and she was sure they would. Someone had to show Captain MacRae that he could be wrong. Crossing her arms, Hannah turned away from the accusing looks and headed to her cabin. Not because the captain told her to go there, but because she wanted to go.

And I'm not afraid!

Once in her cabin, though, Hannah's courage crumbled. That big, fierce, angry man was going to be in her cabin any minute, and he was going to yell. Certainly that was all he would do. Captain MacRae wouldn't hurt her, wouldn't put her in irons and place her in the hold. Would he? She bit her lip knowing that she was being a hypocrite and not caring one bit. She wanted to be treated as a member of the crew, to be respected as if she were a man. But at that moment, she didn't want to face the punishment a man would face for questioning an order with such belligerence. At that moment she wished she was any place but in her cabin waiting for James MacRae to give her a dressing down.

The knock, when it came, was surprisingly polite. Taking a deep breath, Hannah opened the door.

"Before you say anything, Captain, I'd like to explain my position. As a member of this crew . . ." A large calloused hand covered her mouth, causing the rest of her words—for she did continue talking—to sound quite muffled.

"Shut up." Hannah, her brows creased, her eyes spitting daggers, tried to pull his hand from her mouth, and she continued to try to talk.

"Shut up. Now," James said, as if not quite able to believe she was still trying to talk. When Hannah tried to bite his hand, he pulled it quickly away.

" . . . so you see, I wasn't out of line. I simply felt . . ."

"If you say one more word, I will not be responsible for my actions," James shouted, clearly frustrated that this woman would not obey the simplest of commands.

"But, Captain, if you don't listen to what I have to . . ."

All James knew was that he wanted her to stop her infernal jabbering. He acted without thinking, doing the only thing he knew that would be sure to stop a woman from talking. He kissed her, hard and fast, then thrust her away from him as if it were the most disagreeable thing he'd ever done. It worked. Hannah's mouth gaped open, then closed, slowly, settling down into a little "o" shape.

"There. That's better," he bellowed.

"Why did you do that?" Hannah demanded. "I hope you remember that I am a woman engaged. That . . ."

"I'll do it again if you don't shut up." Her mouth snapped shut. "Now, Miss Wright. If you ever again question my orders in front of my crew, I will throw you in the hold and to hell with your being a woman. If you weren't such a fine navigator, you'd be there now. But I find it more important to get to San Francisco on time than to punish a spoiled little brat. I'm convinced it would do no good in any case. That boy got the punishment he deserved."

"You didn't have to wield the whip yourself. You make me sick," Hannah spat. She found it slightly disturbing when he looked away, for it was almost as if she'd hurt him with her words. Impossible to hurt such an unfeeling brute, she quickly decided.

"Your opinion of me is of no concern," he said with little emotion. "I only care that this ship continues to sail well, that we reach our destination. If I find that your presence on this ship puts anything in jeopardy, you will no longer be part of this crew." James gave her a hard look, which Hannah met without flinching, though Lord above knew she wanted to look away. "Do not disobey me again. Do not."

"I may, Captain. If I disagree."

James clicked his tongue against the side of his mouth. "I do not understand you. Why do you continue to try to thwart me?"

Hannah looked at him and then away, her eyes fastened on a point somewhere behind his left shoulder. "I will try not to. But, Captain, you didn't have to whip him yourself. You didn't have to force me to watch."

Hannah didn't think he was going to respond, but just as he walked from her room, he said, "Yes, Miss Wright. I did."

The winds continued strong for days, but everyone knew it was only a matter of time before the ship hit the doldrums and wallowed in the heat near the equator. Hannah avoided James, still in a sulk and hating herself for it. Her conscience was a nagging thing, telling her she had overreacted, that she had been wrong. Certainly the crew thought she had been in the wrong. Where before they had been unfailingly polite, almost fawning, now they either ignored her or worse. Just the night before, she'd picked something simply awful and indefinable out of her stew and heard snickers coming from the pantry.

Hannah braced her elbows on the forehatch, far away from everyone, and argued the merits of apologizing to the captain. If he hadn't been so—polite, she would have. He no longer blustered or yelled or looked at her as if he were glad she walked toward him. He didn't slap her back or give praise or even look at her with that twinkle in his eye that she'd thought she'd hated but now found she missed. She might have been a piece of tackle that sometimes got underfoot, for all she seemed to matter to him. He was angry. Disappointed even. And it was driving Hannah mad. What was wrong with her that she needed his admiration? He was allowing her to do her job, he nodded when she gave him her calculations, asked polite questions, even asked her opinion on when she thought they'd hit the doldrums. James MacRae was being the perfect gentleman, the perfect captain.

Then, why did she want to cry?

Hannah let out a sigh so long and hard, she was surprised it didn't fill one of the jibs snapping in front of her. She heard him then, his voice that carried with seemingly little effort. He was talking to one of the passengers, entertaining the man with a lively story about a cat—a ship's mascot—that survived a fall overboard. Hannah tried not to listen, but found herself engaged by the amusing story about the cat who fell off the ship while chasing a mouse. It seemed the crew thought the feline lost at sea until, two days later, they heard meowing coming from the bow. The poor cat had been clinging to the bow for two days, bobbing in and out of the water, before it was rescued.

Hannah caught herself smiling, then forced a frown. James MacRae certainly could be jovial when he wanted to be. Just not with her. She tensed when she heard his familiar steps coming toward her.

"By my watch, Miss Wright, it is eleven-forty-five."

"Thank you for telling me the time, Captain," Hannah said. Then he walked away without another word, leaving Hannah feeling like a shrew. She stared down at the water rushing beneath her, at the foam created by the ship's passing. Apologize. You were wrong. Wrong. Wrong. It's what he is waiting for. But she just couldn't, and for the life of her didn't know why she was being so stubborn.

She thrust herself from the railing and headed to the chart room and her sextant. It was time for the noon reading. Sextant in hand, Hannah stood near the binnacle and awaited the sun to hit its zenith. She knew the moment James came to stand nearby, his hands behind his back.

"I was wrong before. I apologize," Hannah said quietly. To her horror, she felt her throat close up.

"Too late, Miss Wright."

More than anything, Hannah wanted to whip around and glare at the stubborn man, but the sun was about to reach high noon and it was critical that she keep her eye on her sextant.

"That is not very chivalrous of you, sir," she said between her teeth. "When a lady apologizes, you are supposed to accept."

"When a lady apologizes, I usually do."

Hannah pressed her teeth together, calling herself an idiot for leaving herself open to such a remark. If she had been able to turn to him, she would have seen that look in his eyes that had the effect of warming her insides. But because she had to take her reading, all she heard was his emotionless tone.

"High noon," she shouted, then turned to him. "I won't apologize again."

It was James's turn to be shocked. For in her eyes he saw that he'd angered her. And hurt her. Blast it, he hadn't meant to do that, only to teach her a lesson. God above knew the girl needed a lesson in behavior. He watched her walk away with as much dignity as a person can when they are on a rolling, pitching ship. Hell, he thought. She was mad at him again. While his anger toward her had lasted about four hours, he suspected she'd be able to hold on to her anger a bit longer. Damn me and my lessons, James thought, with one last frustrating look at her back as she headed down to the chart room to make her calculations.

The past few days had not been pleasant. He'd been annoyingly distracted, something that made James uncomfortable and irritable. For some reason the thought that Hannah Wright disapproved of him, was angry with him, bothered the hell out of him. It shouldn't, but it did. When he'd heard that apology—brief as it was—the elation he'd felt seemed far out of proportion to what he told himself he should feel. She hadn't been stewing about him, she'd been stewing about her own behavior these past days. And that pleased him. Too much, he realized. Now she was angry with him again. One of the jibs fluttered loudly, taking his attention away from Hannah and putting it where it should be: his ship.

In the chart room, Hannah snapped her sextant case closed with an angry slap. So this is how it was going to be. Fine. She forced herself to calculate the ship's position, then determined approximately when they would cross the equator. They were already at the tenth parallel, a point when the doldrums often started. Already she had felt a softening of the air, a balmy, tropical feel. The ship was making excellent time. She could be in San Francisco in just two months, sixty days. Allen would be there—somewhere. Then her life could begin.

For some reason, that thought depressed her. Hannah reasoned that any life would seem dull after this trip. What was she to do? Stay at home, entertain, buy clothes, bear children? She would do what all women did. Chin on hand, eyes fixed on the brilliant blue sky showing through her porthole, she tried to make herself look forward to such a life. It wasn't so very long ago that it was exactly what she thought she wanted. Life with Allen, safe, solid, unchanging.

"It's what I want," she said aloud. Hannah closed her eyes and thought of her mother. How she had loved Austin Wright, her gallant sea captain. Her mother had loved him so much, Hannah was convinced she had died because she thought he was lost at sea. No doctor could convince her otherwise. Hannah loved her father dearly and would never let him know, but she blamed him for her mother's death.

Mary Wright fell ill the winter of 1841 and was forced to bed, but her sickness did not turn serious until that awful day when the shipping company owner came to tell them that they'd had word the *Annabelle* had been lost in the North Atlantic. Her mother had already been worried, for the ship was overdue, but when she heard the news the ship had gone down, she simply gave up. At least Hannah was convinced that she had. It seemed her mother cried until there couldn't have been tears left, an impossible amount of tears seeping even through her closed eyes.

Mary Wright's funeral was held two days before Austin Wright's *Annabelle* limped up the East River. Her mother had died because her father wasn't there, had died because she loved a man too much to want to live without him. At twelve years old, Hannah vowed two things: she would not marry a sea captain nor a man she loved. As she got older, Hannah amended her vow, excluding only sea captains from her list of potential husbands. It was ironic, she'd thought more than once, that she was sticking to her girlish vow, after all. Allen certainly would never be a sea captain, and she did not love him. Hannah knew what love looked like, what it must feel like. She'd seen it in her mother's eyes every time Mary Wright looked at her husband.

She realized her quest to find Allen was somehow wrapped up in what happened when she was twelve. Allen, by disappearing into the California countryside, had left her. And that could not happen. Not with Allen, not with a man she wanted to spend the rest of her life with. She had to prove to herself that a mistake had been made. Allen was dependable, solid. He would always be there. He would never leave her there, standing on a dock, with tears in her eyes as she tried to smile.

Allen was not a sea captain. And that, more than anything, would make him the perfect husband.

She heard James's voice through the open portal then and smiled. It was only natural that she be attracted to him, she finally admitted. My goodness, he was probably the handsomest man she'd ever met, a man of high integrity, charming in his own blustering way. There was nothing wrong with finding Captain MacRae attractive, of even developing a tiny crush. She was certain, by their blushes and giggles as they dined, that Mrs. Coddington and Mrs. Davis had even succumbed to his charms. Perhaps it shouldn't hurt so much that she was no longer in his favor. Perhaps she had allowed herself to like the man too much. That would all stop now. She had apologized, and he had refused, and they would continue to be the polite strangers they had been for the past few days.

Hannah knew she should be pleased, just as she knew the thought that Captain MacRae would not smile at her again made her want to weep.

Chapter Eight

Just twenty days into their voyage, an amazingly short time, the *Windfire* crossed the equator with much fanfare and celebration. The crew was moody and dispirited, having spent four tedious days as the ship languished in the doldrums. But when the tiny island of St. Paul's Rocks was spotted, the men gave a hearty shout: *Windfire* was about to cross the equator, the first true milestone. Spirits were brought to new heights when James announced with flourish that there would be an initiation. Hannah knew that green sailors were often made to do simply disgusting things as their ship crossed the equator. It was a passage into manhood, a tradition that she was not surprised Captain MacRae was following. The ship's four apprentices, faces already wary yet filled with a strange excitement, were gathered on the main deck between the binnacle and the after house. Other crew members were attempting to gather two other sailors, older and far grumpier, who were seasoned sailors but had yet to cross the equator in their travels.

Hannah, with Mrs. Davis and Mrs. Coddington by her side, stood with other passengers on top of the after house to get a better view of the ceremonies. They held onto the longboat strapped atop the cabin for balance. The ceremony was all silliness, really, something to break the monotony on the ship that seemed to stand still in the calm seas.

Barely a breath of wind moved to fill the light sails. For three days it had been hot and humid and dull as a rock. So little did the ship move, that many of the crew jumped into the warm tropical waters for a swim while others kept an eye out for sharks.

These doldrums were expected, and though wind was scarce, the *Windfire* had sailed so well, no one was worried that she had barely moved since hitting these calm waters.

"Men," James said, waving his arm dramatically in front of the six men who awaited their fate. "In great charity, I will give you a choice of penalty." Many crew members who surrounded the six hapless souls chuckled, knowing what was coming. "You may have your head shaved by Mr. Lodge with this," and he brandished a wickedly sharp, fish-gut encrusted knife. More guffaws from the crew as the six men eyed the knife with sick expressions. "Or you may lick the boots of your officers." The men, Hannah noticed with amusement, were beside themselves with glee. The men, that is, who were not facing such a choice.

She noted with reluctance, that the captain looked un-usually handsome, smiling that charming, eye-glittering smile of his. He was enjoying himself, purely relishing this event that put his crew into such high spirits. Next to Hannah, Mrs. Coddington muttered, "Oh, my," but it was clear that she, too, was tickled by this lively diversion. The two older women simply loved the doldrums, and had told Hannah they didn't care if they ever reached their husbands if they could sail in seas this calm for the rest of the journey. Hannah didn't have the heart to tell them that in a matter of weeks they would face their greatest collective nightmare as the ship rounded the Horn.

Todd Engle, whose hero-worship of James was more than irritating to Hannah, considering she had tried to spare him his sentence, stepped forward. "I'll lick the officers' boots, sir." He rubbed his white-blond hair thoughtfully. "My father was bald, and my grandfather before him, so it's my thinking I'll not have my hair much longer. I'd like to keep all of it as long as possible."

The men were delighted by this speech, and further by the comical way Todd Engle kneeled before the mates, making much of licking the officers' boots. Hannah wrinkled her nose, but couldn't help but join in the laughter. The boy was a surprise, entertaining the crew and passengers with his seeming relish for boot-licking. The officers good-naturedly pointed out portions of their boots that the boy had missed. The remaining five also opted for boot-kissing, to the disappointment of the crew. They had anticipated seeing a head shaven with the unsavory knife. After the final boot was licked, James raised the knife like a scepter and began pronouncing the ceremonies over when Timothy Lodge stepped forward interrupting him.

"Sir. It has come to my attention that one crew member has not stepped forward for initiation."

"Oh?" James appeared genuinely surprised by this announcement and began scanning the crew. "Who would that be, Mr. Lodge."

"Your navigator, sir."

Hannah gasped. Surely she would not be expected to . . . no. She would not lick *his* boots. She'd refuse. Surely the second mate was just taunting her. She shot a look over to James and saw nothing in his look that showed he was in the least reluctant for her to undergo the equator initiation.

"Mr. Lodge," James said, "I think that under the circumstances . . ." And that was when George stepped forward. Hannah smiled. George, thank God, would put a stop to this. Already members of the crew were shooting her hostile looks, and the two ladies standing next to her were tut-tutting and shaking their heads in disapproval.

"Captain, it is only fair that all green members of this crew undergo the same initiation." George's words were directed to the captain, but his eyes were pinned to his cousin, a challenge clear in his expression.

With a little jerk of her chin, Hannah climbed down from

the after house without a word and stalked over to Captain MacRae. She spared not a look to her traitor of a cousin.

"I choose to be shaved rather than lick the officers' boots," she announced, anger in her voice. She heard the females gasp and the crew members mumble.

"She's just tryin' to get out of it," grumbled one sailor.

Hannah snapped her head around. "I am not." She turned to Mr. Lodge, her mouth set with determination. "Do it." Oh, God, she thought, someone stop him. The sailor who had shouted had been right. She didn't believe in a million years that Captain MacRae would allow the second mate to shave her head. Surely he would put a stop to it.

But with a gleam in his eyes, as if knowing what she was about, James said, "Proceed, Mr. Lodge."

Hannah couldn't stop the soft gasp of breath at his words.

"Just lick our bloody boots," George hissed.

"I'll not. I'll not lick his boots," she said, darting a hard look toward James, who smiled and bowed slightly. Oh, that man! Now she would never, ever lick his infernal boots.

"Hannah." A plea tinged with impatience from her cousin.

"You made your point quite clear, George. I am a member of this crew, and I shall be initiated." Someone, please stop this. Oh, goodness sakes, what have I done now?

Mrs. Coddington yelled down, "Captain, surely you won't allow this."

He shrugged and gave the woman his most dazzling smile, and Hannah scowled at him. "I'm afraid, dear Mrs. Coddington, the decision has been taken from me. The lady wishes for a haircut."

Oh, no, she doesn't, thought Hannah desperately. But just as desperately, she refused to think about licking his boots. The thought of kneeling before him, his face smug, those damned eyes twinkling as if a million stars lit them from within—she couldn't do it. She couldn't. For the rest of her days, she would remember that humiliation, the crew's delight over her put-down. They all hated her, were all delighted to see her put into this position. But wouldn't they feel simply awful to see her walking about the deck with nothing but stubble on her head.

"Do it," she repeated to the second mate. Hannah plunked herself down onto a barrel that was set up for just this purpose.

And so with great relish, Timothy Lodge whipped up the shaving cream and began putting it onto her hair. He stood before her, looking mean and hateful. He's trying to frighten me, Hannah thought, and he's being terribly successful. The men watching became restless, shuffling their feet, mumbling among themselves, clearly uncomfortable with how this was turning out. And Hannah, hating herself for her stubbornness, sat on the barrel, her throat burning, waiting for him to begin. She closed her eyes, not wanting to look, and two tears escaped.

"Jesus, Cap, you really want me to do this?" Timothy Lodge asked, the knife inches from her forehead. Mr. Lodge, for all his fearsome looks, apparently was a sucker for a woman's tears.

James must have nodded, for she hadn't heard a word, and then felt the knife placed with surprising gentleness against her forehead just where her wispy first hairs had turned blond from the sun. "Miss, I'll try to be gentle," came a gruff voice by her ear. He began to move it upward, cutting away those first fine hairs.

"Oh, bloody hell," Hannah yelled. "I'll lick their damned boots." The knife was immediately withdrawn, and the crew members, who had held a collective breath at the first touch of the knife upon her head, now let it out. Hannah couldn't help thinking that the breath exhaled was the stiffest breeze the ship had felt in days.

She stood, knowing she looked a sight with her hair filled with foam, her blouse slightly damp from sweat. Stalking over to the four officers, she began by giving the tiniest lick to the third mate's boots, then to Timothy

Lodge, who turned out to be a much nicer man than her
cousin or the captain. She gave her cousin a scathing look
before licking his blasted boots, then moved to the captain.
And there she hesitated. She dared not look into his face,
for if she saw him smiling at her, even if only in his eyes,
she'd put the lout overboard. Hannah moved to him and
stared at his highly polished black boots for a long moment.

"Maybe she'd like to kiss something else," came a yell,
and Hannah blushed purple.

"It's not necessary," came a soft whisper in her ear. His
face was there, right next to hers, for he had bent over so no
one would hear him. He was so near, she could smell the
bay rum he'd splashed on his face that morning after his
shave. Hannah turned, expecting to see amusement in those
blue eyes, but instead saw something . . . else. Regret or
compassion or something. But at that moment, his eyes
held no laughter. Kindness. That was it, that was what she
saw glimmering in those beautiful depths. Hannah's heart
turned over, she bent her head, and darted her tongue out
just enough so the tip touched his left boot. She did the
same with his right.

Then she stood to cheers and backslaps, and suddenly
Hannah was smiling. She'd done it, finally. She'd got the
crew to like her again. Suddenly, inexplicably enjoying the
moment, she took a wad of shaving cream and flung it at
her cousin. That was the start of an all-out war of shaving
cream, until the deck was slick with the stuff, until not a
man or woman did not have at least the tiniest fleck of the
white foam on their person. Several men dove in to calm
seas to clean themselves off, others brought up buckets of
seawater to do the job.

"I don't think her father knew what he was asking of me
when he agreed to allow her on this trip," George muttered
to James once most of the ruckus had calmed. The two men
were watching Hannah, her head still covered with shaving

cream, along with her clothes, as she made her way to the companionway. "She can be so stubborn."

"I find her rather delightful," James said without thinking. Then realizing his first mate might misconstrue his remark—or rather that he might construe his meaning accurately —he quickly said, "She's like a ship's mascot. We needed one this trip. They're good luck, you know."

"I'd rather have had a cat myself," George grumbled. "She was going to let Timothy cut her hair. She was going to let him do it. Thank God she finally saw reason."

"She was probably expecting me to stop it. Which I would have done, by the way. Couldn't have her walking about the ship with a bald pate, now, could we? Her dislike of me overcame her reason. At least for a time." James felt inordinately sad admitting such a thing aloud.

George let out an impatient huff. "My cousin is stubborn when it comes to you, Captain. Ever since the lashing, she's acted like a child. I should speak to her, demand that she apologize. The thing of it is, sir, she knows she is wrong."

"She's already apologized, Mr. Wright. I refused to accept it. I was . . . teasing her."

"And she thought . . . I see now. I imagine you ruffled her feathers a bit with that one."

James narrowed his eyes as Hannah laughed at something one of the passengers said. He was a good-looking young man, with clear gray eyes and light blond hair, and was being rather over-friendly to their navigator. They stood cozied together in the entrance to the companionway. In fact, now that he thought about it, it seemed Miss Wright had been spending quite a bit of time talking to the young whelp. If he recalled correctly, they had sat next to each other in the dining hall on more than one occasion. Christopher Easton. That was the man's name. A Yale man on an adventure, following the path of several of his classmates to the gold fields of California.

"Ruffled her feathers? Yes, I suppose I did," James said distractedly. "If you will excuse me." Moments later James

found himself standing with the young couple, who were
talking so animatedly. They each acknowledged his presence politely enough, then continued to talk about
Nabucco, a Verdi opera that James had actually seen, and
loathed. These two, apparently, had enjoyed it.

"Christopher Easton, isn't it?" James asked when the two
had taken a breath.

The young man smiled showing even white teeth. "Yes,
Captain. I'm pleased that you remember."

"Yes. Well, Mr. Easton, I'm afraid you will have to continue your discussion on Verdi a bit later. Perhaps at dinner.
Miss Wright has duties she must attend to."

Easton, all politeness, nodded and retreated toward the
ship's bow. Hannah turned to James, her eyes wide. A bit of
shaving cream was spattered across one smooth cheek.
Cream on a blushing peach. He lifted his hand and brushed
his knuckles against her cheek, wiping the cream away.
Yes, exactly like a soft, soft peach. Hannah pulled back a
bit, her eyes going wider.

"You are a mess," he said to negate the intimacy of his
caress. He stepped back from her. "Go clean up. I imagine
your calculations have not been completed for the day with
all this distraction."

"Uh. No." Her voice sounded slightly hoarse.

"Then, I'll see you at dinner. We'll discuss our position
then. The ship's position," he added self-consciously.

She gave him a slightly puzzled look. "Of course, sir."

Sir. Captain. Call me James, he wanted to say. "You are
all right? I mean to say, that this . . ."

"I'm fine. I made such a to-do about it. I should have
simply licked your boots and gotten it over with."

He gave her a crooked grin. "But that wouldn't have
nearly been as much fun."

Hannah scowled at him. "Would you have stopped it?"

James looked away, not liking the distrust he saw in her
eyes. This was dangerous, what he was feeling. He wanted
to touch her cheek again. He wanted to kiss her. Hell, he

wanted to take her to his cabin and ravish her. "No," he lied. "I wouldn't have stopped it."

And with a glare that cut him, she said, "I didn't think so."

Chapter Nine

Hannah stood near the bow of the *Windfire*, looking out into the inky blackness of the sea, made darker by the sheer brilliance of the stars overhead. The ship had been in the doldrums twelve days—long days in which the crew had nothing to do but ready the ship for its trip around the Horn. In systematic thoroughness, each sail was inspected, each rope, chain, cleat. Everything. It was George's job to inspect the spars and masts, Timothy Lodge's to determine that the heavy sheets were ready to face gales that could rip the sturdy canvas like tissue. It seemed impossible that within a week, the air would be chilled, the wind strong. And within a month, they'd be battling gales that brought snow and ice.

Hannah tugged at her blouse, which stuck uncomfortably to her clammy skin. At that moment she would have welcomed a cold blast of air. Instead, she got her meddlesome cousin.

"I was looking for you. We need to discuss your attitude."

Hannah let out a heavy sigh.

"You must get over this stubborn dislike you have of the captain," George said, taking her arm and making her face him. He spoke quietly, for sound traveled well on the water.

"I don't dislike the captain," Hannah said.

"It certainly seems as if you do. Some of the crew notice

it. The officers, at least. When the two of you are together,"
he paused, uncertain how to explain himself, "it is clear that
you, neither of you, are yourselves."

It was true. Hannah could think of numerous times she
had come upon a laughing James MacRae, only to have him
immediately walk away at her appearance, or become subdued. It was painfully obvious the captain wished he had
never allowed her on his ship. But beyond apologizing, she
didn't know what to do. Perhaps she had not seemed overly
sincere in her apology. She still was angered by Todd
Engle's lashing and by the fact the captain had given the
final five blows. The equator crossing did nothing to endear
him to her.

"It is difficult to be myself in front of a man who so obviously dislikes me. I've done what I can. I apologized for
my behavior over the boy, although I still believe he was in
the wrong."

Again, she had made George angry. Though it was too
dark to clearly see his face, she could tell by his rigid stance
that he was trying to control his temper. Why was he forever taking the captain's side of things?

"You little fool," he whispered harshly. "The captain
spared the boy by taking up the whip. If you hadn't turned
away like such a coward, you would have seen that the
blows he dealt the boy were nothing. They barely raised
welts. Do you think he enjoyed whipping that boy? Do
you? Captain MacRae is the fairest, most decent man I have
ever met. If I am ever half the captain he is, I will be
proud."

Hannah looked away from her cousin's anger. "I didn't
know."

"How could you? You were too ready to think the worst.
And," he said, poking his finger rather painfully into her
shoulder, "the man you think of as so callous would not
have allowed your head to be shorn. He told me so himself."

"He told me otherwise." Thinking back, remembering

how kind he had been, Hannah knew that he would have stopped Timothy Lodge. "Oh, George, I have been horrid, and I know it. I don't know why I am so disagreeable to him." And then, suddenly, she did know. When *Windfire* reached San Francisco, she would never see James MacRae again. She would find Allen, and they would marry and live their sedate and comfortable life. Dear Allen would make her happy. James MacRae, if she allowed him to, would break her heart. She must dislike him, she thought with determination. *Surely I can guard my heart for two more months.* Her handsome captain wasn't *that* irresistible. She remembered George's warning to her as they stood by the railing the day their journey began. He had warned her of this, and she had thought him ridiculous.

"George." Something in her voice made him relax. She took a deep breath. "I know I've been disagreeable. I'll try to follow your advice. All of it."

He let out a small laugh. "You, Hannah? Listen to me? Why, the only advice you've heeded thus far is my command that you not fall in love with him." To Hannah's horror, her face flushed red beneath George's sharp gaze. "Oh, Hannah, tell me you haven't fallen in love with him."

Her face grew impossibly hotter. "I haven't," she said forcefully. "Of course I haven't. But I admire the captain. He's an admirable man."

"And handsome."

"Well, of course there is that. I'm going to marry Allen, George. I know that." And then she said more strenuously: "I am going to marry Allen."

"Of course you are." He said it as if there were no doubt in his mind. "Hannah." He gave a sigh like a parent about to give a lecture, and lay a light hand on her shoulder. "I've seen far more sophisticated women than you fall for the captain. But, Hannah, he never returns the feelings. Never. Timothy has told me stories that I could . . . well, perhaps I'll share them with you another time. Captain MacRae is a man who enjoys women, all women. I wouldn't want you to think that he . . . that there was a chance of him falling in love with you."

"I wouldn't. Truly, George, I have no interest in the captain, and I am just as certain he has no interest in me," Hannah said, suddenly wanting her cousin to shut up. "As I said, I am marrying Allen. I know this. I also know there can never be a future with a man like James MacRae, and not for the reasons you think. I would never marry a sea captain, George. My mother died a little every time my father sailed away. When she didn't think he was coming home to her, she truly died."

"Don't say that, Hannah."

"It's true. I will not have the life my mother had. If you could have seen her, heard her when she thought he was lost to her. I will never forget the pain, pain I hope never to feel. I am very much like my mother, George. If I loved a man the way she loved my father, I think it would destroy me, too."

"You don't love this Allen Pritchard?"

Hannah looked away.

"No." The two stood together for a long moment. George finally brought one arm around her shoulder and gave her a tight squeeze.

"I think I ought to talk to the captain and try to make amends. Don't worry, George, I'll guard my heart well."

"He's just gone down to my room to rest. Well-needed rest I might add. Perhaps your apology should wait."

Hannah nodded and said good night to her cousin, who would be up most of the night so James could rest. She planned to talk to James in the morning, but when she saw a thin slice of light coming from the cabin door, decided to get her apology over.

She knocked on the door. "Captain, it's Hannah Wright." She heard shuffling inside, and the door opened.

"I was just about to get some sleep, Miss Wright. Is something wrong?"

Hannah, for a moment, could not speak—not with her

jaw locked open. He wore only his pants and a shirt, opened
and untucked and revealing his muscled chest and flat, cor-
rugated stomach. Hair, dark and thick covered his chest . . .
his chest, my God, she was staring at his chest. Hannah
snapped her mouth closed and moved her gaze safely up to
his face. His mouth was stern, but his eyes crinkled at the
corners, as if he'd enjoyed her shock.

"I, um, I came to . . ."

"Yes, Miss Wright?"

Her eyes drifted back to that magnificent chest, and she
shook her head. "Don't you have a robe, or . . . something?" She blushed red at her transparent request, but as
long as he stood there half naked, she knew she wouldn't be
able to get out what she came here for. Instead, she just
might do something entirely insane, like give in to the terrible temptation to see what that hairy chest felt like beneath her fingers.

James moved back, buttoning his shirt as he did, but
leaving the cuffs loose and the tails untucked. "Yes, Miss
Wright. How can I help you?" Hannah couldn't help but
note his impatient tone.

"George has indicated to me that I have been uncharita-
ble toward you." She bit her bottom lip. Her eyes locked
onto the canvas-covered porthole, so she didn't see how
James's own gaze was fixated on her mouth. "Actually,
George has nothing to do with this. I know I have been un-
cooperative. I want to apologize."

One side of James's mouth lifted. "I thought you already
had."

"Yes. But, if you recall, you did not accept. I can only
think you did not because you did not believe me to be sincere." A small bit of pique crept into her voice.

"Ah." He leaned against a small writing desk beside the
bed. "So you are sincere this time."

"Yes, sir." For some reason, James immediately scowled.

"Your apology is accepted." It was a terse sentence.
"Good night, Miss Wright."

"Yes, then. Good night." Hannah left the room feeling oddly disappointed. It seemed as if nothing had been resolved. Captain MacRae had seemed tense and moody and not at all forgiving. He must truly dislike her, she thought. Hannah went to her cabin, closed her door, and threw herself onto her bed. She couldn't wait until this damnable trip was over.

James awoke with a jolt, instantly and completely awake. Wind. They were in some damned good wind. He quickly dressed and went on deck, feeling a sharp cold breeze hit him full force. The doldrums were over.

"You should have awakened me, Mr. Wright," he called, a smile lighting his face.

Dawn was beginning to lighten a sky that was heavy and gray with clouds. James was always amazed at how quickly the weather could turn from balmy to frosty in a matter of hours. A strong southeast wind drove the ship toward the Horn, and it would be only a matter of days before the ship hit the area of the ocean known as the "Roaring Forties," where gales would buffet the ship for days at a time.

One by one the passengers escaped their rooms and headed to the maindeck. Most, surprised by the chilly air, returned to their rooms to fetch warmer clothing. The cool air seemed to invigorate the crew, many of whom had become short-tempered as the ship made its tedious way through the doldrums. The entire ship seemed to snap with excitement. Only Mrs. Coddington and Mrs. Davis peeked their heads up fearfully and looked at the full sails with loathing. For most, a strong wind meant they would arrive sooner in San Francisco, where they could begin gathering up bucketfuls of the gold that awaited them. But for the two older women, strong winds only brought sickness.

Days and days of strong winds followed, days in which the ship cut through cold and choppy waves at fourteen knots and better. James strode about the ship like a proud father, slapping crew members on their backs, shouting orders with such pure joy, the men smiled and hurried to do his bidding. Only one thing could bring a frown to his face: the unexpected sight of Miss Hannah Wright.

If he knew she would be there, he could control his reaction. At dinner, for example, he could be pleasant and exchange niceties with her as he would any of the ship's officers or passengers. But if he came upon her suddenly, he was rather . . . put out. He became irritated with her, with every aspect of her. Why did she have to wear those pants, for instance? Didn't she know they showed every curve she had, and that the eyes of the crew members, despite his warning, were pinned to her enticingly round bottom? And her hair, flying about, sometimes fluttering softly against his face as she moved past him in the hall. Did she have to look so appealing? Did she have to smile? And hell! Did she have to talk to that goddamn Yale boy at every dinner he attended?

James made a point of eating with the officers and passengers daily when the weather allowed. Now that the seas were rough once more, the numbers dining diminished, and the hearty few remaining became fast friends. But damn if Christopher Easton didn't have a stomach made of iron. Even in the roughest seas, he shoved food into his mouth as if it were his last meal, doing so with remarkable grace. Not a crumb was allowed to fall onto his lapel, not a bit of sauce ever graced his chin. He would dab a pristine white napkin, that never seemed to become soiled at the corner of his mouth, after every bite without seeming prissy, as if good manners were so ingrained, they were effortless, like breathing.

James, on the other hand, was constantly wiping crumbs from the beard he began to grow since hitting the southeast trades. Though he disliked wearing facial hair—it was damnable itchy at times and messy as hell during meals— he was always grateful to have hair on his face when the air turned bitter cold. Easton was clean-shaven, lean of jaw, with the kind of soulful gray eyes that made women swoon. And those eyes were fastened on Hannah more often than

not. Hadn't the girl told the cow-eyed child that she was engaged? If she had, the boy certainly hadn't been discour-
aged in his pursuit. Not that he cared how she comported
herself. He cared not a wit.

But did she have to laugh at everything the boy said? Did
she have to touch his wrist and allow him to grasp her
elbow as they sat for dinner? As if Hannah Wright, with sea
legs nearly as sure as his crew, needed assistance sitting in
a chair.

Thank God the ship kept his mind where it should be.
The *Windfire* had been in the strong trades for a week, and
James knew their first gale was already overdue. Eight days
after hitting the trades, George came up from the chart
room, his face filled with excitement.

"Barometer's been dropping all day, sir. Looks like we're
in for it."

The storm hit just as the already dark skies were dim-
ming to dusk, a wind-shrieking tempest that heaved up
enormous waves that crashed onto the deck, pummeling all
who worked to keep the *Windfire* on course. The sails were
shortened only when it became apparent the ship would be
in danger if they were not. James MacRae was known as
one of the best captains in a storm; he was fearless, but not
foolish. As the storm intensified, more and more sails were
reefed, which seemed to have little effect on the speed of
the ship.

"Mr. Wright," he shouted over the roar of the storm. "I
want her speed. By God, she's flying." George heaved the
log overboard and began counting knots in the rope that
passed through his hand while James kept an eye on the
hourglass. "Now!" he shouted when the sand ran out. "How
fast, Mr. Wright?"

"Eighteen knots, Captain. She's going eighteen knots."
An impossible speed, a wonderful speed. In his joy he
grasped his first mate's arm. That is when he heard the
woman's scream, and his heart nearly stopped.

"Stay here. I'll go." What the devil was one of the

women doing atop, James thought, his heart pounding madly in his chest. And then it came again, that scream ripping through him, sounding chilling over the storm's howl. Hannah. It was her, he knew it. He could just make out that hat of hers, still tied around her neck, whipping wildly behind her. His body, already cold from the frigid sea and rain, went colder still. He made his way toward the bow in agonizing slowness, battling waves that crashed over him, taking his breath away. His hands, numb from the cold, gripped the rail awkwardly as he lurched toward where he thought the screams had come.

He saw her in the dim light, between waves that nearly swept him away, clutching the shrouds near the foremast. She must be terrified, he thought. And then: What the hell was she thinking to come on deck in the middle of a gale? The ship dipped suddenly, plunging deep into a valley between two monster waves. My god, he thought, she'll be swept away before I get to her. She'll not be able to bear the force of the wave. He watched in horror as the ship cut through the sea, as the wave lifted up and began its descent toward the deck. He was still twenty feet away when the wave crashed down, tearing at him, making him strain to keep his place on deck. Another scream, and then only the roar of the sea.

And then laughter. High-pitched and melodious. Laughter.

What the devil?

She was there, his brave girl, still clinging to her ropes. Laughing. When he reached her, she was silent, blinking away the salt spray from her eyes and clutching the ropes with all her strength.

"Miss Wright!" he shouted, the wind whipping his voice away, turning it into a whisper.

Hannah turned when he touched one hand to her sopping shoulder. "Isn't it glorious, Captain?" she shouted into his ear. "Did you see that last wave? She drove through it as if she were in a bathtub. My goodness, I've never felt so wonderful in all my life." She turned away, again pointing her lovely face into the storm.

In that moment James realized a horrible truth. He was deeply and forever in love with Hannah Wright.

Chapter Ten

"What the hell happened up there?" George shouted two days later as Hannah checked her sea and wind current charts. The storm, as storms went near the southern tip of South America, was not a fierce one. But the storm that remained still needed to be dealt with.

"Nothing, George. I was just enjoying the storm, and the captain came to make sure I was all right. I've apologized for frightening him, but he seems rather put out. Truly, nothing happened. I think we must face the fact that Captain MacRae cannot abide me."

George scowled at his younger cousin. "Something must have happened. The man's been in a bad temper ever since. I knew this was a mistake."

Hannah looked up from her chart, unable to ignore her cousin's last statement. "Why must this be my fault? Perhaps the captain is simply tired and taking it out on the crew. God knows the man needs his sleep. Two hours sleep in nearly three days is not enough rest for any man." She was worried. James looked almost haggard the last time she'd seen him, with deep circles under his eyes in a face that appeared almost pale. "Now that the gale is over, I don't see why he shouldn't get some rest. He can have his own bunk if he wants it. I won't be in my room until this evening."

George shook his head. "He won't be going anywhere until after the noon reading. After three days of cloud cover, he's anxious to know our position." He stroked his beard thoughtfully. "You're probably right. He is tired. But I also know he's angry, and there's only one person on this ship who makes him angry with any consistency, and that, my dear cousin, is you."

"I swear to you, George. He came up to me, and I told him I thought the storm was wonderful. And that was the entire contents of our conversation. We barely exchanged two sentences. It isn't fair that he be angry with me for riding out the storm on deck. After all, I am part of the crew. I've proven my worth and my expertise."

George gave his cousin a smile. "You are probably right. Captain MacRae is a reasonable man. There must be something else behind his foul mood. Fair warning, though, Hannah. He's been giving you some rather dark looks. If you are telling the truth . . ."

"If!"

George held up an apologetic hand. "There is something else, Hannah, and I am certain it has something to do with you. Perhaps you should talk to the man again and . . ."

Hannah gave a little huffy moan, like a child who is happily playing and is told it is bedtime. "When did you become such a diplomat?" she said, scowling at her peacemaker cousin.

"Anything that interferes with the running of this ship . . ."

"Yes, yes, yes. I know. You win, George. I'll speak to the captain."

Hannah's stomach was a nervous jumble for the next several hours. What her cousin said was true. The mood on the ship was tense, with the crew members tiptoeing around a captain who looked menacing and mean . . . especially whenever she was within sight of him. Hannah even tried smiling at him, but he gave her the queerest look—almost as if he were going to be sick. Then he swiped an angry hand through his hair and turned away, shouting an order to the helmsman. Captain MacRae, a man who couldn't hide his

mirth, also couldn't hide his pure dislike of his lady navigator. It hurt. Hannah, despite her resolve to protect her heart,
found it quite unbearable to know that he did not like her.
And nearly as unbearable was knowing that the crew members she had finally won over were looking at her with ac-
cusation. She could see it in their eyes: What has she gone
and done now?

The early September day was glaringly bright, but cold
with the sharpness of a New York winter day. Just before
noon, Hannah was ready near the helm with her sextant. The
officers were anxious to know how close they were to turning the corner of Cape Horn. For once they were around the
Horn, it was a wonderful and fast sail to San Francisco, in
strong northeast trades. Hannah shouted that it was high
noon, and eight bells were struck.

With the look of a woman on a grave mission, Hannah
walked toward the captain, whose back was to the binnacle,
effectively trapping him into a confrontation. His hair was
getting long, touching the collar of his heavy woolen
sweater, and his beard, darker even than his hair, had filled
in entirely, making him look even more the part of a sea captain. A very handsome sea captain, who happened to be
scowling quite heavily at his ship's navigator.

"Captain, if you don't mind, would you assist me with my
calculations today?"

Surrounded by his officers, James had no choice, as Hannah knew. She walked along the deck of the rolling ship to
the companionway, half fearing he would ignore her and
stay on deck. But she heard his footsteps behind her on the
steep stairway that led to her cabin and the chart room. Once
inside the chart room, Hannah turned to him, her heart in her
throat. It must simply be weariness making him such a
crank, she thought. Look at him. She could see how tired he
was; he was past exhaustion.

"George is under the impression that I've done something
to anger you, and I am the reason for your . . . foul mood. If
I've done something to make you angry, I apologize." It

galled Hannah to apologize for something she was unaware of, but for the sake of peace, she was willing to do it.

He sat down heavily onto a swiveling chair that was attached to the chart room floor, making Hannah all the more worried. "I am not angry with you, Miss Wright." He sounded angry, and she frowned.

"Oh. Good." Then what? "Simply tired?"

He looked at her, his gaze steady and disquieting. "Yes. I'm tired. So goddamned tired, I don't have the energy to discuss it. Now. Can we get these calculations done so that I may rest?"

Hannah could feel her face heat to be spoken to so abruptly. "Of course, Captain." She watched as he clenched his jaw.

After several moments, Hannah spoke. "We're just one hundred miles from the mouth of the River Plate." She looked up. "George tells me that's where we'll see our roughest weather."

"Yes, Miss Wright. Weather so rough, I don't expect to find any screaming females on the bow of my ship."

With that, he turned and left, leaving Hannah staring after him. George was right, something was wrong with their captain, but she was not completely convinced it had anything to do with her. He'd denied he was angry, admitted he was tired. Perhaps that was all there was to it. Then again, he had, in a rather caustic tone, reminded her of that exhilarating experience during the gale. It had been thrilling, marred only by the thought that her actions had angered the captain. If he was angry, why not admit it? Hannah had convinced herself that it was simple weariness that was driving the captain's mood, until dinner later that night.

"Thought we could kill our first pig tomorrow," George said, frowning down at his plate of salted codfish. It had been several days since there had been any fresh food to eat at the dining table.

"Wouldn't do it," cautioned Timothy Lodge. "Let's wait until we're past the River Plate. Bad luck to kill the first pig

before that. What if we get stuck rounding the Horn. Then
what? I tell you, it's bad luck." Mr. Lodge had taken great
pleasure in telling Hannah and other green crew members
tales of ships who "hit the wall" trying to get around the
Horn, languishing for weeks and even months and making
little progress.

Hannah smiled, thinking about the succulent taste of
freshly butchered meat. "It would be good to have fresh
meat," she said wistfully.

"Don't see the harm. We're already nearly halfway done
with the trip. I'm with you, Hannah. I can taste that pig right
now," Christopher Easton said, wrinkling his nose at his fish
and giving it a poke with his fork.

"Wouldn't do it," Lodge mumbled. "Bad luck."

"Oh, Mr. Lodge, you think everything is bad luck," Hannah said, smiling at the second mate. "Why, just this morning you said seeing a lone albatross is bad luck. If that is the
case, nearly every ship rounding Cape Horn would be
doomed."

Lodge grinned sheepishly, but wouldn't relent. "Still say
we save the pig."

"But it's been so long . . ."

"The pig won't be killed until we've reached the Horn,"
James said, his eyes hard and steady on Hannah, as if killing
the pig had been her idea. Hannah felt chastised, and those
dining fell into an uncomfortable silence. Feeling somehow
responsible for the tension at the table, Hannah tried to think
up another topic of conversation that would not irritate the
captain.

"Christopher," Hannah said, not noticing the captain's
frown when she used the young man's given name, "I'd like
to tell the story about the ghost ship. You don't mind hearing it again, do you?"

"The squall story?" Easton turned cheerfully to the captain. "Oh, you'll enjoy this, Captain. It happened on Hannah's father's ship during an Atlantic crossing. Quite eerie."

The passengers leaned forward, and Christopher leaned

an elbow on the table so that he might comfortably stare at Hannah as she told her tale. "I've got the shivers already," he said with a wide grin, which Hannah returned.

James stood, half his meal still on his plate. "If you'll excuse me, I'm needed on deck."

His tone was polite, but for some reason, Hannah again felt chastised. He tossed his napkin onto his plate, bowed to the passengers, and exited the dining room. Suddenly, Hannah didn't want to entertain those remaining with the story. The truth was, she'd tried to think of something that would please James, and now that he'd gone, telling the story had lost its appeal. She told it anyway, thrilling those who remained, and fairly terrifying the superstitious Timothy Lodge.

"Bad luck to tell a story like that. Oh, we're in for it now," he said dramatically. Hannah ruffled the older man's bushy hair. Ever since the shaving incident, the two had been fast friends and enjoyed baiting each other.

"I'll tell you what's bad luck, Mr. Lodge. Claiming everything is bad luck."

With that, she headed to the main deck, her eyes automatically searching out the captain in the muted light of dusk. She saw him near the bow, adjusting one of the halyards himself, his forearms bulging under the strain. Even from a distance, his movements seemed angry. Hannah sighed. The good captain had lied to her—he was angry with her. What else could explain his terse attitude?

His back was to her as she approached him, and she moved around him so that they might talk. When he noticed her, he straightened and frowned.

"Captain. We need to talk," she said.

He leaned his forehead against one hand that still held the halyard and seemed to study the planked deck. "I've told you, Miss Wright," he said, looking up, "there is nothing to discuss."

Jutting her chin up stubbornly, she thrust a hand toward the after house. "I will meet you in the chart room in five

minutes. If you are not there, I will seek you out and force
you to speak to me where I find you."

His eyes widened in surprise, and Hannah thought she
saw a gleam of admiration as well.

"Just who are you, Miss Wright, to be giving me orders?"

"No one, sir. But blast it, I'll have this out with you.
Now." If there had been more light, Hannah knew the blush
that tinged her cheeks from swearing would have been visible, diminishing her strident tone. "I'll not be the object of
your scowls and dark looks anymore." With that, she turned,
feeling his eyes bore through her back, not sure whether she
wanted him to follow her or not.

When she reached the chart room, he was directly behind
her, his large body filling the narrow hall. With his dark
beard and wind-whipped hair, James looked downright fearsome. Entering the room and lighting the lamp, she noted he
also looked incredibly weary, as if he still hadn't slept. Suddenly, she felt foolish and self-centered. The man was tired.
He had a ship to run and certainly wasn't sparing her a
thought.

"What is it now, Miss Wright?"

Hannah's heart turned in her breast at his weary tone.
"I . . . You should rest. Take your room tonight. I'll sleep in
George's. You'll do no one any good if you collapse or become ill." She went up to him and gently placed a cool hand
on his brow. James jerked away, as if her touch was painful.

"I'm sorry"—her face heating at his reaction to her touch.
"I just wanted to determine if you had a fever." She stared at
his taut profile for a moment, uncertain. "I thought . . . That
is, at dinner and earlier, I thought you were angry with me.
I realize you are simply tired."

James was silent a long moment, his body turned away
from her. "Your fiancé. What is his name again?"

Hannah blinked, momentarily confused by this sudden
change of subject. "Allen Pritchard."

"Ah. Pritchard."

She creased her brow. "You know him?"

James shook his head, turning toward her and leaning against the desk. "Hannah Pritchard. Your name will be Hannah Pritchard."

"Well, yes. I suppose it will be. I really hadn't given that much thought."

"That's odd. Usually girls in love will write their new name over and over. My sisters, for instance, will try out a new name before they are even properly introduced to a gentleman. But only those men whom they love at first sight." He laughed, but his eyes, for once, were not smiling.

"I simply never thought to," Hannah said, a bit defensively.

"Could it be that you do not love your Allen Pritchard who has so effectively disappeared on you?"

"For one thing, it is none of your business whether I love my fiancé or not. However, I daresay my traveling fifteen thousand miles to find him speaks for itself," she said, secretly satisfied she'd found a way to remain ambiguous. "And secondly, Allen has not disappeared on me. He simply is . . . unavailable."

"So, you do love him." Words said so softly, Hannah barely heard them.

"Actually I . . ." Something in his eyes made her lie, a challenge, a dare, she wasn't certain. But she lied to him, perhaps only to find out what his reaction would be. "I do love him," and she raised her chin. "Very much."

"I see. It certainly is good to love the man you plan to marry. And he loves you?"

Without hesitation Hannah said, "Oh, yes. Allen loves me."

"How happy for you both." His Scottish burr was thicker than usual.

"Indeed. We are very happy."

James chewed on his thumb knuckle, while his other fist gently tapped his thigh, apparently deep in thought. Suddenly he slapped one hand onto the desk. "Well, then.

Good." He straightened. "One thing before I go, Miss Wright. Just something I need to get off my chest."

Hannah smiled despite the earlier tension, for James seemed like his old self again. "Be my guest, Captain."

He came to her, and suddenly those laughing eyes weren't laughing but filled with something Hannah immediately recognized. Before she knew it, she was being kissed.

"There," he said, his lips still against her mouth. "I just wanted to get that out of my system. Perhaps, one more. You don't mind, do you, Miss Wright? I'm afraid if I don't kiss you just once more, I might go mad, and I shudder to think what will happen to *Windfire* if I'm shackled in the hold."

Hannah was too stunned to speak, and then by the time she got her wits about her, his mouth was on hers again, driving from her mind any sensible thing she was about to say. It started as a simple enough kiss, not quite like Allen's, for there was something about the captain's mouth that was infinitely more . . . exciting. His mouth grazed her sensitive lips as one hand went to the nape of her neck. And then the kiss was deeper, desperate, somehow. Needy. His tongue, oh, his tongue licked her lips, teasing them open, and she welcomed him, slanting her head to allow him entry to her mouth. That hand on her nape tightened convulsively, the other was fisted by his side, not touching, as if not daring to touch. He let out a low groan when Hannah leaned into him, and she was lost for the moment in the feeling of him wanting her.

Oh, she thought, her mind drugged, how could he want her when he hated her? How could he make her feel so wonderful? Oh, this was . . . Hannah's mind snapped back into place. *How could he?*

Hannah shoved him away. "Stop it, Captain."

"James," he muttered, his brilliant eyes half closed with desire.

Hannah struggled to push him away. "Stop it, *James.*" With her forearm against his throat, she pushed him away, glaring at him and his unreadable expression. He stepped back.

"I will forget this happened, Captain. But I will not forgive it. How dare you insinuate yourself on me? I am affianced. We were just discussing my Allen, and you dare to . . . What sort of a man are you? I thought you were honorable."

He stood before her, his expression closed, his hands clenched by his sides, but something in Hannah told her it was not anger that made those large hands curl into fists. James jerked his head downward in a quick bow.

"I apologize, Miss Wright. As I said, it was something I needed to get out of my system. It will not happen again."

"I should hope not." Why, Hannah thought, did that sound like a lie to her own ears?

My God, what have I done? James thought moments later as he stared at the whitewashed ceiling of the first mate's quarters. He could still taste her on his tongue and might never again know what it was like to hold her in his arms. She would be wary of him, angry with him—as she had a right to be, he admitted. It was craziness to kiss her, to allow himself that one small pleasure that only made him want her more; a small torture having held her, even so briefly, in his arms. Arm, he corrected ruefully. One hand on her neck, feeling that soft hair, that smooth skin. One hand pulling her up against him, that lithe little body fitting so perfectly up against his own.

Why her, of all the beautiful women who had looked up at him with adoration in their gaze, why the one who was unavailable, who looked at him with anything but the awe he so liked to see in his women? Perhaps that is why I want her, he thought, closing eyes so tired they burned. She is a challenge to me. A beautiful challenge. A passionate, lovely woman. The thought that Hannah was simply a challenge pleased him. That frightening feeling that had overwhelmed him the day of the storm was not love, but lust for a woman who rejected him. Didn't his reaction to what was a simple

kiss prove he had been nearly overcome by that lust? He'd
been swept away like a teenage boy feeling his first passionate rush. Her reaction only proved his theory, for she,
too, had responded, and certainly she did not love him. Yes,
she'd enjoyed the kiss, he thought with masculine smug-
ness.

But then she'd pushed him away. Angry with him. Disappointed in him. James hated this feeling of uncertainty,
hated that a woman could so distract him he'd been lax in
his duties as captain. Never again, he thought with new resolve. Lying there, so tired he couldn't sleep, James convinced himself it was mere lust he felt. A beautiful woman
in such close proximity was bound to attract him. Of course
he admired her, too. Her strength and bravery and spunk.
Imagine standing near the bow of a ship being beaten in a
gale, he thought with a chuckle. Remarkable woman.
Damned remarkable. No man would be immune to her, and
certainly not a man who loved women as much as he did. He
loved all women in a manner of speaking. Hannah Wright
was no different, no better, no more beautiful.

The ship gave a sudden lurch, and he immediately sat up,
his entire body taut and alert. He waited, but the ship continued on its course. James smiled, glad to have his senses
back. Then he lay down and slept, deep and long, sparing
not another thought to his navigator.

Until the dream.

She was standing on shore waving good-bye, a bright
smile on her face. Beside her was a faceless man, tall and
thin. James was on a ship sailing toward her, but seeming to
get no closer. The wind was strong, yet the seas were remarkably smooth beneath his ship. He sailed alone, manag-
ing to navigate the large ship single-handedly. But no matter
what he did, he got no closer to her, and she continued to
wave good-bye. Then she turned away. He was desperate to
get to shore, desperate to make her turn around. And then he
was alone in the middle of the sea, sailing, sailing. Toward
nothing.

James awoke feeling drugged and groggy. He rubbed his eyes with the heels of his hands, letting out a tired groan. He could tell by the angle of the ship that she was in a good wind, and he lay still for a long moment, enjoying the feel of his *Windfire*. He didn't like to spend too much time belowdecks, felt he was too far from the ship. Sometimes, though, he would go below and listen to her creaks and groans, to the muted sound of the waves hitting her hull. Now, instead of his ship, he heard the sound of a cabin door shutting, and knew it was the captain's quarters. Knew it was her.

Aw, damn, he thought, feeling his gut clench, his heart pound. Damn me to hell.

Chapter Eleven

Hannah didn't have time to dwell on that kiss. The ship reached the River Plate late the following day, and once again it was buffeted by strong winds. The barometer had been falling all day, and the gray clouds that made for a bleak and dreary morning grew darker and heavier as the hours passed. Seagulls, which hovered and screeched at the ship's stern, headed to shore, a certain sign of a coming storm. Four albatross lifted out of the roughening sea, soaring silently overhead, riding the wind as if hung suspended from the heavens.

James ordered stronger ropes to tie down the lifeboats on the forehouse and longboat that rested on the after house, and by dusk, the topsails were reefed to give the helm more control. Darkness fell, and the wind grew ominously stronger.

Hannah visited Mrs. Coddington and Mrs. Davis, whose fear was nearly palpable. Those poor ladies, Hannah thought, what were their husbands thinking to send them so unprepared on such a trip. Though also a woman, Hannah saw herself separately—for she was a girl who had grown up on ships, who knew what to expect. They had tried to be brave since leaving the doldrums, had even made it up for dinner on a few occasions. But seasickness continued to plague the two women, who refused to heed Hannah's advise to spend more time on deck. The sight of the undulating sea was enough to send Mrs. Davis into a swoon. With a storm nearly upon them, they were forced to endure the heaving, stomach-churning roll of the ship belowdecks.

"Oh, what have we done to deserve this hell?" Mrs. Davis moaned.

"I ought to whip your husbands for moving to California," Hannah said.

"Oh, no. Don't blame them. We both encouraged them to go. We were so brave in New York, weren't we, Beatrice?" Mrs. Davis said. "So brave."

Hannah, weary to the bones, comforted the two women until they both fell into a fitful sleep. Finally, she went to her bunk and climbed into its cozy warmth, thankful that she could. Most of the crew and all of the officers were on deck battling the storm that seemed to grow more fierce with every passing minute. Though the crew tried to maintain their normal schedule, the call for all hands was often made during a storm, disrupting their well-needed rest. Hannah, who never suffered from seasickness in her life, began to feel a bit queasy belowdecks as the movement of the ship became more violent. Still, she slept, only to awaken at dawn to a sea that had gone mad and a ship that suddenly seemed fragile.

Hannah dressed with difficulty, losing her balance and banging about the cabin in an almost comical fashion, and then headed to the companionway. She lifted the hatch, which flew out of her hands and banged back with a loud crack. Poking her head up cautiously, she took in a scene that was awesome. It was as if the sea had come to life, a ruthless monster of seething frothing water, cold and savage as it tore at the ship. Lifelines were strung from bow to stern along the deck, a necessity, Hannah quickly realized as she watched a wave crash fully over the deck, leaving a trail of white foam behind. The men were blurry outlines in the storm. For the first time Hannah felt her stomach clench in fear—not for herself, but for Captain James MacRae, who at that moment was making his way aft battling waves that pounded the deck so hard, it seemed impossible that even a man such as he would not be washed away. As another wave crashed down, soaking Hannah and the companionway, she realized her foolishness and made a grab for the hatch.

His hands numb from the cold, James made his way toward the stern. The ship had to be tacked so she could run with the wind else the ever-growing waves would crush her. Though most of the sails were either shortened completely or reefed, she still continued to cut through the seas—a beautiful thing to behold. One lifeboat had already been lost, torn from its spot on the forehouse. It was only providence that no crew member had been swept away with it. He knew it was only a matter of time before the second lifeboat and longboat also were torn from the ship. He looked for the outline of the longboat in the early dawn, squinting as salt spray stung his eyes. Then he saw her, or rather her hair whipping above the entrance to the companionway as she struggled to close the hatch. Foolish girl, stay below, he wanted to shout. But he knew his voice would carry no farther than a few feet. It appeared she was trying to do just that, but the wind and waves were making her task nearly impossible.

As if he prophesied the event, he watched with horror as a huge wave approached the ship. He hunkered down, his back toward the curling water, and clutched the lifeline with all his strength. When the wave hit with pounding force, it seemed as if hell had descended with cold fury. The long-boat, with a loud crack, was ripped from its mooring atop the after house—just a few feet from where Hannah struggled with the hatch. When James was finally able to lift his head, he saw nothing. No longboat, no hair whipping in the companionway, no Hannah struggling with the hatch.

"Jesus God," he said as he hurried to the back of the after house. More waves crashed over him, tugging him toward the sea, but he continued on. When he finally reached the hatch, he wiped the salt from his eyes and peered down the companionway. She was there, lying on the bottom on the stairway, surrounded by seawater that continued to drip down on her. Still as death.

James's mind, for just a moment, shut down. All he could see was Hannah. All he could think was that she was dead.

"Sir! Sir!" He felt a tugging on his arm. Felt another wave pound against him, felt the ship lurch wildly, and thought only: Someone must help Hannah.

"Sir! Doc Owen will see to her, sir. The ship, sir!"

He turned to the voice that finally penetrated the anguish that paralyzed him. It was Timothy Lodge, pleading with him, begging him to see to the ship. His ship.

"See to her, Mr. Lodge. We're coming about. We'll ride with the wind." James pushed against the companionway with all his strength, forcing himself to walk away, feeling a pain so sharp in his chest, he thought for a moment he must have been injured. The order was given, the men, exhausted and battered, turned the ship slowly so that the wind was behind her and the waves hit her stern, no longer crashing over the bow. James ordered the helmsmen to lash themselves to the wheel as the heavy waves continue to batter the ship, causing it to shudder. The deck was covered by white sea foam, and the masts, dark silhouettes against the gray sky, heaved back and forth, three fragile fingers pointing to the heavens. The ship, even with most of its sails reefed, was traveling twelve knots, but away from Cape Horn.

Hours later, when the barometer finally began to rise and dusk was again descending on the ship, James ordered another tack and all hands on deck so that more sail could be set out. Seas were still high, but the wind had eased and once again *Windfire* was cutting through the seas heading toward the tip of Cape Horn.

Never had anything been more agonizing than sailing that ship not knowing whether Hannah lived or died. Not even when his brother had died had he felt such a powerful need to leave his watch. George, following a rest, told him only that she was alive and still unconscious. But that was hours ago, hours of forcing his mind to the ship and driving away the image of her lying at the bottom of those stairs. Then, suddenly, it was too much. He must see her, prove to himself that she would live. Make her live.

"The ship is yours, Mr. Wright," he said, satisfied that the storm and the misery of crossing the mouth of the River Plate was behind them. He made his way to the forehouse and the galley, casting a thankful look at the smokestack that still miraculously stood. It was so cold, he could feel the heat from the chimney as he walked past it.

"Doc, how is she?" he asked the ship's cook as he stepped into the warm galley.

The portly man shrugged. "Woke up once."

James's heart soared, but was quickly brought back into place.

"You know I've got no medical training. I can stitch a cut, treat scurvy, set a bone. But a hit on the noggin?" Owen shrugged again. "She ain't moved much, and when she did wake up, it was only for a minute. Didn't talk. Got an egg on the side of her head and that's all. No blood. With the head, you don't know what's going on inside. Hell, Wells looked worse than she does, and he was up and about before the end of the day but for that broken arm."

Owen led James to the tiny infirmary off the galley, large enough to contain only a bed and chair. A lantern, its flame low, swayed above the bunk where she lay.

"If you'll excuse me, Owen," James said, not taking his eyes off the pale form on the bed. When the little man had backed from the infirmary, James fell to his knees beside the bed. Reaching up, he raised the lantern's flame so that he might see her better. She looked perfect, as if he had come upon her sleeping, as if all he needed to do was shake her and she would look at him with her extraordinary eyes.

"Miss Wright." That sounded wrong. He raised a hand that trembled slightly to softly brush back her hair. "Hannah." James swallowed past something odd and thick in his throat. Not even a flutter of her lashes. To his tortured ears, her breathing sounded shallow, strained. Fading. He grasped one cool hand, so small in his, and pressed it to his lips.

"Hannah, love, you must wake up." His voice sounded loud to his ears, commanding. And yet she continued to sleep. Closing his eyes, he moved her hand to his bearded cheek and rubbed it back and forth, a strangled sound coming from his throat. He sat there for what seemed like hours, imploring her to wake up, telling her about the storm, that everyone was safe. Even Todd Engle. Finally exhaustion overtook him, and he lay his head down, placing her hand on the back of his neck, his hand gently holding it in place.

That was how George, nearly dropping from fatigue, found him. After the captain had been gone from the deck nearly four hours, Timothy Lodge began grumbling that the captain had been missing from the main deck long enough. Though the storm had abated even further, the wind continued to howl and the seas to buffet the ship, now sailing on course under full canvas.

"Ain't like the captain to be gone from the ship so long. Where the hell is the man?"

George pointed out that, although he and Lodge had managed to get some rest during the storm, the captain, already fatigued, had never left his post.

"Bah. You don't know the cap' like I do," Lodge had argued.

Reluctantly, George agreed to look for the captain, thinking that he must have decided to rest and then fallen into a deep sleep. He went to his own cabin, then to Hannah's, thinking the captain would take advantage of the empty room with Hannah in the infirmary. Puzzled, he left the after house and headed to the forehouse. Perhaps, he thought, Captain MacRae was checking on the patient. His brow furrowed, George headed to the galley and the little room that held his cousin. He'd been worried sick, but knew he could do nothing for Hannah. She was in the best hands the ship had with Doc Owen. Knowing the captain's history, George forced himself to stay on deck, all the time telling himself that a bedside vigil would do Hannah no good and could do the ship harm. That is why when he finally found the captain, sleeping with his head nestled beneath Hannah's hand, he was momentarily dazed.

He tiptoed to the bedside, careful not to disturb the captain, and touched his cousin's shoulder. "Hannah," he whispered in her ear, "it's George." He was vastly pleased to see her eyes open sleepily.

"George?" For some reason her right hand wouldn't move, so Hannah brought her left hand up to her pounding head. "Head hurts. What happened?" Then her eyes traveled down to see why she couldn't move her right hand. Her brow furrowed.

"Is that the captain?" she whispered, realizing that someone had fallen asleep by her side.

"Apparently he came to visit and fell asleep."

A ghost of a smile touched her lips. "Should we let him sleep?"

With a sudden jerk, James was awake, his eyes immediately going to hers. A brilliant smile lit his face, which was creased on the left side from a wrinkle in the bedcover.

"You are well," he said with such force, it almost sounded like an order. He spared not a glance to George.

"Well, not entirely. My head hurts. I feel a bit . . . fuzzy. What happened?"

James closed his eyes briefly, as if he did not want to recount the accident. "A wave ripped the longboat from its lines and must have struck you on the head. Either that or you struck your head falling down the companionway."

"The storm," she said sleepily, and her eyes fluttered shut.

"Hannah."

She could hear his voice from a distance, recognized a note of panic. Odd. As odd as finding him sleeping beside her.

"Hannah."

Please let me sleep. So tired. "Tired," she managed, before once again slipping away. She felt a hand, large and warm and gentle, touch the side of her face. And then something soft. Warm and soft on her mouth. How very strange. Someone is kissing me. She slept.

George watched this impossible scene silently, feeling like an intruder. He loves her, he realized, and felt an overwhelming sadness. This could not be good, this love. Not with Hannah engaged. Not with James MacRae leaving San Francisco, leaving Hannah behind a month after their arrival to sail back to New York.

James stood, looking at George directly and without embarrassment. He looked back at Hannah's sleeping form and let out a small sigh.

"She doesn't know," James said softly.

George felt it his duty as Hannah's chaperon to remind the captain of her near-married state. "Sir, Hannah is . . ."

"I know what she is, Mr. Wright. God help me, but I don't care." With one last look at Hannah, James turned and left. George could only think that Captain MacRae had been right all those weeks ago: This was going to be a trip they'd not soon forget.

Chapter Twelve

Hannah awoke to the sun streaming through the portal and the smell of pork frying, and smiled. Her head ached only slightly as she tried to sit up on the narrow bed set up in the small room off the galley. She could hear Doc Owen moving about the kitchen, humming under his breath as he worked. Her movement brought him to the infirmary's entrance.

"Up and about? How's the head?" he asked, moving back into the galley to continue cooking.

Hannah put a tentative hand to the still-swollen area. "Still hurts a bit. How long have I been sleeping?"

"Were unconscious for a while. Drat!" he said as he dropped something with a loud clang. "Then you woke up after a few hours. Been sleeping near twelve hours now."

"Twelve hours. I've missed both readings," Hannah said, throwing the covers from her and bringing her legs over the side of the bed.

Owen was in the room in seconds. "Oh, no, girl. You stay abed until the captain says you can get up."

Hannah scowled. The captain was probably angry with her for poking her head above deck during the storm. It had been a foolish move, she realized, trying to recall precisely what had happened. Her mind was blank, recalling only her struggle with the hatch and a monster wave crashing down.

"Was anyone else hurt?" she called to Owen's retreating back.

"Naw. Just some bumps and bruises. Helluva storm, she was. Lost one lifeboat and the longboat. Two sails ripped to shreds. Lucky we didn't lose a mast."

"Hmmm." Hannah sat cross-legged on the bed, wanting nothing more than to relieve herself, wash, change her clothes, and eat some of that pork that smelled so delectable. Though she had spent long hours in the company of men all her life, she still was unsure how to delicately put what she had to say. She spied a chamber pot in the room's corner and began easing herself out of bed.

"Oh, no you don't, miss. I've got my orders."

"Do your orders include allowing your patient to use the chamber pot?" Hannah smiled with satisfaction at the red blush that appeared on Owen's already heat-flushed cheeks.

"Suit yourself," he said gruffly, and closed the door with a bang. Hannah chuckled as she went about her business, sobering only when she heard *his* voice. Hastily finishing, she quickly sat on the bed and pulled up the covers, even though she was fully clothed.

Though Hannah had no recollection of the last twenty-four hours, her last meeting with the captain was vivid in her mind. Just thinking about that kiss made her angry. She could never again relax with him alone in a room. Those hours they'd spent discussing the best course to take would not continue. Hannah wondered how long the captain had wanted to kiss her before he finally succumbed to temptation. She dismissed that first kiss, accepting it for what it was: a means to shut her up.

But that other kiss. That long, slow, burning kiss. How could she forget that? How could she stand next to him, feel his heat, and not remember that kiss? He'd gone and ruined everything. Hannah found it perfectly acceptable that she'd desired him, but now that she knew he desired her and had the nerve to act on it, she was a bit annoyed.

And flattered. Of course, she was flattered that a man

such as Captain James MacRae, who could probably have
any woman he wanted, desired her. Perhaps, she thought
with a frown marring her pretty face, *desired* was too strong
a word. Just because a man kissed a woman didn't mean he
fully desired her. Did it? She kissed Allen all the time and
rarely felt she wanted to take it further. She'd never before
felt that melting sensation she'd felt in the captain's arms.
She heard his voice again, and her scowl deepened.

Why did he have to kiss me? Why did he have to show me
that there was something more to a kiss? That's the crux of
it, my girl, Hannah thought. You're not angry because he did
something you didn't want him to do, but because you're
afraid that now that he has, you'll want him to again.

"Guard your heart, Hannah. The man's a cad," she whispered to herself.

The cad politely knocked on her door. "Are you pre-
sentable, Miss Wright?"

"I am." Terse. Polite. Oh, God, it's good to hear his voice.

He walked in, windblown and carrying the scent of the
sea with him. Hannah couldn't help but breathe him in and
savor every tantalizing molecule.

"Doc says you are feeling well enough to complain about
missing your readings." He smiled at her, an open genuine
smile that put her on edge. She didn't like the fact that her
heart stepped up a beat, that she wanted to return that smile,
that she had the oddest desire to hold him to her.

"I am, sir." His smile faltered.

"You needn't worry about doing your readings until tomorrow noon. We've spotted Staten Island. Once we're
'round it, it's westward past the Horn. The storm brought us
only a bit off course." He seemed falsely cheerful as his eyes
swept uncertainly over her.

For some reason his talking of the ship, its course, their
bearing, depressed Hannah. "I suppose I can rest a bit
more," she said, hating the sullenness she heard in her voice.
"How are Mrs. Coddington and Mrs. Davis?"

"Haven't been topside yet."

It was awkward, suddenly, having him there, his big body filling up the room. They had never been awkward together. It must be the kiss, Hannah thought. He regrets it, is embarrassed by it. And I . . . I'm sitting here wishing that he would kiss me again.

Hannah turned her head and gazed out the portal. Oh, fool, fool, how can you want such a thing? Tears filled her eyes, and she did nothing to stem their flow.

"Han . . . Miss Wright. Are you quite all right?"

She heard him take a step toward her and stiffened. "Quite all right. It's my head. It hurts." It's my heart. It's breaking. Oh, God, how did I allow this to happen? How did I allow myself to fall in love with him?

It's the kiss, he thought. It's made her wary of me, made her churlish. James gazed at the barren rocky island off the starboard bow that signaled the beginning of their journey around the Horn. Staten Island's snowcapped peak was a landmark that he always looked forward to—a sign that headway was being made. To cross the island less than two months out was astounding. This trip, the sight of that bleak and forbidding island depressed him. Soon *Windfire* would be in San Francisco, and then he would return to New York to . . . nothing. And she would remain with her fiancé, planning a life with a man James was growing to loathe even though he'd never met him. How Hannah must love him to travel all this way. He realized there wasn't a woman alive he would do the same for, except Hannah. He allowed himself a bitter smile at the track of his foolish romantic thoughts. He would sail a thousand seas for her. Two thousand.

James had never given marriage a thought other than to think that someday he would marry, have children. He'd never met a woman he could imagine waiting at home for him. He would do that with nearly every woman he met, imagine sailing into port with her waiting on the pier, perhaps a baby in her arms, his heart filled with anticipation. None of the myriad women he had met, who had fawned over him and batted their eyelashes at him, could fill his heart with anything. Except, perhaps, lust. And the heart was not the organ doing the talking at that point.

He could imagine Hannah waiting for him. How happy he would be to head toward his home port knowing she would be waiting. And how empty his life would now seem knowing she would never be there. With a shiver he recalled his dream, her waving good-bye even as he tried to make it back to her. It seemed his subconscious had accepted the truth his heart never would.

James pulled out of his pocket the intricately carved whalebone he'd planned to give to Hannah, but the awkwardness between them, the politeness, made him change his plans. His brother had carved a clipper ship on the bone and given it to James as a Christmas present the year before he died. No object held more meaning for James than the carving. He'd imagined, foolishly so, embracing Hannah, kissing her, proclaiming his love. Silly man, to imagine such an impossible scene. Still, he'd gone to see her with that carving in his pocket, ready to give it to her, ready to let her know the depth of his feelings toward her.

No one approached James MacRae as he gazed with hard eyes at Staten Island. His loyal crew was edgy these days, not knowing what to make of the captain's strange behavior. They discussed it at length in their bunks, arguing back and forth, and usually coming to the conclusion that it was either the new first mate's doing—though no one could say why— or more often, blaming Hannah, their beautiful navigator. Never was it thrown out that the captain was in love with her and that was the cause of his changeable moods. Many had been with the captain long enough to know that no woman could distract him once he stepped foot on his ship. They'd seen female passengers literally throw themselves at him with little success.

Said one sailor three days after sighting Staten Island: "I remember on a leg to France, this beautiful girl stripped stark naked and lay waiting for the captain in his bunk. Well, we'd been in rough weather for days, and finally he went down to get some rest. That's when our mainsheet decided to tear. Now, what would you have done with a choice between going up on a cold deck or staying nice and cozy with a beautiful bit of woman? I'll tell you what the captain did, he left her there angry as a kitten without milk. Told the first mate to get the chit out of his cabin 'cause when he did go down again, he wanted to make damn sure he got some sleep."

The men hooted out their approval of the story, and agreed that tender feelings toward Miss Wright had nothing to do with Captain MacRae's scowls. Instead, they agreed that Miss Wright must have done something to irritate the captain, an offense for which, had she been a man, she would have been punished. The general conclusion was that the captain's foul moods were because he was frustrated by his inability to throw their lady navigator into the hold. And so, while Hannah recovered from her wounds, the tide gently turned against her. No one even thought to question their sudden about-face. It soon became fact: Hannah Wright needed to be punished, and the captain was too much of a gentleman to do the deed. A fine man, that captain. The only foolish thing he'd done was hire on a female navigator. Only a few noted that, thanks to their navigator, it looked as though they'd make record time to San Francisco. The officers were unaware of these debates, for they were not deemed trustworthy. The first mate was Miss Wright's cousin, after all, and the second mate behaved like a besotted idiot whenever Miss Wright was in view. No, this was best kept among the men.

Hannah, ready to resume her duties within days, instead spent long hours talking with Mrs. Davis and Mrs. Coddington, mostly about Allen Pritchard. Hannah wanted to drive James out of her mind, out of her heart. By the end of that week, Allen was again placed on a pedestal lovingly built by Hannah. He was witty and handsome and so cultured. Yes, he was wealthy, terrifically so, but Hannah wasn't marrying him for that, she said. Allen was everything she wanted in a husband, she explained. He was steady, he loved her, he would never leave her. Hannah carefully edited out the precise reason for her sudden trip to San Francisco, the desperate nature of her decision, and she was grateful the two old women never pried about why she was traveling to California as a crew member rather than a passenger.

One week to the day of being struck by the longboat, Hannah was on deck, sextant in hand, for the nine o'clock reading. It was a clear, bitterly cold day with wind that cut through even her thick fur-lined woolen coat. She hadn't seen the captain except in brief glimpses since the day he visited her. Hannah had systematically eliminated all thoughts of the captain from her mind, convincing herself that what she felt was only the schoolgirl crush she'd thought it to be all along. A little distance was a wonderful thing, she told herself. She was proud of herself. So she was completely taken aback when she saw him standing there near the ship's wheel and her knees almost buckled at the emotion that swept through her. She clutched the railing, her sextant digging painfully into her hand, as she tore her eyes away.

"Jesus Christ, what the hell are you doing on deck if you are not well." Hannah was almost relieved to hear him bluster at her.

Without looking at him, she said, "I am quite well, Captain. I simply lost my balance. My sea legs aren't quite what they should be." Blast and damn, she thought fiercely. I can't be as weak as all that. She forced herself to look at him, and immediately wished she had not.

Oh, he's beautiful, she thought. How can a man be so beautiful?

"You don't look well, Miss Wright," James said, and raised one hand as if to steady her.

"No, I don't . . . No, I'm fine," she said with conviction, backing away from that outstretched hand. She swallowed.

"I'm fine." But she turned away and clutched the railing as if she would fall if she did not.

"Shouldn't be up top anyhow," she heard one sailor grumble, and was surprised to hear several grunts of agreement. Hannah, her emotions already raw, was wounded by the comment—not by the words but by the dislike she heard underlining them. She was quite sure the sailor who'd made the comment was Todd Engle.

"Go about your business, sailor," James bit out.

Hannah whirled around. "Don't chastise him. He's right. I shouldn't be here. I don't know what I was thinking." Without a thought to what she was doing, Hannah thrust her sextant into James's hands and moved toward the companionway as quickly as she could on the shifting ship. She only knew she had failed miserably, utterly. Stifling a sob that the wind whipped from her mouth, she headed down the steep stairs so quickly, she skidded down them, landing hard on her rump. Behind her she heard: "Good riddance." Then she jumped up and ran to her cabin.

"Didn't have to make her cry, Engle, you sod," Timothy Lodge growled. The other sailors suddenly looked ashamed. "You ever think what it must be like to be her? With everyone growling at her all the time? You all ought to be ashamed." Lodge darted an angry look toward the captain, letting everyone on the ship know where he cast true blame for Miss Wright's tears.

"Mr. Lodge," came James's booming voice. "Take the reading." Hannah's sextant was shoved into his startled second mate's hands.

Within seconds James was pounding on Hannah's door. "Miss Wright, open this door. Now." On the other side of the door, Hannah dashed her tears away and did as requested.

"Yes, sir," she said, not looking up at him, but focusing her eyes on his pea coat lapel.

"You signed on as navigator to this ship. Against my better judgment, I hired you on. If you cannot perform your duties, you will be responsible for half fare."

Hannah brought in a shaky breath. "Yes, sir."

"I expect you to be on deck at high noon, Miss Wright. If you have a problem with that, I pray that you . . ." He faltered when Hannah finally garnered the courage to look him in the eye. He continued more softly. "I pray that you tell me. It is my wish that you will continue as navigator."

Hannah dropped her gaze from those intense blue eyes, pausing on their downward trek when she noticed his ice-encrusted beard had begun to drip, leaving rivulets of water streaking down his coat. He wanted her to continue as navigator. How nice. "Yes, sir," a response to his words, not the answer he was looking for. She thought she heard him curse beneath his breath.

"I am not sorry I kissed you, Miss Wright," he said with an angry jerk of his head. "If you are awaiting an apology, you will not get one. I am only sorry that it was so very disagreeable to you."

Hannah shot her head up. "It wasn't entirely . . . disagreeable."

"That is quite gratifying to hear," he said sharply. "It was not, after all, intended to be. Nonetheless, I realize that from your prospective, my kissing you, perhaps, was not the proper thing to do. Suffice it to say, I will not attempt to . . ."

"To be entirely honest, I rather liked the kiss." Hannah could have swallowed her tongue at that moment. Imagine, admitting such a thing when all she had done for a week was try to forget it, try to convince herself she was angry with him for it. "What I mean to say is that, I don't expect an apology. Sir."

"I think when we are discussing something as personal as a kiss, you might call me James," he said, a smile touching his lips.

"I thought we were discussing whether I would continue on as navigator," Hannah said, being purposely obtuse. She watched as his eyes dropped to her mouth, and she tingled there, as if he were caressing her with more than just his eyes.

"No. The kiss. That was the subject."

"Captain. James. Are you about to do something for which you will not apologize again?"

James lowered his head. "I believe I am." Just as he was about to finally, finally taste her again, Hannah brought her hand up to cover her mouth, so that instead of her mouth, his lips met the back of her hand.

"I'm engaged," she whispered, her eyes above her hand filled with panic.

"I don't care," he said, trying to draw her hand away.

She stepped back. "But I do. I do care."

"Hannah, I . . . Hell." He brought both hands up to clutch his hair, clearly frustrated by her withdrawal. "Whoever the hell this chap is, he better well make you feel the way you feel when you're kissing me. He'd better love you the way . . ." He stopped. And Hannah's heart stopped. "He'd better love you the way you ought to be loved," he said finally, harshly.

"Allen is a wonderful man. Truly he is." *He'll be there for me. He won't leave. He won't break my heart.*

After James left, Hannah sat on her bed for a long time, thinking about her choices. Certainly Allen, by succumbing to gold fever, had not proved himself to be the dependable man she'd thought he was. But Hannah was certain once she found him, brought him back to San Francisco, he'd realize his mistake and stand by her forever. If he didn't, she could return to New York, resume her life, her only regret being that she wasted too much time depending on a man who could not be depended upon. Her heart would be intact. Already her heart was breaking over James, and all they'd shared was a single kiss.

"No more," she said aloud. "My heart can't take it." To James, kissing her was little more than a game. He was attracted to her and so wanted to kiss her. His heart was not at stake. He'd gloated about how he had drawn a reaction from her, and crudely predicted Allen would not make her feel the way he would be able to. For one flashing moment Hannah had thought James was about to declare his love. She flushed with embarrassment over her vivid and fanciful imagination. He had only been strutting like a male rooster.

She let herself dream about what it would be like to have James proclaim his love, then quickly pushed such soul-damaging thoughts away. It would only make things worse if James loved her, she thought reasonably. Could she marry Allen knowing James loved her and loving James the way she did?

"Yes. I could." It didn't matter anyway. She knew she would never be faced with that decision.

Chapter Thirteen

Weeks passed, weeks filled with strong southwesterly gales, that pushed the *Windfire* safely around the Horn and sent her streaking northward toward San Francisco. The Pacific doldrums came and went, hot, sultry days in which the crew spent spiffing up the ship. For Hannah and James they were weeks filled with polite exchanges and impersonal glances. Except when with her, he was back to his boisterous, blustering, boyish self, she thought, leaving no doubt in her mind that his interest in her had been short-lived.

Hannah scowled at him from across the dining room table. Once he discovered she was not an easy mark, he apparently discarded thoughts of her as easily as Doc Owen discarded fish guts off the side of the ship. She couldn't have made much of an impression, she thought grumpily, for him to have so easily given up his pursuit. Not that he had ever truly pursued her. One kiss, one attempted kiss and the contest was over. He must not think her much of a prize. She was glad of it, she told herself. Relieved to not have to worry that every time they were together, he would be tempted to kiss her.

Everyone at the table—including the besotted Mrs. Davis and Mrs. Coddington—was smiling at James, listening with rapt fascination to one of his sea tales. He told the story of how an English gentleman, out on a drunk and looking worse for the wear after fisticuffs, was mistaken for a crew member and ended up spending a year aboard various ships before he was able to make his way home. By that time he was presumed dead, and his estate had fallen into the hands of his loathsome nephew.

Hannah tried not to admire how well he spun his tale, how he entertained the diners, how handsome he looked with his black beard now shaved revealing his strong jaw. How those sparkling eyes seemed to look at everyone at the table except her. She tried not to think about how much she missed him, their long talks as she was plotting a course. She told herself a million times she didn't love, couldn't love him. Her insides were twisting, her heart was slowly breaking, and all he could think of was silly sea tales. She was miserable, and he was . . . he was . . . untouched. Had she imagined those searing looks he used to give her? Had she imagined that kiss which still kept her up at night?

Hannah poked at the tuna one of the crew members had caught earlier that day, flaking off bits and shoving them around her plate.

"Don't care for tuna, Miss Wright?" Another polite inquiry. She thought she might scream.

"Oh, I think the tuna is delicious," she said lightly, even though she hadn't yet taken a bite.

"Captain, you must pass on my compliments to Mr. Owen," Mrs. Coddington gushed. "Do tell us about the Orient, Captain. I find it so interesting." There were murmurs of agreement among the diners. He flashed a grin meant to melt hearts.

Really, Hannah thought, Mrs. Coddington is a married woman and almost elderly.

"If you'll excuse me please, everyone. I'm not feeling well." Though Hannah felt quite well, hours later it was as if she prophesied what was to come. Everyone who ate that tuna became violently ill. It started with a low fever that was hardly noticeable. But by morning, nearly everyone on ship had bright red faces, swollen hands, more than queasy stomachs. Nearly everyone but Hannah, who hadn't touched her tuna the night before.

"Ptomaine poisoning," George said, looking rather pathetic as he made a dash for the railing. Doc Owen, to everyone's disgust, had neglected to test for ptomaine before cooking the fish and was forced to barricade himself in the galley for the duration of the minor epidemic to protect himself from the irate crew.

James, who had eaten heartily, was as sick as the rest, but stayed on deck and continued to command the ship as best he could. It had been left to Hannah and a few others who had not eaten the fish to administer bicarbonate of soda, which did little to alleviate the symptoms. She watched as James swallowed heavily, trying without success to command his stomach to be still.

"This will help," Hannah said, keeping her eyes on the amber bottle and tin of water she held outstretched.

He took the remedy without a word, taking big gulping swallows, only to succumb to his sick stomach seconds later.

"Blast and damn," he muttered, spitting into the sea. "I'll kill Owen. My whole ship brought down because the man's in too much of a hurry to test for the poison." He braced himself on the rail, his head hung low, as Hannah stood awkwardly behind him, not knowing what to do. It was oddly disturbing to see James so weakened.

"Perhaps you should rest, Captain."

"Who the hell will run this ship if I'm below. You?"

Hannah attributed his surliness to his discomfort and tried not to let his harsh tone wound her. "No, sir. I just thought . . ." And then he heaved again, cursing between retches. Hannah placed a hand on his shoulder as he vomited, only wanting to comfort him. He wrenched away, looking at her as if she were the cause of his illness.

"The last thing I need is you hovering around me. Keep away from me, Miss Wright. Keep your comfort and compassionate looks the hell away from me." His gaze nearly

sliced her in two before he spun away, one fist to his gut,
leaving Hannah bewildered and hurt.

Where had that come from? she wondered, hating that her
throat was burning and closing up. All this time, had James
been hiding his animosity toward her, his dislike of her, behind smiles? The politeness of the past weeks now seemed
forced. False. Certainly he'd noted that his dislike of her, his
anger over his rejection, had turned the crew against her.
Hannah knew any rift in the crew was bad for the sailing of
a ship. Had all the politeness been a calculated effort to keep
the crew in line? The thought made her want to take a dose
of the bicarbonate.

Like a wounded animal, Hannah avoided the thing that
had caused her hurt. Long after the crew had recovered, she
kept her distance from James. She began discussing the best
courses with George, giving no explanation why she no
longer wished to deal with Captain MacRae. If the *Windfire*
kept at her current speed, they would reach San Francisco
Harbor in eighty-eight days—a speed unheard of and one
that surely neither the *Flying Cloud* nor the *Challenge* had
beaten.

On the seventieth day of their journey, the day broke
clear, with fair winds and mild seas. Hannah continued to
search for the best currents and wind, rejoicing when they
overtook ships that had left long before they did. Each time
they passed a clipper, they would signal their home port and
date of departure and the ship they passed would signal
theirs. James demanded that the crew display the utmost restraint and dignity by not shouting out victory when learn-
ing just how much faster they were than most ships they
passed. There was much masculine gloating, much back-
slapping, once the slower ship was a dot on the horizon.

Hannah, brimming with happiness, refused to feel disappointed when James failed to congratulate her on her navi-
gational skills. He would have before. Before the near kiss.
When the latest clipper was far behind them, Hannah headed
to the chart room, filled with renewed excitement. Sunlight

filled the small whitewashed room, crammed with charts and instrumentation. Unfurling a chart, she glanced at the barometer. Fair weather today, it seemed, and she smiled. Fifteen minutes later, she again gave the barometer a glance and was startled to see that it had dropped markedly. Hannah glanced out the portal. Nothing but blue sky and sunshine. The liquid seemed to fall before her widening eyes.

Hannah rushed from the chart room and headed to the main deck, tripping up the stairs in her haste. Her eyes looked about frantically for an officer, finally resting on George and James, deep in conversation by the foremast.

"Captain!" Hannah shouted as she ran toward the officers, the brim of her hat flipping back in her haste. "The barometer's falling. Fast. I've never seen anything like it."

James immediately looked to the west, his eyes sharp and narrowed, searching for a reason for the sudden drop. George immediately ran to the chart room to confirm Hannah's news.

"She's right, Captain. The glass is falling like hell," he shouted when he returned.

And then James saw it. A white cloud scudding toward the ship, a froth of boiling water beneath.

"Jesus God, a white squall," James whispered. "All hands to shorten sails," he shouted, and suddenly the deck was filled with men, their fearful eyes on the oncoming storm. James marched up and down the deck, shouting orders, helping the men with the sails. Two men were ordered to hold the wheel, and when it became clear that not all sails on the mizzenmast could be hauled in before the white squall hit, he ordered the men to abandon their efforts. Then he saw Hannah, foolish woman, standing by the after house, her eyes peeled excitedly on the approaching storm. Fear filled his gut with the speed of a gale. He'd been in such squalls before, with winds so strong, legend held that a man once opened his mouth to shout and was turned inside out by the force of the wind. No one was safe on this ship during such a storm, especially not such a slight woman.

"Get below, Miss Wright. Now." He stalked over to her, angry that she didn't immediately move.

"I'm perfectly safe where I am, Captain." He saw the stubbornness in her eyes that so infuriated him. He'd be damned if he allowed her to become harmed.

"You'll obey my orders, Miss Wright. How many times must you be hurt before you heed me." When she set her jaw, he did the only thing he could to keep her safe. He picked her up like a sack of flour—a squirming sack—holding her under one arm as he made his way to the companionway. Then he shoved her down the hole, making sure only that she was not harmed by her rather rough tumble. "By God, you'll not disobey me again. I don't have time to nursemaid a foolish girl." With that, he closed the hatch just as the storm hit.

All anyone could do was hold on and pray the ship could take such a fierce wind without coming undone. James's ears were filled with the roar of a wind that sounded as if it came from the depths of hell. The ship heaved sickeningly as the wind shrieked and lifted the sea onto the deck like a child making waves in a bath. James spied George clutching the rail, and made to speak, only to have the wind fill his mouth with such force, he could not make his jaw work or drive a sound through his lips. The ship shuddered violently, and then he heard a shriek that was not from the wind, but was the unmistakable sounds of a man in the midst of terror. Suddenly, James was surrounded by halyards, tangled in ropes, and struck hard on the shoulder by something solid that drove him to the deck of the ship.

And then it was over, the ship left bobbing in a calmed wind, as if the storm had never been. James felt a weight on him, taking only a moment to determine what had happened. He found himself pinioned by a spar, which could only mean the mizzenmast had split in the storm. He heard shouts, men calling for him and the man who had surely fallen into the sea.

"Here!" came a call. George, sounding frantic.

"Get this blasted thing off of me," James shouted, know-ing the sound of his voice would calm the crew. Within min-utes they dragged him clear of the wreckage and were helping him to stand. The sight before him was immensely depressing. The mizzenmast had broken in two and was clearly unrepairable, the man who had been caught still on the mast when the ship hit, had been lost. Although a lifeboat was immediately dispatched, all knew the man hadn't a chance to survive in the cold rough sea. A half hour later, the dejected men on the lifeboat would return having found no sign of the fallen man.

The *Windfire* could continue to sail without the mizzen-mast, but the remainder of the trip would be far slower. No record would be made, the bonus in jeopardy. The *Windfire* would limp into port, for they were too close to San Fran-cisco to bother putting into a closer port for repairs.

"Any injuries?"

"No, thank God," George said, eyeing the wreckage.

"Then, let's clean up this mess, men. We've still got a ship to sail." He tried to sound hearty, but failed miserably. A man lost, his ship nearly crippled. That's when he noticed that the mast, which had crashed through the railing on the port side, lay at the precise spot where Hannah had stood. All the frustration, sorrow, and anger over losing a man, over having his dreams of setting a record around the Horn, centered on one silly woman who had tried his patience one too many times.

He turned to George, his face a mask of fury. "Go get your cousin, Mr. Wright."

George simply nodded and did his captain's bidding, though it was clear from his expression that he did this duty reluctantly. When George returned with Hannah, James rel-ished the horror he saw in her eyes as she looked at the wreckage. And when James walked up to her, he saw fear, and he relished that, too. Without a word, he walked up be-hind her and put a hand on each side of her head. He felt her stiffen, almost smelled her fear as he turned her head roughly to the spot where the mast had crashed through the rail.

"You would have died, you little fool," he said softly and close to her ear so that none of the crew who were pretending to ignore them could hear. "Do you know what that mast would have done to your pretty little head?" He tightened his hold, and she let out a small sound. "You have become a liability on my ship, Miss Wright. You are relieved of duty."

He dropped his hands and moved to the front of her, his heart clenching at the sight of her tears. She was too big a distraction. While he was tossing her down the companionway, one of his crew became stranded in that mizzenmast. He told himself he could have done nothing to save that man. But the fact that he had been nearly paralyzed with fear that she would be harmed and spent precious seconds watching over her, was unforgivable.

He stood inches from her, so close all he could see was her pain-filled eyes.

"Stay away from me, Miss Wright. When I am on the bow, you will be at the stern. When I dine, you will not. I don't want to see your face, I don't want to hear your voice. Just stay the hell away."

"I hate James MacRae," Hannah said, tears streaming down her face.

George let out a long sigh. "Why? Because he gave perfectly sound orders that you go below? Because he has had the patience of a saint in dealing with you? Because . . ."

"Because I love him," she wailed, and flopped down onto her back atop her bed.

"This is bad."

She bit back a sob. "Very bad."

George smiled down at his cousin's grief-stricken face. It occurred to him then that Hannah was still so young and likely in the throes of her first real love. At twenty-two she was in love with one man and engaged to another. Yes, this would seem quite awful to Hannah, but George knew something Hannah did not. This was not some tragic unrequited love scenario. He was quite certain James MacRae loved Hannah, and was just as certain that as long as Hannah pretended to be in love with Allen, MacRae would do little about his feelings.

"Perhaps this is not so bad as it seems," George said cautiously. He knew he walked dangerous ground here by meddling in Hannah's life.

"Oh? How could things possibly be worse? The man I love hates me. And with good reason," she said brokenly. "I've been simply awful to him. It's a wonder he hasn't made me walk the plank."

"Hannah, you silly idiot, I believe the man's in love with you."

She rose up onto her elbows, giving George the full force of her bereft, tear-filled face, and sniffed. "What man?"

"James MacRae."

To George's dismay, she began shaking her head in horrified denial. "Don't tell me that, George. Oh, nothing could be worse than for him to love me." With that, she flopped back and turned over, sobbing into her bedcovers.

"I'm not certain if he does or not," George hurried to explain.

"Well, what is it, George, is he in love with me or not?" she shouted.

"I am."

Hannah's red-rimmed eyes shot to the door where Captain James MacRae stood, his solemn gaze fixed on Hannah.

"Well, stop it," she said ridiculously, and James smiled.

"I have tried, Miss Wright."

George, looking exceedingly uncomfortable, excused himself, ignoring Hannah's plea that he stay. Left alone with her, James suddenly found himself at a loss. For the first time in his life, he was proclaiming his love for a woman, and he apparently was doing a poor job of it. The lady did not look at all happy.

"If I was angry with you, if I said things that hurt you . . ."

Her face filled with panic, Hannah put up a hand to stop him. "Please don't say anything more, Captain."

". . . it is because I find myself in love with you." Hannah gave a little squeak of distress. "Is that really so bad, Hannah?"

Hannah furrowed her brow. "It's because we're on this ship together. The closeness. We've spent an uncommon amount of time together. I daresay I know you better than the man I plan to marry. The man I will marry." James frowned, but let her continue. "Once we're on land, it will go away." And then, softly, "Won't it?"

"I wouldn't know. I've never been in love before. But I suspect it is not a whimsical thing. I suspect that I will always love you. You are in here," he said, moving a hand to his heart. "And I suspect that's where you will stay."

Hannah shook her head. "You mustn't think such things. You mustn't say them."

"Why, love?"

Hannah cringed at the endearment. "Because I am engaged to another."

Thus far, James's tone had been even, his soft burr almost hypnotic, but now she could see that she angered him.

"You don't love the man. You don't, do you?"

"No."

It came out as a choking sound, and her eyes widened when James strode toward her. Sitting on his heels before her, he put a hand on each side of her head, and this time the gesture was gentle.

"You love me, Hannah. Tell me you love me."

Hannah wanted to collapse against those hands, to let him hold her, but instead she stiffened her back. "I may not love Allen, but I am going to marry him."

"You haven't answered me," he said, his voice becoming hard.

"That is my answer, Captain."

He abruptly dropped his hands and stood. "James! By

God, when we are together like this, call me by my first name."

"How could I love a man who is constantly hollering at me," Hannah said just as loudly and coming to her feet. All trace of sadness and insecurity had vanished.

"Like this," he said, putting one hand behind her head. "Just like this." He pulled her toward him, and she felt his hardened strength. For one agonizing moment, his lips only a breath away, he held himself from her. And then he kissed her, a wonderful, bruising, glorious kiss. Hannah closed her eyes, and for a moment allowed herself to feel, to be loved by the man she loved. *How can I leave this behind? How can I?*

His firm mouth moved away from her reddened lips to kiss and nip her jaw. "I can't help myself, love. I'm sorry." Then his mouth was on hers again, moving slowly, as he licked her lips. Hannah opened her mouth, allowing him in, wishing she could swallow him up, inhale him into her body. Their tongues rubbed gently and then ungently, and then it seemed the entire world, their whole existence, was their mouths, their tongues.

"I'm not sorry, love. I'm not." He moved a hand to cover one breast, inhaling sharply. "My God, girl, you tempt me." He moved a thumb over her nipple, which instantly hardened.

"Oh." Oh, she hadn't known. Allen had never . . . Oh. Hannah felt herself arch her back, felt then his arousal against her hips, and dropped her head back. Her braid snaked from one shoulder to hang behind her as he dipped his head and put his mouth where his thumb had been. She felt his hands at the buttons of her shirt, knew what he wanted, and in that moment knew that she wanted it, too, wanted his mouth there on her nipple without clothing as a barrier.

"Sir. Captain, sir." George, the chaperon.

"One minute, Mr. Wright," James said, lifting his head

from Hannah's breast. His eyes were blazing when he looked at her.

"You undo me, Hannah love." His Scottish burr, nearly imperceptible most times, was thick with passion.

Hannah straightened, embarrassed, mortified, confused. James looked down at himself and made an adjustment, lifting his head and grinning at her. "You unman me, love," he said wickedly, and Hannah blushed scarlet. "I'll see you on deck," he said, clearly happy with the events that had just passed. He gave her a quick kiss on the cheek, a possessive gesture that was unnerving. Hannah remained silent and unsmiling as he walked from the room, for she had never been more frightened in her life.

Chapter Fourteen

The captain was courting her, and Hannah hadn't a clue, other than to be cruel, how to stop him. He acted like a man besotted, and Hannah let him. Not that she could have stopped his blazing gaze, his transparent efforts to get her alone so he could steal a kiss. Not that she wanted to stop him. Hannah, so in love with him she felt giddy, told herself it would do no harm to let herself love him—if only for a short time. But in the back of her mind, and not so far back as she would have liked, she knew that when James sailed away, she would not be with him. She felt torn to pieces, loving each smile, each touch, and regretting them with all her being. By the time the ship met the tug that would pull the *Windfire* into San Francisco Harbor, Hannah's nerves were frayed and her heart thoroughly captured.

At first she'd tried to avoid the captain, but he would have none of it. He continued to captain the ship; however, it was clear to all on board that the captain was distracted by her presence. He made no attempt to hide his feelings toward her, something that mildly surprised Hannah. She had not thought he would want his crew to know he had succumbed to love. The first time he'd called her "my love" in front of Timothy Lodge, Hannah thought the poor man would choke to death. She'd pulled James aside and whispered, "I don't think you ought to use such endearments in front of the men, sir. James."

James looked thoughtful. "And I don't suppose I should do this, either." And he'd kissed her, quick and hard, his mouth smiling against hers. She'd sputtered and pushed away, and turned lobster red at the hoots she heard from the men. As she tried to walk away, he put a possessive arm around her waist, pulled her against him, and nuzzled her neck.

"Oh, stop it, Captain," she said purposefully, but he chuckled when she tilted her neck to give him better access. Realizing what she'd done, Hannah pushed away with earnestness.

"James," she admonished through gritted teeth. But she soon found herself smiling at his foolish grin. James shrugged, cocking his head to one side, a silent plea for forgiveness. Before Hannah could give it, he was striding away from her, shouting an order.

Since the time George had abandoned them in her room, and then reasserted his powers of guardian, he became the couple's shadow. They were rarely left alone for more than a minute or two, just long enough for James to give Hannah a kiss that would leave her gasping. It was mortifying. And thrilling. And horrifying. For Hannah knew, even if James did not, that it would all end as soon as they reached San Francisco.

Now, with the fast-growing city in their sights, Hannah felt the beginnings of an ache in her heart that seemed to grow the closer they got to the city. The steam tug pulled them through a harbor so crowded, it at first seemed an impossible task to bring a ship as large as the *Windfire* through the mess. Hundreds of naked masts, so many they obliterated the blue sky above, thrust into the air. Ships, abandoned for lack of crews, lay rotting in the harbor. The lure of gold was so great, it was only the most loyal crews that re-upped and made a voyage home.

It took several tedious hours to maneuver the ship to its pier. While they made their slow progress, rough and rowdy men in skiffs approached the ship in droves offering crew members pints of rum, which they were forbidden to buy. James prowled the ship, keeping a sharp eye on his men, who looked near ready to dive off the deck and into the harbor. James knew it was intoxicating to be so close to land, so close to women and rum, and not be allowed to get at it. The *Windfire* hit the pier at ninety-eight days, ten hours from the time it had left New York. James had learned from other ships that Captain Josiah Creesy's *Flying Cloud* had made the journey in a record-breaking eighty-nine days, twenty-one hours. The *Challenge*, whose crew had tried mutiny and whose captain faced charges of murder, made it to port in one hundred eight days.

James's disappointment over not setting the record was lifted a bit with the realization that even without a mizzenmast for part of the journey, he'd beaten Robert Waterman and the *Challenge*.

Shortly after the ship was secured to the pier, the crew, shaved and combed and wearing their best, gathered on the deck, eyeing the gangplank like teenagers eyeing their first naked lady.

"You are the finest crew I have had the pleasure to sail with," James shouted above the sounds of the Union Street Wharf. "I know that some of you will not return with me. But I would be honored to have you all return. Those who do, will receive a one-hundred-dollar bonus the moment they step aboard ship." James knew it was a huge sum for men who earned just twenty-six dollars a month. "The *Windfire* leaves port on November twenty-second. I'll see you then. Enjoy your leave, men." With a shout, they headed for the gangplank, James eyeing them like a fond parent saying good-bye to his children. The men were paid as they left, and James knew he'd likely see less than half of the same faces when it was time to return to New York.

As he watched the men walk away, their pockets full, their heads already filled with women and rum, he felt her come up beside him long before he saw her. It was the strangest thing, he thought, this unfathomable love he felt

for her. Each kiss, each touch only made him long for more.
Hannah had done something that no other person other than
his family had ever done—she had stolen his heart. No, not
stolen, he amended with an inward smile, for he gave it
freely.

"I expect my uncle will be here," she said formally. Hannah had written to her aunt and uncle before leaving. The
letter, which made its way to San Francisco via Panama,
likely had arrived weeks before *Windfire* made port. James
turned to look at her, disturbed by what he saw. Hannah
turned fully toward him and thrust out her hand. Only the
slight trembling of that hand betrayed that this was more
than a woman saying good-bye to an acquaintance. James
stared at that hand and frowned, then lifted his gaze to hers.

"I'm sure I can manage a visit after *Windfire*'s cargo is unloaded," James said, and tried to make himself smile.

She looked away, and his heart began a slow, painful thud
in his chest.

"I will be very busy in the next few weeks. I . . . I have to
find Allen, you see. It is what I came here for. To find
Allen."

James forced himself to remain still, when what he
wanted to do at that moment was pull her into his arms and
kiss her until she forgot about her damned fiancé.

"You want to find him, to say good-bye." He hated the
uncertainty he heard in his voice, the fear.

She remained silent. And then she was smiling and waving at an older couple in the crowd who were talking animatedly with George. "My aunt and uncle are here. James,
I'll . . . I'm sure I'll see you again before you depart."

"Of course we will," he said to her back. What the hell
was going on? She was acting as if they might never see
each other again. Didn't she know that she'd be returning to
New York with him as his wife? As he helplessly watched
Hannah run down the gangplank to greet her relatives, he
realized what a fool he'd been. Hannah couldn't know that
was what he expected. How could she? A woman wanted a

proposal, a ring, a promise. Frustration welled up in him as he realized he was trapped aboard ship until the cargo was unloaded. Already the stevedores had begun the work that would take at least ten days. For nearly two weeks he would be shackled to this ship, days in which Hannah would likely find her lost fiancé. Duty, never shirked, never before resented, suddenly felt like an iron choker around his neck.

Once Richard Wright greeted the niece he had not seen in five years, he strode up the gangplank, one beefy hand extended in greeting. Richard Wright was a big man, towering over most men and certainly outweighing them. His hair, curling to his shoulders, was a shocking white, and his beard, thick and lustrous, was that same pristine color. He was a hard-drinking, backslapping sort of man, who rarely was seen without his big-bowled ivory pipe.

"James. Thank you for taking such good care of my niece. She looks hale and hearty." He glanced up at the wounded ship. "Ninety-eight days with a broken mast. I'll be damned, MacRae, that's good sailing."

"Your niece is a fine navigator," James said. "And your son a fine mate."

"Couldn't believe that bit when I read it in Hannah's letter. Though she's had as much experience as some first mates I've seen come into this port." Richard looked at the graveyard of ships rotting in San Francisco Harbor, disgust clear in his face.

"In my day, a crew would die rather than leave their ship to rot. Seamen have no loyalty."

"I've a good crew, but I expect even the best will feel the lure of gold," James said, his eyes straying to Hannah as she talked to her aunt.

"Gold. Love it. Hope they find boatloads. Making me a rich man, with all these fools traipsing here from all over the world. Even real gold is fool's gold, I say." Richard lowered his voice. "Found the damned fiancé, scoundrel. Can't understand why a girl like Hannah would come after such a man."

Curiosity ate at James. "She seems to think he'll make a good husband," he choked out.

"Bah! A wastrel." Richard shrugged. "There's no telling what makes a woman do what she does. Just look at Prudy, there. A better, more refined woman you'll never find. Never could understand what she saw in the likes of me. I'm as rough as they come, but I've never been able to ruffle her feathers. God knows I've tried. Damned infuriating, it is." But James saw in the man's gaze the enduring love of a man for a woman he's been married to for decades.

Richard swung his gaze back to James and clapped the younger man hard on the back. "You'll come to dinner one night when you can?"

A smile split James's face. "It would be my honor to, sir."

Hannah stood alone with her aunt, a woman with poise and grace, who rarely smiled, wishing duty had not called George from his mother's side. She was a stranger to Hannah, this distant, remote woman. Prudence Wright—she pretended to dislike her husband's nickname of Prudy—greeted her niece with politeness but little warmth. Hannah remembered that her mother was slightly in awe of her sister-in-law when both families lived in New York. She could still remember her mother's nervousness at the prospect of a visit from Prudence. The house was made spotless, the meals flawless. Hannah had always been admonished to be on her best behavior. She had watched her aunt, the way she ate, sat, spoke. While her mother was all warmth and smiles, her aunt was as cool and inviting as marble.

Now, standing by her as an adult, her hair windblown, her face and hands turned brown from wind and sun, her dress impossibly wrinkled from its stay in her sea chest, Hannah again felt like a ten-year-old girl. Hannah had an almost poignant need for Allen at that moment. His comforting presence, his suave confidence, the effortless way he was able to instantly put her at ease in difficult social situations, would have been more than welcome. She realized that she had missed Allen. He was her best friend, her confidant.

Hannah felt herself relax. This leaving James would not be as difficult as she'd thought. Simply stepping from the ship, feeling the solid earth beneath her shoes, gave her the distance she needed. By the time *Windfire* sailed away, surely this thing she felt for James would have dissipated. It was fading already, she told herself. Already she looked forward to seeing Allen, already . . . And then she heard his laugh, and her heart nearly exploded. She turned away at the sound, putting her back to the ship, to James.

"Are you quite all right, Hannah?"

"Yes, Aunt. I'm simply anxious to get settled in." Hannah forced herself to look at her surroundings, at the busy port, the stevedores, their thickly muscled bodies heaving cargo to and from dozens of ships on the wharf. She could hear shouts in several different languages and concentrated on identifying as many as she could. French, Italian. German. Spanish.

From the side she saw her aunt signal her husband, and within minutes her uncle was escorting them to an awaiting carriage. Once seated inside, with Hannah sitting across from them, Richard grumbled, "Could have walked faster than it will take to get this blasted thing through this mess."

"Please don't swear in front of your niece," Prudence said calmly.

"I'm sure she's heard worse than that in the past few months."

"I have," Hannah said, laughing. "And some of it from my own mouth." Richard leaned forward and slapped his niece's knee, but became instantly sober when he saw his wife's disapproval.

As Richard waited with obvious impatience for a heavily laden mule to get out of their path, Hannah turned to look back at *Windfire*, her eyes searching for James. It came to her suddenly that she hadn't said good-bye, hadn't even shaken his hand. It was possible that they would not see each other again, she thought, panic beginning to grow. One hand clutched the window frame, open to let in the sharply cool October breeze, and her once calm search for James became almost frenzied, her eyes moving over the ship in a desperate way. Oh, where is he?

"I have to . . . I didn't say good-bye to Captain MacRae. I never had a chance to thank him . . . to say good-bye." Just then, the mule was successfully maneuvered from their path and the driver tapped on the reins. As the carriage began moving away from the wharf, Hannah was nearly paralyzed with the fear that she might never see James again. This wasn't what she wanted. She wanted to at least say good-bye. Her eyes suddenly filled with tears, and her throat closed painfully. She blinked rapidly, fearing that in that one moment of teary-eyed blurriness, she might miss seeing his beloved form as he strode upon the deck. The carriage moved forward slowly, jostling in and out of deep ruts, her hands gripping the windowsill almost painfully.

Then a hand covered hers, strong and brown and heartbreakingly familiar. James walked quickly beside the carriage, his hand engulfing hers as he moved directly beneath the window. Hannah, ignoring her aunt's outraged gasp, half stood and poked her head and one arm through the small opening so that he could hold her hand.

"I will see you, Hannah," he said. "It will be a few days. The ship's cargo . . . I've been invited to dine with your aunt and uncle." Hannah drank in the sight of him, his smiling face, his deep blue eyes.

From within the carriage Hannah could hear her aunt say, "Richard, perhaps we should stop the carriage before one of them harms themselves." And then her uncle's loud reply. "No need, dear. They seem to be doing just fine."

As the carriage picked up speed, James moved his hand to the back of her head, pulling her down. Hannah didn't know how they managed to kiss like that, but she found her mouth being pressed by his for a few wonderful moments before the carriage hit yet another rut, driving them apart. Then the vehicle picked up speed, leaving James behind, a huge grin on his face, his teeth flashing white against his tanned face.

"I love you Hannah Wright," he shouted to her as the carriage moved on. "Don't forget that, lass."

Hannah heard, and her heart expanded as she hung out the window until the carriage turned a corner and he disappeared from sight. She sat back, one hand on her wildly beating heart, suddenly aware that her aunt and uncle were sitting in the carriage with her, both shocked at her behavior. She looked from one to the other, her mouth slightly open as if she were ready should either demand an explanation.

"I was under the belief that you were here to find your fiancé. Have I been misinformed?" Her aunt's voice was cool.

"No, Aunt. I still plan to find Allen."

"And you still plan to marry him?" That from her uncle, who was unable to keep the disbelief from his voice.

Hannah looked down to her lap, where she held the hand that James had just held. "Yes, Uncle. I do."

Thankfully, her aunt and uncle were quiet for the rest of the ride. Hannah knew she would have succumbed to the tears that burned in her throat had they forced her to speak.

San Francisco was a city in the midst of an explosion. Everywhere one looked were signs of construction, of the growth that had made her uncle a rich man. Her uncle lived in a three-story brick house, one of the finest in the city that not five years ago was a desolate place with little more than a collection of ramshackle structures that passed for homes and businesses. Her aunt had insisted that, although they were forced to live in an uncivilized city, they would build a home of grace and elegance—and one that would not easily succumb to the fires that plagued the city.

The massive front door, with its finely etched beveled glass and intricate floral carvings, had once graced their New York mansion. And as Hannah moved about the home, she recognized other fine pieces brought from New York— a bronze statue, the fancy carved newel post on the staircase, and a dazzling silver chandelier that held nearly one hundred candles. A staircase, whitewashed with a red runner trimmed with gold, swept up to the second floor, nearly encircling the chandelier. A large gilt mirror was strategically hung just below the second-floor balcony to reflect the chandelier.

"It's lovely," Hannah said, twirling around like an awestruck child. And then a large gray dog, scruffy and straggly, came bounding into the hall, its nails clicking loudly on the wood floor. The elegant coldness of the area was suddenly quite changed as her uncle greeted the ecstatic hound with enthusiasm.

As the dog twisted and whined a greeting to her aunt, she placed a gloved hand on the dog's head, patting it with seeming reluctance. "Yes, yes. We are thrilled to see you, too, Beggar." Hannah smiled at her aunt's reticence, for it was clear from her fond gaze that the lady loved the dog almost as much as it loved her. Though her uncle's greeting was unreserved, it was Prudence the dog hung about, leaning its body lovingly against her aunt's pristine skirts, its tongue lolling.

Hannah hunkered down, heedless that her skirts fell on the floor, and held a hand out to the dog. "Hello, Beggar. I'm Hannah." The dog lowered its head and tentatively sniffed her outstretched hand. Then, apparently deciding it was safe, moved to greet Hannah with a wag of its skinny tale. A small woman appeared, her swarthy skin telling of her Italian ancestry, and silently took their coats and gloves.

"Rosala, I'd like you to show Hannah to her room once you have disposed of the coats."

The little maid bobbed an unpracticed curtsy, and moved away.

"Her father is still working in a mine," Prudence sighed, looking after the girl. "He banished her when she fell in love with a Jewish boy. She is Catholic, you see. She was nearly starved when I found her. Such a sad little thing."

Hannah looked at her aunt sharply, suddenly reassessing the woman she'd thought was so unforgivingly hard. As if reading her thoughts, Richard said, "Your aunt has a soft spot for foundlings. Who else would take in that mutt. Or me for that matter?" and he gave a hearty laugh.

"That mutt has royal bearing," Prudence said with a sniff, and Hannah smiled, suddenly liking her aunt.

"What happened to the boy she loved?" Hannah asked.

"He died of diphtheria."

The conversation ended with Rosala's reappearance. With a shy smile she turned and led Hannah to her room. It was large and elegant, like everything else in this house. Butter-yellow, accented with white, it was a sunny, pleasing room. Though Hannah preferred richer tones, she liked the room at first glance. Her trunks arrived within hours, and the remainder of the day was spent with Rosala, shaking out gowns and storing away her rather large wardrobe.

"Goodness," Rosala said in heavy accents. "So a-many clothes for one lady."

Hannah blushed. She'd never thought much about clothes until meeting Allen. Now she was embarrassed by the volumes of dresses she owned. She already knew by looking at the women she'd seen during their carriage ride that the few women living in San Francisco dressed far more informally here than in New York.

Though used to long hours at sea, Hannah found herself quite exhausted by the time dinner was announced. Wearing an evening bodice of yellow silk over a yellow tartan skirt, Hannah paused before the full-length mirror attached to a closet door. She left her hair in simple braid, which she coiled up at her nape. Sun-brightened tendrils framed her face, and Hannah was pleased with her appearance. As comfortable as her shirt and pants were, it felt wonderful to wear a dress again, to feel like a pretty woman. As she gazed at her reflection, her thoughts drifted to Allen. He had helped pick out this outfit, saying the color made her hair seem more golden. Just as she was about to leave her room and head down to dinner, a knock came at her door.

"Aunt Prudence. I was just about to go down for dinner."

Her aunt gave her a coolly assessing look, and Hannah was instantly tense. "We need to discuss your behavior of this afternoon," she said finally, and Hannah's stomach knotted.

Hannah let out a weary sigh. She truly was much too tired for a lengthy lecture on social etiquette. "I realize it was . . . improper."

"That is the least of it, Hannah." Prudence gave a try at a smile, failing miserably. She sighed. "Of all people, I understand the lure of a sea captain. And Captain MacRae is no doubt an outstanding man. Your uncle does go on." She waved a hand, as if erasing that thought. "I want to know . . . that is, I am here to ask. Oh, goodness, it is so much easier raising boys."

Hannah frowned, confused at her aunt's discomfort. "Aunt Prudence, if you are concerned that I plan to renege on my promise to Allen, you can be assured that . . ."

"No, Hannah. Allen Pritchard is not my concern. You are my concern, child." She tapped an elegant finger against her lips. "How to ask this . . . I suppose I should just come out with it." Lifting her chin, she blurted, "Have you had relations with Captain MacRae?"

Hannah's face instantly heated, a blush that moved with agonizing quickness from her neck to the root of her hair.

"Oh, goodness," Prudence said, and sat upon the nearest chair.

Alarm set in as Hannah looked at her aunt's pale face. "Aunt Prudence," she said hurriedly. "I'm afraid I'm not certain what you are asking. Captain MacRae *has* kissed me."

She could see the relief flood her aunt's face. "And that is all?"

Hannah thought about James's hand on her breast, his mouth there, kissing her through the layers of thin cotton, and again her face heated.

"Oh, Hannah!" Prudence said with impatience. "Have

you lain with him? Has he . . . Have you lost your innocence?"

"My innocence?" And then Hannah, thinking she must be the most obtuse woman born, realized what her poor aunt was trying to ask her. "I am still a virgin, Aunt Prudence," she said.

Her aunt sagged. "Oh, thank God for that." Then she stood, shaking out her burgundy skirts, and said in a voice so calm Hannah nearly laughed, "Dinner is ready, Hannah. We shall speak no more of Captain MacRae."

Hannah's smile faded as she followed her aunt from her room. *We shall speak no more of Captain MacRae.* As if it were a frivolous thing, as if not speaking of him would make him disappear. How could it, when she could still feel his lips on hers, still feel his hand clutching hers? Still hear him shout words that warmed her heart. *I love you, Hannah Wright. Don't forget that, lass.*

She would always remember it, always simply close her eyes and hear him call out to her. Even when she was Allen's wife.

Chapter Fifteen

After much discussion it was decided that once George was free from his duties, he would escort Hannah to the site of Allen's claim. He shared the claim with three other men, men Allen apparently had met on the passage from New York and from whom he had caught gold fever. By the time George sent a note saying he would be ready the next day to escort Hannah to Allen's claim, more than two years had passed since she had seen or heard from Allen. Two years suddenly seemed like such an awfully long time, she thought, her brow furrowing. Her aunt had handed Hannah a bit of needlepoint, which she dutifully attacked with predictable results as she let her mind wander.

"Having trouble with a stitch, dear?" her aunt asked, apparently noticing her frown.

"No, Aunt." Hannah sighed, and for the first time looked at the stitches she had laid, grimacing.

"Those kinds of expressions will put premature lines in your face, Hannah," her aunt said from across the pretty parlor in which they sat. Her aunt, as it seemed she did everything, was an excellent stitcher, an artist truly, Hannah thought, who would have been horrified to see what she had done to her simple design. She lowered her hands into her lap and stared at the fire, bright and warm on this damp and chill San Francisco night.

Allen. She could scarce remember the finer details of his

face, only that his eyes were brown and lively, his hair chocolate. As long as she had known him, he wore a mustache. In fact, the only aspect of his kisses she could recall was that his mustache had tickled her upper lip to distraction.

Hannah spent her first days in San Francisco writing letters home to her father and to old school friends who would enjoy hearing about her adventure. She saved writing Althea Pritchard until after she saw Allen.

Two years. Would he still want her? Would she still want him? She had been barely twenty years old when he'd departed, a girl swept away by a sophisticated older man. Allen was twenty-five, and now was twenty-seven. Their parting seemed like so long ago. They were strangers. Hannah gulped down a knot of fear, that was part humiliation. It struck her hard that she had traveled fifteen thousand miles for a man who hadn't bothered to write a single word to her, a man who had promised to marry her. Was she the biggest fool God created for risking nearly all to find him?

It wasn't as if Allen had purposefully disappeared, she told herself. He had simply gone into the gold fields as so many others had before him. There were no formal records of claims, for a man could simply drop a shovel and make that spot his own. It had been the purest luck that Allen had been found. The man her uncle had hired to find Allen, and who had given up his search, happened to sit next to a Harvard student who was heading back home. After a few whiskeys, her uncle's man had discovered quite by accident that the student had shared a claim with Allen. The student was one of hundreds to get a strong dose of reality and had hightailed it back to his former life. But Allen, at least according to the student, remained.

"Aunt?"

"Yes, dear." Her aunt did not look up from her needlepoint.

"What do you think of my quest to find Allen?"

Prudence's needle stopped in mid-stitch. She relaxed her hands and looked up. "I'm not sure what you are asking."

"It has been two years since I saw my fiancé. He hasn't written. I didn't even know he lived until I arrived and Uncle told me he had been found." Hannah's gaze went from her aunt's cool assessment to the warmth of the fire.

"You are thinking, perhaps, that you have made a mistake coming to San Francisco?"

Hannah's eyes glittered in the firelight as her eyes filled with tears. A mistake? No. If she had not traveled here, she would not have fallen in love with James, and she would never, ever regret that.

"Was it a fool's errand, Aunt?" she whispered brokenly.

Prudence softened her tone. "You won't know that until you see your fiancé, Hannah."

"I suppose I am simply nervous. I don't know what I will find when I find Allen."

"If he begs off, Hannah, he was not worthy of you. Remember that," her aunt said forcefully. "Your heart will mend. They always do."

Hannah's lips curved up, hinting at a bitter smile. "My heart," she whispered. My heart will never mend.

Allen Pritchard scratched his groin, cursing the vermin that had taken up residence there. Then he scratched his tangled beard, his tangled hair, and stretched, welcoming another day. This, he thought, would be the day. He stepped from his shack, little more than a lean-to scratched into the side of the rocky hill, and walked down the scarred slope to the stream of silty water that had yet to make him a rich man. For God knew, he was not, and probably never again would be, a rich man. Unless he found gold. That thought, as he splashed the cold water from Weber Creek onto his face, is what kept him going. By his calculations, the money his mother spent so freely would be gone within two years. Unless he found gold.

All around him, it seemed, men were finding the stuff.

Everyday someone would pass by with a grand story of a ripe vein found just upstream, just downstream. He ignored the complaints he heard that the American River and the creeks and streams feeding it had long been picked clean. Instead, it seemed everyone was getting rich but him and his two remaining partners. Ralph Potter and Graham Smith were still sleeping off their drunk started a week ago when Josiah Ambercroft threw down his pick for the last time and announced that, like his brother Daniel before him, he had had enough of hunting for gold. With a shrug and a casual wave, Josiah bid good-bye to his friends. What did it matter to him, or to Ralph or Graham for that matter, Allen had thought bitterly. This was just a lark, an adventure. Eventually, they would shave, wash years of grime and vermin from their bodies, and sail home to their rich parents, laughing about their silly plans. Not Allen.

All he had left behind was a mother too stubborn to listen to the truth, and a lovely fiancée he was too ashamed ever to see again. The Pritchards, thanks to their opulent house, their many servants, the jewels, the parties, the clothes, the carriages, the *everything*, were quickly going broke. Upon the death of his father, Allen had continued to spend as recklessly as his mother, never dreaming that at some point, the well would run dry unless it was refilled. By the time he looked at the family's finances, it was too late. His salary as attorney for one of the most prestigious law firms in New York, would only put a dent in the amount they would need to continue living as they had.

In the firmest tones possible, Allen told his mother the dire news, but she refused to listen. Simply refused. It had been quite maddening, driving Allen to near tears at her obstinance. The woman still controlled the purse strings, and would until he reached thirty. The opportunity to go to San Francisco and become part of Hannah's uncle's enterprise had seemed like a gift from heaven. Partnership was hinted at—partnership in what was quickly becoming a huge enterprise. And then he met those four chaps from Harvard and

had been swept away by their enthusiasm, their total conviction that they would all find enough riches to last a lifetime. None of them would have to work again. They had
brought with them news clippings and pamphlets, all with
firsthand accounts of men finding pounds and pounds of the
gold nuggets. By the time their ship had docked, Allen was
convinced the only way to save his family's fortune was to
hunt for gold.

He'd planned to write to Hannah when he was a rich man.
As the weeks, then months, passed, he continued to tell himself that the next day would yield him the riches he needed.
When that day passed, he put his hopes on the next day. He
never wrote, refused to write, until he had discovered the
vein that would make him a rich man. Then, so many days
passed, so many months, that writing to Hannah seemed
ridiculous. What, after all, would he say to her? That instead
of a fine businessman, instead of establishing a home for
her, he was the proud owner of a rickety shack and a passel
of worthless rocks?

He found just enough of the gold to feed himself and feed
his dreams. Just enough to hope that the next cradle of mud
and silt would reveal nuggets as big as a robin's egg.

Already, even though the sun had been above the horizon
only a few minutes, the air was filled with sounds of miners
hammering away at their dreams. It was a sound that once
filled Allen with exhilaration, but now filled him with a sort
of dread—that somewhere along this piddling stream, someone was striking it rich while he washed his face and
scratched his groin. All along the creek, men like him
emerged from shacks like his and began the backbreaking
work of trying to get rich. After a hasty breakfast of coffee
and stale cornbread bought from a girl who baked and sold
it to miners along the stream, Allen headed to the Long Tom,
a long wooden trough that would separate the worthless
rocks from the gold he sought.

Grabbing a shovel, he heaved a load of gravel onto the
wooden contraption, letting water from the creek drive it

down to a sieve. It wasn't long before Graham poked his head out of the shack, his bloodshot eyes glaring at Allen for having the audacity to wake him up before he was good and ready. Like Allen, Graham's blond hair was long and tangled, his scraggly beard snarled and matted into spikes at the ends. That is why when he spoke with his cultured Eastern accent, Allen almost always smiled.

"I say, Allen, what the devil are you doing working at this time of night?" he asked, even as he squinted against the early morning sun.

"Some of us actually must work for a living, Graham," Allen said good-naturedly.

"I keep telling you, my dear man, this is not work. It is adventure. The moment you convince me that we are working, I'm afraid I will have to depart as Daniel did. Now, leave off a few minutes, will you? I just need a bit more sleep, and I'll be right beside you. Fair enough?"

The distant clanging of a pickax downstream made Allen's decision for him. "Sorry, old friend." He heaved the pickax easily, using muscles that no longer ached at the end of a day. He was lean and sinewy, stronger than he'd ever been in his life. His mother would have fainted dead away had she known her son was engaged in manual labor. As he let the pickax fall once more, he felt a twinge of guilt about not writing to his mother. She had been against his traveling to California all along—even when she believed he would become part of a growing wholesale enterprise. She'd thought even that work beneath him. She would not recognize her son now, he thought with a certain amount of satisfaction. Hell, he wondered if he'd recognize himself if he were presented with a mirror.

The sun rose higher, taking the chill off the morning. Graham and Ralph joined him, grumbling a bit as they examined the tiny bit of fine gold dust clinging to the bottom of the Long Tom's sieve. It would be enough to buy another piece of stale cornbread.

Ralph Potter was thin to the point of looking frail, and yet

was a man who possessed amazing strength. Of the three
men who remained at the claim, Ralph was the only one
who tried to keep up his appearance. Once a month he
would take a knife, and by feel, could cut off hanks of hair.
Without a razor he was forced to let his beard grow longer
than he would have liked, trimming it in the same manner he
did his hair. The result was that he appeared as if some animal had taken great bites out of his thick hair and beard,
leaving him lopsided and rather mad-looking. Graham and
Allen hadn't the heart to tell Ralph that his efforts to maintain his appearance were disastrous.

It was near noon when Ralph looked upstream and
straightened his long body. "Looks like we have visitors,
gentlemen. Shall I heat up the tea?" Ralph was forever making such dry remarks.

All three stopped their work to watch the two figures maneuver their mounts along the rocky path. Passersby usually
brought news of gold and were much anticipated. As the pair
grew closer, it became clear that they were not miners—they
appeared too clean, their clothes too fine. And they hadn't
any equipment to speak of. By the time they were fifty yards
from the miners, it also became clear that one of the riders,
despite the pants worn, was a woman. Allen's stomach knotted painfully as recognition finally dawned. Hannah Wright
had come for him.

Hannah eyed the three dirty men with curiosity and a bit
of wariness. They looked mean from this distance, standing
there silently waiting for George and her to approach their
camp. Hannah looked over to George, who gave her a tentative smile. It was clear he was no more sure of their reception than she was. When they were still ten horse lengths
from the staring men, George spoke.

"Perhaps you gentlemen can help us," he began, but
stopped when one of the men stepped forward.

"Hannah."

Hannah furrowed her brow. That voice was familiar, but

the man . . . My God the man was not. Not at all. It couldn't be.

"Allen?"

"Hannah Wright. To what do I owe this pleasure?"

"Oh, my God. Allen." A whisper. She swallowed hard, shot a quick look over to George, who looked more angry than stunned to find her fiancé was this dirty-looking miner. The man who must be Allen took another step forward, a crooked smile on this face that was horrifyingly familiar.

"Do I look all that terrible, my dear?"

Behind Allen, one of the other men, the blond one, let out a hearty laugh. "Oh," he said, "this is grand. The fiancée has come to take you home, Allen." He laughed loudly, slapping the thin man next to him, who also grinned broadly.

"Perhaps champagne is more in order than tea," the grinning man said.

Allen turned and gave his friends a withering look, and they both made a show of trying to control their mirth.

Hannah jerked her chin up. Though she knew Allen had been mining for gold, the reality of finding him thus was like a slap in the face. Illogically, she had hoped that he would be injured, that he had been in an accident which left him an invalid and ashamed of his condition, explaining why he had not written. But to find him healthy, carefree, and among friends, to see that he was able to smile up at her with that same confident smile, filled her with rage. She had worried. She had defied his mother, her future mother-in-law. She had traveled fifteen thousand miles to see him, and all he could do was say, *To what do I owe this pleasure*!?

With a hard pull on the reins, Hannah jerked the horse around without saying another word. That man had called her "the fiancée," as if they had talked at great length and with great humor about the poor jilted girl back in New York City. A dirty hand grabbed the reins and halted her confused mount, causing it to skitter sideways.

"Hannah, please."

She looked down into that face, into those brown eyes,

and what she saw made her stop her flight. Those eyes and
that crooked smile were the only things in this man's face
that she recognized. But they were Allen's. Her fiancé's.
They belonged to a man who would never have done what
he obviously had done.

"Why, Allen?"

He looked down as if ashamed. When he raised his head,
his eyes were filled with tears. "I'm poor, Hannah. Near
broke. I wanted to be rich. I wanted us to be rich." He
shrugged and turned away, looking toward the mining camp.

"But why didn't you write? I was so worried. I came here
thinking you were hurt or dead."

"Look at me, Hannah." He let out a bitter laugh. "How
could I write to you. What would I say? I planned to send for
you when I found a good vein. It's here, I know it is."

Hannah nearly winced at the excitement in his face.

"All up and down this stream, they're finding gold. All
we have to do is keep trying, keep carving away this
riverbed."

Hannah dismounted and gave her cousin, who remained
mounted near the two men, a reassuring smile. "But it's
been nearly two years you've been looking." She watched as
his expression closed. "Allen, I know I could convince my
uncle to hire you. He's still in need of a right-hand man. It'll
take some talking, and you'd have to promise to never again
look for gold . . ."

"Hannah," he interrupted angrily. "I'll be able to buy your
uncle out as soon as I find that vein."

Hannah was momentarily stunned by the bitterness and
anger she heard in his voice. "You need to consider the possibility that it's simply not here."

He turned away, his body tense. Hannah noticed for the
first time how he had changed in other ways. He was no
longer soft and pale. Allen was hard and tanned and more
stubborn than she'd ever imagined. She could see corded
muscles along his forearms as he stood with his hands on his
hips looking at the pile of rubble he called his stake.

"I've considered that there is no real gold. Every night I consider it. And every morning I wake up, and I know—I know this will be the day. I know," he said, pounding a fist in the air.

"And every day, you are wrong."

He let out a sigh and let his head hang. "I don't know if I can quit, Hannah. I don't know if I want to."

Hannah moved in front of him and watched as his eyes moved over her face. In that moment she knew that part of him still loved her. "Come with me to San Francisco. Just for a month. You can always come back to your mine if you decide it is not what you want. If your partners find gold, it will be yours, too, won't it?"

"Yes."

"And you trust them?"

"With my life," he said, glancing at his two friends who were deep in conversation with George.

"Then, come to the city, Allen. See if you really want to go back to the mine. If you do, then we will say good-bye."

"Good-bye?"

"I will not go with you, Allen. I'll return to New York. My father needs me."

"I need you."

Hannah smiled her disbelief, and Allen blushed. "Come away. For one month, Allen. Just for one month."

Allen let out a sigh. "All right, darling. I'll go with you."

Chapter Sixteen

He wore his finest. Dark gray pants, fitted perfectly by his New York tailor, draped smoothly over his highly polished shoes. His jacket covered a lighter gray silk vest that peeked just below his jacket when buttoned. A silver watch chain, cut so that it glimmered in the light as if it were bejeweled, and a loosely tied cravat completed his attire. And in his jacket pocket, giving him both courage and comfort, he carried his brother's scrimshaw. He bent his head to make sure his newly trimmed hair was neat, that the barber had given him a fine, clean shave. As he straightened, his eyes moved to the bed that she once slept in, the bed they would share for their return journey. He pictured her there, her brown hair made gold by the sun fanned out on the white sheet, her stormy sea eyes sleepy with invitation. He grew hard simply thinking about her, simply imagining his mouth on hers, on her breasts, on every part of her.

James's stomach gave a nervous clench, and he twisted his mouth sardonically. He hadn't been this unstrung since he stepped aboard his first ship as captain. That sick, excited feeling in his stomach, the lurch that feels like you are dropping off a cliff, surprised him. He loved Hannah, and he was quite sure she loved him, though she'd never said it aloud. He had thought, rather smugly, that he could tell when a woman loved him. But now, after ten days of not seeing her, of wondering why she hadn't stopped by to see him, he was not so sure. Damn, he was not sure at all. It was that blasted fiancé, the man she obviously intended to search for. He understood. After traveling so far to find him, it was only common sense that she seek him out to tell him that she loved another, that she must officially break it off with him. Not that the fool deserved an explanation, he thought with a deep scowl.

But what if . . .

What if she saw this Allen Pritchard and realized she loved him after all? James let out a shaky breath, damning his soul for falling in love so hard, so completely. It addled the brain, it unmanned him. By God, she stirred his blood. Heaven help him if she ever found out how very much he loved her. He laughed aloud. She'd likely scowl, put her little fists on her sexy hips, and tell him he should quit such nonsense this instant. If only he could.

James stepped from his cabin with a broad smile on his face. In minutes he would see her. He might even get a chance this evening to kiss her, to hold her against him. Ah, he'd take what he could get for now. They had a lifetime together for more serious kissing and touching.

"I'm off, Mr. Lodge," he shouted to his second mate. The older man, lounging by the mainmast, waved and gave him a grin.

"Give her my hellos," he shouted back.

James walked down the gangplank, his strides sure and strong. Though by his dress he could have passed for a successful businessman, by his manner, he was all sea captain. He walked with confidence, with the slight swagger of a man used to keeping his balance on a rolling ship. He walked with the buoyant step of a man in love.

"James," she said, a sparkling smile lighting her face, "I'd like you to meet Allen Pritchard. My fiancé."

Hannah watched as the broad smile that lit James's face faltered slightly. For the first time she saw that, although his mouth was pulled up at the corners, his eyes were hard.

James had walked into her uncle's house all energy and vi-
brance. He practically threw his hat and gloves at the butler,
his eyes scanning the entranceway. Hannah knew he was
looking for her, and her heart wrenched. She took in his fine
clothes, his freshly shaved face, that smile. Though James
was completely unaware of it, he was elegant in a devastat-
ingly masculine way. She drank in the sight of him, feeling
the sudden urge to run across the floor and launch herself
into his arms. The way he stood there staring at her when he
spotted her, sent her heart pounding, pounding in her breast.
It was a painful beat, hard and real. For even as she wanted
to pull James to her, she was agonizingly aware of Allen
standing next to her completely innocent as to what she
meant to this man.

"Fiancé. I see."

She watched as his jaw tightened and something passed
through his face before he spoke again. "Captain James
MacRae at your service, Mr. Pritchard," he said, with a little bow that Hannah found oddly disturbing. It was the type
of gesture a man made to another after having lost a bet.

"I've heard much about you, Captain. Thank you for taking care of my Hannah. I hear it was a rough passage."

Hannah looked at Allen with gratitude.

Once cleaned up, Allen looked remarkably like his old
self—except he was even more stunningly handsome with
his tanned, chiseled aristocratic features. His teeth flashed
white when he smiled, as he thrust out a sun-browned and
work-callused hand to James. The two men shook, and Hannah looked away. Seeing them together, the man she would
marry and the man she loved, had the qualities of a disturbing dream. Allen, relaxed and his old pleasant self, drew
James away with him. Allen had a wonderful way of putting
nearly everyone at ease, men and women. It was one of the
things she had missed about him, his great ability to mesh
with nearly everyone. Even her uncle, who made a great effort to dislike Allen, found himself smiling at his amusing
tales and dry humor.

Three days after she had brought Allen back to San Francisco, she introduced him to her uncle and aunt, and prayed the subject of gold would not be broached. Of course, the first thing out of her uncle's mouth was, "So, you're one of those young fools who thinks they can get rich digging for gold. It's all fool's gold," her uncle said, booming out his oft repeated sentiment.

"I'm beginning to suspect you are right," Allen had said, a self-deprecating smile on his fine lips. That took the wind right out of her uncle's sails.

Allen was not the man she remembered. He was not the thoroughly confident, thoroughly relaxed man she'd known in New York. The two years digging for gold, two years of backbreaking work, two years of failing, had toughened Allen. She saw it in his manner, in his eyes, which often seemed troubled.

"I don't know where I belong," he'd told her the day they arrived in the city. Indeed, he seemed a little lost, and Hannah's heart went out to him. A bath, haircut, and shave did wonders for his appearance, but his eyes were haunted, his face tense. He was not a happy man, and Hannah wondered if the Allen she had known was lost forever. He had held her to him and cried, begging for forgiveness for his abandonment, and Hannah returned his embrace, like a mother holding a child. She forgave him. How could she not?

"If I'd only found the gold," he'd said brokenly. "I know it's there. I know it."

To Hannah's ears, he sounded like a gambler down on his luck, praying for the win that would break a losing streak.

Each day away from the mine, Allen became more like the man she remembered. He'd been in San Francisco a week now, and days had passed without the mention of gold. She prayed no one would bring up his failed venture, just as she prayed Allen would not bring up their renewed plans to marry and settle in California. She found out quickly enough that it was too much to ask.

Her uncle was holding the dinner in honor of Captain

MacRae. Among the invited guests were the Coddingtons
and the Davises. It happened that, as publishers of one of the
most oft read newspapers, her uncle knew the husbands of
the women Hannah befriended on the trip. After a brief visit
with his parents, George had headed to Monterey to visit an
old sea captain he'd sailed with for two years who had been
left crippled by a falling spar, and so was not present. Also
invited was a business associate of her uncle's, Stuart Hall,
who brought along his wife, Edith, and their lovely daughter, Susie. Susie, with her brown hair and blue-gray eyes,
was a pretty girl, Hannah thought begrudgingly. The moment she saw Captain MacRae, the only single gentleman
invited to the dinner party, her eyes grew wide and her face
took on that awed look that Hannah knew had been on her
own face the first time she'd seen him. It was extremely irritating.

They were to be paired for dinner, of course, and Hannah
knew she should be relieved that there was no question of
whom she would sit across from at the dinner table. Allen
was her fiancé, and James was, as far as her aunt and uncle
knew, simply a man with the audacity to kiss their niece on
a public street. Hannah realized that her aunt and uncle had
not taken James's declaration of love seriously. After all,
what sort of man shouted something like that to a girl who
planned to marry another?

The guests gathered in her aunt's large parlor. As guest of
honor, James was the center of attention. The Coddingtons
and Davises surrounded him, the Halls hovering close
enough so that their daughter was within his sight—if he
cared to look. To Hannah's relief, it seemed he did not care
to look. Instead, he darted his eyes to her, quick, heated,
questioning looks that made Hannah want to shout for him
to stop. Finally, unable to bear it, she turned her back to him
and pulled Allen to a corner. Still, she could almost feel
James's eyes on her, a warmth on her back, at the base of her
neck, as if he stood inches from her, breathing hotly on her
sensitive skin.

"Why does Captain MacRae look at you so proprietarily, Hannah? It's rather . . . obvious the man has feelings for you," Allen said, barely keeping the anger from his voice. Hannah could feel her face flush, but she waved a dismissive hand.

"Oh, Captain MacRae fancies himself besotted. It's really quite charming, in an annoying sort of way." Hannah let out a laugh that sounded false, even to her own ears.

"I'm not a fool, Hannah, though you think me one." Anger flared, unconcealed and bright in his eyes, and Hannah stiffened.

"I wouldn't know what you are, Allen. I barely know you anymore." It was the first time since they'd returned to San Francisco that she acknowledged her anger over his disappearance.

Allen swore softly. "I don't want to argue with you, Hannah. I am fully aware what I have done to you. I can only say I am sorry. You know that I am." He grasped her hands and pulled them to his mouth. And to her shame, all Hannah could think was: Please, God, don't let James see.

"And are you in love with him?" he whispered hoarsely, his eyes filled with pain as he looked at her over the hands still pressed to his lips.

Hannah gently pulled her hands down, allowing him to continue to hold them. With a steady gaze and a firm voice, she said, "I am going to marry you, Allen."

He looked down at their joined hands, obviously disappointed in her response. "I am grateful," he said softly.

Hannah closed her eyes briefly, hating that she seemed to be hurting everyone she loved. And she did love Allen, as a friend. A best friend. We will have a good life together, she thought.

"Allen." He looked up. "If we marry, you must never leave me again. I will not be abandoned while you go off to hunt for gold. If you cannot promise me that, I cannot marry you."

Allen hesitated an instant, and said, "I promise you, Hannah." But his eyes shifted away, and Hannah knew, she *knew*, she could not trust him to keep that promise.

No one looking at James knew that he was filled with a murderous rage. It was not easy for him to hide his feelings, for he was a man who never found it necessary to shield himself from others. If he was happy, he smiled. If he was angry, he yelled. But this was not mere anger, this was a roiling, seething, burning thing. It was torrid. It was unbearable.

When he saw that . . . man . . . take Hannah's hands and pull them to his lips, he took a stilted step toward them before remembering himself. Hannah had made it clear that James meant nothing to her. Every smile she gave the man, every touch, was like a red-hot brand to James's heart. It hurt, Jesus God, it hurt. Beside him, that silly girl was looking up at him as if he were Jesus Himself come down to give her His personal blessing. That sort of look used to please him, but now he found it extremely irritating. She flinched every time he raised his voice, moving a fluttering hand to her throat if he gestured a bit too broadly. And all the time looked at him with adoring eyes as wide as saucers.

What the hell were they talking about over there? His eyes moved over Hannah, relishing the sight of her, wishing he could stroll up to her and move back in place that bit of hair that hung loose from her coiffure. He liked her looking like a woman, all soft and pretty, her dress accenting just the things it should. She wore a forest-green velvet evening gown that left the tops of her shoulders and small amount of chest bare. Still faintly discernible on her chest was the V made from the sun on those long days at sea. A wide collar of ivory lace-trimmed neckline and a series of elaborate flounces decorated the full skirt, revealing ivory lace at the very bottom that matched her collar. She looked more than lovely, he thought, and far different from the little hoyden with trousers and a floppy straw hat who ran so confidently about the *Windfire*. He wondered if her fiancé had ever seen her thus, had ever kissed her the way he had, had ever felt her nipple against his tongue.

"Blast and damn." He said it softly, but with seething emotion.

"Is something wrong, Captain? Some injury that pains you?" Susie asked. She sounded almost hopeful.

He looked down, startled to realize that, not only was the silly chit still standing next to him, but that he had spoken aloud.

"If you'll excuse me, Miss . . ." He'd already forgotten her name, so left the title hanging in the air, and the young woman's mouth hanging open in disappointed bewilderment.

Allen watched James advance upon them, and smiled. "Ah, speak of the devil," he said, his tone almost as light as he'd intended.

"Mr. Pritchard, Miss Wright."

"Please, no formalities, Captain. Call me Allen." James ignored the man.

"Miss Wright. I need to speak to you privately." He almost enjoyed the panic he saw in her eyes.

"I don't think that I . . ." She was saved by a maid announcing dinner.

James watched Allen hold out his arm for Hannah. Without looking again at James, she slipped her hand onto Allen's forearm. As they walked away, James was suddenly reminded of his dream, of that tall, faceless stranger who had taken Hannah away from him. He felt that same desperation, the same terrible sense of helplessness. Only now the man had a face.

"Why?" It boomed out of his mouth before he could stop himself.

Hannah turned, a brittle smile on her face. "Because dinner is ready, Captain. If you would be so kind to escort Miss Hall?" Then she turned away, her hand in the crook of that man's arm.

"Have you any idea what a brave girl you have for a

niece?" Beatrice Coddington gushed to Hannah's uncle after the party had been seated for dinner. It seemed that now that Mrs. Coddington was on dry land, the true memory of their trip had been completely erased from her brain. Mrs. Coddington was full of funny and harrowing tales about the voyage, so many that Hannah was left stunned. When did Mrs. Coddington have a chance to experience anything with her head in a bucket for most of the trip?

"Fool girl, ask me," her uncle said, but he flashed Hannah a grin.

"Here, here," James said, putting a wineglass to his lips and taking a large swallow.

"Oh, posh, Captain. You must admit that Miss Wright is an original."

"An original what?"

Mrs. Coddington ignored James, apparently deciding it was useless to talk to the man. "You remember, Winifred, I'm sure, that day of the squall?" At Mrs. Davis's nod, she continued. "It was Hannah who predicted it."

Feeling slightly embarrassed to be reminded of that tragic day, Hannah said, "I simply read the barometer." She didn't want James reminded of the day he lost one of his men, or that her own foolishness had nearly cost her life.

"Captain had to drag her from the deck." Mrs. Coddington giggled. Apparently the woman had imbibed in too much wine, for a giggle followed each sentence she uttered. Hannah wished the older woman would stop talking so much.

"And the mast fell, and would have landed directly atop of our dear girl if Captain MacRae hadn't forced her down below."

"We all make mistakes," James said, his eyes glittering.

Mrs. Coddington giggled, then stopped abruptly, as if suddenly realizing that what the captain said was quite awful.

Hannah could feel her face heat, and grow hotter still when she realized Allen was about to come to her defense.

She tried to shoot him a warning look, but he either ignored her or did not see her imploring gaze.

"Are you saying, Captain, that you wish you had not saved Hannah's life?"

"Not at all, Mr. Pritchard. Had I not saved Miss Wright's life, we would not all be here enjoying her wonderful company. Such a delight." His words had an awful bite to them, and Hannah felt her eyes burn with tears she refused to shed. She looked down at her plate and studied the creamed spinach for a long moment. Strangely, everyone else at the table relaxed, taking his words at face value.

"You are one lucky man to have a woman such as Miss Wright agree to marry you," James said, sounding almost as if he meant it. But Hannah knew better.

"Yes, Captain, I am."

Hannah closed her eyes, feeling suddenly faint. Stop it, James. Please stop.

"A lucky man," he repeated softly.

"Oh, Mr. Pritchard," Mrs. Coddington blurted, "Hannah went on and on about you during the voyage. We were beginning to think we would find a halo about your head when we met you, didn't we, Winifred?"

Winifred Davis nodded. "It was always, 'Allen says this,' and 'Allen says that.' It was getting a bit boring," she laughed, and Hannah managed a smile. Allen glowed to hear such anecdotes.

"I suppose you didn't tell the two ladies about your fiancé's adventure with the gold," her uncle said.

"Richard, really," Prudence said, giving her husband a small shake of her head.

"Well, it's obvious to me that she didn't. All seems well now, but poor Hannah didn't know what she was going to find when she arrived in San Francisco."

"Gold?" Mrs. Coddington asked. Hannah gritted her teeth.

"Yes, Mrs. Coddington," Allen said with a weak smile. "Gold. I succumbed to gold fever. Quite willingly, I might

add. I and two partners—there used to be five of us—have a
stake on Weber Creek on a stream that's been making plenty
of men rich. We haven't hit our vein yet, just enough to get
by, but we will, mark my words." His voice faded, and he
shot a guilty look to Hannah. "What I mean to say is that,
my partners will find gold. Now that Hannah and I are marrying, I won't be going back to the claim."

"You've set a date, then." This from James, and Hannah
thought she might throw up the creamed spinach she'd managed to force down her throat.

Allen smiled intimately at Hannah. "We thought Thanksgiving or the New Year at the latest."

"How wonderful!" Mrs. Coddington beamed. "This calls
for a toast." She made a wobbly grab for her glass.

James stood immediately, his wineglass raised in a toast.
"To the future bride and groom. I hope . . ." He worked his
throat. His mouth opened and closed. His eyes hit Hannah
with a force that nearly knocked her from her chair. "I hope
you are happy with your choices," he finally managed.

"Here, here," came the responses.

Dinner continued, the guests chatting animatedly. Allen
told several amusing stories about his days at the mine, win-
ning over nearly everyone at the table. Allen was, if nothing
else, extremely likable. Hannah ate her meal hearing only a
dull roar in her ears, the guests' voices merely muffled
sounds, as if she were on deck the *Windfire* in a stiff wind.
She'd thought that once James knew, she would feel relieved. Instead, she felt as if her entire body had been ruth-
lessly pummeled, her heart beating painfully in her breast. It
was difficult to breathe even. I'm dying, she thought, I'm
dying because he's going away and I love him so. But the
feeling only gave her strength, for this is how she would feel
every time he went away if she were married to him. A slow
death, each parting.

Hannah finally garnered enough courage to look up at
him, all the love she felt clear in her eyes. James flinched,
almost as if she'd struck him.

He stood then, abruptly and so violently, his chair was nearly upended. "If you'll excuse us. Miss Wright and I must speak privately regarding some unresolved business."

Hannah, ignoring Allen's small sound of protest, stood and began to follow James out the dining room door.

Chapter Seventeen

James dragged her behind him, though she would have gone willingly. Something inside her unfurled, that tiny bit of mendacity twisting in the pit of her stomach that insisted she would forget him. With a single gesture from him, her resistance dissolved, setting her free, if only for a few moments.

Behind her, she heard her uncle growl, "Sit your ass down, Pritchard."

And then her aunt's cultured voice. "Richard, really. Try to curb that tongue of yours. We do have guests. Do sit down, Mr. Pritchard." She heard Allen mutter something, but by the time he spoke again, James had dragged her too far to hear.

His hand clasped her wrist as he made his way down a long hall, stopping periodically to thrust open a door, only to decide the room he saw was not adequate for his "discussion." Just so he wouldn't think her completely willing, Hannah pulled back, giving a token resistance, but he simply pulled her with him effortlessly. Her stomach curled with excitement and a small amount of trepidation, for she could tell James was quite angry. He finally came to the kitchen, paused, and then walked through the door, ignoring the curious stares of the kitchen staff. He maneuvered around a sack of potatoes, and headed for the back door. And then they were outdoors in the chill October air, dew wetting their shoes.

James headed deeper into her aunt's garden, all without saying a word, walking quickly toward a shed tucked in one corner. With a grunt of satisfaction, he opened the door, pulling Hannah in behind him. He stood there, breathing heavily, not touching her. Though it was dark, she could tell he was glaring down at her, his whole body rigid. She told herself he would not harm her, not with dinner guests so close by, but the back of her neck tingled with the tiniest bit of fear. Then suddenly, Hannah found herself in his embrace, his mouth ravaging hers, his hands pulling her so close she could barely breathe.

Hannah let out a little sound of surprise and then lost herself in his consuming kiss. She wanted this, she wanted to kiss him, to hold him, to feel his muscles bunch beneath her hands. James moaned, a sound she felt more than heard, and she pressed herself even closer. He dragged his mouth away from hers, attacking her jaw with nips and licks, then her neck. Her breath was jagged, raw, her body liquid as he molded her against him fully so that she felt the proof of his desire. Hannah was about as innocent to what happened between a man and a woman as a girl could be, but she knew instinctively that what she felt against her hip meant he wanted her. She pressed against him, delighting in the delicious sensation the erotic movement sent shooting through her body. He sucked in his breath at the movement, halting his kisses.

"You don't love him," he said harshly, his mouth against hers. He dragged his mouth to her temple, her forehead, and back to her lips. "Tell me you don't love him, Hannah. You don't, do you."

"No, James," Hannah said, finally, breathlessly. "I don't."

"Hannah, I . . ." With one motion, he brought her bodice down, baring her breasts. Before Hannah could even think to protest, she was whimpering, begging him to never stop. His mouth, greedy and hot on one nipple, nearly caused her

knees to buckle. It felt so wonderful, his mouth there, sucking, his tongue licking. His hands were on her bottom,
kneading and pulling her toward him so that her groin was
flush against his rigid member. It was that spot, that center
of her, that felt so . . . alive. She pressed herself against him,
wanting more but not knowing how to go about it other than
to press harder. It felt good, so she moved again, smiling
when James moaned and moved his hips, thrusting against
her, sending such sensations through her body, she thought
surely she would die. She dimly wondered if this was something that women should allow a man to do, and let out a
giggle thinking: I should not allow any of this.

James brought his head up at the sound of her laughter.
"Am I amusing you?" he asked roughly. Even in the darkness, she could see that he smiled.

"No. You are doing something else entirely," Hannah
managed to say. She was oddly short of breath.

"Am I?" He kissed her, long and deep, his tongue moving
with hers as his hips moved in the same intoxicating motion.
"I can't," he groaned. "Hannah, I have to . . ." His lips en-
veloped one nipple, and he drew it hard into his warm
mouth. ". . . stop. I have to stop." He moved away from her,
breathing heavily through his nose, staring at her with such
fire, that even in the darkness Hannah could almost feel the
heat shooting from his eyes. She gave a little sound of
protest, a small gesture of her now-empty arms, and James
let out a gruff laugh.

"You don't know what you're doing to me, darling. I'm
not a man of great restraint, believe me." James turned from
her and began rummaging around in the dark shed, finally
striking a match and lighting a small lamp that hung from a
nail on the wall.

Hannah stared at him, breathing heavily, loving the feeling of the cool air on her naked breasts. She did not cover
herself even in the lamplight, and she wondered if he had
truly drugged her with his kisses. "Kiss me again, James."

He moved forward as if to honor her request, his eyes

fixed on her upturned breasts, then stopped abruptly, his jaw
clenching, his lips pressed tight. He tapped his thigh with a
clenched fist. She watched as he forced himself to relax. He
took a step back, putting a hand in one pocket. Out of his
jacket pocket, he brought an exquisite scrimshaw carving of
a clipper ship. "I . . . I suppose I should have had a ring"—
he smiled, looking like a young boy—"but this means more
to me than anything I own. My brother gave it to me." He
placed the whalebone in the palm of her hand. It felt heavy
and dense. "You see, it's a carving of my first ship, *Patriot's
Lady*. He gave it to me shortly before he died." He let out a
shaking breath.

"Marry me, Hannah."

Pure joy flooded Hannah's heart, but the moment was
shattered almost instantly by a brutal reality. What was she
doing here, baring her breasts, allowing him to do things
she'd never dreamed of doing with Allen, and suddenly
could not imagine doing with anyone but James. She turned
slightly away from him and moved her stiff, boned bodice
back in place. She felt his warm hand on her shoulder and
shivered.

"I can't marry you." She turned back to him, her eyes imploring him to understand, knowing in her heart he would
not.

He swallowed. "I love you, Hannah. Marry me." He put a
strong hand on each shoulder and gave her a gentle shake.
"You don't love him. You've just said you don't. Why are
you doing this?"

His voice broke, and Hannah's heart felt as if a sharp
splinter was piercing her heart. His eyes, his beautiful eyes,
were filled with anguish.

"You wouldn't understand. I can't marry you. Please
don't love me. Please. It only makes it more difficult to say
good-bye." She refused to tell him her reason, for she feared
he would rashly promise anything. Hannah would not ask
him to leave the sea for her. In her soul, she believed taking

James away from the sea would do his heart far more damage than her refusal. She would not make him choose.

"You don't love me, either, do you?" he asked in a voice gone flat and emotionless. Hannah drew in a sharp little breath, then turned her head away.

James felt desperation consume him when he watched her turn away. For the first time in his life, he was failing. He couldn't make her love him. He looked at her, her full mouth, her eyes that glittered with unshed tears, memorizing each detail. Would he remember the tiny lines like little commas appearing near her mouth when she smiled? That her chin dimpled when she frowned? He hadn't realized it would feel this way, that he would become the type of man he'd sneered at before—a man who would do anything, say anything, to convince the woman he loved to love him in return. His pride lay shattered at his feet. James knew only one thing: Without Hannah, his life would be empty, worthless. If he had to beg, by God, he'd beg.

"We don't have to say good-bye," he said gruffly, pulling her against him. "Marry me. Sail home with me. Please, love." He felt her relax against him and was heartened. His words fell from his mouth, rapid, desperate. "We'll make it to New York in record time, we'll fly, Hannah. I can smell that sweet sea air already, I can hear the snap of *Windfire* sails. I need you with me, Hannah. I need to know that you'll be waiting for me, that you'll always be there."

Hannah pushed him forcefully away. "No. No. I won't. I won't wait for you, don't you see? I will not wait. I will not marry you." She ran to the still-open shed door and disappeared into the night.

James took a step to follow her and stopped. Save some of your damned pride, you fool, he told himself bitterly. His words came back to haunt him, his voice, strained and cracked and . . . begging. To hell with her, then. To *hell* with her. He'd not waste his love on someone who would not love him back.

He walked out of the shed and slammed the door loudly

behind him, and then slammed into her. She hadn't left. His heart soared.

"James." Her voice sounded small, frightened. "I think you should take this back." In her trembling hand she held the carving, her fingers curled slightly as if she were reluctant to return it to him.

Rage filled him, fueled by hurt and pain and a love that he feared would never die. He slapped her hand away, sending the whalebone flying. Other than a sharp intake of breath, Hannah said nothing. She looked at him, and he thought he saw pity before she turned and headed back into her uncle's home.

Hannah was on her hands and knees, her face streaked with tears and dirt. "It has to be here. Has to be." She sniffled, moving the back of her hand across her nose, not caring that such a gesture was entirely unladylike and would certainly leave a smear of dirt on her face. Groveling in the dirt was not ladylike, either. Letting a man kiss your breasts . . . Oh, where was it? She'd been searching nearly an hour and was about to give up, when her eyes spotted a bit of white hiding beneath a broad leaf in the overgrown pumpkin patch. The relief she felt when her hand wrapped around the cool smooth surface let loose another deluge of tears. She rocked back and forth on her knees, clutching the carving to her breast.

"Hannah? What is wrong, darling?"

Hannah stiffened, instantly stopping her tears. She grasped the handkerchief Allen offered her and sopped up her watery face, her head turned away from her fiancé.

"I thought I lost this. But I found it," she said, smiling.

Allen studied her swollen, red-rimmed eyes, the dirt streaks left on her face from her tears, before glancing down at the whalebone. "It must mean a great deal to you," he said finally.

"Yes. It does. It . . . was a gift."

"From the captain?" Allen did not seem angry. Only hurt.

"Yes."

He let out a long sigh. "I can see you are not going to make this easy on me, Hannah. I suppose it is what I deserve." When Hannah didn't argue, he smiled fondly at her.

"When did he give it to you?"

Hannah looked down at the carving, her eyes once again filling with tears. "Last night. He asked me to marry him, Allen. I said no."

"I see."

She grasped one arm. "Oh, no, Allen, you don't see. I don't want to marry him. I don't. I want to marry you."

He began walking, and she moved beside him, her hand still on his arm.

"But you love him?" It was a question. "I asked you before, but you didn't answer me."

"I'm sorry, Allen."

"Sorry that you love him, or sorry you did not answer me."

"The first one," she said, not wanting to say the words aloud. "I tried not to. And I'll get over it," she said forcefully. "All girls do. They fall in love with the wrong man, and then marry the right one. And after a time, they forget the silliness altogether. That man they thought they loved becomes a fond memory, if even that. It happens all the time."

"Are you trying to convince me or yourself, darling?"

He was being so good, so gentle and understanding, Hannah felt all the more wretched. If he had ranted and raved, it would have been easier, she thought. "Both, I suppose."

"And what if it doesn't go away. What if you discover ten years from now that you love him still?"

Hannah stopped. "I'll be a good wife to you, Allen. As long as you stay by me."

Her words seemed to disturb him. "Why must you obsess about me leaving. I am a partner in that claim. It is only natural that I would check on its progress from time to time. I hope you don't mean to forbid me to visit my mine, a legitimate business venture."

Hannah's heart sank. "You promised me."

"I promised that I would not go digging. I did not promise to ignore an investment." He sounded petulant, hostile. "I think you expect too much of people, Hannah. You always did. It is so easy to disappoint you, isn't it?"

"That's not true," she said, hurt by his angry words.

"What is it about the captain that makes you turn away from him? What is the grand flaw that makes you send a man you love away? What small thing will it take for you to turn me, who you do not love, away from you?"

Hannah winced at his words that were too true. "He would leave," she shouted. "He would leave me behind." She turned and made to run, but Allen's strong hand stopped her. He pulled her against him.

"I'm sorry, Hannah. Please. I'm sorry. It just hurts to know you love him. Hurts like hell, to be honest. I promise. All right? I promise I won't go back to the claim. After we're married," he amended quickly.

She turned into his arms and let him hold her, her best friend. "I'm so sorry Allen. I wouldn't hurt you for the world. And I do love you. I'm simply very confused and quite out of sorts at the moment. Forgive me?"

"Of course," he said, tucking her head beneath his chin. But his brown eyes were filled with sadness.

James wanted to hate her. God, how he wanted to. But he could not. He need only think of her face, and his heart would fill with a longing that was painful. Physically painful. It was odd, really, that love could hurt so much. He wondered when it would go away, this emptiness that she'd carved out of his soul. The pain centered around one irrevocable fact: She did not love him.

"Hell. Everybody loves me," he muttered. It was true. Captain James MacRae was a thoroughly likable man with confidence that bordered on arrogance. Without boasting, he could honestly say he'd never met a woman that didn't want him, like him, want to bed him. For the woman whom he loved to reject him was as incomprehensible to him as it was painful. Why? Why wouldn't she marry him? Why didn't she love him?

He tipped back his half-empty bottle of rum and took a long swallow. James was not a drinking man, though he'd been known to get drunk now and again, always regretting it in the morning. He could count the number of times he'd drank himself silly on one hand. This was number four. And he planned to fill the rest of his hand tomorrow and the next day and eventually move on to his toes. He wanted to be drunk and oblivious for a good long time. He wanted everything and everyone to go away. So far it wasn't working, but he knew if he drank long and hard enough, it would.

He took another swallow.

"Captain. Little early for that, ain't it?" Timothy Lodge said, eyeing the sun that had barely made an appearance on the horizon.

"A little late, I'm thinking," James said good-naturedly. See? Things were already looking up.

"Never seen you tipping the bottle before the sun was up, sir. Hell, can't say as I've seen you ever tipping a bottle."

Lodge was beginning to irritate him mightily. "First time for everything." It was not every day, after all, that a man asked a woman to marry him. Why, he was celebrating, that was all. Celebrating his narrow escape of marital bonds. Lodge sat down beside him atop the forecastle, groaning as he did.

"This damn damp San Fran weather's got my bones aching," he complained. He held a hand out for the bottle, and James gave it up. Lodge took a swallow, winced, and handed the bottle back. "Seen Miss Wright last night?" he said in overly casual tones, but James was already too drunk to pick up on Lodge's obvious fishing trip.

"That I did, Mr. Lodge," James said heartily, but Lodge

saw a flash of anguish in the younger man's eyes before he lifted the bottle to his lips for another swig. "Asked her to marry me."

Lodge looked away from his captain when he saw tears in his eyes. It's the drink, he thought, making the man so emotional.

"She said no," James said unnecessarily.

"She's a fool, then," Lodge said, always loyal.

"Ever been in love, Mr. Lodge?"

The older man shifted uneasily. "I was married once. A long time ago, it was. I was nothing but a boy. She died." He grabbed the bottle and took a long draw, and his voice softened, growing wistful. "You know, even though we were only together a short time, I still dream about her. It's the strangest thing, it is. Sometimes it's so real, I wake up thinking I'm nineteen and she'll be there next to me, all smiling and sleepy. Funny thing . . . in that moment I still love her, and then I miss her something awful. Guess it must have been true love." He laughed and took another swallow. "Haven't hardly looked at a woman since. Not that any would have me. Always thought my Paula was a silly girl for loving me so." He was silent a long moment. "But that was years ago," he said gruffly. "I got over it."

James looked at Timothy Lodge's profile, and knew the man lied. He hadn't gotten over his wife, and never would. Just like he would never stop loving Hannah. How could he? She was in his heart, embedded there, like a tough barnacle on the bottom of a ship. He could scrape her memory away, but a part of her would always remain to haunt him, to visit him in his dreams and leave him with a yearning that could never be assuaged. He was suddenly sober, suddenly aware of just what he was losing, and bitterness filled his heart.

Damn her cold heart.

"Let's get drunk," he said, slapping Lodge on the back.

"I thought that's what we were doing."

"We're not even close, my good man. Not even close."

Chapter Eighteen

For days Hannah walked about in a haze, a lump lodged in her throat that no amount of swallowing would dislodge. It was a ball of grief that seemed to grow bigger each day. Soon the *Windfire* would set sail, and then the aching clot of grief would disappear. During the day, Hannah stayed busy, visiting with her aunt, exploring the city with Allen. But at night, she would tuck herself into her window seat and stare and stare at the bay, the moon shimmering on its distant black surface. She could see the outline of masts against the moon, but could never be sure if she was looking at the *Windfire*, if at that moment, she might actually have her eyes trained on James and not know it. She would sit there for hours, sometimes closing her eyes, to try to recall every detail of him, from his gleaming black hair, to his startlingly blue eyes, to those fine lines that marked him as a man who often smiled. When the wind was right, she could smell the sea, and sometimes, if she tried hard enough, she could almost breathe him in, that man, sea, wool smell. She could almost feel his eyes looking at her, almost feel his lips pressed against hers. Once, in the midst of her dreaming, he seemed so close, she found herself searching the street for him. Of course, he was not there, he would be on the *Windfire*, lying on the same bed she once lay on.

In those moments of longing, Hannah would begin to

imagine that life wouldn't be so bad as a sea captain's wife, as James's wife. When he was in port, they would spend every moment together, they would laugh and make love and make children. Such thoughts would always make her smile. But without fail, they would immediately be replaced by images of him leaving, of him waving good-bye distractedly, his mind and his heart already with the sea. And she would picture herself standing there, watching the ship grow smaller and smaller on the horizon, knowing it would be months and months before she saw him again. That is when she knew that the heartache she was now feeling was nothing, nothing compared to what it would be later when she realized she hadn't the strength to say good-bye again.

Allen, who was staying at a rather rough boardinghouse on Battery Street, was a constant companion. But if Hannah were honest, she was beginning to find his soulful, hurting looks a bit irritating. She wanted to shout: "I've chosen you, haven't I? Stop looking at me like such a whipped dog." It wasn't until the topic of his working for her uncle came up that Hannah realized the hangdog look was not one of heartbreak, but of growing gold fever.

They were finishing up breakfast. Hannah, an early riser, had waited for Allen's arrival before eating. Her uncle had long since disappeared to his huge warehouse near the Union Street Wharf, her aunt was helping a friend plan a Thanksgiving Day ball.

"When do you think you'll begin accompanying my uncle to work?" Hannah asked. While Allen was meticulously well mannered, he seemed to consume an inordinate amount of food, as if he hadn't eaten a thing in the two years at his mine.

He lay down his fork, wiped his mouth, and smiled. "I've been meaning to discuss that with you."

Something about the way he said those words, or perhaps because his eyes shifted away, left Hannah filled with foreboding. Allen tapped his fingers on the pristine linen that

covered the table, accidentally hitting a fork tine and sending the utensil flipping through the air. It landed on Allen's
well-filled plate with a little plop. Hannah frowned.

"Since we won't be married until at least the New
Year . . ."

"I thought we'd also discussed Thanksgiving," she said,
even though the New Year seemed much more appealing.

"You must admit, dear, that a Thanksgiving wedding is
cutting it a bit short. Not nearly enough time to plan. Your
aunt would have my head if I put that on her." He smiled
again, but she could tell he was irritated by the tightness
around his mouth. She'd seen that smile before, yet it had
always been directed at his mother.

"I thought perhaps something very small." Hannah was
left wondering why she was arguing for an early wedding,
a wedding that would be held when James was still in port.
Thanksgiving was less than a week away, and it suddenly
seemed utterly absurd to have the wedding so quickly. "Oh,
you're quite right, Allen. A New Year's wedding would be
much better. But you were saying?"

"Yes. I thought perhaps that until the wedding, since
everything has been decided, I could go back to the claim
and complete some business there." He made a great show
of delicately picking up his fork from his food. As if the discussion were closed.

"No, Allen. You promised."

She could almost hear his teeth grind together. "Yes, I
promised to not go to the mine when we were married. But
I clearly stated to you that I might go to my claim prior to
our marriage."

Gold. How she hated it. It had taken the Allen she knew
away from her. It had brought her here, it had been the
cause of everything. She fell in love with James because of
gold. And she was losing the Allen she'd known because of
it. Though she wasn't even sure if she wanted this man sitting across from her as husband, something inside made her
give the ultimatum. "If you go, the wedding is off. All I ask

is that I not be deserted, Allen. I don't understand you. I don't understand what's happened to you."

Allen, in a very unAllen-like manner, slammed down his fork, sending bits of egg flying. "I became a man, that's what happened to me. I will not bow to you or to my mother or to any woman again. I tell you I will leave the mine when we marry, and I will. Until then I'll do as I please."

After her momentary shock at the unbelievable sound of Allen's raised voice, Hannah jerked up her chin. "Do not speak to me so, Allen. You abandoned me, made a fool of me. I traveled all this way fearing something terrible had happened to you, and it seems that something terrible did indeed happen. Two years, Allen. Two years. I waited for you. And you cannot give me two months." She stood, tears hot in her eyes. "Go, then! Go and good riddance to you. Find your blasted gold. I hope you choke on it."

Hannah whipped around at the sound of polite applause from behind her. George, a grin on his face, stood giving her an ovation.

"Go to hell, George," she said, and stalked from the room.

George, who knew his cousin perhaps better than anyone, simply laughed.

You've made Hannah angry, Mr. Pritchard," George said, walking to the sideboard and inspecting the remaining fare. Grabbing up a sweet bun, he turned to face Allen, who sat like a sullen child.

"She doesn't understand. The gold is there. I know it is. I just need a few more weeks, perhaps a few months. I'm so close," he said passionately.

George walked casually up to Allen, and with the speed of a falcon swooping down for his prey, hauled the man up from his chair and slammed him into the fine oak wainscoting that graced the breakfast room's walls. The sweet bun, still in George's hand, crumbled against Allen's jacket and fell to the floor.

"You listen to me, you fool. If you leave Hannah, I will

personally see to it that you are incapable of finding anything, including the buttons on your pants so you can piss."

George, shooting daggers at Allen, who tried his best to
appear bored by this attack, shook him so hard that his head
banged painfully against the wall and raw fear filled his
eyes. "She has been through hell to get here. God knows
why, but she wants to marry you. I've tried to talk some
sense into her silly head, but she's certain that you will
make her a good husband. And you goddamn better, you
son of a bitch. If you love her at all, you won't leave her
again. Got that, Pritchard?" He shook the man again. "Got
it?"

"All right. I'll stay." But it was said through gritted teeth.

"See that you do," George said, and pushed him again
for good measure. Allen rolled his shoulders and straightened his vest and jacket.

"You're a sorry bastard, you know that Pritchard?"
George said with pure disgust.

Allen looked down at the fine parquet floor, then met
George in the eye. "I know exactly what I am." His words
were filled with honest bitterness.

George found Hannah in his mother's parlor sitting at a
writing desk, a blank piece of stationery before her. She
raised her head when he came in and smiled.

"You didn't beat him, did you?"

"Not as much as I wanted to," he said, then laughed at
her look of horror. "No, Hannah, I did not give your so-
called fiancé the beating he richly deserved."

Hannah tapped the inkless pen against the paper. "He's
truly a good man. Or was. I can't believe he has changed so
much. It's the gold. If I can just get him away from it, we'll
be fine."

George's silence told Hannah he was skeptical. "What of
the captain? Have you seen him since we've been in port?"

Hannah looked down at her hands. "He was here for a
dinner. It was just that once." She could feel her face heat,
her heartbeat quicken at the thought of him, at the thought

of what they had shared. And then that sick feeling washed over her that always came when she remembered that she would not see him again, that he was lost to her forever. The lump in her throat grew so thick, she was not sure she could speak.

"So that's the way of it. You love him still. And yet you plan to marry that . . . that . . ."

Hannah raised her head, her eyes glittering with unshed tears. "George, I am fully aware of what I am doing. My heart is breaking because of what I am doing."

George placed his fists upon the desk and leaned toward his cousin. "Then, why, Hannah. Why put yourself and the captain through this?"

Hannah looked away and bit her lip to stop the sob that threatened. "James will survive this. I will, too." She turned to him, her eyes beseeching him to understand. "But I could not survive a lifetime of it. Don't you understand? This one heartache is horrible enough. I won't suffer it again. I won't!"

George pushed away in anger and frustration. "The captain's gone missing. It's why I've returned so early."

"W-what?"

"According to Mr. Lodge, he's gone on a drunk. Mr. Lodge saw him last five days ago. The cargo's nearly in the *Windfire* hold, the mizzenmast's repairs will be completed within five days. We're scheduled to set sail in one week's time, and our captain has gone missing. Because of you."

Hannah let out a small sound and shook her head. "He'll be there. No matter what, his ship will always come first," she said, trying to make her voice strong.

"That's what we all thought," he said, giving her a look that was slightly accusing. At Hannah's stricken look, he softened. "I'm not blaming you, Hannah. I'll not excuse the man for abandoning his duty. But from the way Timothy told it, he showed up here expecting you to be free to marry him and you presented him with a fiancé. Rather heartless, I'd say."

Hannah closed her eyes and swayed slightly. "It was the cruelest thing I've ever done," she whispered, and ran from the room.

Chapter Nineteen

Thanksgiving Day dawned clear and crisp, reminding George of autumn back home. After two days of rain that left the city's streets no more than rutted stretches of thick mud, the sun's appearance was enough to raise even his flagging spirits as he made his way toward the ship. The *Windfire* was scheduled to sail tomorrow, and her captain was still missing. Timothy Lodge, who had haunted every tavern and brothel in the city, reluctantly gave up his search so that he could assist George in preparing the ship's crew and cargo for their Journey back to New York. They feared that Captain MacRae was either dead or had been forced to crew for another ship, mistaken for a common sailor and taken aboard when he was unconscious or drunk. Crews were so hard to come by, that drunks were often grabbed up and turned into instant crew members. What a surprise that captain would have, they joked uneasily, when he discovered he had kidnapped Captain James MacRae. It would have been amusing had the two men not been so genuinely worried that the captain had met with some ill fate.

As George placed a foot on the gangplank, Lodge appeared on deck, his face solemn. "He's back."

When George went immediately to search the captain out, Lodge put a hand out to stop him. "Leave him be, son."

"I'll not," George bit out angrily. "Someone has to let him know that this ship's been dealt with while he's been off on a drunk. If he wasn't the captain, I'd thrash him to within an inch of his life. He abandoned his ship and his crew. He shirked his duties and abused his office." George tried to go around Lodge, but the older man gripped his arm with surprising strength.

"He's suffered enough," Lodge growled. "Leave off, Wright."

"He is not a child. He is captain of this ship and . . ." Suddenly George found himself slammed against the after house, Lodge's enraged face inches from his own.

"No one knows more than Captain MacRae what he's done. He's never shirked his duty. Never. Not when his brother died, not when he was younger than you and was captaining a ship in one of the most hellish storms my eyes have ever seen. All his life he's been seeing to duty. This time, something got the better of him. This time he was laid low. I won't even pretend to know how a man, who can sail a ship while the brother he loves more than life itself is dying, can be driven to such depths."

"Over a woman," George said, looking to Lodge for an answer. It was clearly baffling that a man such as James MacRae could be nearly destroyed by a woman. Baffling and damned frightening.

The second mate shrugged and released him. "I can't explain it, Mr. Wright. He ain't himself. Hasn't been himself since your damned cousin put her dainty little foot on this deck."

George sighed. "Is he drunk?"

"Nah. Sober as a judge. Well, nearly so. Came aboard 'round two this morning looking like the devil."

George made to move past Lodge again, and this time the old man let him go. He made his way down the companionway, letting his eyes adjust to the dimness, before knocking on his captain's cabin. "It's your first mate, Captain. I've come to discuss our departure."

"Enter."

The voice was strong and sober, and George relaxed as he

walked into the room. The cabin's skylight allowed in enough light so that the cabin was well-lit, even at this early hour. James was at his small desk, his back to George, going over cargo records that George himself had written.

"Fine job, Mr. Wright. Everything is in order. Mr. Lodge tells me the tug will arrive at seven bells." He sat back in his stool that was attached to the floor, turning his body so that he was in profile to George. "This time tomorrow, we'll be heading back home. Got enough crew. Barely. Fine job on that, as well."

George cleared his throat feeling exceedingly uncomfortable. Something in the captain's voice, his manner and bearing, was missing, and it was damned disconcerting. "Mr. Lodge handled the crew, sir. A surprising number are returning with us. Apparently they've had their fill of this place."

"So I saw. Thirty of the forty-five. And ten others. We should be in fine shape." A long bit of silence stretched between them. "Mast looks good."

"Yes, sir."

More silence. James flexed his jaw and moved one hand slightly off the desk, as if he had been about to get up and then decided it would be too much effort. His face was covered with a new beard, his hair was unkempt, and the one eye George could see was stained purple underneath. For a sailing man, his skin looked pale, and there was a new sharpness to his features.

Ah, hell, George thought, here goes nothing. "I'll be attending a Thanksgiving ball with my parents this evening."

James looked down at his hand laying limply on his desk, and curled it slowly into a fist. As George watched that fist, he felt the tiniest niggling of fear.

"I saw Hannah yesterday," he said cautiously, his eyes on that fist which clenched even tighter.

"And how is your dear cousin?" James said, sounding casual, but the tendons in his arms became markedly visible.

"Actually, not well," George said, moving to the bed so

that he could look directly at the captain—and put himself at more of a distance. "You see, tomorrow the man she loves is about to sail away and her heart is breaking."

George watched, his gut twisting, as James's face hardened and his tortured eyes turned to blue ice. "Pritchard is leaving?" he asked, his gaze impaling George.

"Hell, James, she loves you. Surely you know that."

James jerked his head, his entire body. "She told you that?"

"Yes, sir."

James stood abruptly and pounded his fist against the desk so violently, the ledger sitting atop it bounced. "She's a goddamn liar. Because when you love someone, with every breath, every heartbeat . . ." He stopped, swallowing visibly, and George prayed the man would not weep. "If she loved me, Mr. Wright, she would marry me. Me!" He pounded his fist against his chest.

"Hannah does love you, sir. She loves you so much, she's letting you go."

James let out a harsh sound that almost sounded like a laugh but wasn't quite. He turned his back to George and gripped his desk. "Get out of here, Mr. Wright. Now."

George nearly ran to the door. But before he eased out of the captain's cabin, he said, "She'll be at that ball tonight. Just thought you should know."

"One more word and you're fired, Mr. Wright," James yelled to the closing door.

It seemed as if every candle and lamp available in the city had been brought to the Perrymans' house and lit, a bright beacon to those attending the Thanksgiving ball. A long line of carriages sat in drying muck in front of the house, and carpets, laid to protect their guests from the mud, were laid out beside them.

James stood across the street staring at the house, tearing out his heart, one minute taking a step toward the house, the next nearly running back to the *Windfire*. What kind of fool was he, to come to this place, to once again lay his heart out for her? For that is why he was here. Once more he would try to convince her to come with him. He had not even bothered to try to convince himself that was not why he was here. Hell, he was wearing his finest clothes, the uniform of all successful men: black swallowtail jacket, trousers, pristine white shirt, bow tie fixed loosely about his stiff standing collar, and a black satin vest. He clutched his silk top hat in one hand and banged it against his thigh.

A thousand times that day he had changed his mind. But in the end, it was his heart that had won out, that demanded he at least see her, if not talk to her, one more time. He would seek her out and watch her with Pritchard. He would see if she smiled at her fiancé the way she had smiled at him, or if she looked sad, as her cousin said she was. Perhaps that would be enough, a silent good-bye. But he knew better. If he saw her, he would want to speak to her, if only to let her know that . . . what? That he loved her still? That he did not? He supposed it depended on whether she looked sad or happy. Hell, he didn't know what he was going to do.

He angrily stepped forward, stopping immediately when his foot sank two inches into the mud. With a small curse, he pulled his foot out with a sucking sound and searched the street for another's tracks that he could follow. By the time he was across the street, his boots, shined to a brilliant finish, were covered with mud. He tried ineffectually to wipe the mud off, using one of the carpets laid on the road, then gave up with an impatient oath. The ball was in full swing, the reception line long dispersed as he made his way into the home. A servant, eyeing his fine clothes, simply inquired if he should let his master know of his arrival.

"You may tell him Captain James MacRae has arrived, but I will not be here long." His eyes were already scanning the crowd as he stepped farther into the home. The large, brilliantly lit entryway was circular, with a short staircase at the center leading to a landing with two hallways on either side cutting back diagonally. At the center, more steps led upward to the home's small ballroom. James could hear the rumble of male voices as he made his way up the stairs toward a mass of people milling about the French doors that were opened to the room. A small orchestra, surrounded by ferns and other leafy plants so that it looked as if it were sitting in a jungle, was playing but the dancing had yet to begin. Men, some wearing rough clothes, others in formal wear, made up the vast majority of the crowd. Here and there, a feminine splash of bright color would break up the blacks and browns worn by the men. It was almost sad, this attempt to bring refinement to a city so rough and lacking in things refined.

"Captain MacRae. How nice to see you again." Hiding his irritation, James looked down to see the girl who had attended the Wright's dinner party. What was her name? Miss Hill?

"You've forgotten my name," she said, playfully batting him on the arm with a closed fan. She was a pretty girl he thought, and she knew it well. "It's Susie Hall. I thought perhaps you would have departed for New York by now."

"I leave tomorrow morning," he said distractedly, looking over her head. "Have the Wrights arrived?" he asked finally, not caring at all that he was being rude to the girl. She immediately frowned.

"I haven't seen them, but it's such a crush here. Why don't we stroll about and see if we can find them?" she asked, all innocence.

James forced a smile. "Thank you for your kind offer, Miss. . . ." Blast, he'd forgotten her name again.

"Hall." She did not bother to smile.

"Yes. Miss Hall. I'm in a bit of a hurry. If you will excuse me." He hurried from her, not even pausing when she called his name. Where the hell was Hannah? Damn her cousin to hell, they'd better be here. And then he saw her aunt amid a group of older women and hurried to her, brushing rudely past people, shouting apologies over his shoulder. Prudence's eyes flickered up and spied him, and she gracefully withdrew from her friends.

"Captain MacRae. How nice to see you . . ."

"Where is Hannah?" At her raised eyebrows, James apologized. "I am leaving tomorrow morning at half past seven, and it is vital that I speak with Hannah tonight."

Richard Wright came up to them, and the two men exchanged greetings. James gritted his teeth and forced himself to be civil.

"Hannah is not here, Captain," Prudence said. "She was feeling . . . unwell."

"She's all right? She's not ill is she?"

"Hannah is fine. Just didn't feel up to all this hubbub," Richard said, giving his wife a meaningful look. James just wished to hell he knew what the meaning of that look was.

Prudence lifted her chin, a gesture that gave her a regal air. "I pray, Captain, you do not intend to visit Hannah now. It is quite late, and she is alone at our home. We shall not be returning until very late. It would not do at all for you to go to our home at this hour." She raised one eloquent eyebrow.

James opened his mouth and closed it. A hint of a smile formed on his lips. "You can count on me to do the correct thing," he said with a little bow.

Prudence nodded, and James left the couple.

"I say, Prudy. You practically invited that boy to ravish our niece," Richard blustered.

"Ravish, Richard? Hardly. I specifically told the captain that it would be highly improper for him to visit Hannah at this late hour."

"And let him know she was alone. And that we would be quite late in returning home." He watched James disappear down the stairs. "Do you think, my dear, that there will be two Wrights home for supper tomorrow evening, or three?"

"Two, I think."

"By God, I hope you're right." And he kissed his wife's cheek right there in the middle of a crowded ballroom.

*   *   *

Tomorrow. He was leaving tomorrow. Hannah sat upon her window seat and stared at the distant silhouettes of the masts until her eyes burned. It was late, perhaps eleven o'clock. Surely he would be abed by now. She wondered if he was thinking of her the way she was thinking of him. She wondered if he was fighting a terrible urge to see her, as she was fighting, fighting. She called herself a fool to give up on this love. Moments later, she would call herself wise. She was so torn, it felt as if she were ripping in two.

Hannah had planned to attend the Thanksgiving ball. But one look in the mirror earlier that evening, and she knew she couldn't bear to be in a roomful of happy people. Her face was pale and drawn, her eyes red-rimmed. Grief was written on her face so clearly, even her aunt had not argued when she'd told her of her decision to remain at home.

She drew up her knees and lay her forehead down upon them, pressing hard to stop the tears that once again threatened. "I can't bear it. I can't, I can't," she whispered raggedly. Something, a sound or simply a feeling, she was not sure, made her lift her head and look out her window. He was just a shadow, but she knew it was him, standing in the dewy grass beneath her window. Her heart beating rapidly, she pushed open her window.

"James?"

He stepped forward out of the shadows and into the moonlight. His top hat was tucked beneath one arm, his gloves dangled in his hand. "I've come to say good-bye."

"Oh." It was a sound of anguished joy. "I'm so glad, James."

He stood there silently for a moment, then moved toward the house stopping directly beneath her. "Come down and let me in." It was a command.

"No, James. My aunt and uncle are not here. They're at a ball."

"Come down and let me in, or I will come in through your window."

Panic filled Hannah. She knew if she were to let him in,

he would kiss her and she would let him. "No. You can't. Say good-bye from there."

He swore beneath his breath. "I lied. I don't want to say good-bye. I want to kiss you." He sounded almost angry.

"I know. That's why you can't come in."

"Hannah, please," he said wearily. "You're killing me, lass." Never had he sounded more Scottish than at that moment.

Hannah bit her lower lip and disappeared from the window. She paused to light a small lamp by her bedside, and moments later she was letting him in through the front door, a finger over her lips admonishing him to be quiet. "I don't want to wake the servants." She waved him up the stairs and toward her bedroom, fully knowing what she was doing, what she was inviting. At that moment she did not care. Her blood was singing, her heart rejoicing. He was here, and for one night he would be hers. If it was all she could have for the rest of her life, she would take it. Suddenly, the thought of living and dying never having loved him was unendurable.

Hannah wore only her nightdress and a soft wool wrapper. Her feet were bare and noiseless on the stairs as she led him to her room. Grabbing the lapel of his coat, she pulled him inside, pausing to look up and down the hall to make sure no one had seen her furtive activity. She closed the door and turned.

"Hello, James."

He nodded. "Hannah." A broad grin split his face, and she flew into his arms. "Ah, girl, I missed you." He wrapped his arms around her in a crushing embrace, his nose buried into her hair, which was soft and smelled of lilacs. He pulled back, and placing his thumbs beneath her jaw, his hands surrounding her head, he tilted her face up to him. His kiss was soft, tentative, lips brushing lips. He sucked at her full lower lip, gently, and his tongue darted out to taste. At the touch of his tongue, Hannah let out a small sound, startled that it escaped her. If only this didn't feel so good, if only I didn't love him quite so much, she thought, moving her arms up to wrap around his neck.

"Open your mouth, love. Let me taste you," he whispered against her lips. She did. She would do anything he asked of her this night. Anything, anything. He drove his tongue into her mouth, and it seemed to Hannah it was the most erotic thing a man could do. He slanted his mouth over hers, moving back and forth, tongue thrusting against hers, as he moved one hand to the small of her back and pressed himself against her. Her breathing became shallow, her body pliant. She could even feel the startling sensation of liquid between her legs, the place that was hot and tingling.

James pulled back, nipping her lips. "You'll come with me tomorrow. Hannah, say you'll come with me."

Chapter Twenty

Hannah looked at him, his heart so clearly in his eyes, that beloved face, and in that moment of want and need and love, she meant it when she said simply, "Yes."

He crushed her to him. "Oh, God, thank you." His voice broke, and Hannah's heart soared. This was right, so right.

Then he was kissing her again, long and hard, thrusting his tongue as he pressed his full, hard sex against her. His hands were beneath her wrap, hot and strong as they molded her bottom and pressed her even closer so that she gasped from the sensations he was creating. Her hands pulled back his jacket, and it fell to the floor. She was greedy to touch skin, and tried to work the buttons of his shirt, but her hands were crushed against him in their embrace.

James stepped away. "Hannah. I want to make love to you," he said, his breath shaking. He swallowed audibly. "Do you know what that means?"

"I think so."

"We can't be married until we get to New York. I don't want to wait, but we'll not do anything you don't want. Do you understand? We'll wait if that is what you want."

James could not trust himself to touch her, not now, not when he wanted her so much he was close to shaming himself simply by looking at her. Her lips were slightly swollen, her eyes filled with the same passion he felt, her jutting nipples were plainly visible through her thin gown.

He felt himself swell almost painfully as his eyes swept over her.

"I want to love you now, James. If that is all right."

James let out a bit of hysterical laughter, joy and relief bubbling up inside him. He reached up and placed a hand on one breast, and watched as she slowly closed her eyes and took a deep breath. He could feel the nipple against his palm.

"I will try to be gentle. I . . . Hell, Hannah, I've never been with . . ."

"A virgin?"

He let out a small laugh and drew her to him in a gentle embrace. "I will hurt you, and I don't want to."

She lifted her head up, and he nearly drowned in those eyes of hers, dark and dusky and a color he had no name for. "Kiss me, James." And she looked down at her breasts, telling him where she wanted that kiss.

"Jesus God," he muttered, and did as she asked, first through the thin cotton of her gown, and then, with a swift movement, he brought the garment up and over her head. And brought his greedy mouth onto one nipple, sucking deeply. She let out a sound and let her head fall back, so her hair brushed the back of the hand that pressed the small of her back. He moved her to her bed and sat her down and knelt between her legs. He felt her try to close her legs, but he gently pulled them apart, and brought his lips up to kiss one nipple while his hand caressed the other. He moved one hand down her belly, then lower to brush the soft, curling hair between her legs, nearly driven mad by the sounds of pleasure coming from her. But when he moved his hand lower, she tensed.

"James, I . . ." He looked up to see her face flushed with embarrassment and passion.

"What, love?"

"Do you have to . . ." She bit her lip. "It's just that I'm . . . perhaps you shouldn't touch me there." Hannah looked so mortified, James nearly laughed.

"You're wet for me, Hannah." She looked uncertain, and he smiled. James stood and slowly undressed, feeling Hannah's curious gaze on his body as if she were touching him instead of simply looking at him. When he was fully naked, her eyes darted down to his arousal, then shot up to his face and his smiling eyes. He took one of her hands and put it on his member, sucking his breath through a clenched jaw at the feel of her small, warm hand on him.

"That is what you do to me," he gritted out.

"Oh." And then her face, moments before filled with only curiosity, was then filled with comprehension, and she giggled. "Oh," she said again, finally putting the two things together. James was stunned at just how innocent this girl was.

With her hand still around him, she looked up and smiled. "How fascinating," she said. She moved her hand, and James sucked in a harsh breath. She jerked her hand back. "Was that wrong?"

James let out a shaky laugh and pulled her hand away, breathing out as he did. "No. Nothing you do to me is wrong. Now. Lay down for me. Let me love you, Hannah." He fell onto the bed with her, kissing her as they went. He kissed her breasts and moved one hand up and down her body as if soothing her, but in truth, he was simply driving her mad.

Hannah could barely keep still beneath his hands. His very touch was electric against her skin that had suddenly become overly sensitive. She felt the cool blankets beneath her, she felt her hair slipping off one shoulder, she felt his hands, his wonderful hands everywhere. He lay one hand between her legs and pressed, and Hannah lifted her hips against it. All the while, he made love to her breasts, her neck, her mouth. That hand began to explore, making her hips move against it, making her feel things she never imagined. When he pushed one finger into her, she arched her back and cried out, nearly frantic to feel more. And there was more, much more, she learned mo-

ments later when his thumb moved against one particular
spot.

"James, James, what is happening?" She shook her head
back and forth, denying these feelings even as her hips
moved in a rhythm she couldn't have stopped even if she
wanted to. And then, then she was flooded with it, her body
filled with a wondrous sensation, her heart exploding. She
felt him move on the bed, was vaguely aware of one hand
between her legs, the other spanning her hip. She felt something, him, moving between her and then inside slowly,
slowly opening her.

"So damned tight," he said, sounding as if he were in
pain. "Oh, God, Hannah, I'm trying, love. Trying." And then
he was in, past the barrier. A sharp pain and then a dull
throb. Inside. He's inside me. It was stunning. Wonderful.
James's breathing was harsh in her ear.

"I'm going to move, Hannah. This shouldn't take long."
He laughed, but Hannah didn't know why. He was so thick
and big, and he was inside. Hannah smiled against his shoulder. At first he moved slowly, his entire body shaking, his
back slick with sweat. He moved in and out of her, creating
a sensual rhythm, and Hannah wrapped her legs around him,
wanting to get even closer.

"Hannah, I can't. I can't." And she wasn't sure what he
meant, until he began thrusting harder and harder, pounding
into her, and it was thrilling. His entire body grew rigid, and
he let out a hoarse sound of pain and joy, before he collapsed
against her heavily. His breathing still labored, he said, "I
love you. I love you. I love you."

Hannah opened her mouth, then closed it, feeling sick inside. Tell him. Tell him you love him, she shouted to herself.
But she remained silent. He withdrew and gathered her
against him. "So tired," he muttered. "Sleep just a little
while." It was only a matter of minutes before James's
breathing was soft and even. He was asleep. And then, she
was, too, wrapped up in his cocoon, safe and warm.

Hannah awoke with a start, looking around the room fearfully. She relaxed when she looked out the window and realized it was still night. The bedside lamp had gone out. Perhaps that was what had awakened her. And then she heard the sounds of someone in the yard and was again filled with panic.

"James," she whispered harshly. "Wake up." He mumbled something and drew her down to him. "James." Hannah pushed him away, then grabbed his shoulders and shook. "My aunt and uncle are home. You have to go. Now."

"Aunt and uncle," he said sleepily, then shot up straight in the bed. "Blast it, I didn't mean to sleep for so long." He hurried from the bed and began a mad search for his clothing. "Light the lamp," he whispered.

"I can't. They'll see the light and then wonder why I'm still up and then they'll see me and they'll know."

She heard him stifle a laugh. "It's not written on your forehead, love."

"Oh, just hurry up and find your damned clothes." Her head whipped toward her door when she heard their voices coming up the stairs. He tsked, tsked over her foul language, and Hannah gave him a scowl she knew he couldn't see. James was tugging on his pants. He'd never be dressed by the time they got here. What if her aunt came in to check on her? She had been worried about her. She just might want to see how she was. Hannah leapt from the bed, grabbed James's hand, and tugged him toward her window.

"Go."

"But I'm not dressed." He was laughing at her. She could see his eyes crinkling in the moonlight.

"Blast it, MacRae, get the hell out of my room. They may come in here. Go! I'll throw your things down to you."

He got one bare-footed leg through the window before tugging her to him and kissing her soundly. "We leave at seven bells. Be there by six. That should give you enough time to pack a few things and tell your aunt and uncle good-bye." He kissed her again. "I love you, girl." He disappeared over the side, and Hannah heard a small *womp* as he landed. Frantically, she gathered up the rest of his things and threw them out to him. Some he caught, others lay scattered on the lawn. She'd just found his last shoe when she heard her aunt whisper, "Should we check on her?"

Her heart in her throat, she waved good-bye, silently closed the window, and ran to her bed. To her vast relief, her aunt and uncle apparently decided not to check on her. It was several moments before the mad beating of her heart subsided to a level that wasn't painful. She gingerly got out of bed and looked out her window to see if he'd gone. The yard was empty. Letting out a heavy breath, she began to mentally think of what she should bring with her. Walking over to her dresser, she lit the lamp, and was startled by the girl she saw reflected in the mirror. She was wild-eyed and wild-haired. Her lips were puffy, her cheeks flushed. Hannah smiled, her stomach fluttering with happy nervousness.

Opening her dresser, she quickly selected the items she could not part with and lay them on her bed, ready to be packed into her bag. Her hand fell upon the scrimshaw she'd hidden with her undergarments, and she stopped dead. Picking it up, Hannah gazed at that carving of the clipper ship sailing in rough seas, its sails billowing. James's most cherished item, given to her. She placed it softly on the smooth wood of her dresser, her fingers lingering on its cool surface. Hannah's gaze touched the pile of clothes she had hastily deposited on her bed, then slowly moved back to the carving, her lips turning up slightly in something that might have been a smile, but was not.

"Tug's ready to go, sir," Timothy Lodge said, pretending he didn't know what was happening, pretending he didn't see that look of dawning comprehension on his captain's face.

"Yes, Mr. Lodge. Just a few more moments, please."

James's gaze wandered the wharf, willing his eyes to see her slight form hurrying toward him. He could almost see her, wearing her men's clothes, one hand clamped on that straw hat, heaving a large bundle on her back. He could almost picture her expression, harried and excited, as if he were to blame for this hasty departure. James went through a mental list of what she needed to do to make it to the ship on time. But no matter the list, he couldn't fathom it taking so long to get down to the ship. She would pack her things. He gave that task perhaps an hour. She must say good-bye to her aunt and uncle. Another generous hour. She should be here. Even if it had taken her twice that long, she should be here.

Unless she was not coming.

James pushed that thought away, closing his eyes and recalling her warm body curled up next to his, the way she trailed her finger down his body, the way she'd nuzzled against his neck. Something had delayed her. She was coming. He refused to believe that after what they had shared, after he again and again told her how he loved her, that she would remain. It was not possible. His hands gripped the rail almost painfully as he felt the sun beating down upon his head. Hannah should have stepped up the *Windfire* gangplank long before the sun was high enough to beat down. He knew that if he did not leave soon, he would be forced to stay another day, and that was something he would not do.

The crew hung about, talking among themselves, keeping their distance. George Wright and Timothy Lodge stood by the ship's stern talking with the tugboat captain. The thought that they might be discussing the exact reason for the delay was humiliating. Though he had not explained why he refused to leave the wharf, he suspected that at least Mr. Lodge and George knew. Jilted. He was being jilted. By God, he couldn't believe she would do it. His breathing became shallow, his heart an irritating pounding in his chest, every beat a taunting reminder that it was growing later and later.

She wasn't coming.

His hands, still bronzed from the sea, gripped the rail even tighter. To keep him there, to keep him from running down that plank and demanding why. Why was she doing this?

"Mr. Lodge." His voice snapped like a sail in a stiff breeze. "Bring up the plank."

That's when he saw a small boy hurtling himself down the dock toward the *Windfire*.

"Stop," he shouted to the men who were set to heave the gangplank aboard. His heart soared with hope. She'd sent this boy to tell him to wait. He knew it! He knew she would come. The boy, his cheeks flushed from exertion, pounded up the gangplank, gasping for breath.

"You Captain MacRae?" he asked, full of the importance of his task.

"I am," James said, a smile tugging on his lips.

The boy thrust out his hand. "This be for you. The lady that give it to me says to say"—and he screwed up his freckled face in concentration— "She says to say: Tell the captain I'm sorry." Then the boy smiled and wheeled about, pounding down the gangplank with a small wave.

James's heart felt like stone. No, he thought, like ice, cold and sharp, like the ache you get when you swallow too much snow at once. He didn't have to open the delicate handkerchief to know what he held, but he did anyway. He untied the blue ribbon that held it closed with deft fingers and calmly pulled the cloth away to reveal the carving. The ribbon and handkerchief dropped from his hand, the brisk breeze blowing the material about the deck for a moment, before they fell over the side to drift in the murky water.

He clenched his hand around the bone until his hand shook with it, until the pain he was causing himself finally, finally registered in a mind gone numb.

"Pull up the plank," he said in a voice that sounded hard and dead. He shoved the carving into his pocket, his eyes going to the seamen who hesitated in their task. "I said pull up the goddamned plank." The men hurried to do their task.

"We're running late, men," James shouted. "I expect to make up for our delay. Look sharp." Lines were thrown from the wharf, and the tug's steam engine belched in readiness. He smiled at the men who jumped to do his bidding, but it was a smile that did not touch his eyes. They were hard and cold, and the men closest to him, who saw something terrible and fierce in his eyes, were afraid.

Hannah sat upon her bed, eyes dry, until the sun reached its zenith. She wanted to be numb, she didn't want to think. She didn't want to feel. But she could not shut off her thoughts, nor ignore the gnawing pain that filled her with agony. I can still feel him there, she thought, aware of the slight aching between her legs. How long will I feel him? How long?

Her aunt knocked, then let herself in, her eyes filled with concern as if she knew what Hannah was going through. But no one could know, she thought. Except James. She had hurt him. She had broken his heart as surely as she had broken her own. And that, more than anything, was unforgivable. She would never forgive herself, and so she knew in her heart that neither would he forgive her. Not that she would ever have the chance to ask him to.

"I have a note," Prudence said, pulling the note from a deep pocket in her skirt. At Hannah's look of hope, she quickly said, "I believe it's from Allen."

Allen. Her fiancé. Oh, yes, the man she was supposed to marry. Hannah almost laughed aloud, but instead held out a steady hand to accept the bit of paper her aunt held out to her. It was hastily sealed with a hardened blob of wax, which Hannah snapped listlessly.

My dearest,

   *I pray that you forgive me, but I have returned to my
claim. I will write when I can.*

   Yours, Allen

Hannah stared at the note with disbelief, then let out an
hysterical bit of laughter. And then another, holding the note
limply in a hand that was draped, palm up, upon her lap. The
other hand went to her mouth, her fingers held loosely over
her lips.

   "He's gone," she said finally, looking up to her aunt. "Oh,
Aunt, he's gone." And then she was crying. Not over Allen,
but over James, and somehow, somehow, her aunt knew for
whom she cried.

   "Oh, Hannah. You did love him. I thought that you might."

   "More than anything," she sobbed. "More than life." Hannah was grateful her aunt did not push her for an explanation. She simply wanted to be held, to cry against a shoulder,
and her usually stiff and proper aunt became soft and yield-
ing and let her cry her heart out. When the flood of tears had
subsided, her aunt pulled back and tipped Hannah's chin up
with her hand.

   "There is a hill from which you can see for miles. A beautiful view. It's where people gather to watch for ships coming in.
Or leaving."

   Fresh tears coursed down her face at her aunt's understanding. "Tell me where."

   Hannah left her horse tethered to some brush and climbed
the hill her aunt had described. The grass was still brown
from summer, but was turning a brilliant green in places,
creating a splotchy brown and green quilt. Hannah was
grateful the well-worn path was unoccupied as she made her
way up the hill, suddenly afraid that she had waited too long.
But even the *Windfire* could not have made its way out of
the crowded harbor and out of sight so quickly. As she

reached the crest of the hill, her eyes met the brilliant blue of the Pacific Ocean and then the glorious sight of the *Windfire* under full sail. She knew it was his ship, for nothing could be as beautiful as the *Windfire* running with the wind, her bow arching gracefully. For a wild moment Hannah thought to run down the hill to the ocean and leap in and swim, swim to the ship. But in truth, the *Windfire* was miles from shore. She couldn't even make out individual forms on the deck. Couldn't even hope to see him one last time.

"Oh, God, what have I done?' she whispered brokenly, her heart filled at that moment with a devastating yearning to be on that ship. Then she took a deep breath. It is done, she thought, and in the end I'll be glad. Oh, please let me be glad.

As she stood on that hill, drinking in the sight of the *Windfire*, knowing that she looked at James as she did, she could almost hear her mother whisper in her ear: Smile, darling. Don't let him see your tears.

Prudence Wright let her niece mope around the house exactly three days before she confronted her. She wanted to be sure that the girl was truly heartbroken before approaching her with her scheme. Hannah had not eaten, had not slept but for small naps in the early morning hours. Prudence knew, for she could hear her niece crying and pacing and generally being the most miserable person she'd ever seen. The poor girl had made a dreadful mistake and was torturing herself over it. But it was not something that was without remedy.

She wished Hannah's errant fiancé was still about so that she could throttle the self-centered cad. Imagine abandoning the woman you plan to marry not once, but twice. And after the poor girl had traveled thousands of miles to come to him. The nerve of the man! It was nearly enough to force her to violence. Perhaps the devastation of letting James go would have been eased by his presence. Allen Pritchard, for all his faults, seemed to make Hannah happy when he was about. At least the girl had smiled. They'd been easy with one another, like two old friends. Friends, however, did not leave when they were needed the most.

Though Prudence was more than curious to find out why her niece had made the decision she had, she knew Hannah would tell her in her own time. Right now she needed to heal or hit bottom, and Prudence was quite sure the girl had sunk dangerously low. She opened her door without knocking and found her niece precisely where she knew she would be— sitting in her window seat and gazing out to the bay. Though it was nearly noon, Hannah still wore her white nightdress, her bare feet tucked beneath her. Hannah's eyes, for once, were dry. The girl turned to look at her aunt, gave her a weak smile, then turned back to the window.

"I think I shall die," Hannah said matter-of-factly.

Prudence tilted her head. "Do you think so?"

"Oh, yes. Slowly. Wither away." Like *she* did.

"Few people die of a broken heart, Hannah."

Hannah remained silent, her gaze never wavering from the window.

"You'll never forget him. But you won't die of it. Even if you wish you would."

Hannah bit her lip, and Prudence knew she was trying to hold back more tears. The poor girl's eyes were chronically red-rimmed and swollen, and a neat pile of well-used handkerchiefs lay at her bedside. Prudence smiled sadly at that pile of lace-trimmed cloth, proof of the heartbreak she knew Hannah was suffering.

"I don't *want* to die," she said. Then she straightened her back and looked very, very young as she turned again to face her aunt. "It just feels like I am. That's how I know I've done the right thing." Hannah's fist curled against her stomach.

Prudence sat on the bed, and Hannah turned to sit on the window seat so that her feet dangled above the carpet. Her heels made little thump-*thumps* against the whitewashed wainscoting.

"Perhaps you should explain why it is good to feel so badly."

"Because I never want to feel this way again. And if I married him, I would feel this way every time he left. Again and again and again until I couldn't bear it, until I died from it. Don't you see, Aunt Prudence? I love him too much to ask him to leave the sea, and too much to be forever saying good-bye."

Prudence lowered her eyes to her lap, suddenly knowing with shocking clarity what Hannah was saying. "Like your mother."

Hannah's face became animated, believing her aunt understood. "Yes, just like her. She loved my father too much. Like I love James. And it killed her. I know it did, I saw her die, I heard her calling for him over and over, crying and crying until I had to run away so that I couldn't hear her anymore. I'm just like her, Aunt. I couldn't bear it."

To Hannah's surprise, the understanding look left her aunt's face.

"Oh, what poppycock," she said, waving a hand at her. "You, my dear, are nothing like your mother. Don't forget, I knew her when she was your age." Prudence stood, her face once again rigid, but her eyes were still warm as she made her way over to Hannah and sat beside her.

"Your mother was a beautiful girl, like you. That is true. But that is where the similarity ends. My goodness, Hannah, do you think your mother would have signed on as navigator of a ship, sailed thousands of miles to a place she'd never been to find a man she wasn't sure was even there? Do you think your mother could have stood up to a man like Captain MacRae? I loved Mary dearly, like a sister, but I saw what she did to your father. She clung to him, suffocating him so much I think he actually looked forward to leaving."

"That's not true," Hannah said, hating what her aunt was saying. Hating it because she knew in some deep part of her that what her aunt was saying was true.

Prudence placed a gentle hand on Hannah's clenched fist. "It is true, dear. Oh, your father loved your mother. I'm not saying that he did not love her. But your mother . . . It was more than love, Hannah. It was a need, an obsession. A weakness."

Hannah looked down at the hand that clung to her aunt's. "But that's the way I feel about James," she said softly.

Prudence smiled. "I know you love him, but the fact that you had the strength to let him go says to me that you are strong enough to bring him back."

Hannah hated the fierce racing of her heart and shook her head against the surge of hope her aunt had planted. Prudence stood and placed a hand on each upper arm, squeezing Hannah almost painfully. Hannah looked up at her aunt with astonishment.

"Don't let him go, Hannah. If you do, you will regret it for the rest of your life. Love, the kind you feel for James, is so very rare. And he loves you with all his heart. That man wears his heart on his sleeve, and it's one of the biggest hearts I've ever seen. Don't throw that away."

A new rush of tears flooded Hannah's eyes. "But I already have. I can't . . ."

Prudence gave Hannah a little shake. "You can, Hannah. You can beat him back to New York if you travel over the isthmus. You can meet him at the pier."

That surge of hope which had been so unwelcome just moments before, became a terrifying thing. It pulled her, it begged her, to try. Her aunt's words created an image in her mind, of her standing on that pier, of seeing James. He would be shocked, perhaps still angry, but he would also be glad to see her, to know she had hurried back to him. Surely he would still love her, surely he would forgive her. He must, he must.

"But what if . . ."

Her aunt wouldn't let her finish. "Blast it, Hannah, just go!"

Chapter Twenty-one

The *California* bobbed at anchor in Panama Bay, its passengers bored and irritable under a canopy that protected them from the constant drizzle. The air was warm and heavy, so thick with moisture, Hannah could almost imagine her lungs filling with water. She stood on the top deck with the rest of the first- and second-class passengers and watched as dozens of natives, their dark skin shining from the rain, paddled their canoes toward them. By all accounts—and Hannah had gotten many accounts about traveling the cross-land route—the rainy season should have been long over. The continued rain meant an unpleasant trip on a journey that had already been exceedingly unpleasant. At least for Hannah.

She tried to be fascinated by the city she could see before her, its ancient stone buildings, the busy port, but all she wanted was off this blasted ship once and for all. She had been stuck in San Francisco for three weeks before a steamship became available. The Pacific Mail shipping company sailed out of San Francisco twice monthly, and the *Panama* had been booked solid but for steerage. Hannah, desperate to leave as soon as possible, was forbidden by her uncle from traveling in steerage, where unsanitary conditions had been known to spread disease. As a single woman, it had been unthinkable to travel in steerage, which was almost exclusively male, and Hannah reluctantly agreed to wait for the next departure.

Now Hannah was not certain if it would have been better to sail on the *Panama* and take her chances on traveling in steerage. The *California* had been beset with mechanical problems from the start. Though it had two masts and could travel under sail power, the ship was ridiculously slow without its steam engines working to spin the side-wheel. The ship limped first into San Diego for repairs, then San Blas, each delay adding several days to what should have been a twenty-one-day trip. She mentally counted the days since James had departed—fifty-nine days. The *Windfire* could be already around Cape Horn and heading up the South America coast toward New York. This cross-land trip to New York, which could be done in as little as forty days under optimum conditions, had already taken thirty days, and she was just now reaching Panama City. It was exasperating.

The only pleasant part of the trip was her room and meals, which she begrudgingly admitted were far superior to that served on the *Windfire*. The *California* was built for the comfort of its passengers, whereas the *Windfire* had been built for speed and cargo. Hannah's stateroom had two bunks, a mirror, toilet stand, and washbowl. She was served a full bottle of fresh water each morning shortly after breakfast, one of the privileges of first-class travel. The floors were carpeted, the walls whitewashed with teak trim, the fixtures shining brass and etched glass. If it wasn't for the incessant bobbing and lurching of the vessel, not to mention the loud throb of the engines and the *ker-chunking* of the side-wheel, it could have been pleasant.

Her cabin mate was a young woman, whose husband slept in second class, on the wheel side of the ship. When she wasn't bemoaning the fact that she missed her husband, who was just across the dining hall and through one door, Anne Stiles was rather pleasant company.

Now she stood clutching her young husband's arms, looking into his eyes dreamily. They were newlyweds and were going to his home in Boston. She had left her family behind. Hannah looked at the couple and was so filled with envy, she was ashamed. She hadn't seen James in nearly two months and had no idea of her reception. How she wished she was standing next to him on the *Windfire*, clutching his arm and looking up at his face with all the love she felt shining in her eyes. She vowed she would never, ever get angry at James if he would forgive her the insanity that kept her from his ship that fateful day.

"Won't be long now, Hannah." Allen came up beside her to watch the bungos pull up to the boat. Hannah gave him a weak smile. Allen, who had come back to her too late. Allen, who was going home to face his mother and his bankruptcy.

He had gone back to his dig to find that his friends had abandoned the mine. For two weeks he tried to dig himself, finally realizing the futility of his efforts. It had been a hard, humiliating lesson. He returned to San Francisco, to Hannah, only to learn he had finally lost her. He accepted his loss with grace, and insisted that he accompany Hannah on her long journey home. And Hannah, who'd needed a friend, accepted. Only once had Allen broached the subject of his feelings for her. He'd had too much wine in the dining hall one evening, and came sobbing and banging on Hannah's stateroom.

She'd opened the door a crack. "Allen, do be quiet. You'll awaken the entire ship."

"But I love you, Hannah," he'd slurred out, then smiled sloppily. Allen rarely drank, but when he did, the results were almost always disastrous.

"I love you, too. Now, off to bed you go."

"You love me?" He swayed, stepping backward to catch his balance. "Will you be marrying me, then, instead of that fiancée-stealing bastard?"

"James did not steal me. You gave me away."

He'd looked wounded and shocked. "I dint!" A shout, and Hannah winced. "He stole you right from under my nose." He tried to point to his nose, but instead his finger ended up pushed against one cheek. "Nose." He smiled finding the correct facial part.

"Allen, go to bed. We'll discuss this in the morning."

"Promise."

"Yes. Now, go."

But they hadn't discussed it. Allen, his head aching, had apologized, and Hannah had accepted. She was glad Allen was with her, despite their history. Many of the men on board were a rough sort, though they mostly behaved themselves on board ship. Some were returning home as failures, some with huge caches of gold locked in the ship's safe. They were young and hardened and wise to the world. Hannah felt a kinship with these men, for she, too, felt much wiser than when she first stepped foot aboard the *Windfire*.

Anne Stiles was suddenly in front of her, wearing a pretty white dress with wilting blue bows down the skirt. Hannah had worn her pants and shirt, something that a veteran of the isthmus recommended to her.

"I wanted to say good-bye to you both, for I may not see you again once we are on land." Anne hugged Hannah and Allen. "Please write, Hannah. I consider you one of my dearest friends." Hannah watched the girl turn to go, surprised and flattered that the young woman considered her a friend, but knew that once separated, they would soon forget one another. A ship had a way of turning two strangers into fast friends in a matter of days, she thought, and the land had a way of erasing friendship. That thought left Hannah stricken. Is that what happened to James and her? Would they be strangers when they finally saw each other again? Would he be embarrassed to find her there at the dock waiting for him like some besotted child when he had gone on with his life?

Hannah pushed those doubts away as another bungo pulled up to the ship. While most passengers required two bungos, one for them and one for their luggage, neither Hannah nor Allen had much with them and only had to hire one canoe. They were silent on the bungo, their eyes on Panama, which Hannah found surprisingly large and developed.

The drizzle stopped, and the sun shone weakly from a milky sky when they reached the pier. She'd expected something like San Francisco, but Panama was an ancient city, teaming and crowded and very American. It seemed, as their boat pulled up to the pier, that the whole of Panama was enmassing at the pier to greet the passengers from the *California*. There were men trying to be hired to carry baggage on their backs, on mules, in handcarts. Men were trying to lure passengers into hotels, bars, and gambling halls. Women, with huge bundles on their heads, walked gracefully among the traffic. It was noisy and hot and humid, and Hannah couldn't wait until they were settled for the night in the American Hotel, which one passenger had recommended.

Allen and Hannah looked at each other and smiled, sharing their wonder and dismay at the city and its inhabitants. Allen hired a boy to haul their luggage with a handcart, refusing to pay him until they reached their destination. They had been forewarned not to give anyone any money—or at least only half—before a task was completed. Hannah, who was extremely uneasy about crossing the tropical land, had sought the counsel of those who had passed overland on their way to San Francisco. She heard horror tales of men who promised to deliver luggage, only to realize their baggage was stolen, or bungo owners who took full fare then disappeared without delivering their passengers to their destination. Allen had laughed at her cautiousness, but Hannah refused to be taken advantage of.

As they made their way down a paved street toward the hotel, Hannah noticed the city had all the conveniences of an American city, with its barbers, butchers, restaurants, bakeries, fish markets, and hotels. Many people were as finely dressed as one would find during New York in July, though the natives were garbed in what Hannah considered much more practical clothing. Steam rose from the street as the sun burned away the remaining puddles, and Hannah could feel her clothes sticking uncomfortably to her skin. A large group of people had gathered about a man who appeared to be auctioning off goods, and they stopped to see what all the interest was about.

"Needed money to get to San Francisco," one man said, seeing their curiosity.

Allen shook his head. All about them were fresh, excited faces, and he wanted to shout at them, to tell them they were too late. They all had that innocent, eager look he knew he'd had when he'd stepped foot in California. His clothes had been clean and pressed, his face scrubbed and shaved, his eyes bright. He paused in the street to listen to the auction, scanning the crowd.

"You can tell the new ones from the old," he said. He could see Hannah looking about the crowd to see if she could as well.

"You're right. The ones traveling to California are rude, the ones coming from it are . . ."

"Hardened."

She smiled up at him, and his heart quickened before he could stop himself. "I was going to say they seem more world-weary. Not hard. You certainly aren't hard, Allen. If anything, you are nicer. I haven't heard you say one cutting remark about anyone's attire or note the filth on some of these men."

He gave a short, bitter laugh. "There were times, dear Hannah, when I would have made these men look downright pristine." It had been difficult, but Allen had come to grips with his failure—or rather, his failures. He fully blamed himself for losing Hannah, and now regretted that loss with a deep and growing pain. He had been such a stupid fool to allow himself to be lured by dreams of finding gold. With the distance of time, it was difficult to believe that the man at that claim had existed, with his dirty beard and insane obsession. He had lost himself, his self-respect, and Hannah. He mourned all three equally and with greater clarity the farther he traveled from California.

They finished their walk to the hotel, where the boy with their baggage waited patiently for them to arrive.

"How much?"

"One dollar."

Allen grimaced, but handed over the dollar. From what he'd heard, everything cost money crossing the isthmus, and if a person were not careful, they would not have enough cash to finish the journey. His eyes went back to the street, where the auctioneer continued to hawk some poor soul's worldly goods before walking into the hotel beside Hannah. The hotel lobby was large and well-appointed, with rich-looking sofas and Grecian columns extending three stories. A fountain, water gushing from a nymph's water pitcher, was surrounded by tropical plants. Colorful parrots flew about the large lobby, ignored by most in the room. It was ungodly hot, and he couldn't fathom why so many of the women he saw insisted on wearing their heavily petticoated dresses. Hannah, smart, modern girl, didn't care what anyone thought.

"Surely no one would expect me to favor tripping over my skirts and swooning from the heat over being safe and comfortable in my pants," she had said when she made her appearance on ship wearing her men's garb.

But from the censorious looks several of the women in the lobby were giving Hannah, it seemed as if they would rather have her swooning and tripping. He overheard one woman say loudly enough for the entire lobby to hear: "I'd rather die than to shame all of womanhood by exposing myself to the natives." He watched as Hannah stiffened, then plastered a smile on her face, as her eyes sought out the woman who made the complaint.

"You may get your wish in this heat, madam," she said coolly, then turned back and placed her hand on Allen's arm. He escorted her to the front desk as if she wore the most exquisite ball gown.

* * *

Hannah swatted a mosquito. "I thought mosquitoes weren't supposed to be a problem after December," she grumbled, and began scratching her arm. Their mule driver, a silent man in his twenties, mumbled something in Spanish when Hannah knew darn well the man spoke English as well as she did. She'd stopped asking the man questions about the unusual birds and plants two days ago when it became clear he planned to ignore the couple trailing behind him. It cost them forty-eight dollars for the three mules they needed to travel on before reaching the Chagres River, where they would ride the rest of the way aboard a small steamship. Taking the advice given them, they hired a man from a well-established transport company, Zachrissen, Nelson and Company, but insisted, after some debate, on paying the man only half the fee until they reached the small city of Gorgona. The man at the transport company had cautioned them that, because the wet season had lasted longer than usual, they might have to take bungos from Cruces to Gorgona. If the river had decreased enough, they would take the mules all the way into Gorgona, where they would board the *William H. Aspenwall* and travel on it all the way to the Atlantic Ocean. Barring delays, they could reach the mouth of the Chagres in one week, where they would board the first steamship available.

Hannah smiled, despite having her backside abused by the jarring gait of her mule. If all went well, they could be in New York by January thirtieth—a date that almost guaranteed they would be home long before the *Windfire* was pulled to its pier on the East River. At odd times Hannah would feel anxiety wash over her, for another significant delay could mean James would almost certainly reach New York first. She knew it was unlikely the *Windfire* would make consecutive trips in less than one hundred days—especially with a less experienced and smaller crew.

The mules' hooves slopped and sucked in the still-moist ground as Hannah slapped at another mosquito. She thought she saw the young man smile. Behind her, Allen was having his own difficulties, for he was taller than most and kept getting hit in the head with branches and leaves. The path they rode on was narrow, the jungle threatening to overtake the well-beaten strip man had carved out. As fascinated as Hannah was by the foliage and the sounds of the jungle, she wanted only to see the sea stretching out before her, to smell the salt air, to hear the crash of waves on a shoreline. This slow-plodding progress was maddening, when every other minute she was picturing the *Windfire* going eighteen knots in a gale.

That evening, they stayed in a tiny village of Obispo, just a half a day away from Gorgona. Allen and Hannah shared a hut with another group of travelers who were on their way to San Francisco. Hannah was relieved to see two other women among their group. For the first three nights staying at other villages, Hannah had been the only female traveler, and she realized again how grateful she was to have Allen with her. They slept in hammocks, which Allen favored, but she loathed. She was in constant fear that she would turn over in the night and end up with her face mashed into the dirty floor. Since they had been warned to eat as little food in these villages as possible, Hannah and Allen existed on a diet of dried beef and sea biscuits, though Hannah couldn't help but think the pleasant smells emanating from Panamanian kitchens would have been far more appetizing.

Hannah awoke feeling groggy and ill, something she attributed to her poor night's sleep in her hammock. But by the time they reached Gorgona in mid-afternoon, it was clear Hannah was more than simply tired. She sat upon her mule, feeling oddly separated from herself, from the mule, as if she were floating above everything. She tried to focus on Allen, who was helping take their baggage off the pack mule, but found she was unable to focus on anything other than trying to stay atop of her patient mule. Allen walked over and looked up at her with a bemused expression.

"For four days you've been getting on and off that mule by yourself, and now you expect me to play the gallant gentleman and assist you simply because we've found some civilization?" he asked, a teasing grin on his face.

Hannah turned toward Allen. He was saying something. Something important? No, he was smiling.

"Allen. I feel rather odd." And she slipped from the mule in a boneless heap into Allen's arms.

Allen, stunned to find Hannah's limp body in his arms, looked about frantically for help. "Hotel?" he asked their guide, who backed up a step from the couple. Allen knew cholera was greatly feared by all in the isthmus, but he was fairly certain it was not what afflicted Hannah.

"It's not cholera," he said with conviction, though he was not certain of that fact. "Tell me where the closest hotel is." The man pointed to a small, two-story building with a gold-leaf sign tacked to the front proclaiming it to be the Tropical Paradise Hotel. He strode across the paved street and into the lobby, ignoring the startled looks from the guests and workers.

"I need a room," he said. "My . . . wife is ill. I'll need a doctor, as well."

Within minutes Allen was laying Hannah down on one of the two small beds in the clean but simple room. Opening a window to allow some of the oppressive air into the sti-flingly hot room, he looked down onto the street to see if he could pick out a doctor among those walking toward the hotel.

"Allen?"

He rushed to her side. "Yes, darling."

"I think I'm sick." Her skin was bathed in sweat, her face flushed from more than the day's heat.

He smiled despite the fear gnawing at his gut. "I've sent for a doctor. I believe you have a fever of some sort." Please God, he thought, don't let it be yellow fever. Among the tales of woe many of the passengers related, were stories of how people had died of the mysterious disease while travel-ing across the isthmus. More recovered than succumbed to the disease, he'd been told, but Allen could not take comfort in that knowledge. But in minutes his fears were realized.

The doctor was an American, deeply tanned with curly steel-gray hair that fringed his bald pate. His nose was large and red and bulbous, and he reeked of alcohol so strongly, it was as if the stuff were seeping from his pores. Hannah lay still as the doctor felt her head, then asked her a series of questions, all of which she answered with a nod of her head.

"Yellow fever. Nothing I can do. Just keep her comfortable." And he walked from the room.

Allen stood still for one moment, then hurried after the old boozer, grabbing his wrinkled cotton shirt roughly. "What do you mean there is nothing you can do. Surely there is something."

The old man must have seen something in Allen's eyes, for he gentled his voice. "I'm speaking truthfully to you, young man. There is nothing I can do except make her comfortable. She'll begin vomiting. Try to get her to drink. Call me again if her gums begin to bleed or her skin takes a yellow cast."

"You'll help her then?" he asked, in so hopeful a voice the doctor grimaced.

"Son, if that happens, it means she's worsening and there still will be nothing I can do for her. I will know, however, when to send for a priest." With that, the doctor turned to go, and Allen let him.

Chapter Twenty-two

For three days, Hannah suffered from blinding headaches, chills, and an unrelenting fever. She was never too sick to complain that they were wasting time because she was too sick to travel, and Allen was heartened. On the fourth day, it seemed as if her fever had gone altogether, and Hannah complained only of sore muscles from the body-racking vomiting.

"By tomorrow, Allen, we'll be able to leave tomorrow." Her voice sounded raw, and her words came out just above a whisper.

"Absolutely not, Hannah. We are not leaving until the doctor says you are ready to travel."

Hannah waved her hand weakly. "That doctor knows nothing. We've got to go, Allen. Tomorrow." She held on to his hand and squeezed his arm. "Please. Even if you have to carry me. Please let us leave tomorrow."

"Damn it, Hannah."

She smiled at him. "Thank you, Allen." And then she closed her eyes and slept. Two hours later she was again racked with a fever, her body shaking convulsively. "C-cold," she managed, and Allen's heart wept. It was hot as blazes in the room. There was no way she could feel cold, but he covered her with more blankets anyway. Minutes later, her face bathed in sweat, she was throwing off the covers, thrashing about nearly out of her mind with fever. She moved her head to the side, and when she lifted it, she left a small amount of blood on the pillow.

"Oh, Jesus have mercy," Allen said through a raw throat, looking at that blood, his stomach churning in terror. Hannah bled through her nose, and a quick and horrifying check of her gums showed they, too, were bleeding.

"Hannah, I've got to go get the doctor. I'll be right back, okay, love?"

"James? I tried, James. I'm so sorry."

"It's all right, Hannah. You've made it in plenty of time."

"So sorry. So sorry." She thrashed again, blood streaming from her nose.

The doctor, his eyes red and bleary, let out a heavy sigh. "Just a matter of time."

"What the hell does that mean?"

"She'll either live or not. If I were a betting man, I'd say you'd better have a priest standing by."

Allen looked helplessly over at Hannah, who suffered even though she was nearly out of her mind with fever. Rage filled him—against himself, against Panama, against whatever had attacked Hannah's body, and against this old doctor who stood swaying on his feet and telling him Hannah would likely die. He grabbed his collar, sweaty and dirty from an unwashed neck, and shook him. "There's got to be something you can do, you old drunk. Save her. Do something."

The doctor's eyes widened in fear, and Allen released him with a disgusted push.

"Get the hell out of here." He turned back toward Hannah, filled with frustration and a grief that touched his soul.

"Even sober, I couldn't save her," the doctor said softly from the door before he closed it behind him. Allen bowed his head and cried.

Two hours later he walked to the door to answer a soft knock, so weary he wasn't certain how he'd moved his body even that far.

"I am Father Guerres. Doc Randall told me there was a woman who needed the Lord's comfort."

"She's not going to die, Father. Though I thank you for your time."

The priest looked around Allen to the girl in the bed. She looked as if he were already too late. "To say a prayer for her will not mean she is going to die, Mr. . . . "

"Pritchard."

"Mr. Pritchard. But should the Lord choose to take her, her soul will be prepared."

"Hannah is not Catholic, Father."

"It matters not to the Lord."

Allen looked at Hannah, so quiet, so very still. Her breathing was shallow, her pulse barely perceptible. Allen had tried his best to clean her, but a bit of dried blood was still caked around her mouth. She was going to die, and there was nothing he could do about it.

"Say your prayers, Father."

The priest moved over to Hannah, speaking softly in Latin as he made the sign of the cross over her forehead. He prayed for just a few minutes before straightening, his face sad. "It is in God's hands." And then Allen was alone again.

"Allen."

He heard Hannah whisper to him in his dream, and he smiled. The priest had come to issue last rites two days ago, and Hannah had clung tenuously to life. She hadn't moved, she hadn't uttered a sound—not even one of pain, and Allen accepted that he was on a death watch. He'd held her hand, thinking that somehow she might know that he held it, that when she finally did die, she might realize she had not died alone.

When he was too weary to sit and hold her, he would sit in a chair and doze for a few hours, always waking with the gut-wrenching fear that when he checked her, she would be dead. Two times he had awakened and looked over at her, certain she breathed no more. He had to hold a finger wet by his tongue to her mouth to be assured she breathed.

"Allen?"

His eyelids felt heavy, as if weighted. So real, he thought of his dream. Suddenly, he snapped open his eyes and jerked awake, turning immediately to Hannah. To an alert and smiling Hannah.

"Oh, Hannah, darling. You're awake. You're ... " He grabbed one limp hand and pressed it to his lips.

"Why are you crying?" she whispered.

"You were very sick, and I was worried," he said, trying to keep the fear from his voice.

"Oh. How long?"

He smiled, knowing what she was thinking. "One week."

Her eyes widened slightly. "Got to leave tomorrow," she managed.

"Of course," he said, knowing that the devil himself couldn't have made him put Hannah on the *William H. Aspinwall* the next day—or the day after that. "Here, have something to drink. You've become dehydrated from your fever." He lifted her head and helped her drink a small amount of water. She lay her head back down as if the act of swallowing had exhausted her. And again, she fell asleep.

It was days before Hannah could walk haltingly from the bed to the chair not six feet away. It seemed like miles as she shuffled her way weakly to the cushioned chair, her eyes focusing on a bit of stuffing poking from one corner. Letting out a shaky breath, she braced her hands on either armrest and carefully sat down, amazed that she was still so light-headed.

"I'll never make it. Never," she said between little gasping breaths.

"You did make it," Allen said with false cheerfulness.

Hannah gave him a dark look. "To New York, you idiot." Her words lacked any venom, and Allen smiled.

"Glad to see you returning to your old self, Hannah darling," he said, then proceeded to straighten the skirts of her dressing gown so that her ankles were neatly covered. Hannah smiled at his ministrations. When he looked up and saw that look of bemusement, he flushed.

"No sense forgetting modesty simply because you're ill," he said.

"I'm not ill. I've recovered." Hannah tried to make her words come out strong and was dismayed at the lack of force behind them. "And I'm going to be on that steamer when it arrives tomorrow."

"Hannah."

She ignored the warning note in his voice. "I will, Allen, if I have to hire someone to carry me, I will be on that boat. Two weeks! I can't wait another four days before departing. We'll miss the *Cherokee* if I wait, and then who knows how long we'll be stuck in Chagres waiting for another steamer. I've still a chance to beat James back if we leave tomorrow. But after that, it's hopeless."

Allen let out an angry sound and turned away from her. "I won't have you become ill again, Hannah." He made a great show of straightening the covers on her bed even though a maid was expected at any moment to change the sheets.

"I'm going. With or without you," Hannah said, knowing she was hurting Allen by her insistence that they leave. He'd been having a difficult time hiding his true feelings for her in the past few days, and Hannah had been filled with guilt. No matter how many times she reminded herself that Allen was the one who abandoned her, who made it possible for her to meet and fall in love with James, she still hated to see him suffer. Hannah sat in the chair and watched him angrily bring the blanket up over the pillow, then he stopped and hung his head, one hand curled into the pillow mussing the work he'd just done.

"I'm sorry," he choked out.

"Oh, Allen, don't be."

"It's just that you can barely speak without getting exhausted," he said, turning to her. "I watched you almost die, Hannah."

She waved a hand at him, refusing to believe she had been that seriously ill. "I'm better now. I'll admit I'm still weak, but I'm well enough to travel. I feel better each day. By the time I get to New York, I'll have roses on my cheeks and a bit more flesh on my bones. Please, Allen. I want to go home. It's not just for James. I'm sure my father is going mad with worry over me.,"

"I sent him that letter saying you were getting well."

"Yes, I know. But he'll worry anyway. Tomorrow, Allen. Promise me."

He clenched his jaw. "I promise."

Chapter Twenty-three

Austin Wright stood at Pier twenty and watched as the steamship *Cherokee's* crew members lay down the gangplank to allow the passengers to disembark. They were nearly all men, and yet Austin could not pick out his daughter among the rag-tag group that made its way down to the pier. His daughter, bless her, would never know the agony he felt when he received that note from Allen telling him they would be delayed because Hannah had contracted yellow fever. Only common sense had made him stay in New York when his heart screamed out that he should immediately travel to Panama. But he knew if he had departed, he would have found either a corpse or would have passed her on her way home. He waited for a letter, feeling sick and empty, fearing when it came it would be from Allen telling him his little girl had died. When a letter came in Hannah's fine handwriting telling him that she was coming home, he'd buried his head in his hands and cried.

Austin craned his neck, not caring that he was directly in the path of disembarking passengers who jostled him in their haste to get off the ship. He saw Allen first, his chocolate brown hair longer than he remembered. And then, her head just reaching Allen's shoulder, he saw her and nearly cried again. It was so clear that Hannah had been through something hellish. She huddled next to Allen looking like a faint shadow of the girl who'd lifted her skirts and ran aboard the *Windfire* so many months before. Aw, Hannah, girl. He swallowed and tried to smooth the worry from his face. It would do no good to let Hannah know just how upset he was at the sight of her.

The two made their way down the gangplank slowly, the last of the passengers to leave the ship. Hannah's skin was still tinged yellow, and it held a greenish cast, as if the girl had been seasick. He saw her lift her eyes, saw her catch sight of him, and the joy and relief and pain he saw in her eyes made his heart stop. Pushing away from Allen, Hannah lunged toward her father and threw herself into his arms.

"Oh, Daddy. I'm so glad I'm home." Austin blinked back the tears. His poor little girl. She hadn't called him "Daddy" since she was four years old, having announced sternly that use of such a title was for babies. He held her against him for the longest time, wishing he could give her some of his strength. She was so very frail beneath him. When she finally lifted her face, new tears rushed down her cheeks as she realized he, too, had been crying. Dark circles smudged her eyes, her lips were pale and slightly chapped. Austin looked up toward Allen, who hovered behind Hannah, and gave him a smile.

'Thank you for bringing her home to me," he told the younger man.

Allen's cheeks flushed red. "Please do not thank me, sir," he said, his voice strained. "If it wasn't for me, none of this would have happened."

Allen met his eyes with solemn strength, and Austin realized that, whatever else had come of it, Allen Pritchard had become a man on his journey to and from California. Austin did not argue with Allen, but simply jerked his head, acknowledging the truth of his statement. Allen's brown eyes flickered to Hannah, then back. They stood awkwardly for a few moments.

"I'll see to my bags," he said, nodding at the pile of baggage on the pier that other passengers were picking through. "I have to go home to see my mother." He grimaced slightly, and Austin smiled. Allen turned to Hannah, leaned forward, and kissed her forehead lightly. "I'll call on you tomorrow."

Hannah shook her head. "Give me a few days, will you, Allen?"

Allen nodded, looking sad and infinitely weary as he turned toward his baggage.

With one hand still around his daughter's back, Austin drew her away and toward the carriage. "You're looking fine, daughter."

Hannah smiled at the blatant lie. "I look awful, and I know it. Now that we're on dry land, I'm sure I'll feel better." At her father's raised eyebrows, she laughed. "I got seasick on that blasted belching tug they call a ship. They don't cut through the waves, they plod through them with great bouncing jerks. They're noisy and they smell. I don't know why they are becoming so popular."

Austin threw back his head and laughed, glad Hannah was showing some spirit.

It was an effort. Hannah was amazed at how weak she still was, and blamed it on the rough trip northward. She was cold to her bones, even though she wore a fur-lined coat to ward off the raw February wind whipping off the East River. The ship's heating system—one warm water pipe laid beneath the floor—was far from adequate. There had been times on that three-week trip when she'd thought she'd never feel truly warm again.

Despite the cold, Hannah was glad to be home, glad to have one chapter of her life completed. When James arrived in New York, she would look well and hearty. She would greet him wearing her prettiest winter cloak, the burgundy wool with rich satin lining. It was not her warmest, but perhaps when James arrived, spring will have touched the northeast air with a bit of warmth. It was the thought of him, wind-tousled, his rugged face burned from the sun and winter gales, striding up and down the *Windfire* as it was pulled into its pier, that kept Hannah's spirits up. She would watch him for a time, then make her way closer to the ship, close enough so that all he had to do was look down onto the pier and he would see her. Just thinking of that moment when she would gaze into those blue eyes was enough to make her heart pick up a beat. She didn't think past that. She refused to think that he would turn away from her in anger. Instead, when she allowed herself to think beyond that first look, she pictured him bounding down the gangplank, while she ran toward him. Perhaps they would stop before they embraced to drink in the sight of one another. Or maybe they would just throw themselves into each other's arms and hold each other for hours.

As if reading where her thoughts had gone, her father said, "Heard about the *Windfire* and your Captain MacRae?" He had settled himself into the carriage opposite her.

Hannah nearly stopped breathing at his question. His tone was light, so it could not be bad news. She forced herself to answer. "No."

"He's gotten his record. San Francisco to New York in eighty days. Should have taken the *Windfire* back to New York, Hannah. Would have been home more than two weeks already. Damned fine sailing, if you ask me. You should have seen the crowds that greeted him. A regular hero." Her father was puffed up and proud, as if his own son had accomplished the feat.

With all her strength, Hannah tried to hide her disappointment and shock upon hearing the news. He had beaten her back. Even as she lay ill in Gorgona, she feared he would, though she tried to block out that possibility. She could not see him now, not looking as she did, wasted and frail. "That's grand. He must be so happy."

Hannah felt a telltale burning in her throat, but refused to let more tears fall. She so easily cried since her illness, as if the disease had ravaged not only her body, but her heart as well. She could not help thinking that if she had not become ill, she would have arrived shortly before the *Windfire*, she would have made it even with the ship's amazing speed. Eighty days. It was an unheard-of feat.

All her fantasies shattered into painful shards of reality. He had come home, and she had not been there. He had come home to an empty pier, an empty home. In all the scenarios Hannah had conjured up, none had encompassed this possibility. She had refused to believe he could make another journey in less than one hundred days.

"I had thought I would beat him back to New York," she said, her voice shaking only slightly.

"That ship's got wings, it has. They're saying the *Flying Cloud's* record to San Francisco is written in sand at low tide, with the *Windfire* and MacRae added to the mix. I hear tell he's looking to buy his own ship, another McKay and one that's supposed to be the fastest yet."

Hannah barely heard her father. She was putting all her concentration on not crying. He was home, here in New York, where she could run into him, where she would read about him in the newspaper. Somehow this made everything impossible. What would she do, send over a note and request an audience? He could and probably would, refuse. What then? Ambush him as he made his way out of his home? Her plan had been perfect, the stuff made of fairy tales. Would she see him at the opera? Would he be with another woman? Hannah responded to her father's enthusiastic gushing with monosyllables, suddenly lacking the energy to even pretend she was happy about James's success.

I just need to get well, she told herself. *I have to be strong when I see him.* A week, maybe two. Then she would be ready.

James looked at the growing pile of invitations with irritation, knowing that his celebrity would be short-lived once word spread that he was engaged. All the poor mamas and papas who'd hovered about him in the past four weeks, daughters trailing behind them, would slowly disappear. And good riddance to that. It was one benefit, among many, that he would get from his marriage to Sandra Sheffield.

He'd known the Sheffields for years, had danced with

their daughter on a few occasions before his triumphant return to New York, and had attended their son's wedding. He'd been home just three days when he was invited, with several other guests, to the Sheffields' home. It had struck him suddenly, as he spooned béarnaise sauce onto his filet mignon, that Sandra Sheffield would be perfect as his wife. She was petite, and had black hair and blue eyes like his own. They would have black-haired, blue-eyed children. And she looked at him with those big blue eyes in a way that helped erase from his mind other eyes which had haunted him for months. She was, in nearly every way possible, the complete opposite of Hannah Wright. She was soft-spoken and delicate. She would no doubt get seasick simply stepping aboard his ship. She was pretty in a classic way, her features dainty, her mouth a perfect little bow that she had the habit of keeping just slightly open. She didn't argue, she didn't talk back. She didn't make him hard for her with a single glance. Sandra Sheffield, was indeed, perfect.

With a sigh he lifted the pile of mail and began sifting through the invitations, some so old it would be impossible to accept them now. His hand stopped suddenly at a simple white envelope with bold writing. It was from Austin Wright, who no doubt was likely unaware of his daughter's perfidy. He stared at the envelope a long moment, pausing to scratch his eyebrow with one thumb, a conscious effort to appear nonchalant even though he was alone in his study. With a swift movement he opened the envelope and quickly read the invitation. A dinner to be held in honor of his engagement. He and Sandra Sheffield and her parents were to attend. James tapped the invitation lightly against the surface of his desk.

Why not? he thought. He'd nothing against Austin Wright. In fact, he liked the man. Surely he would not hold his daughter's behavior against him. James knew the subject of Austin's daughter would come up, and he told himself he did not care. He was over that bit of insanity. He'd convinced himself on that wickedly fast trip from San Francisco, that he no longer loved her. For to love her still would be to admit he was a fool, and it went roughly against his grain to admit such a thing. He chose to ignore that sharp pain that came upon him almost daily, hitting him with the swiftness of a white squall on a calm summer day. It knocked the breath out of him. As well he ignored that each morning when he wakened, loneliness weighed down on him so heavily, it was only the greatest of efforts that made him rise and face another day. Of course he was lonely. He was a single man—a fact he was soon amending.

He sighed. No doubt Austin Wright would likely have news of his daughter. And, he thought suddenly, of her marriage to Allen Pritchard.

James's gut twisted with such violence, he was momentarily dazed. Rage against himself quickly followed. He didn't care if she'd married every derelict miner in California. Hadn't he learned his lesson? That hellish trip from California had taught him one thing about himself. He would never, ever let a woman make a fool of him again. He loved all women, not one in particular. Not one with a stubborn little chin and eyes the color of a stormy sea.

Dear God, he could not go through such pain again and survive. Some who knew him were of the opinion he *had* died on that last trip around the Horn. George had called him a madman with a death wish. He brutally remembered that awful moment when George and Lodge had threatened to take his ship away from him, claiming he was putting his crew and the ship in mortal danger. He'd denied it at the time, angrily. Now, he could be honest. He had been a madman, driven there by memories of a love that never existed. In the middle of one of the worst gales he'd ever sailed in, James had climbed to the top of the mainmast, two hundred feet above a churning sea, with hands so numb from the cold, he'd had to bang them against the spars to get feeling back in them. He'd stayed there, wind and sleet lashing him, yelling into the wind until his voice was hoarse, screaming out his pain, exorcising his soul of Hannah Wright. George and Timothy Lodge had confronted him after he'd come down, weary, half dead. And he had given them his ship for two days while he lay in his bunk wracked with fever and chills, refusing to see anyone and secretly wishing he would die.

When he was well, he gave his officers a curt apology, and they gladly gave him the helm. He could tell they were shocked when they saw him, but he didn't care. James hadn't died from fever, but something inside him did die in that gale. Hope or that light that seemed to shine from him.

He was a good captain, tough but fair. He watched the horizon, he plotted the course, he listened to his ship. But his eyes that once looked up at the *Windfire* sails like a man looking at his lover, were strangely devoid of anything. He didn't seem sad or angry. He was empty. And he didn't care. Being empty was better than being in pain.

And so, when he saw Sandra Sheffield, the perfect material for a sea captain's wife, he quickly courted her and asked her to marry him. She, of course, was madly in love, but a little afraid of the man who asked her to be his wife without smiling, without even a tender word. A part of James knew he was being cruel to Sandra by making her his wife. She was marrying a man incapable of loving her, a man whose ravaged heart had been left at that wharf in San Francisco.

Hannah smoothed her dress before her full-length mirror. The gold silk gown with its fitted bodice and full skirts was slightly loose, but Hannah was more concerned that it didn't make her skin appear yellow. The jaundice was gone, but her cheeks were still too pale. She leaned forward toward her reflection and pinched them, wishing for the first time for a bit of rouge. She wore her hair gathered at her nape in a style that allowed much of her golden-brown locks to trail down her back, left bare by the dress. Intricate embroidery covered the bodice, that was rounded at the waist before the plain full skirt trailed down to her slippered feet.

"How do I look?" she asked Joan, her maid.

"Frightened," she said honestly.

Hannah whirled back to the mirror and saw a pretty girl, eyes wide and a face so pale she did, indeed, look frightened. She let out a little moan.

"Oh, not so bad as that, Miss Hannah." Joan, her squat little body making Hannah look almost delicate, came up to Hannah and gave her cheeks a painful squeeze.

"Ow!"

"Yes, ow, ow, but now look?"

Hannah gave her bossy little maid a scowl, but smiled when she saw the result. "You'll have to stand by downstairs so you can pinch my cheeks when they become pale again." For as she watched, the bloom on her cheeks faded.

"Oh, that blasted yellow fever," she said, balling her fists. Truly, it had ruined everything. And here she was, trying to look beautiful, trying to take James's breath away when he entered the dining room with his fiancée, and she'd never looked more horrid in her life. She wished Allen could have come to lend her support, but he had told her, his voice oddly strained, that she was asking too much of him. Feeling horribly guilty for even asking him, Hannah had understood.

Hannah sat down at the edge of her bed, taking care to spread out her gown so that it would not become overly wrinkled before her grand entrance. She suspected her father knew something had happened between her and James, but knew he would be shocked to learn the full truth. She wasn't certain who her father would be more angry at—her, for letting James sail without her, or him, for taking his daughter's innocence. Probably her, she thought with a frown. After all, what her father had planned had happened. They had fallen in love, but Hannah had foolishly thrown it away. All she could do was try to win James back. Some time in the past week, she decided that is what she wanted to do. And looking like a washed-up rag doll would not help matters.

Standing with more confidence than she felt, Hannah

strode out of her room, stopping only when she reached the stairs that led down to the entrance hall. She painfully gripped the old ship's railing that made up the banister, her fingernails leaving behind faint half-moons in the wood. His voice. She'd heard his voice. Standing there, looking down, her breath coming in short gasps, she thought she'd surely faint and tumble down those stairs. Just from hearing his voice.

"Please God, just let me get through this night. Give me strength."

She waited for the panicky feeling to go away, for her palms to dry, for her heart to stop its wild beating. Slowly, slowly, her breathing became normal, and she shook her head, stunned at how close she had come to swooning. One hand pulled up the hem of her dress, one foot stepped down, then the other, until she was halfway down the stairs, her eyes steady on the simple chandelier in front of her. She did not look left or right, but straight ahead, her hand moving down the banister, sticking a bit because her palms were not quite dry. She heard a woman's giggle, a man's bland reply. No. Not just a man's. *His.* He was talking again. His voice. His voice.

And she fainted.

Chapter Twenty-four

Hannah was only out for a matter of moments, but it was enough to cause a stir among the guests. She opened her eyes to see her father hovering worriedly over her, as he quickly explained to his concerned dinner guests that his daughter had recently suffered a bout of yellow fever as she crossed the Isthmus of Panama.

Hannah waved a hand at her father, wishing he would stop talking and simply help her to her feet.

"I'm all right. Truly, Papa." She heaved herself up onto her elbows, suddenly horribly embarrassed to find herself sprawled out at the bottom of the stairs. Why could nothing go as planned?

"You should go to your room and rest, Hannah. Everyone will understand."

Hannah shook her head. "No, Papa. I am fine." He grabbed her beneath her arms and lifted her up—straight into James. She brought in a sharp breath before recovering, if one could call your heart bursting through your chest recovering. Hannah would have smiled if he'd given her the slightest reason to. But his eyes held nothing, not even recognition.

"Miss Wright." He nodded politely. Hannah found herself nodding back just as politely.

"Captain MacRae." Hannah could feel that awful blood-rushing feeling that came just before her eyes rolled back into her head, but she closed her eyes against it. She was dimly aware that James had taken a step toward her, before her father's hand was once again wrapped around her arm.

"That's it, young lady. You're still too ill to be socializing."

Hannah looked up at her father beseechingly. "I'll sit in the parlor for a few moments. If I'm still feeling unwell, I'll go upstairs. I promise." She even smiled, something she knew her father would not be able to resist.

"One more fainting spell and up you go," he said sternly.

"Yes, Papa."

Then her mother's old friend Edna Price was by her side, leading her into the parlor, excitedly asking her about her adventures of the past eighteen months. She wanted to look back, to see if James was watching her, to see if, perhaps, he wanted to speak to her. But Edna dragged her along and physically pushed her down onto a sofa by the fire, tsking and tut-tutting and generally being motherly. Poor homely Edna Price, who Hannah suspected had been in love with her father even before her mother died, chatted on and on about New York society and all that had happened in the past year and a half. Hannah found herself nodding as Edna droned on, grateful that the older woman did not again demand to know about her own experience. She simply was not up to talking about her grand "adventure" and pretending she was happy when she was not.

How could she be happy when the man she loved pretended she was a distant acquaintance. *It's what you deserve, it is God's punishment for breaking his heart.* Then a new thought came to her: Perhaps his heart hadn't been broken, after all. Perhaps Captain James MacRae was exactly the kind of man everyone warned her he was—a man who loved all women equally, but let none into his heart. He certainly did not seem to be a man tortured by the sight of her. Her body flushed with humiliation. My God, she had traveled halfway across the world for a man who thought so little of her, he was getting married to another woman just months after professing to love her.

She brought a fist up to her mouth and pressed hard.

"Hannah, dear, are you having another spell?" Edna's hands fluttered about her ruffled and laced neckline, before settling on her lap to fiddle with one of the many bows that covered her pink dress. Edna had a habit of wearing frilly, heavily ornamented gowns that only made her long narrow face appear even more homely. She smiled tentatively at Hannah.

"Oh. No, I'm fine, Edna."

She looked doubtful, so Hannah smiled, though her face almost hurt with the effort. It could not have been a frivolous thing James had felt for her. She had seen his eyes, felt his body cover hers, heard his words. He must still love her. He must.

Then, why when I look into his eyes do I see nothing? James, who always had such a terrible time hiding what he thought. Hannah wanted to scream and scream and scream to purge herself of her maddening uncertainty. She felt a bubble of hysterical laughter press against her throat.

"It looks as if they are going in for dinner, dear. Are you up for keeping company?"

Edna smiled, and Hannah was struck that her smile almost made Edna, with her solemn dour looks, seem pretty. It was unfair that Edna had been cursed with those droopy eyes and loose, long features, for a more giving, less dour woman Hannah had never known.

"I'm up for anything," Hannah said with false bravado.

It was a small party that gathered about the long dining table. Her father, who felt uncomfortable sitting at the head of the table, sat next to Edna. Across from them, the Sheffields, and then Sandra and James. Sandra's brother and his wife sat across from them, leaving Hannah awkward and alone at the end—a single in a company of pairs. Sandra's brother's wife, Clara, leaned over to Hannah while they were in the middle of eating their wild mushroom soup.

"This soup is delicious, Miss Wright."

Hannah smiled, but noticed that the woman had eaten only the broth, leaving the mushrooms at the bottom of the bowl. Hiding a smile, she looked up and locked eyes with James. For a fleeting moment she thought she saw something in his eyes, perhaps a smile, before he looked down, his black lashes hiding whatever it was she saw. Hannah's heart began hammering again, a pounding in her ears. You can do this, she told herself, though she wasn't sure what she wanted herself to do. Simply get through the evening? Prove to James that she wasn't destroyed by the fact he was sitting next to his fiancée? Or prove to James that she still loved him, loved him enough to make a fool of herself right here in front of her guests, in front of the woman he had pledged to marry.

Hannah noticed her hand holding the spoon began trembling, so she gently placed it on the white lace tablecloth. She pushed her pinkie finger through one of the holes in the lace, concentrating on the smooth feel of the wood, and frowning when she noticed she had pulled the lace apart, leaving a small hole.

"Hannah." Her father's voice boomed over them. "Mrs. Sheffield was inquiring about your trip through the isthmus," he said, leaning back to allow a servant to remove his soup plate.

"It was beautiful, exotic, rainy, and warm," Hannah said as lightly as she could. "I rather liked it."

"Were you very ill?" This from Sandra Sheffield, her blue eyes wide with interest, her mouth open slightly. A pout, just as Hannah predicted.

"Just a touch of yellow fever," Hannah said as lightly as possible. "I'm quite over it now. It's rather like the flu."

"She almost died."

Hannah whirled to see Allen leaning up against the dining room door. His brown hair was slightly mussed, but he was dressed elegantly in a chocolate-brown suit and brown-and-tan-striped vest. Hannah's first feeling was one of relief, that

Allen would be there to field questions, to help avert a disaster, to stop her from saying something that she would regret for the rest of her life. But as he walked toward the table, gracefully accepting her father's invitation to join them, she knew something was wrong. He walked into the room with the exaggerated care of a man who has had too much to drink.

"Died?" Sandra said, her eyes going impossibly wider. She glanced at James to share her astonishment, but his face remained impassive.

Hannah gave Allen a tight smile that held a warning, which he saw and ignored. "I was hardly close to knocking on heaven's gate," she said with a little laugh.

"They sent for a priest to issue her last rites," he said breezily. "I'd say that was pretty close to heaven's gate."

Hannah looked at Allen with shock. She hadn't known.

"We didn't think the priest would get there in time, but he did. Obviously." Allen laughed at his own joke.

"It must not have taken," Hannah said with a little laugh. "You see, I'm Episcopalian."

There was some uncomfortable laughter. Hannah shot a look at James, but he was looking at Allen, his expression unreadable.

"Ah, yes," Allen said on a sigh. "We almost lost our Hannah. They said it was a miracle that she lived. But I say it was her iron will."

"Allen." She held a warning note in her voice.

"You see, Hannah wanted to come home. Wanted it more than anything in the world. Such determination." His words, said lightly, held a bitter note. "Even when she was so weak she could barely swallow, she whispered how she had to get home, had to reach New York before . . . "

"Allen, please."

He glanced at her, and Hannah saw raw pain in his eyes.

Sandra had leaned forward in her chair. "Before what?" she asked breathlessly.

"Before spring," Hannah said quickly before Allen could answer.

"Ah," he said. "Yes, it was something like that, wasn't it Hannah? Before spring. We left long before she should have, but then she was half out of her mind in a fever, and weak as a lamb. Imagine loving spring in New York so much you'd risk your life to get to it. I think if Hannah hadn't loved spring quite so much, she would have died. I'm quite convinced of it."

Oh, bless you, Allen Pritchard. Even if it took a few drinks to work up the courage, thank you, thank you. Now James knew why she'd come home. He had to know, for it was so clear to her what Allen was saying and for whose benefit, she couldn't imagine James not understanding. But when she looked at James, she saw nothing, not even casual interest. Allen could have been boring them all with a discussion of rock formations.

"Spring?" Edna said, her forehead heavily wrinkled in confusion. "Why spring won't be here for at least another six weeks, Hannah. You had plenty of time to . . . " She stopped when Austin placed a hand on her wrist. "Oh. I suppose it had something to do with the wedding."

For one confusing moment, Hannah thought she was talking about James's wedding to Sandra, but when Allen stiffened beside her, she realized Edna was referring to her own wedding plans.

"Should you tell them or should I, my dear?" Allen asked, lifting a glass of cabernet to his lips.

"Allen and I have broken off," Hannah said flatly.

Edna let out a small sound, her eyes going from one to the other, clearly wondering what Allen was doing sitting beside Hannah if they had no plans to marry.

"It was quite mutual, so no need to become upset, Mrs. Price," Allen said easily. "Still . . ." And Hannah tensed. "I was quite, and still am, quite willing to marry her." Allen laughed then, and stood, pushing his chair back carefully. "This whole thing is rather like a Shakespearean tragedy, when you think of it. Who is happy in all this?" he asked, suddenly sounding as drunk as he clearly was.

The Sheffields, as if realizing that Allen was inebriated, put on affronted looks. Hannah bowed her head onto a hand, too weary to stop whatever it was Allen was going to say.

"Is Hannah happy?" He laughed again. ""My God, look at her. *Look* at her," he repeated, his eyes again going to James. "I, obviously, am not happy. And our good captain, here. Engaged to be married. Happy news indeed." Everyone was silent. "Everyone's so damned happy," he said, his voice breaking.

Mrs. Sheffield gasped, Mr. Sheffield muttered his protest. Ignoring them both, Hannah turned, her heart aching when she saw that Allen's face was a mask of misery.

"I could have made you happy," he said. "I still could." He gave Hannah a little shrug and a watery smile before turning and leaving.

"Well, he was certainly in his cups," Mr. Sheffield said with a sniff.

"He's not a drinker," Austin said, leaning back in his chair, his worried gaze going to his daughter. "Do you know what that was all about, Hannah?"

"Obviously, the poor man's upset about being jilted," Mrs. Sheffield said. And Hannah wanted to slap her face for the censure she heard in her voice. Allen had been drunk, Allen had made the scene, and she had the nerve to somehow blame Hannah?

"Allen has known for some time of my feelings, Mrs. Sheffield. I apologize for his behavior, and I'm sure Allen will feel simply awful come tomorrow. It was very unlike him." She couldn't help it, she looked again at James, but he was looking at his fiancée, his blue eyes warm. It hurt, that look. He'd just learned that she'd nearly died coming home to him, and he couldn't even look at her. Perhaps he didn't care.

Edna, seeing the engaged couple gazing at each other, sighed. "Was it love at first sight between you two?"

Sandra blushed crimson, and James smiled. "I've known James for years," Sandra said, her voice soft and musical. "I was twelve the first time I saw Captain MacRae . . . James." She blushed again. "And then it was love at first sight." She smiled and looked down at her lap.

"It was all the girl talked about," Mr. Sheffield said with a fond smile for his daughter.

Hannah swallowed past the burning in her throat. He couldn't love her, he simply couldn't. She was meek and shy and blushed if you looked at her. And she was so young. Hannah looked at the girl, suddenly picturing James covering her with his large body, torturing herself with those images that left her feeling a bit sick. She looked to her plate, where her now-cold ham sat untouched. Would he do the same things to this girl that he had done to her? Would he make her body clench with pleasure, would he tell her he loved her over and over until it sounded like a prayer?

"I hope you don't mind all this talk of weddings."

Hannah lifted her eyes to the girl's blue-eyed gaze, and she wondered how much this girl knew. Could she be as innocent as she seemed?

"I love weddings," Hannah said lightly. "I go to them all the time."

"We'll be sure to include you on the guest list, won't we, Mother."

"Of course," Mrs. Sheffield said. "My goodness, the guest list grows daily." There was something about that exchange which made her think the two of them were being condescending.

"Thank you, but I'm going to be out of town that weekend. It's one of the reasons I wanted to invite you here to dinner, so that I might wish you well," Hannah said, her face reddening slightly at her lie. The thought of watching James wed this girl was unbearable. She gave her father a quick look, and he narrowed his eyes, making Hannah blush even brighter.

The conversation went off in the direction of business and

investments, and Hannah relaxed for the first time that evening. When dessert was finished, the tension came rushing back when her father asked to see her before he joined the men in the study for a smoke. He led her to the breakfast room, now dark but for a single lamp her father lit.

"So. You love him." There was no doubt what her father meant.

"Yes."

"And you let him leave without you, regretted it, and then went chasing half the world over for him."

Hannah swallowed. "Yes."

"And now, after all that, you're going to let him go."

Hannah's throat was so closed, she could only nod her head.

"By God, girl, I won't have it!"

Her father's shout made her jump, and her eyes went to the door, a silent plea that he lower his voice. The study where James and his future father-in-law were waiting was only two doors down and across the hall.

"He's engaged," she said miserably.

"So were you."

Hannah winced.

Austin moved to his daughter and placed his large hands on her shoulders. "Hannah. If you love him, you've got to fight for him."

"But"—her breath caught—"he"—a sob—"doesn't"—another sob—"love me!" And she threw herself into her father's arms and cried and cried.

"There, there, now, girl. You don't know that for certain."

"Yes, I do," she said wetly against her father's once pristine lapel. "He didn't even care that I almost died." This she said rather loudly. Loud enough for James, who was about to enter the study, to hear.

Didn't care. That little fool of a girl, to think such a thing. Hell, when he first saw her, saw how pale and thin she was, he'd known something horribly wrong had happened. James tried to tell himself he didn't care. Didn't care, didn't care.

Blast and damn, but he did. He more than cared. Through the red rage, through the pain that still kept him up at night, he knew he still cared.

She had come home. For him. He was certain of it, but uncertain how he felt about it. Seeing her again, when he thought he never would, when he didn't expect it. It was unnerving. He hadn't been prepared to have her here, to have her looking as if she were wasting away.

"What's that caterwauling I hear?" Maxwell Sheffield said, poking a head out into the hall where James still stood, his cigar held loosely in his right hand. "That the Wright girl? She must have a weak constitution, that one. That fellow ought to thank his lucky stars to get rid of her."

James wiped his face of emotion. "She's the bravest lady I know," he said, then turned and walked into the study.

"Brave, you say?" Sheffield called after him. "Bah. Flighty. Imagine, nearly killing yourself so you get home in time to see a New York spring. You'd never see our girl doing something like that."

"Our girl?"

"Sandra. Girl's been taught better than that. And I can't say much for a girl traveling alone with a man who used to be her fiancé. That's how reputations get ruined."

James gave a hard look to the man he was quickly coming to dislike. "Reputations are ruined by wagging tongues."

Sheffield took a puff on his cigar. "That's the truth, my boy. That girl's as good as ruined. Mark my words."

James shrugged. What did it matter to him whether Hannah Wright's reputation was ruined or not? She had used him, betrayed him, left him there on that ship hurting with a pain that was soul deep. A few tears and sorrowful looks would not be enough to pump tender feelings back into his heart. He'd be damned if he succumbed that easily.

Chapter Twenty-five

Hannah stood at Allen's front door, her embossed calling card in her gloved hand, and waited what seemed like an eternity for someone to answer her ringing. Finally, a small maid opened the door with a smile, and Hannah couldn't help but smile back. She was so used to the stodgy old butler opening the Pritchards' door, looking down his nose as if she were a street peddler, it was a pleasant surprise to find this grinning girl instead. The maid waved away Hannah's card.

"Oh, you don't need that, Miss Wright. I knows who you are. I'll get Mr. Allen straight away, if you doesn't mind waitin' in the hall here."

Hannah's smile faltered when she noticed Althea Pritchard hurrying toward the door, her face unusually flushed, her hair looking slightly less than perfect.

"Allen is indisposed," she said, her voice cold. Despite her flustered appearance, Althea looked at Hannah with the haughtiness of a woman who is convinced she is someone's better.

"I imagine Allen is indisposed, but I do need to speak with him, Mrs. Pritchard, if you don't mind."

"I'll get him," the maid chirped, as if unaware of the nearly tangible friction created by the two women.

"You'll do nothing of the sort," Althea snapped, and the girl simply shrugged.

"Got a bit of a bowel problem," the girl whispered to Hannah, as a way to explain Althea's bad mood.

Two bright spots appeared on Althea's face, but she said only, "Polly. Leave." The girl gave another shrug and sauntered off toward the back of the house. The older woman watched the maid walk off, a deep frown marring her features, before turning back to Hannah.

"Allen has forced me to fire nearly all our servants. How that girl ended up being one of the few to remain, I'll never know."

"She makes me laugh, Mother," Allen said from the stairway. "Hello, Miss Wright."

Hannah smiled. "Hello, Mr. Pritchard."

Althea let out a sound of disgust and shot daggers at her son before walking from the entrance hall, with a stiff back.

"Mother is very angry with me," Allen said, smiling still. "I fired all but five servants, put the house on the market, and plan to auction some of her wardrobe. She was spitting nails at me for days, but I think she finally realizes there is no other way."

"It must be difficult for her to accept," Hannah said, not feeling as sympathetic as her words made her out to be. Allen smiled, seeing right through her.

"To what do I owe this early morning visit. I'm surprised, considering what an ass I made of myself last evening."

Hannah followed Allen into the richly appointed library, her shoes tapping on the entrance hall's marble before sinking into the library's thick Indian carpet. "Eleven o'clock is hardly early, Allen. And you did not make an ass of yourself. You were wonderful."

"So I take it all is well between you and Captain MacRae?" He asked the question lightly, but he shifted his gaze away from her.

"No, things are not all well. He didn't speak to me directly all evening. He barely looked at me, and when he did, there was nothing. Oh, Allen," she said, hugging her arms about her shoulders. "When he used to look at me, it was

like fire. It was . . ." She shook her head, unable to describe
the warmth, the heat, the desire, and the love she'd seen in
James's eyes. "But last night, it was blank. As if I were a distant acquaintance. No, it was worse than that. It was as if I
were not there at all."

"I'm sorry."

"Oh, Allen. Don't be," Hannah said, realizing with a stab
of guilt how difficult it would be for Allen to hear her go on
about another man. "I just came over to thank you. And to
tell you good-bye. I will be traveling out of town soon."

"Some traveling that coincidentally corresponds to a certain wedding date?"

Hannah flushed, and nodded her head. "I couldn't bear
being in New York, hearing church bells and wondering if
they were ringing for them." She went to Allen, her dearest
friend, and hugged him close. "Thank you for being such a
good friend."

Allen drew her back with a wistful smile. "You know,
even though I was drunk, I meant what I said. If you change
your mind . . ."

Hannah leaned forward and kissed his cheek. "Good-bye,
Allen."

He knew then that Hannah was lost to him forever.

After Hannah said good-bye, she walked a bit, huddling
closer into her coat to shield against a brisk March wind. For
the first time in her life, Hannah knew what it was like to
feel lonely. The days stretched out before her, days filled
with longing, with emptiness. Days filled with the fear and
terrible hope that she might come across James and his
beautiful new wife. After all, her father shared many of the
same acquaintances as James and his future in-laws. How
could she bear seeing them together? But then, how could
she bear not seeing him at all? They would have children,
they would have a life. Perhaps, after all this, she should return to San Francisco, go to a place and start anew. As soon
as she thought of the idea, she cast it aside. She wanted to

stay home, where everything was familiar. Where she might see James. Might hear his laughter. It would be worth the pain, she thought, just to have a chance to see him.

Hannah stopped suddenly, her hands resting on a granite hitching post outside a three-story brick house that appeared to be abandoned. She held on to that post as if she might collapse from the grief that weighed her down, her pale yellow silk gloves becoming ruined on the rough stone. For the thousandth time, she pictured herself sitting on her bed in her aunt's house watching the sun come up. She willed that image of herself to move, to run as fast as she could to the *Windfire* and to James. She pictured it in her mind, her hair flying loose behind her, her skirts lifted high, mindless of the looks, of the muddy streets. And she saw him, his face at first worried that she would be late, and then breaking into a wide grin when he saw her. She saw herself running up the gangplank, heard the hearty hellos of the crew members, and felt the wonderful embrace as James finally, finally, took her into his arms. Standing there buffeted by the sharp March wind, she could almost feel his arms around her.

Her hands moved over the stone mindlessly, gripping and ungripping as she willed that dream to come true. Move, move, run to him, her mind shouted to that foolish girl who sat on that bed and watched the sun rise. But she hadn't moved, she'd left him there standing on the deck, searching the wharf for her. Left him there until finally, finally, the truth dawned on him. She could see it all, could almost feel his agony, for it was so much like what she was feeling now. She saw the sympathetic looks, heard the curses muttered by George, whose disappointment in his cousin would be immeasurable; and Timothy Lodge, who loved James nearly as much as she did, would suffer for her cowardice, as well, to see James hurting so.

As if conjuring him up with her thoughts, she looked up to see a spiffy-looking Timothy Lodge walking toward her.

"Oh, Mr. Lodge," Hannah said, and threw herself into the older man's arms. Lodge's face at first flushed with pleasure

at her enthusiastic greeting, but as if he suddenly recalled
what she had done, he stood stiff, his arms by his side, his
face turning stony. Embarrassed by her display, Hannah
stepped back, laughing at herself, sobering instantly when
she realized he was less than pleased to see her.

"It's so good to see a familiar face," Hannah said, ignoring the fact he obviously was angry with her. "And don't
you look fine in that new suit." Lodge almost looked like a
society man with his beaver hat and forest-green suit, his
fancy tan embroidered vest sporting a gold watch fob. But
despite his fine clothes, Hannah had no trouble recognizing
the second mate. Lodge blushed and shifted his feet.

"What're you doing in New York? Thought you'd be married making up house in San Francisco." His voice held a
slight sneer, and Hannah's heart wrenched.

Hannah shook her head, mortified to feel tears pricking
her eyes. "I came home," she said quietly.

"For him."

"Yes." Hannah didn't stop to wonder how so much meaning could come from so few words. "I love him," she said,
surprising herself.

"Aye." He looked down and kicked one booted foot at a
stone. "I suppose that's why you left him there waitin' for
you."

"I thought I was doing the right thing. But I was wrong. I
tried to beat him back to New York, to meet him at the pier.
I imagined him blustering and ranting, but I never
thought . . ."

Lodge grunted. "A man like Captain MacRae has a long
memory." He shoved two fists into his pants, ruining the elegant effect of his clothing.

"He's getting married," Hannah said.

"So I heard." He glanced off to the distance and returned
his gaze to her almost reluctantly. "You been sick?"

"Yellow fever in Panama."

He grunted again. "I got to be going now."

Hannah felt like crying. She'd been so happy to see

Lodge, and now he was turning away from her, too. She let him walk a few feet away, before calling after him.

"Mr. Lodge." He turned to her, cocking his head to tell her he would listen to whatever it was she had to say. "I made a mistake. One I'll regret for the rest of my life. I hurt the man I love with all my heart, and there's nothing I can do to change that. I do know one thing—he's getting married, and I know that I'll never marry. I'll go to my grave loving that man." Her voice broke, and she spun around to walk quickly away.

James looked up from his desk and scowled at the two men entering his office without so much as a knock. Timothy Lodge entered first, followed by George, who had been out of the city these past weeks looking over a new McKay ship in Boston.

"How does she look?" he asked, ignoring the two men's grim expressions.

"Like hell," George said, crossing his arms.

"Worse than that," Lodge said, scowling first at George and then turning his glittering eyes James's way.

James bit the side of his mouth in irritation. He knew what—or rather who—the two men were talking about, but he chose to ignore them. "McKay said it's his finest ship so far. Better even than *Windfire*, though that's hard to believe."

"Ain't talkin' about the ship," Lodge offered. "We're talking about . . ."

"I know what you are talking about, Mr. Lodge. But what I am talking about, and what we in the future will be talking about, is that goddamn ship I'm thinking of buying from McKay. Is that clear?" James gave them both an icy glare before settling back into his leather chair. His office, once a tiny room in a ramshackle building tucked beside a warehouse, was now in a much finer building near the piers. Its walls were whitewashed above teak wainscoting, the floor covered with thick carpeting. Fine marine oil paintings graced the walls. He had a separate room for his charts, but a few were rolled up and leaning against his large teak desk.

"Should I tell him?" Lodge asked, looking up at George, who simply shrugged.

"This better be about that McKay ship," James warned.

"She told me she loved you," Lodge said stubbornly. "Said you cannot have loved her if you're so willing to marry that bit of fluff you're calling your fiancée. Said . . ."

"Enough."

"Ain't enough. Not nearly enough. That girl's heart broke. And sick. Ain't she sick, George?"

George shuffled a bit uneasily. He didn't like going against his captain, especially when the man was about to buy a ship and would need a good officer to serve her. But he'd seen for himself what Hannah had looked like, and although they hadn't talked about her reasons for returning so abruptly to New York, he suspected he knew the reason.

"She was sick," George said. "Now she's just heartbroken."

James gave them both a withering look and began tapping his thigh with one hand. "I am engaged, gentlemen. And unlike some people, I plan to honor that commitment. This conversation is over."

George looked into the captain's eyes, waiting to see a twinkle, waiting to see anything other than that hard nothingness.

"Perhaps if you understood her reasons," he ventured.

James slapped his hand onto his desk. "Blast and damn, I've had about enough of this, ladies. One more word and . . ."

"She was afraid."

Despite himself, James's head snapped up at George's words. "Hannah's never been afraid of anything," he said.

Timothy Lodge gave George an encouraging nudge.

"She was afraid she loved you too much." He ignored James's snort of disbelief and continued, his heart racing madly in his chest. "Her mother died waiting for her father to come home to her. When Hannah's mother falsely learned her husband had died at sea, she died within days. Hannah is convinced that her mother would have lived had her father returned home. And she is—or at least was—equally convinced that it would be the same for her. She didn't want to marry someone who would leave her, time and time again. She was willing to give you up rather than face that kind of heartache the rest of her life. That's how much she loves you, sir."

James turned to gaze out the window, his face hard and seemingly unaffected by George's impassioned speech. "That's a very touching story, but it changes nothing."

Lodge muttered an oath under his breath.

"Now, gentlemen, about that ship . . . Oh, good God, give me strength."

Austin Wright, his face grim, entered James's office at that moment. The older man ignored his nephew and Lodge and strode directly to James's desk, pointing an accusing finger at James.

"You, sir, are no gentleman. The damage you have done to Hannah is irreparable, sir, and I want you to answer for it."

James had only one thought: My God, she is pregnant. And then: I've made a girl pregnant, and here is her irate father come to confront him with his great sin. The news rattled him, left him nearly speechless for a few agonizing seconds as he looked helplessly into the face of a man he respected almost more than any man he knew.

"Sir, it was only that once, and I planned to marry her."

Austin Wright's eyebrows snapped together so quickly, it was as if someone had tied a bit of twine to them and pulled with a jerk. Confusion turned to shock turned to outrage.

"Are you telling me, Captain, that you have stolen my little girl's innocence?" he bellowed so loudly the other three men in the room winced. James felt suddenly sick.

"Isn't that what you came here for?" he asked weakly, his face going pale.

"You . . . you . . . fornicate with my daughter and then become engaged to another girl less than three months later? What kind of monster are you?" Austin placed two beefy fists on James's desk and leaned forward, forcing the younger man to lean back.

Timothy Lodge gave a sniff, as if he was the overseer of good form for all of New York.

James clenched his jaw. "I asked her to marry me, sir, before we . . ." He trailed off when he saw that Austin's face was becoming more and more red. "She abandoned me, sir. I had every intention of . . ."

"When, Captain? When did you plan to marry her?"

"Upon our return to New York," James said. Even as he said the words, he realized how damning they were.

"Let me get this straight, Mr. MacRae," Austin said, purposefully leaving off his title of captain. "You fornicate with my little girl. Then you plan to sail back to New York, with her aboard ship, and what? Leave her untouched for those three months? A fine mess it would have been if she had become with child, stepping down from the ship with a growing belly."

"Then, she's not pregnant."

Austin's eyes widened at the slight note of disappointment he thought he detected in James's expression.

"No! And we only have the grace of God to thank for that, apparently. Of course, there is no question what your responsibilities are now." Austin looked to the other two men facing James, who both shook their heads in overexaggerated scorn. But neither George nor Lodge could help the happy gleam from entering their eyes.

James looked up at Hannah's father, his eyes bleak. "I understand what you are saying, sir. But since she did not become pregnant, no harm's done."

"No harm!" Austin bellowed. The two other men also looked appropriately shocked. "She's tainted goods, sir. Her reputation is already sullied by her broken engagement, and by that Pritchard's ridiculous theatrics the other evening.

What do you think her future husband will do when he realizes he has married a woman who is not a virgin?"

James could not get beyond the thought of Hannah marrying, never mind what would happen in her marriage bed.
"She would not have me, sir," he said quietly, driving all the
bluster out of Austin.

"My boy, that girl loves you more than you deserve, if
you ask me."

James's eyes grew fierce. He pounded his thigh almost
painfully. "And what if I no longer love her?"

"It's of no consequence whatsoever. You must do what is
right."

"I am engaged."

"Break it. Today."

The three men filed out of his office, leaving James feeling as if he'd just been in a barroom fight. He had no choice
but to marry her now. No choice at all.

"You what?"

"I got him for you, girl. Hook, line, sinker."

Hannah stared at her father in utter disbelief. "But I don't
want him," she shouted, flinging her arms wide. Austin
Wright's smug expression faltered a bit.

"Hannah, I'm afraid I'm a bit confused. Weren't you the
girl who was crying on my shoulder just a few nights ago
because you thought he was lost to you?"

"Yes," she said with obvious reluctance. "That was me."

"Please explain to me why you are angry."

"Because I don't have him. *You* have him. You forced him
to marry me. I don't want to marry someone who doesn't
love me."

Austin waved a dismissive hand. "He loves you."

"He said that?"

Austin looked away from the hope he saw blooming in
Hannah's eyes. "Well, not in so many words. But he didn't
fight it all that much. Not as much as a man would who truly
didn't want to marry you."

"Oh, that warms my heart considerably."

Austin walked up to his daughter. "Hannah, girl, I thought this was what you wanted."

"It is. It's just that I didn't want to force him. He hates me, and now he'll just hate me more because he's been forced to marry me. What if he loves Miss Sheffield?"

"You don't believe that," her father said gently.

Hannah bit one knuckle. "I don't know what I believe."

Chapter Twenty-six

Tears streamed down her face unchecked as Hannah said her wedding vows three weeks later. She did not know the man who stood next to her, the man whose cold blue eyes swept over her without even the hint of welcome. He said nothing when she came to stand next to him in the church. He hardly looked at her. And that's when the burning in her throat began, a burning that quickly turned to tears when she glanced uncertainly at his hard, uncompromising profile.

Behind her, only a few family and friends sat in the pews. It wouldn't have been in good form to hold a large wedding, given that the groom had just recently broken off with another girl. As it was, three weeks had been barely enough time to have a wedding dress made. There would be no wedding ball. There would be no wedding trip. And Hannah was quite certain there would be no wedding night.

He said his vows without emotion, without anger, and certainly without gladness. When the ceremony was finished, he looked at her, his eyes taking in the tears that continued to drip from her jaw, and said, "You'll ruin your dress."

Hannah looked down, and indeed, her tears had stained the ivory satin of her exquisite wedding gown. She dabbed ineffectually with her kerchief, and when she looked up, he was already stepping away from her, shaking hands with her father, his face grim. Timothy Lodge and George also gave James hearty handshakes, then turned to kiss the bride. The two didn't seem to realize, or chose to ignore, that this wedding they seemed so pleased about was not a happy event.

"He'll come 'round," George whispered into her ear. "The fool loves you."

Hannah gave her cousin a tearful smile, then turned to James, who stood waiting for her, his blue eyes hooded. Hannah wished he did not look so magnificent in his wedding finery. She wished she did not love him so. She wished, she wished, he would look at her and smile. If only with his eyes.

Instead, when she reached his side, he simply nodded and began walking from the church, leaving Hannah to follow him. Suddenly, anger, hot and raging, filled her. She clenched her fists by her sides and remained where she stood. He should at least have had the decency to hold out his arm for her to take. He should at least give her that much. It took a few moments before James realized he was walking alone toward the church doors. Behind her, Hannah knew everyone was watching her humiliation, and her anger grew until she was quite unsure what she would do if he chose to continue walking away without her.

But James turned and smiled. "I seem to have lost my wife already," he said, and someone chuckled behind her. He held out one white-gloved hand, but Hannah simply threw up her chin and moved not an inch. The smile, that never quite reached his eyes, disappeared altogether. With her heart in her throat, Hannah stood stock-still as she watched him stride toward her, his face hard as stone. When he reached her, he stared down, and Hannah thought she saw admiration in his gaze—or perhaps imagined it—before he turned and offered her his arm. With the grace of a queen, Hannah placed her hand gently in the crook of his arm, and walked sedately out of the church next to her new husband.

"You may not like it, James," she said so that no one would hear, "but we are married. I am your wife, and you will treat me with respect." He remained silent, but she felt the muscle beneath her hand bunch.

The carriage ride to his house was made in silence. Horrible, awkward, silence. A hundred times Hannah wanted to say something, anything to knock that grim expression off his face. Was this what their marriage would be like? Would he forever hold this against her? So disturbed was she, that she barely noted his home when the carriage pulled up. She had a perception of brown stone, of a large porch, a bank of mullioned windows, and then she was in a dark, wood-paneled hall. A man hurried toward them, but James waved him off.

"I will show Mrs. MacRae to her room," he said, dismissing the servant. Mrs. MacRae, she thought, I am Mrs. MacRae.

He led her up a broad beautifully carved staircase that was lit by an intricate stained-glass skylight three stories above them. The stairs creaked loudly beneath the silent couple's feet. He moved her toward a door at the end of the hall, opening it with one hard push.

"I hope it will be adequate. I didn't have much time to prepare it." Hannah stood at the doorway, her heart plummeting. Her own room. It was lovely, and Hannah hated it on sight. It was a woman's room, with lace and ruffles and a pretty pale blue carpet partially covering the parquet wood floor. James stood in the center of the room, Hannah hovered just inside the door, her eyes sweeping over what were to be her sleeping quarters.

"How long are you going to punish me?"

James raised his eyebrows as if he hadn't the foggiest idea what she was talking about. He looked about the room, an exaggerated gesture. "I thought the room quite nice," he said.

Hannah hated that tone, the sarcasm she heard, the slight mockery in his expression. She didn't much care for this James. She wanted the old James back.

"It's fine," she said coldly.

He bowed to her. "Then, I'll leave you to settle in." He left then, sauntered, really, as if quite pleased with himself. That red-hot rage filled Hannah again. Her eyes scanned the hated room, the pretty things, and settled on a particularly lovely flowered vase. Picking it up, she threw it with all her might against the door where James had just disappeared, smiling when she heard the most gratifying crash.

"I'll leave you to settle in," she mimicked angrily. She strode to the bed and sat down, slightly amazed at the anger that continued to surge through her when not an hour ago she stood at the altar weeping. "Do you want me to say I'm sorry?" she shouted so loud her throat hurt. "All right, then, I'm sorry."

The door flew open with a crash. He stood there, fists clenched by his sides, looking fearsome. "For what?" he asked, his voice as cold as a Cape Horn gale. "Breaking an expensive vase? Or forcing me to marry you?"

Hannah looked at him, and blinked rapidly. She raised one hand limply off her lap. "For breaking your heart, I apologize," she said finally.

His head jerked downward, as if he saw something immensely interesting at her feet. Echoing the words he'd said to her on his ship, he said, "Too late." And then he left her there, quietly closing the door to her room behind him.

Morning touched Hannah lightly, softly whispering to her to come out of her slumber. She snuggled into her covers with a contented sigh. And then the hammer came down, pounding her head with memories of a miserable wedding night spent alone. Her eyes, gritty and swollen from a brief but torrential storm of tears, snapped open obliterating any feelings of contentment she'd had.

Hannah had stayed awake, her ears straining to hear his footsteps, until she finally convinced herself that he would not come to her. Somehow, even though she knew he did not love her, she didn't believe he would stay away on their wedding night.

But he had.

She tortured herself with guilty thoughts that she was experiencing a little bit of what he must have felt waiting on the deck of the *Windfire*. The foolishness, the hope. The disbelief. And finally, the acceptance that the person you love must not love you. That was when she'd cried. She had no way to call back her actions, no way to convince James that letting him sail away had ripped her heart in two. She heard a knock and had just a moment to wipe the misery from her face before an elderly woman in a gray housekeeper's uniform poked her head through the door.

"The captain will be in the dining room in twenty minutes. He requests that you join him for breakfast." All this was said as the older woman's eyes swept about the room, looking everywhere but at the sleepy-eyed bride sitting alone in her bed.

"Thank you . . . "

"Oh, my manners. Mrs. Holland. I'm the housekeeper. My husband is butler, valet and all-around man. Our daughter Hope is the upstairs maid, but she's helping cook right now. And our son, Harold, well, he's everything else. All in the family, you might say."

"How nice."

"Sometimes." And Mrs. Holland's eyes twinkled.

"Please tell the captain that I will not be joining him." As he has refrained from joining me, she longed to add.

That seemed to rattle the plump woman, whose rosy cheeks bloomed even brighter. She took a few tiny steps forward, and leaned conspiratorially toward Hannah. "I truly think you should reconsider," she whispered, and took another tiny step. "I don't know if you've ever seen our captain in a snit, but it's a sight to be seen. And heard. For the sake of all of us Hollands, it would greatly be appreciated if you went down."

Unused to arguing with servants, Hannah was momentarily taken aback. If the old woman had been with James for any amount of time, she knew the captain was more bluster than bite. It was James the old woman was thinking of, not Hannah, and certainly not the servants. Hannah forced a smiled.

"Very well."

With a satisfied nod, Mrs. Holland departed, and Hannah flopped back onto her pillow to stare at the ceiling high above her head. Why would he demand to see her at breakfast when he hadn't wanted to see her last night? Hannah dressed with some difficulty, tugging on her corset laces as best as she could and choosing a dress that fastened in the front. It seemed to take forever to dress without the help of a maid, and Hannah gave herself a mental reminder to send for Joan as soon as possible.

Smoothing down skirts that didn't need smoothing, Hannah left the sanctuary of her room, stepping uncertainly into the hall that led to the wide stairs. The stained-glass skylight left squares of muted color on the carpet, a broken rainbow scattered onto the steps. She watched as her hand, trailing down the banister turned yellow, then red, then green, as she descended. At the bottom of the stairs, she paused, trying to hear the telltale tinkling of silver on china that would indicate the direction of the dining room. Then her stomach tightened when she heard his voice.

"You did tell her twenty minutes, Mrs. Holland."

"Yes, sir. I'll go check on her, Captain."

Hannah stepped into the room. "No need. I'm here."

James snapped his head around. "So you are."

Hannah ignored his scowl and went to the elaborately carved sideboard laden with various meats, poached and scrambled eggs, and sweet buns. She wrinkled her nose at the dead stag, rabbit, and pheasant carved into the sideboard's walnut surface, thinking that animal corpses hovering above one's food was not very appetizing.

"It was a gift. We can get rid of it."

"No. It's wonderfully done. Just a bit gruesome for my tastes," Hannah said, giving her husband a tentative smile that was not returned. She forced herself to turn back to the fare laid out before her, but none of it looked appealing to Hannah, who was nervous and angry. And hurt. She poured herself some tea and sat at the opposite end of the table from James, ignoring the setting placed adjacent to his spot at the head of the table. He shot her a look of irritation after gazing pointedly at the place setting.

"I asked you here this morning to let you know I'll be departing today for two weeks."

"Thank you for informing me."

James tapped one fist lightly against his thigh. "I'm sailing on a schooner with a skeleton crew to bring my ship home. It's in Boston. Because I have so few men, we'll be under reduced sail. It could take longer."

"Mmm." She sipped a bit of tea and gently placed it upon its saucer.

"I was going to give George the honor of her maiden voyage. But recent events have made it possible for me to captain her. Which I plan to do. Once she's here, it will take six weeks to find a crew and load up a cargo."

Hannah felt as if her chest were being crushed beneath a great weight. "You mean her maiden voyage around the Horn." It was a statement.

"Yes."

"How . . ." Hannah swallowed, refusing to let him know how this hurt her. She lifted her chin and looked directly into his challenging gaze. "How long will you be gone, do you suppose?"

As if unable to look at her, James glanced down to his plate. "More than a year."

Hannah could not stop the little gasp that escaped, nor the look of despair that touched her eyes in that moment before she regained control.

"We'll be sailing to San Francisco, then to China."

"Then to London," Hannah finished for him.

"Yes. So you see . . ."

Hannah glared at him. "Yes. I see." She stood up abruptly and began walking from the room.

"Hannah."

She stopped but did not turn.

"I think it's for the best. Don't you?"

Hannah turned to him slowly. "No. I do not. You have hurt me, James. You have cut out my heart. Now neither of us has one. I hope you are pleased with yourself." And she walked from the room.

Chapter Twenty-seven

James found little joy in his ship. He admired it for its sleek lines, for its beautiful grace. He was proud, but he was not happy. He called the ship the *Bold Lady*. At the time, he told himself he was naming her for his intended, Sandra Sheffield. But he'd known in his heart even then that when he named it, he was thinking of another lady, as fearless and as brave as her namesake. His sister had smashed the champagne on her bow, to the great cheers of the throngs of Bostonians who were on hand for the christening of McKay's most beautiful ship. It was an honor that should have been bestowed upon Hannah, and it was another tiny bit of revenge that he'd thought he would find satisfying but did not.

Her hull was black, her trim white and gold. She was modern and luxurious, with large staterooms for passengers and ridiculously extravagant captains quarters. James loved her at first sight. And like a man looking at a beautiful woman, he wondered instantly if he was worthy of her. Though he had yet to put her under full sail, James knew she would challenge even the fastest of ships. The last of the sails were being furled as the tug that would bring them to the pier came into sight.

As the mouth of the East River drew near, James could only think about how much he missed Hannah, how much he wished she would be there at the pier waiting for him. He

knew she would not be, knew he had no right to even hope
it. All the joy of sailing his first ship was gone. He caught
himself looking forward to showing the *Bold Lady* to Hannah. How she would admire the ship, he'd thought. No
woman alive could appreciate her sleek lines the way Hannah did. But it was too late. He'd already turned the ship into
something ugly, something that would drive them apart.
When he'd announced he would take the *Bold Lady* on her
maiden voyage, he'd meant it. It had felt good to tell her.
Until he'd seen her eyes. Suddenly hurting Hannah hadn't
felt good at all; he'd felt sick inside, ashamed. But he'd left
anyway, and without saying good-bye.

Despite everything, his eyes still scanned the huge crowd
that had gathered at Pier 16 to see Donald McKay's latest
masterpiece. When the gangplank was lowered, he couldn't
stop himself from checking time and time again to see
whether she was walking onto the ship. Gradually the crowd
dispersed. The small crew worked to secure the ship; a few
would stay on board to guard her. James found himself reluctant to leave the ship. Going home certainly was not appealing, and he briefly considered staying on board until the
ship's voyage.

"Captain, all is secured," George reported unnecessarily.
George had stayed in New York recruiting crew and taking
care of cargo while James went to Boston to retrieve his
ship. When James was silent, George added, "My uncle's
expecting me this evening, sir."

"You're dismissed, Mr. Wright." James watched George's
mouth open and close, and wondered for the hundredth time
why he'd hired this meddlesome man. "You are dismissed,
Mr. Wright," he repeated succinctly.

"I visited Hannah while you were gone, sir."

James gave George a hard look.

"Hell," the younger man muttered. "I don't know why I
bother. You can fire me for saying this sir, because some
things are more important than a position."

James eyed George's clenched fists with speculation.

"You don't care what you do to her, do you? You truly don't care. I wouldn't have thought it of you, sir. I told you before, and I'll tell you now. She didn't come to you in San Francisco because she loves you. If you're too pigheaded to understand that, then you're not worthy of her love."

"You've said quite enough, Mr. Wright," James said through clenched teeth.

"No. Not nearly enough," he said bitterly. He stomped away.

"You're dismissed," James bit out. But George kept walking as if he'd suddenly gone deaf.

When he returned home, he was informed immediately that his wife was in her room and had asked that she not be disturbed.

"Fine," James had shouted, throwing his hat and coat in the general direction of the hall stand. Mrs. Holland huffed, but said not a word as she picked up his things. George's words whirled about his head nonstop. As if he needed that pup to tell him what he already knew. He was beginning to hate himself. His mind tried to shut off all thoughts of Hannah, but his heart and his body refused to listen. He throbbed. He ached. He goddamned hurt from wanting her, all the while cursing that part of his body that shouted at him to consummate his marriage. Tonight.

James let out a strangled sound of frustration. Why not? Why not go to her, spread her legs, push inside her hot, tight . . .

"Blast and damn, James. Get ahold of yourself, man," he said aloud, raking trembling hands through his hair. He tried to remind himself that he didn't love her anymore, but he was so sick and tired of being miserable. It was like a fog covering his brain. He didn't like himself, didn't enjoy being surly or mean. He knew he had been wretched to her, something that was so far against his nature, it left him feeling even more surly. But dammit, she'd hurt him. She'd let him wait there for her, she'd let him believe that she loved him as much as he loved her. She'd made love with him so

sweetly, that just the thought of those few magic moments
had been enough to nearly bring him shameful release. He
didn't love her. Refused to love her.

She's your wife.

He had the right to share her bed, the right to ease the terrible aching in his loins. He'd be damned if she kept him out
of her bed.

James stalked to her room, knocked once, then entered. It
was dark, but he could see her shadow in her bed.

"James?" She sounded startled, slightly fearful.

"I don't love you," he said, his voice sounding harsh even
to his own ears. She struck a match and lit the bedside lamp.
He cursed that flame that allowed him to see her. Her hair
was down, long and wavy, glimmering gold in the light. Her
eyes, smoky and wary, looked at him, her hands clutched the
bedcovers. He walked to the bed and glared down at her.

"I don't love you," he said again.

"I heard you the first time," Hannah said, lifting her chin.
"But I love you."

James blinked. "Don't. It's a waste of energy. I ought to
know." He stood there, staring at her, thinking only that he
was being mean and not knowing quite why he was doing it.
She looked so damned lovely, looking up at him, her stubborn chin lifting even higher.

"Is that all you had to say? Are you finished? Because if
you are, I'd like to get some sleep. I'm tired." He watched
as she made a great show of snuggling down into her covers. She pounded her goose down pillow and turned her
back.

"Tonight we consummate this . . . marriage. There'll be
little sleeping tonight," he said coldly. Hannah turned and
sat up, and he nearly winced at the pain he saw in her eyes.

"Please, James."

He grabbed her upper arms, lifting her partially off the
bed. "Please, what? Please leave? Please stay?" He gave her
a little shake, hating what he was doing to her. Her eyes glittered with unshed tears.

"I'm sorry, James. I'm sorry for what I did. If I could erase what happened, I would, but I can't. Please don't hurt me."

James dropped his hands, fearing he was, indeed, hurting her, even though he somehow knew she meant for him not to hurt her heart. The anger was still there, though he wasn't sure whether he was angry with himself or with her. He bent over her, his face only inches from hers.

"I want to hurt you. I want to take your heart and squeeze it and squeeze until you feel what I have felt for the past three months. I want to make you scream the way I screamed. I want . . . I want . . ." He stopped, his breath coming out harshly. And then he pulled her against him with a hard jerk, his face buried in her hair, his mouth near her ear.

"I don't love you," he whispered, but his mouth moved over her jaw, and his hand moved to the back of her head to hold her against him. Hannah let out a sound of joy or anguish, he couldn't be sure. Either way, he wanted to stop that sound, so he smothered her mouth with his, letting out a groan. Hannah clutched his shoulders, her fingers digging in, as she turned her mouth to deepen the kiss.

"Hannah, Hannah," he said raggedly against her mouth. "I don't . . . I don't . . ."

"I know, James. I know. But I do."

He moved his frantic mouth to her throat, licked her there, a quick, darting tongue, and reveled in the feel of her, the scent of her, in his arms. Some emotion he was afraid to recognize washed over him. Her fingers were at his shirt, working at the buttons, and he moved away, pulling the half-unbuttoned shirt over his head. Within moments he was naked, standing beside the bed with Hannah looking at him with those drowsy eyes he had tortured himself remembering. She grabbed the hem of her dressing gown, already hiked up to her thighs, and slowly drew it over her head. She didn't smile. She didn't try to hide herself, but knelt boldly upon the bed and looked at him—all of him. He felt her gaze like a

caress, his body heating where her eyes touched him, and he
grew so hard, so painfully hard.

James moved onto the bed, forcing Hannah back, and she
lightly lay one hand on his shoulder. They were silent, only
their breathing and the sound of her hand skimming over his
chest interrupted that silence. He kissed her lightly, almost
chastely, nipping her full bottom lip, sucking in gently, as
his fingertips rested on her chest just above the swell of her
breasts. Slowly, a whisper of touch, he moved his fingers
down, skimming her hard nipples, going lower and back,
making her shiver. Her breathing was becoming more
ragged—or was that him? She had dropped her hands from
him, lost in the sensations he was creating with his feathery
touch, her arms laying by her side. And then he felt her
warm hand wrap around him, squeezing, moving. He let out
a choking sound, but let her continue touching him, making
him sweat with the exertion of not throwing her down and
entering her. He dipped his head, drawing a nipple hard into
his mouth, and she gasped, involuntarily squeezing his erec-
tion even harder as he suckled.

"God, Hannah," he groaned, and lifted her hand gently
away from him.

James pulled her to him, his mouth capturing hers almost
violently, his hands cupping her bottom and pulling her
against him until they were nearly joined. They moved together, legs entangled, mouths becoming bruised, hands
clutching and caressing. Suddenly he was over her, looking
down into her eyes, his body straining toward her, his heart
pounding, pounding. He was lost in her gaze, in the love and
trust he saw. He swallowed past something hard lodged in
his throat.

"Dammit! Don't make me love you, Hannah."

"Is that what I'm doing?"

He breathed harshly, in, out. "Yes."

She smiled. "Don't expect an apology."

And then he smiled. But only with his eyes.

He entered her, filling her, loving her. And he thought: It

was worth it, the pain, the emptiness, if he could have her this way forever. James began moving, felt her legs wrap around him, heard her breath become more and more ragged, her movement more and more frantic. His hand found its way between them, and he almost shouted aloud in pure happiness at her pleasured gasp. No words could tell her how he felt, his body, his heart, and so he remained silent but for his breathing, harsh against her neck. When she arched against him, her body taut, he reached the stars, the rainbows, that burst around him.

Blast and damn, he thought as he lay panting and spent, his face tucked between her jaw and shoulder, still feeling her clench convulsively around him.

"James?"

"Hmmm."

"Did you mean, before when you said that—did you mean that you love me?"

Sounding as if he'd just stepped out of the Scottish Highlands, he said, "You know I do, you little fool."

Hannah awoke to find her husband scowling down at her, and she smiled.

"You've done it now, girl," he grumbled. He was leaning on one elbow, his chin resting on his hand. The blankets left his torso uncovered, and Hannah couldn't help but sweep her gaze along that powerful upper body before looking back at his beard-roughened face.

"What have I done?"

"You've made the prospect of sailing away in six weeks highly disagreeable. Thought I'd be looking forward to the journey, but now you've ruined it for me," he said.

Hannah could tell he was trying to make light of it, but she couldn't force herself to play along. Waking up beside James, knowing that he loved her, was more wonderful than she could have imagined. How he could joke about going away on a trip that would take him from her for more than a year, she could not fathom.

"I don't want to talk about it," she said, turning her head away. She felt his hand fall gently on the side of her face as he tried to turn her head toward him, and she resisted for a few moments before relenting. He kissed her, softly, then lifted his head, his eyes filled with sorrow.

"I know you don't, Hannah. But I want you to know that what has happened between us will not alter my plans for my ship."

"But you hadn't planned to take her on her maiden voyage before. Why must you now?"

"What does it matter if it is now or one year from now. I will still sail away from you. I will still leave. You've married a sea captain, darling. Do you think I look forward to leaving you here when I've just gotten you back?"

Hannah crossed her arms over her breasts, which were still covered by the blanket. "Yes. I do. I think you go down to the pier, and you look at your ship, and you imagine her in a gale. I think you breathe in the salt air, and you feel that sharp wind even standing along the smelly East River. Yes, James, I think you do look forward to leaving."

James lay back down, his hands tucked beneath his head as he gazed up at the ceiling. "This trip . . . I need to know I can leave you. I need to know that my love of the sea is as strong as my love for you. If I find no joy in this journey, I'll know it is time to set my feet on the land permanently."

"That won't happen."

He sighed. "Probably not. Even now, I can hear her calling to me, I can feel her pull." He turned to look at Hannah. "But if you asked me, Hannah, I wouldn't go. I want you to know that."

Hannah would never know what stopped her from shouting for him to stay. The words were there, in her throat, aching to be released. But when she opened her mouth, something else entirely came out, and she wanted to cry.

"I would never ask it of you." She closed her eyes briefly against the pain those words brought, and against the smile that immediately lit her sea captain husband's face.

"I want to show her to you today. She's grand, Hannah. Her mainmast is two hundred feet, her lines are sleek and sharp." He sighed as if describing a beautiful woman. "Ten thousand yards of canvas." Hannah saw the look of rapture on her husband's face and knew he was picturing his ship under full sail. Despite herself, she found herself smiling at his enthusiasm.

"If you ever have that look on your face when you describe me, I'll know you truly think I'm beautiful," she said, and kissed the tip of his nose.

He let out a hearty laugh, so full of joy that Hannah's heart ached. She could not be happy, not totally so, knowing he'd be leaving her. She remembered how she'd felt standing atop that hill in San Francisco watching *Windfire* become smaller and smaller on the horizon, and thought the pain she'd feel watching James sail away this time might be worse. How could she bear it? She told herself that hundreds of sea captains' wives bore it well. Certainly she was as strong as they. She turned to James, pressing herself against him in a desperate way. She felt his smile soften as he realized she'd not intended an ordinary kiss. She needed him. Now. Desperately. She needed to forget he was sailing away. She wanted to drive from her head the words she longed to scream: Don't leave me, never leave me.

Chapter Twenty-eight

The bon voyage party was one of the largest to be held in New York. The *Bold Lady* was departing in one week's time, and as the ship had been proclaimed by the New York newspapers to be the fastest vessel ever built, the excitement surrounding her was frenzied. Josiah Creesy of the *Flying Cloud*, just returned from an around-the-world trek, had graciously agreed to host the event at the Astor House, one of New York's premier hotels.

The offer from Creesy was unexpected and gracious beyond measure, considering that reporters were claiming that Creesy had met his match with the young upstart, James MacRae.

"How do I look?" James asked upon hearing the rustle of his wife's skirts coming up behind him. She had just entered their bedroom from her dressing room, and she watched with some amusement as his worried gaze went to the full-length mirror Hannah had brought from her father's house. He tugged on his cravat and scowled.

"You might think you were meeting the President of the United States," Hannah said with an indulgent smile.

"Creesy's more important than the King of England, as far as I'm concerned," James said, tugging down on his waistcoat. "Are you certain these tails aren't too long?"

Hannah sighed. "According to your tailor, they're the latest thing. By the way, how do I look?"

"Fine," James said, still scowling at his own reflection. Then he looked up, and his mouth fell open. "Jesus and all the saints," he muttered. "You'll be wearing a shawl, no doubt."

Hannah looked uncertainly down at her front to determine if too much of her chest were showing. "This is perfectly modest," she said, then plumped up her breasts so that even more cleavage showed.

"Blast and damn, woman, you pull that dress back up where it belongs."

Hannah shot him an innocent look. "It is where it belongs." She could feel the heat of his gaze on her, and she flushed.

Giving her a knowing look, James took the two steps separating them, his eyes never leaving that exquisitely displayed chest. He placed two fingers between the material of her dress and her breasts, skimming along the cut of the neckline, his blue eyes shuttered. With one small tug, he exposed a breast, and Hannah gasped.

"Perhaps I did have it too low," she said huskily.

"Mmmm." He dipped his head, tasting her. "I find it not so objectionable now," he muttered, laving her nipple with his tongue. His hand moved to the other breast, gently pulled the material down, exposing her completely. "How long will it take you to get out of this thing?"

Hannah swallowed heavily. "Not long. With help."

He smiled wickedly, turning her around to begin tackling the long row of buttons down her back. A knock at the door stilled his hands, and Hannah immediately lifted the dress to cover her breasts. With a small sigh of resignation, James called, "Enter."

"Your carriage is ready, sir," Mr. Holland said. "Shall I tell the driver you will be departing soon?"

James shot a look at Hannah, who smiled with regret. "We'll be down momentarily," he said.

Hannah jerked the neckline even higher. "Will this do?"

"Hannah, darlin', I know what's underneath. I'm afraid

you could wear a potato sack, and you'd not be safe from me." He kissed her deeply, a promise of what would come when they returned home, and pulled away reluctantly. "Shall we?" he asked, extending his arm. And Hannah, the little temptress, took his arm and pressed it firmly against the breasts he'd just been loving.

Astor House took up an entire city block on Broadway, its grand facade telling of the elegance of its patrons. Doric columns flanked the impressive entrance to the granite building that soared skyward six stories, dwarfing the finely dressed men and women stepping into the hotel from a line of carriages.

It hit Hannah hard as she looked up, dazzled by an impossibly large chandelier glittering far above her head—they were here to say good-bye. The rumble of voices, laughter, and soft music were all of a sudden harsh and painful to her ears. She was here, standing next to James, so that New York could say bon voyage to its latest hero. New York had forgiven James his dropping of socialite Sandra Sheffield for the lesser-known Hannah Wright. Many stared with open curiosity at the woman who managed to snatch James MacRae from one of the most highly sought-after New York debutantes. As if sensing this perusal, James placed an arm about her waist, tugging her to him before releasing her and placing a comforting and warm hand at the small of her back.

No formal receiving line was formed, so the MacRaes were assaulted throughout the night by well-wishers and men who hoped to invest in the *Bold Lady's* voyage. Hannah's father, beaming happily, gave her a quick and awkward embrace before heading off to talk to several of his old seafaring friends. The room looked like a grand meeting of sea captains, their bearded faces, their weathered skin looking at odds with their formal garb. Hannah knew many of the men and was comfortable in their company. They spoke a language she understood, they stood with legs planted wide, a familiar and oddly endearing posture.

Faces red from the brandy being served and from whiskey carefully concealed in silver flasks, the old sea captains made up a raucous bunch who formed a semicircle at the far end of the ballroom. She could picture James like that some day, his dark hair snowy white, his blue eyes glittering happily from some remembered adventure. And she would be . . . Hannah scanned the room, looking for the wives of this bunch. Ah, there they were. Sitting quietly together, sturdy old matrons, who often gave the rowdy bunch an indulgent glance. Hannah scowled. For the life of her, she could not picture herself among that group of women. She was inexplicably drawn to the men. She was nearly upon the group when she realized that, though she had grown up with these men, her entrance into this group might be unwanted.

Turning away from her father and his friends, Hannah looked for James, and her stomach twisted. He was among a younger group of sea captains, his head thrown back in laughter. How he was enjoying this night, Hannah thought. Instead of being happy for him, her stomach twisted with some emotion she did not immediately recognize.

Unfair.

The word came blazing from somewhere, harsh and searing. Hannah shook her head, trying to rid herself of unhappy thoughts. She was so proud of James, of his success. But she recognized that a part of her was jealous of the attention he was receiving. He was the great and brave Captain MacRae. And she was . . . she was . . .

His wife.

It should have made her proud. It should have made her content to be known as Mrs. James MacRae. A hundred women would readily take her place, she knew. Then, why did she feel this sudden surge of resentment? It was ugly, but once recognized, Hannah could not put it out of her mind.

Dinner was a huge and sumptuous buffet, but Hannah could barely bring herself to swallow past the growing lump in her throat. No matter how much she chastised herself, she could not help feeling more and more depressed as the night wore on.

"If one more person comes up to me and tells me what a wonderful husband I have and how lucky I am to have captured him, I think I shall scream," Hannah said through tight lips to her cousin.

George chuckled. "Do you mean you don't agree? I thought things were finally going well between you two."

Hannah crossed her arms and shot a dark look toward her husband, who appeared to be having much too grand a time for a man who was about to leave for nearly a year. "Well enough," she said begrudgingly. Then she looked at George, her eyes welling with tears. "Oh, George, I don't think I can bear being in this room any longer."

George frowned, looking quickly around to make certain no one saw Hannah's distress. He quickly led her to one of the hotel's quiet salons and helped her to sit. "So, that's the way of it."

Hannah could only nod, a handkerchief pressed to her mouth to stop the sobs she knew were ready to burst from her throat.

"And I suppose you've been hiding it from him?"

"I didn't know myself until tonight. I was really quite proud of myself. But now I realize I was hiding my feelings even from myself."

George let out a heavy sigh. "Hannah. Many sea captains' wives have been in similar spots and have survived. Women not half as strong as you."

Hannah looked up at him. "It's not that. Not anymore. I know I will survive his absence."

"Then, what is the problem?"

"It's so unfair. He gets to go off on that ship of his. He gets to have adventure, travel around the world. And I'll be stuck here like some meek little miss." Her fist curled around the handkerchief. "What am I supposed to do, George? I swear to you I have actually contemplated stowing aboard and not showing my face until we're a week out."

Her frown deepened when George let out a laugh. "Here I was thinking you were suffering from a broken heart when it's boredom you fear."

Hannah stood, her body stiff with anger. "I do have a broken heart. I shall miss him terribly, but I've come to grips with that. This feeling of resentment has been completely unexpected. I feel churlish and . . . and angry. On the other hand, doesn't it seem rather unfair? I love the sea as much as he does, as much as you do. But simply because I have said some vows in a church, I am suddenly expected to become a dutiful wife."

Still obviously suppressing a smile, George asked, "Do you plan to tell James of your feelings?"

"He wouldn't understand. He wants me to be a wife, not a ship's mate. He's told me a number of times how much he looks forward to this trip, knowing that I'll be home waiting for him. If he wanted me on board, he would have asked."

"Not necessarily. I don't believe it would have occurred to him that you wanted to go with the *Bold Lady*, only that you didn't want him to leave."

Hannah slumped back down on the sofa, her skirts billowing up around her, and rested her chin on her hands. "I suppose I simply have to get used to the idea. I'll work on my needlepoint. That ought to keep me occupied at least ten minutes of the day," she grumbled.

James was in his glory. He'd shaken more hands and slapped more backs than he had in his entire life previous to this evening. A few reporters had sneaked into the ball, and he was happy to tell them about the *Bold Lady*, deftly leaving the questions concerning the *Flying Cloud's* record unanswered. After all, Josiah Creesy was hosting his party, and it would have been unpardonable to even hint at a rivalry between the two captains. Seeing Creesy from across the room, James excused himself from a group of reporters and headed his way.

"Captain. I wanted to extend my gratitude for your hosting this affair," James said when he'd reached the older man.

"No need," Creesy said. His eyes scanned the crowd like a hunted man before he narrowed them with obvious distaste, his bearded face flushing. "Damned reporters. Been clamoring at me for the past three days about the *Flying Cloud* and that record trip to San Francisco. And about you, damn your hide," he said good-naturedly. "Can't wait to get back to Marblehead. I'm leaving tomorrow to get out of this infernal city. Can't imagine why you'd want to live here, MacRae."

James smiled at the man's gruff monologue. "It's close to my ship," he said with a small shrug.

"That's one hell of a gamble you're taking, MacRae, investing so much in a ship. But she's the prettiest ship I've seen McKay build. Walked down to the piers yesterday to take a gander at her. Made my blood run hot, she did. Oh, hell. Here comes one of those scalawags from the *Tribune*. Listen, MacRae. I'd love to get a closer look at her. Would you mind meeting me at the pier tomorrow morning, eight bells?"

"I'd be honored, sir," James said, flushing with pleasure. There was no captain he respected more than Josiah Creesy. He'd met the man briefly years ago and looked forward to showing off his ship and getting Creesy's opinion of the *Bold Lady*.

"Oh, and bring your wife. Nellie will be with me as we'll be leaving directly for Marblehead."

"Certainly, sir." James began scanning the crowd for his wife and frowned when he could not spot her. Soon, though, he was again surrounded by a crowd of men, many of them investors, and his thoughts inevitably returned to his ship.

On their way home after the ball, Hannah was unusually quiet. She stared out the carriage window, her face turned away from James.

"Tired?"

"A bit. It is three o'clock."

James frowned at her short reply. "I'm sorry I was kept from you all evening. I couldn't get away."

"You didn't want to get away," Hannah said, then smiled to take the bite off her words. But James was not fooled.

"No. I didn't." He waited to see how she would react, but was disappointed when she returned her gaze to the window. "Josiah Creesy and his wife, Eleanor, plan to tour the *Bold Lady* later this morning. I'd like you to join us."

"I'm quite tired, James."

"You haven't seen the *Bold Lady* yet, and I thought this a perfect time to see her. I didn't get a chance to talk with the Creesys for more than a moment. Did you have a chat with Mrs. Creesy?"

"Just a polite exchange. James, I'm really too tired to discuss your wonderful triumph of this evening."

"It was your triumph, too."

Hannah looked at him, bitterness clear in her gaze. "Oh, really? I hadn't noticed."

James looked at her with disbelief. What was bringing on these sharp little barbs? Everything had seemed perfect last evening before they left for the party. Now, not six hours later, his wife was acting cold and belligerent.

"Did something happen this evening that I'm not aware of?" he asked. "If you are angry that I could not spend more time with you, then I have said I am sorry."

Hannah remained silent.

"Are you planning to tour the *Bold Lady* today or not?" James asked when the carriage pulled up in front of the house.

"I have told you, I am tired."

"The *Bold Lady* is . . ."

"The *Bold Lady* can rot for all I care," Hannah said heatedly before stepping down from the carriage unassisted.

That night Hannah slept in her own bed. Or rather, she lay there feeling hellish and staring at the ceiling, her eyes gritty. She knew she was being unfair to James and cringed as she remembered his look of complete shock when she'd told him the *Bold Lady* could rot. She didn't mean it, of course.

Unknown to James, Hannah had seen her. She had not stepped aboard the ship, but she had seen it from a distance at its pier near the foot of Maiden Lane. She was beautiful. So beautiful, Hannah's throat had constricted at the mere sight of her. At the time Hannah had thought that emotion came from her fear of seeing James sail away. But now she knew better.

She loved that ship. She wanted to feel her beneath her feet. She wanted to lead her to the best currents, the fairest winds. She wanted to wrap her arms around the shrouds in the midst of a Cape Horn gale, to hear James yelling orders, to see him stride from stern to bow.

She wanted to be on that ship when she sailed in one week's time, but knew that instead she'd stand on that pier and watch as a tugboat led it out of the East River. And wave good-bye.

Chapter Twenty-nine

James smiled as he approached the *Bold Lady* and saw that Captain Creesy and his wife were already standing at the base of the gangplank. Creesy returned the smile, but pointedly brought out his watch and noted the time.

"I apologize, sir. At the last minute my wife was unable to come, and I was delayed," he lied neatly. In fact, he and Hannah had engaged in a fierce argument. He could not understand her abrupt about-face, and she refused to explain herself. He suspected she refused to tour the *Bold Lady* because she didn't want him to leave, but when he confronted her with his theory, she'd called him an egotistical buffoon and run from the room. It had taken all his willpower not to chase after her and drag her to the pier. Didn't she know how much she was hurting him by not letting him share his ship with her?

"Not all women share my love of ships," Nellie Creesy said kindly.

James raised his eyebrows at the woman. "In fact, Mrs. Creesy, Hannah grew up on ships. I met her on my last trip to San Francisco, and she's a fine sailor."

"Then, I am sorry to have missed talking with her, for it seems we have much in common. I grew up in a seafaring family myself, and have been sailing with Josiah ever since our marriage."

"But you're . . ."

"A married woman?" Eleanor asked, her hazel eyes filling with amusement. "Thankfully, Josiah recognized my skill as a navigator and decided he could not do without me. I've always wondered whether he married me because he loves me, or because I am such an able seawoman." Eleanor cast her blushing husband a fond look. "But shipboard life is not an easy life. I daresay most women I meet think I'm rather eccentric."

James was stunned to silence. He'd not known Mrs. Creesy had sailed with her husband, and although he was aware of other women who sometimes sailed with their husbands, it was not a common occurrence. A thought began blooming in his mind, one that once started, he could not put away.

"Show me your ship, Captain. I want to find out for myself whether she's really as fine as the *Flying Cloud*."

His mind brought back to his ship, James smiled. "Sir, I do beg your pardon, but most of the accounts I've read about the *Bold Lady* put her as finer and faster than the *Flying Cloud*."

Creesy let out a burst of laughter and slapped James on the back, making James stumble forward. As tall and strong as James was, Creesy was even larger, with big beefy hands that had the strength of two men.

The *Bold Lady* was slightly smaller than the *Flying Cloud*, being shorter by five feet, but she was sleeker. Creesy, his gaze intense as he wandered about the main deck, shot rapid-fire questions at James, which he answered in similar fashion.

"She's top-heavy," Creesy announced, gazing up at the mainmast that soared high overhead.

"She carries more sail because of it. She sails like a dream," James said, smiling at the man who was obviously goodnaturedly baiting him.

"That's what they said about the *Challenge*," Creesy argued.

"Now, Captain. You and I both know that given a good

crew and a better captain, the *Challenge* would have fared far better."

"Bah."

The small group headed below, and James again thought of Eleanor Creesy sailing with her husband. He tried to picture Hannah in the large captain's quarters, in the bed that was certainly large enough for two. The quarters even had a water closet attached, including a deep copper bathtub, which Hannah was certain to enjoy. It was a pleasant thought, that he could come in from the sleet and snow and find his beautiful wife luxuriating in the bathtub.

The vision snapped. Hannah would not be drifting in warm bathwater, her hair piled seductively atop her head. His wife instead would be threatening to climb the mainmast in the middle of a gale to repair a sail. His wife would be in the chart room, her pretty brow furrowed, as she tried to find the best course. His wife would drive him insane with her stubbornness, her contrary notions, her complete lack of concern for her own safety. His blood went cold at the thought of her fearlessness. Hannah could not go; he would not be able to keep his mind on his ship if he were worrying about her constantly. Better that she remain in New York. He wondered how Creesy had managed, but decided that the sedate and gentle Nellie Creesy was of a far different temperament than his Hannah.

James shook his head, glad to be rid of the notion that he should allow Hannah to travel with him, and continued his tour.

The *Bold Lady* made the *Windfire* appear utilitarian and almost shabby. His ship was as grand inside as out, with fine inlaid woods, delicate carvings, and extravagant furnishings. The dining salon, wainscoted with satinwood, went the width of the ship with a series of portholes along each end, allowing in sunlight. Large squares of light from the skylight illuminated the polished dining table and the rich Oriental carpet laid underneath. Pride filled James at the exclamations of the Creesys.

"McKay has outdone himself," the captain said, taking in the luxurious salon.

In addition to the ship's creature comforts, it had more water storage, a large iceroom, and enough animal pens to put an entire barnyard aboard her to keep the crew and passengers eating fresh meat and vegetables for months. It was, thought James, the grandest ship he'd ever seen, and he only prayed he was worthy of her.

"You were missed."

Hannah, who had been staring forlornly out the window, started at her husband's deep voice. When she turned to him, she was smiling brightly.

"I should have gone," she said sweetly. "I was simply feeling contrary."

He let out a small grunt of agreement, and Hannah did all she could not to grit her teeth. She'd come to some conclusions in the past hours. When the *Bold Lady* sailed in one week, Hannah planned to be on board. She didn't plan to sneak aboard, either, but would be there at the adamant request of her husband.

Continuing to smile, she indicated a letter in her hand—the letter that had spawned what she'd decided was a flawless plan.

"This has something to do with my good humor," Hannah said. "You do remember Christopher Easton from our trip to San Francisco." From James's frown she knew immediately that he did, indeed, remember the young man.

"Vaguely," he said, and Hannah's smile broadened.

"It seems the fellows he was to meet in San Francisco were no longer there when he arrived. He's expected back in New York . . ." Hannah pretended to scan the letter. "Goodness, in just two weeks."

Hannah held the letter against her breast, hoping she was not overdoing things. "It will be so good to have a friend in New York while you're gone," she said, almost wincing at what she thought was an obvious ploy.

"You certainly have friends in New York other than that Wheaton fellow."

"Easton. And actually, James, I do not. Much of my childhood was spent with my father sailing back and forth between England and New York. Then I was in school. Of course, I met Allen soon after and fell in with his circle of friends. But I think it hardly appropriate for me to maintain those friendships." She could barely suppress her smile at her husband's reddening face.

"Female friends. You must have female friends."

Hannah gave a delicate shrug. "I've always been much more comfortable in the company of men," she said honestly, and watched with veiled delight as James began tapping his thigh lightly with a loose fist.

"Perhaps you are right. You are young and will need an escort, and Easton seems like a nice enough fellow. Perhaps you can become a part of a larger group of young people. I will find it much easier knowing that you are here and not pining away in my absence."

Hannah could not help it when her face fell in disappointment. He was giving her his blessing to keep the company of another man. She suddenly felt like weeping.

"I'm sure I shall keep very busy. I'm sure I will be at parties every evening. At balls each Saturday night. I'm sure the time you are gone will fly by while I flit from party to party."

He smiled at her, and Hannah knew he was onto her game. Crossing her arms with a small huff, she stiffened when he came to her and lay his hands on her shoulders.

"I know you will miss me, love. I already ache inside knowing how much I will miss you."

He kissed her forehead, and she could feel him smiling against her when she deepened her frown. She used all her strength not to beg him to take her with him. It should be obvious that it was the perfect solution. Why should she remain in New York, bored silly, while he was standing at the bow of the *Bold Lady*, wind whipping his hair, tasting the salt and feeling the sting of the sea?

She stepped away from him. "I'll not miss you. I'll not even think of you," she said, knowing she sounded like a child. She wanted to slap his face when he gave her an indulgent smile. "You have no idea what I want," she shouted.

His smile faded, confronted with her true anger. "Apparently not. Why don't you tell me."

"I want to . . ." She closed her mouth.

"What, Hannah?"

Oh, hell. "I want to go."

He shook his head in confusion. "Where?"

"With you. On the *Bold Lady*. I want to be navigator."

"No." It sounded so final, Hannah cringed.

"Why not? I would help you. We could be together. I . . ."

"I have thought of it, Hannah. And decided it would not be in the best interest for either of us."

"You decided?"

"I have."

So that was that. He had decided, and the answer was no. Hannah felt frustration and anger build up inside of her. She wanted to pummel him, she wanted to scream.

She wanted to beg him.

Instead she walked from the room without another word, her fate decided. She was a woman, a wife. She would have to get used to having no say in her life. Her hateful life.

James watched her go, his face grim. He had made the right decision, he was certain of it. For this first voyage, he needed to have his mind and body atuned to his ship, something he would not be able to do with Hannah about, questioning his orders, putting herself in danger. Without realizing he was doing so, he smiled thinking about their trip to San Francisco. He pictured her angry face when she'd thought he would harshly flog the boy, Todd Engle. And he pictured her sitting atop the after house, her knees pulled up against her chin, as the wind whipped her hair.

And then he saw her standing on the deck, the white

squall approaching with ferocious speed. In his mind's eye, he saw her chin jutted up stubbornly as she refused to move, just before the mizzenmast came crashing down crushing her skull.

James swallowed down the bile that formed in his throat. Never. He could never allow it. Seamen died on nearly every trip, of accidents, of disease. He would not put Hannah in such danger. Another thought came to him then. On a trip that would take a year or more, it was possible that Hannah would become pregnant. The Creesys had no children, so it made more sense that they could have allowed the arrangement. He could not imagine his frenzied worry if Hannah were large with child and attempted to move about the deck. Knowing Hannah's stubborn streak, he could well imagine her, awkward and ungainly, trying to take the noon reading in rough seas.

He let out his breath in a long shudder, convinced that he was right.

Chapter Thirty

Hannah stood looking out her window, reminded of another time, another window, another unsaid good-bye. He was leaving tomorrow. Her stubbornness and resolve grew everyday, until she became convinced she was diseased with anger and resentment. Why couldn't she be like other women? Why couldn't she simply accept that he was sailing away without her? She was a sea captain's wife, and like scores of other women, she should accept her role.

But she found to her great frustration, she couldn't.

The worst of it was knowing she was hurting James. Again. But every time she thought to go to him, to hold him against her and beg him to forgive her, something made her stop. He should be the one apologizing to her. After all, he was the one who was leaving. She wanted to be with him. What had changed so much that he suddenly did not want her with him on his ship? He had certainly wanted her there when he sailed from San Francisco. Was he punishing her for that abandonment?

Tomorrow he would sail away, and she would not be there. She would not stand on that pier and smile and wave. She would not travel to Battery Park and watch the *Bold Lady* become smaller and smaller until she disappeared from view, her heart beating painfully in her breast.

She knew James would never forgive her for it. Perhaps she would never forgive herself.

She wasn't coming.

James's gut clenched, a familiar and awful tightening in his stomach. He'd made himself sick by turning again and again to the crowded pier looking for a lovely woman in an overlarge bonnet with skirts billowing about her. Certainly she could not be so stubborn. Certainly she could not kill the fragile love that had blossomed so briefly between them by not coming to say good-bye. She hadn't even responded to his knocks at her door that morning. How could she turn so cold?

What would he find when he returned to her all those months from now? Would there be anything left of their marriage? In the past few days of stony silence, of ice-cold responses to his falsely cheerful questions, he realized just how much he missed his wife, just how painful it would be to leave her. And that realization only fueled his anger now as he gave the crowd one last sweep of his fierce blue eyes.

"Goddamn her to hell," he gritted out, banging a fist hard against the railing. Today should have been the happiest of his life, and he'd be damned if he let her childishness, her stubbornness, ruin it entirely. The steamship was ready to haul the *Bold Lady* from the pier, and he gave the order, turning his back on the cheering crowd.

As the ship made its tedious way from the pier, he kept his back steadfastly to the crowd, perversely hoping she'd decided to come at the last moment only to realize she'd come too late.

But to his complete disgust, James asked for his glass as the ship passed Battery Park. No sign of her. No delicate woman waving frantically. He felt his throat tighten, felt his eyes burn.

She hadn't come.

As the ship passed Sandy Hook, he ordered her sails un-

furled. Where was the joy at seeing her sailing under full
sail for the first time? Where was the thrill of seeing his
crew fumble with their orders, then jump when he shouted
at them, giving them encouragement as he berated them
for failing? The spring air was sharp, but held the tiniest
hint of softness, as it filled the pristine sails. They snapped
overhead, yet they could have been ripping apart for all
James cared.

She hadn't come.

Breathing suddenly became difficult, and he snapped
his head around to see if he could still see New York behind him. One year. Possibly more. He should have forced
her to see him. He should have torn down her door and
kissed her good-bye whether she wanted to kiss him or
not. Where was she now? Still sitting in her room? Or had
she sneaked down to Battery Park and caught a last
glimpse of the *Bold Lady* sailing away as she said she had
done in San Francisco. Was she regretting her stubbornness? Was she crying even now knowing she'd made a
mistake? He could almost feel the distance growing between them, each second passing bringing the ship farther
and farther away. The sound of the sea crashing against
the hull, once a lulling, pleasing sound, became an excru-
ciating thing.

"Come about!"

"Sir?" George turned to him, his face a mask of disbelief.

"Helmsman. Turn this goddamn ship around."

"Sir, I must protest," George said, getting all stiff and
proper.

James pushed by him, muttering, "Protest all you like,
Mr. Wright. We're heading back to New York."

George glared at Timothy Lodge, who was grinning
from ear to ear. "You romantic fool," he said, and then
smiled himself.

The ship groaned, the sails fluttered loudly, as the *Bold
Lady* slowly turned. Seamen heaved on the halyards, their

rhythmic chants sounding like angels' voices to James's ear.

"Where are we going?"

James had been looking up at the sails, but jerked his head down at the sound of that familiar female voice. He stood there, his mouth gaping, unsure whether he should kiss his obstinate little wife or sweep her into his arms.

"Come about, gentlemen," he called, deciding instead to keep his attention on his ship and ignore his wife for the moment.

With some grumbling, the men obeyed his order, and brought the great ship around and back onto its original course. Once all was well, James turned his attention back to his wife, who was looking entirely too pleased with herself. She wore her pants, her blouse, her floppy hat tied with a thick ribbon beneath her stubborn chin. She'd never looked more beautiful.

"Where were you going?" she asked with a smile that told him she'd known exactly what he was doing.

"I was drilling my crew," he said. "A crew that does not include a woman."

"I happen to be a competent navigator," Hannah said. "Would you like a demonstration of my skills?"

With that, James grabbed her wrist and dragged her down into the main cabin.

"The ship is lovely, by the way," Hannah said, hurrying to keep up with her husband. "I especially like the captain's quarters. I imagine that's where I'll be staying."

James ignored her chatter as they walked down a paneled hall that led to the captain's quarters. James, still holding her wrist, heaved Hannah in front of him when they crossed the threshold and closed the door silently but firmly behind him. He looked at her as if he wanted to throttle her, breathing harshly through flared nostrils.

"James? You're not truly angry. Are you?" she asked uncertainly. She shrank back a bit from his blazing gaze.

"Blast and damn, woman," he said softly. "If you ever do that to me again, I swear I'll . . ."

Hannah's eyes suddenly glittered with unshed tears, and she smiled. "Never, James. I'll never leave you."

She walked into his arms, ready to stay there for the rest of her life, knowing she'd be welcome.

EPILOGUE

One year later

Allen Pritchard tossed down his second glass of champagne, his eyes on Hannah and James MacRae as they danced around the ballroom floor gazing into each other's eyes like two love-struck adolescents. He turned away, disgusted with the jealousy that ate at him, ashamed that he wasn't glad to see Hannah so happy. He hadn't seen her since the *Bold Lady's* departure, and had been stunned by his heart's reaction upon seeing her again.

"Allen, you're making a fool of yourself. Again," his mother said, her cold eyes going from her son to the dancing couple.

"Stuff it, Mother," Allen said, then placed his glass firmly down on a nearby table and left his mother gaping at him like a stranded fish.

Depressed, and angry at himself for feeling depressed, Allen made his way out to a small terrace that overlooked the home's gardens. He could see shadows moving about, a flash of dull color, the flow of skirts—lovers taking advantage of the darkness to steal a kiss. It seemed lately that everywhere he looked, there were happy couples and families; and that old longing stabbed him before he could stop such ridiculous emotions. He turned suddenly, unable to bear seeing the couples walking about, and heard a gasp.

"Oh. I'm sorry. I didn't see you there in the shadows." A

young woman, lovely and petite, with dark brown curls and wide blue eyes looked at him. She wore a soft yellow gown that hugged her small frame lovingly, then fell in a dozen delicate flounces to her silk slippers that just peaked from beneath her full skirts. The girl tilted her head at him. "Have we been introduced?"

Allen looked at the girl and found her familiar, but he shook his head, stiffening slightly when she moved toward him. "Oh. I do know you." And she placed her index finger to her lower lip, an enchanting gesture that Allen suspected was not at all intended to enchant. Then she was giggling, one graceful hand covering her mouth in horror. Allen narrowed his eyes. It was quite obvious the girl had just remembered where they'd met, but the meeting continued to elude him.

"We are quite the pair," she said lightly, though Allen was sure he saw something in her eyes other than mirth. She held out her hand. "Sandra Sheffield. We met . . ."

"Oh, my God."

Sandra smiled. "Yes, indeed. They do seem disgustingly happy together, don't you think? Quite irritating, if you ask me."

Allen smiled to find such an ally at this ball. He'd nearly not attended, fearing that the MacRaes, who had just returned from London, would grace this hall. But then he realized that not going would mark him for a coward and would clearly tell the world—or at least New York society—that he had not overcome his humiliation. And here was this brave girl, likely suffering more than he, for she had had a much more public downfall.

"I think you must be quite brave," he said, and was stunned to see tears immediately glitter in her eyes.

"Oh, my goodness. Look at me." She dabbed ineffectually at her eyes.

"You must have loved him very much."

To his surprise, she shook her head. "I thought I did, but now I realize it was just the image of him I loved. And the image of me being married to such an important man. I'm such a vain ninny at times. I'm crying because it has been difficult facing people, and I'm getting quite weary of plastering a smile on my face and pretending all is well."

Allen smiled. He knew precisely what she was going through. He'd seen the looks of pity, as well as the sneers from some men who enjoyed seeing others brought down a peg. No doubt, this girl had suffered much more than he.

"Just think of the stir we would create if we danced together tonight," he said, a mischievous glint in his eyes.

She bit her lower lip. "We could pretend we're quite smitten," she said. "We could look into each other's eyes as if we only saw each other." She clapped her hands, relishing the idea.

It hit him like a brick thrown hard into his gut that Sandra Sheffield was a delightful and beautiful young woman. He smiled down at her, thoroughly enjoying her enthusiasm. "Miss Sheffield," he said, forcing a serious expression on a face that kept wanting to lift into a grin, "may I have this dance?"

She lifted her chin and placed her hand in the crook of his arm. "You may, sir."

And as they danced about that ballroom floor, looking at each other as if all else in the world had disappeared, they each realized they'd stopped pretending the moment he took her into his arms.

"Well, will you look at that. It seems our guilty consciences can now be cleared," Hannah said, eyeing Allen and Sandra as they turned about the dance floor.

"One dance and you are marrying them off already?" James asked, chucking his wife's chin gently.

"I'm quite good at reading eyes. And those eyes are falling in love." Hannah glanced up at James and smiled. "And those eyes are about to fall asleep." It was true, James was exhausted having just finished supervising the *Bold*

Lady's unloading. Home for less than two weeks, they were still getting their land legs after the long journey.

James pulled out his watch. "I suppose we have to stay. We are the guests of honor, after all."

Hannah frowned. She'd hoped James would take the broad hint that she wanted to go home. Desperately.

"I'm sure everyone will understand if I go then?" she asked hopefully.

James looked down at Hannah, lovely and still flushed from the wind and sun. And motherhood. Good God, he only needed to have the vaguest reminder of their child—and how it was born in the middle of a blow off Madagascar—to be filled with gut-wrenching panic. "Perhaps you are right. But I'd hate to send you home alone. I suppose I'll have to accompany you." James spoke as if he were reluctant to leave, but Hannah, who could read her husband so well, knew better.

"Oh, I think it best." She watched with some amusement as he lifted his timepiece up again, still not convinced they should leave. It had been approximately two hours and fourteen minutes since he'd kissed their tiny daughter good-bye. He tapped his thigh with a loose fist.

"She did have the sniffles," she said.

"Did she? Did you call the doctor? Blast it, Hannah, what the hell are we doing here when we have a sick child at home?" He began to pull away, mindless of the stares from those around them. It took all of Hannah's strength to stop him from rushing from the room.

Laughing, she said, "James. Merbelle is perfectly fine. It's just the tiniest bit of sniffles. I only mentioned them to hasten our departure. I didn't mean to send you into a panic."

Collecting himself, James scowled darkly. "I was not panicking. I was . . ."

"Panicking."

His scowl deepened, but his eyes held a glint of humor.

"You *knew*," he said, pointing a finger at his wife, "what my reaction would be. You are heartless."

Hannah smiled smugly. "If that is true," she said, kissing his jaw lightly, "I'm sure you have enough heart left over for the two of us."

He grunted his agreement, and held out his arm, ready to lead his wife to their carriage. She took his arm, ready to follow him to the ends of the earth.

Author's Note

The clipper ships *Windfire* and *Bold Lady*, as well as Captain MacRae, exist only in my imagination. However, Josiah Creesy was the captain of the *Flying Cloud* when it reached San Francisco from New York in just 89 days, 22 hours in 1851; his wife, Eleanor Creesy, was navigator. Eleanor Creesy is credited by many historians as being a key factor in her husband's great success. In 1854, the *Comet* sailed from San Francisco to New York in 76 days. The days of the clipper ship ended in the late nineteenth century when it was replaced by the steamship. It is a tragedy that not a single example of an American-built clipper ship exists today. The only clipper ship still afloat is the *Cutty Sark*, built and berthed in England.